Noble Phoenix

Mark A Pryor

Author website:
www.pryorpatch.com
Email: mark.pryor@pryorpatch.com

Cover design by Katherine Schumm
www.schummwords.com

This is a work of fiction. All characters, locations and
events are either products of the author's imagination, or
are used fictionally.

To Diane

My wife, my best friend, and the love of my life, who has stayed by my side and encouraged me through the good times and the bad.

I am the luckiest man in the world.

Acknowledgements

*To my family and friends for
their encouragement and
support.*

*To my fellow writers who
reviewed my early drafts and
supplied valuable criticism.*

*To Katherine Schumm, one of
my fellow writers, who designed
the cover of this book.*

*To my wife, Diane, who has
always been there for me.*

*And most of all to you, my
readers.*

Contents

Rite of Passage

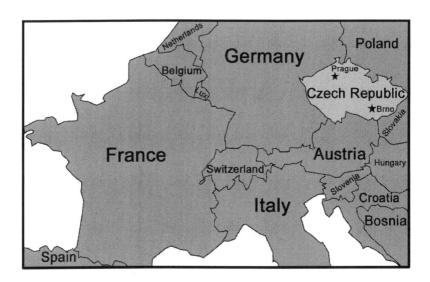

Viktor
Chapter 1

1998 - Prague, Czech Republic

Angry young men with spiky haircuts and shaved heads transformed a cheerful crowd of music lovers into an angry mob. Fourteen-year-old Viktor Prazsky had invited Delia, the prettiest girl in his class, to the Global Street Party. Now they were caught up in the middle of this developing riot.

Delia clung to Viktor's arm, her dark, penetrating eyes shrouded with worry. "I don't like this. Let's get out of here."

Viktor nodded. He searched for a break in the crowd, but the throng of protesters propelled them forward.

An hour ago, Viktor and Delia had been enjoying a music festival at Peace Square. Viktor's father, a lieutenant in the federal police, had warned him not to go, claiming the festival was organized by anarchists. So, Viktor lied to him, saying he was taking Delia to see *Titanic* at the Old Town Theater. They were having fun, even when the bands stopped playing and the party moved to the streets.

Now, they were hemmed in by a gang of young men, raising their fists, shouting, "Reclaim the Streets," and waving signs with slogans expressing the same sentiment. Some men marched with red and black flags, carrying a three-pronged symbol reminiscent of the Nazi swastika.

Most of the protesters were older than Viktor — bigger and taller. Despite the cool day, many were shirtless. Some tied handkerchiefs around their faces, leaving only their eyes exposed. They looked like bandits.

Viktor moved forward with the crowd, Delia in tow, when he spotted something. He turned to her and spoke loud enough to be heard. "The museum is up ahead."

As they threaded their way through the mob, Delia cried out. "Leave me alone." Her grip on Viktor's arm tightened.

He stopped and looked back to see a tall man in a red ski mask holding Delia's other arm, screaming at her. "Black swine! Gypsy whore!"

Viktor's body stiffened and his heart raced. *He thinks she's Roma — Gypsy.* Actually, Delia was Greek, but her dark complexion must have drawn this man's attention. *They hate Roma.* Two Czech men had killed a Roma woman a few months back. The story had been big news in all the papers — telling how those men assaulted her, then threw her into the river.

As the man in the ski mask continued his tirade, the crush of the crowd eased. People moved away from the confrontation, while continuing to march through the streets.

Viktor and Delia stood in the center of a small opening in the crowd, along with the man who towered over them, refusing to release her arm.

Delia struggled and screamed, while Viktor's mind searched for a way out. Police sirens wailed in the distance. He doubted they'd arrive in time. He had learned a few Taekwondo moves, but he was only a novice.

Moving protectively close to Delia, Viktor faced her assailant. "Leave us alone. We don't want trouble."

Crooked, yellow teeth formed a smile that showed through a hole in the ski mask. The man reached into his pocket and fished out a knife — about twice the length of his hand. *Click.* The blade snapped open. He waved it in Delia's face and pulled her closer with his other hand. "Get out of the way, boy. Your damn Gypsy whore isn't worth it."

Gotta do something. Viktor lifted his right knee and delivered a snap kick to the man's groin, causing him to drop his knife and collapse, writhing in pain.

Someone grabbed Viktor from behind and held him in a bear hug.

Where'd he come from? Viktor shouted, "Run, Delia." He struggled to free himself. Despite his attempts, the man at his back held him tighter.

As Delia ran off, the man with the yellow teeth grabbed his knife and stumbled uneasily to his feet. "Bastard!" He pointed the blade at Viktor's face. "I see you met my brother. He seems to like you."

Behind Viktor, a scornful laugh burst out. "You ain't goin' nowhere."

In front of Viktor, the yellow teeth smiled through the mask. "Gonna cut you, boy."

Only one way to break this hold. Viktor twisted to the left. As the man at his back moved his right leg forward, Viktor twisted right again, and stomped his heel on the arch of the man's foot.

With a howl and a curse, the man released his bear hug and shoved Viktor forward — directly toward the knife in the other man's hand.

Viktor instinctively turned his face to the right. *Shit! Too late.*

Something slammed into his left temple. Everything went black.

****

Fifteen minutes earlier, Lieutenant Eduard Prazsky jumped into the passenger seat of the patrol car and buckled up. He knew the street party would turn violent. He was glad he had warned his son, Viktor, to stay away.

Josef Filipek, his new partner, started the engine and turned on the siren and flashing lights as he pulled into traffic. He glanced at Eduard "Wilsonova Street near the opera house. Ten minutes, maybe quicker."

"There could be a lot of foot traffic in that area. You'd be better driving around—"

"I've been driving these streets for years, Lieutenant." Josef kept his eyes on the road. "I can't afford my own chauffeur, so I probably know my way around better than you do."

Chauffeur. Eduard often heard comments like this, but it always made him uncomfortable. "If you want to request a different partner, that's up to you. For now, let's focus on the call."

Josef glanced briefly at his partner and then back to the street, before turning the wheel sharply to the right. "Tell me. With all your money, why do you even bother to work? Can't your friend, President Havel, find something more challenging for you to do?"

It was clear his partner wasn't afraid to speak his mind, so Eduard decided to do the same. "I do this because I hate terrorists as much as you do. The Anarchists of the Black Trinity have been turning these street parties into violent riots all over Europe. They need to be stopped."

Josef continued to speed through the streets and take sharp corners.

Eduard wanted to make this partnership work. They needed to communicate and trust each other. "Listen. I grew up with money and I know our president, but that doesn't make me soft or ignorant. I also spent eight months in Kosovo clearing mines and hunting down war criminals ... so, can you stop being an asshole, and start treating me as your partner?"

A smile appeared on Josef's face. "I think you and I will get along just fine."

The radio came to life with a woman's voice. "Unit twenty-seven, this is base. Assist emergency medical responders heading to National Museum on Wilsonova Street."

Josef made a hard-left turn and accelerated. He flipped a switch to trigger an urgent, wailing siren.

Eduard grabbed the microphone. "Base. Twenty-seven responding."

"Affirmative, twenty-seven. Man down, possible stabbing. Assist with crowd control."

An ambulance came into view from behind, pulling up close, tailgating their police vehicle. Up ahead, a crowd appeared as they approached Wilsonova.

Josef slowed down to avoid hitting any of the desperate crowd scurrying away in all directions, but he didn't stop. He continued to move forward aggressively, forcing people out of the way.

Eduard took the microphone. "Base, this is twenty-seven. Arrived at Wilsonova. Will assist responders on foot."

Josef stopped the car. The ambulance stopped directly behind.

Both officers donned their riot helmets and grabbed their radios and clubs. Eduard grabbed an air horn. They got out of the car and faced a moving sea of young people, marching down the street, most with faces covered and fists in the air.

Two emergency responders in solid blue jump suits rushed toward them from the ambulance, each carrying a red duffel bag. Two more followed, pushing a gurney on wheels.

The man in front shouted at Eduard. "You two lead the way. My partner and I will follow. Don't worry about the gurney team. They'll push their way through. We can't let them slow us down."

Eduard nodded to Josef and pressed noise-suppression plugs into his ears. He aimed the air horn forward and released a loud wailing blast. People moved away from the sound as quickly as the crowd allowed, while the four of them pushed into the empty space.

It took two more blasts before they reached a large opening near the museum. Ten meters away, a man lay on the street. A young couple stood in front of him, obscuring their view. Eduard couldn't tell if he was injured or dead.

The emergency responders rushed forward and knelt beside the victim.

The young couple ran over to Josef, both of them talking at once, saying something about two men wearing masks, an argument, a fight, and a knife.

Eduard glanced at the victim. He looked a bit like Viktor — even wore the same clothes — but the young man's face was turned to the side. A pool of dark liquid stained the street. Then Eduard saw the knife, or rather the hilt. It stuck out of the man's temple. *It's not Viktor. It can't be. He went to the movies.*

The team with the gurney arrived. All four of the emergency responders positioned themselves around the injured man, preparing to slide him on a backboard and lift him onto the gurney.

As they lifted the victim up, Eduard saw his face.

Oh, my God! Viktor!

Desperation
Chapter 2

1999 - Brno, Czech Republic

Nine months later, Eduard Prazsky sat beside his wife, Magda, in Doctor Logan's office at the Moravia Fertility Clinic. The availability of discarded embryos made this the perfect location for Logan's research.

Eduard brushed a stray lock of brown hair from his wife's face and whispered, "I love you." She looked so beautiful, so hopeful — so determined. A highly respected cardiologist, she had reached out to her American colleagues for advice on treating Viktor. One of them told her about the experimental use of stem cells. Before long, she came up with a plan.

Eduard had agreed with his wife, gambling their son's future and his family fortune on the promises of Doctor Logan. All because of two violent degenerates, inspired by hate, who nearly killed his only child, Viktor. *Those bastards should be dead—not just rotting in prison.*

The doctor arrived and settled behind the desk facing them. "Good morning," he said, speaking English with a strong Scottish accent. "I hope you haven't been waiting long."

English. One more reason Eduard didn't trust this man. Any doctor working in the Czech Republic should learn the language.

Despite his wife's optimism, Eduard saw no progress. "What's happening to Viktor? Why do the tumors keep coming back?"

Logan glanced briefly at Magda before focusing on Eduard. "I know this is frustrating, Mister Prazsky." He leaned forward and placed both hands flat on the desk. "The stem cells we injected are creating new nerve cells in his brain, but sometimes they also create teratomas – tumors. This time there's only one small tumor, and Doctor Kaplan will remove it with radiosurgery. No knife."

"That's what you told us last time," Eduard said. "He's not getting better. The stem cells are killing him."

Doctor Logan ran his hand through his thinning hair. "We're fortunate Viktor survived the attack. Even though the knife penetrated deeply into his brain, it didn't affect any life-sustaining functions. Nevertheless, without these cell replacement treatments, he'll be permanently disabled."

It was true. Their son had been lucky — miraculously lucky. The doctors in Prague had brought him back from almost certain death. Eduard and his wife had called Viktor their phoenix — until the extent of his injuries became clear.

Magda held her husband's hand on her lap, and looked at him with her deep blue eyes. "Please, dear. It does no good to second-guess our decision."

Eduard relaxed at her touch. He knew his wife understood this much better than him, even though it wasn't her specialty. "I don't know—"

Magda didn't wait for him to finish. "We knew Viktor had no chance for a normal life unless we tried this. We took a gamble ... a serious gamble. No one has ever done this before. Doctor Logan is taking a big risk with us. He could lose his license, even go to jail."

"Your wife is right, Mister Prazsky. It's still early in his treatment, and I believe this is working. But I can't offer any guarantees."

9

Eduard sat back in his chair and let out a breath. "I know you're right, but this seems so ghoulish. Viktor just lies there, doesn't open his eyes, and doesn't respond when we talk to him. A few months ago, he was a normal teenager. He laughed. He played football." Eduard choked back tears. "Our son doesn't even smile."

Magda squeezed her husband's hand. "Doctor, we're both worried about Viktor's progress. How soon before we see some response? How many more treatments are required?"

"I plan to grow enough stem cells for two more treatments. I wish I could tell you how soon he'll be responsive, but we are in uncharted territory here. There are no past cases to go on."

The door opened, and the faint sound of yells and chants of an angry crowd interrupted their conversation. Most of the sounds were unintelligible, but two words stood out — 'baby' and 'kill'.

A nurse stepped in. "Doctor Logan. There's a rowdy group of people at the front desk demanding to talk to you. Shall I call the police?"

He looked at the nurse. "No, Dana. Tell them I'll be right out." Logan looked at the Prazskys. "Sorry for the interruption, but there are people who don't approve of our work at the fertility clinic. This shouldn't take long." Logan left the Prazskys alone in his office.

Eduard turned to his wife. "Are we fooling ourselves? Does Viktor have a chance?"

Magda pulled a hanky from her purse and brushed it under her nose. "Our son doesn't stand a chance without this treatment — none. Very few people understand stem cells, but Doctor Logan does. He's the only one willing to treat Viktor."

"It feels wrong. We've given him millions of crowns. Hundreds of millions. And we can't tell anyone about the treatments, even though Viktor lies there lifeless. How do we know Logan's not just swindling us?"

"I don't think—"

A loud bang interrupted them.

"Gunfire!" Eduard said. "Quick. Behind the desk."

Magda grabbed her husband's arm and crouched beside him. "The door isn't locked." Her grip tightened. "They can get in here."

Eduard nodded and started to rise.

Three more shots. Screams.

His wife pulled him down. "No! It's not worth the risk. Stay here with me."

Rapid footsteps approached. Maybe only one person, certainly not a crowd.

Dana flung open the door. "Doctor Prazsky!"

Magda poked her head above the desk. "What happened?"

Dana's voice shook as she rocked from one foot to the other. "Doctor Logan's been shot. I think he's dead."

"Where's the shooter?" Eduard asked, moving from behind the desk.

Dana started to cry. "Everyone ran away ... Please help him."

Magda ran toward the door.

Eduard followed her.

****

The following afternoon in their hotel room, Magda dropped the phone and collapsed on the couch. She didn't sleep last night. Doctor Logan was dead. The police had questioned everybody in the clinic, and they asked more questions this morning. Then she pleaded over the phone with Doctor Kaplan at the clinic.

She turned to her husband, tears in her eyes. "Viktor's treatments are over."

Eduard sat beside her and held her hand. "How can they do that? Didn't Logan train anyone?"

"He didn't share his research or methods with anyone. He was afraid he'd be arrested for treating Viktor."

"What about Doctor Kaplan?"

To Magda, this was obvious, but her husband wasn't a doctor. "Kaplan is a neurosurgeon. He doesn't know anything about stem cells."

"He knows what Logan was doing, doesn't he?"

"He claims he has no idea." Magda let out a sigh and shook her head. "He's full of shit. He knows what was going on, but he doesn't want anyone else to know."

"Can't we force him to help Viktor? Would money help?"

Magda stood up and hugged him. Her husband was used to solving problems with money, but she knew it wouldn't work this time. "He can't help." Then she broke down and wept.

Eduard held her until the tears stopped, then brushed the hair from her face and kissed her.

Grateful for the loving support of her husband, she looked into his dark eyes. "You don't understand, do you?"

He shook his head.

Magda looked down at her feet. "Doctor Kaplan can't give Viktor the treatments. No one can." Slowly, she raised her head and stared at the ceiling, tilting her head slightly.

"What are you thinking?" Eduard asked. "I recognize that look."

A weak smile formed on her face. She paced around the room slowly, rubbing her neck. Finally, she sat in a chair. "He's already had five treatments. That might be enough."

"You really think so? Why isn't he better?"

"If Viktor's body has accepted enough stem cells, they're already creating new neurons."

"What do we do now? Just sit around and wait for him to get better?"

"Let's get Doctor Kaplan to remove this tumor, then we can take Viktor back to Prague. I work with several doctors who can deal with teratomas. Logan said he's still at risk. If any tumors appear, the doctors in Prague can remove them."

"Don't they need to know about stem cells?"

"No, they don't. Besides, this treatment isn't approved for clinical trials. We could get in trouble."

As a police officer, Eduard knew the risk. "You're right. I think we should keep this a secret ... forever."

Madrid
Chapter 3

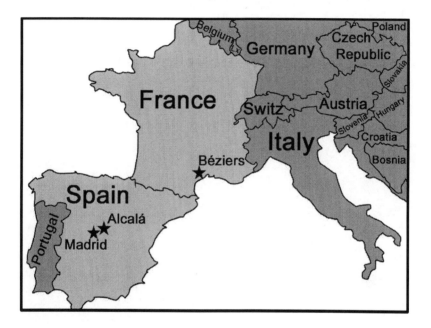

2004 - Alcalá, Spain

Even though the cell replacement treatments ended five years ago, Viktor's health and quality of life steadily improved. It was truly a miracle, one worthy of celebration, but behind it all was a secret that could ruin his family. His parents paid for an illegal medical procedure. They broke the law.

This morning, Viktor completed a series of medical tests at Alcalá University Hospital, near Madrid. After lunch, his parents accompanied him to the office of Doctor Moreno, the most respected neurologist in Spain.

As they pulled up to the curb, Viktor reminded himself to use the name Oliver Klima, the false identity for his medical appointments. He hated the deception, but he knew there was a risk the doctors could discover his illegal treatments, putting his parents in jeopardy.

Viktor stepped out of the taxi and opened the door for his mother.

Magda reached for her son's hand and winked. "You're looking handsome today, *Oliver.*"

"Thank you, Mother." Viktor helped her out of the car.

They entered the modern three-story office building and headed for the elevator. Viktor knew his way. He had been coming here for two years. This was his fourth visit, and he hoped it would be his last.

The 'Klima family' arrived in the reception area and were directed to the doctor's office where a gray-haired man, wearing a white lab coat, met them at the door. "*Buenas tardes.*"

Magda responded in English. "It's good to see you again, Doctor Moreno."

The doctor directed them to the chairs in front of his desk while he took the seat behind it. He glanced at his computer. "I have your test results, Oliver." He looked at Magda and continued, "If you have any questions, Doctor Klima, let me know."

Moreno glanced at the file. "Let me begin with Oliver's vision."

Viktor pointed to the small black patch covering his left eye. His curly black hair was long enough to cover the remaining scar on his temple. "I see nothing with this eye."

The doctor nodded. "The damage to your optic nerve blocks the information between your left eye and your brain. But, you seem to have adapted well to the limitations of your vision."

Viktor's blind eye never improved after the attack, and he had difficulty judging distances with a single functioning eye. Despite this, his parents always requested tests, hoping the stem cells could produce another miracle.

He rubbed his scar. Something he often did when nervous. "I see well enough, but I hate it when people stare at my patch."

"I'm sure your friends and family are used to it. Would you prefer they look at your lazy eye?"

Viktor shook his head and looked at his father. "No, it looks creepy. I prefer the patch."

Eduard spoke up. "He's had eye muscle repair surgery. Both eyes moved together properly for a while, but within a few months they lost the synchronous movement."

The doctor nodded. "That's a common problem with complete vision loss in the eye."

"What about the MRI?" asked Magda.

Moreno turned the computer screen so Viktor and his parents could view it. He pointed with his pen. "On this image, you can see the empty area on the left where the injury occurred. That area is smaller than it was on the scans from previous years."

Viktor studied the image. It was comforting to know the stem cells were still working to heal his brain, but they couldn't let the doctor know the reason for this miraculous growth. Fortunately, his mother knew how to handle this.

Magda nodded. "You mentioned this during our last appointment, but you said we should wait to see how things developed over the next six months."

"That's right, and the damaged section has continued to shrink every six months since our first MRI. We don't know if the same thing happened during the time Doctor Durant was treating Oliver. Those scans weren't conclusive due to the surgical procedures he performed."

Durant. He had been the French doctor Viktor first went to after the stem cell treatments ended. Four times during those three years, a tumor formed and he needed surgery. When Durant's questions threatened to uncover the illegal treatments, his mother decided to change doctors.

Eduard shrugged his shoulders. "Is this a problem, Doctor? Isn't it good to see the area of his injury shrink?"

"In any other part of the body, healing like that would be a good sign. But neurogenesis, the growth of healthy nerve cells, has never been observed in the temporal lobe of any adult brain. The good news is, we haven't detected any growth of unhealthy nerve cells during the entire two years I've been seeing Oliver."

Nothing unhealthy. That's what Viktor wanted to hear. *Two years. Nothing wrong. No more tests*!

Magda took her husband's hand and looked at the doctor. "Are you telling us Oliver has gone two years with no malignant growths, and you're concerned because you suspect his brain is creating healthy cells?"

"That's right. But this kind of new cell growth is unheard of, and I'd like to do some tests."

Magda nodded and rose from the chair. "Thank you, Doctor. We'll have to think this over. Could you give us copies of the results?"

Viktor and his father stood, preparing to leave.

"Certainly, Doctor Klima. The nurse will give them to you on your way out. But I need to tell you about the results of the electroencephalogram."

"The EEG? Did you find something?" Magda took her seat again. Eduard and Viktor did the same.

"Oliver's results are normal ... except for one thing. His brain waves have a higher amplitude than normal — about ten times the average person."

This was nothing new to Viktor or his parents. Doctor Durant noticed this anomaly, too. His mother believed this was most likely a symptom of his newly acquired ability — one they must keep secret."

He had first noticed this ability a year after a man plunged a knife into his head. Whenever Viktor's mother was near him, he knew whether she was happy or sad. The same thing happened with his father, his friends — everyone. Eventually, he realized he was sensing other peoples' feelings.

Magda raised her eyebrows. "You said Oliver's EEG results are normal, but you're concerned because his brain waves are stronger than expected?"

"That's right. The brain consumes more energy than any other organ in the body. Oliver's brain demands even more."

"Is that a problem?"

"We can't be sure without more testing."

"More testing." Magda frowned, then stood. "All right. If you think it's required. We'll set up an appointment with your receptionist."

Viktor knew she would agree to the appointment, like she did with Doctor Durant. But he also knew they weren't coming back. They'd never see Dr. Moreno again. To do so would only draw attention.

****

A few hours later, two blocks from the university hospital, the Prazsky family finished dinner in their hotel and went upstairs for the night.

Viktor sat on his bed talking on the phone with Karla. The door leading to his parents' adjoining room was closed. "We're heading home tomorrow. I'll be back at school on Friday."

He had met Karla the previous fall, when they began their sophomore year at Charles University in Prague. Two months ago, in January, they started dating. They became almost inseparable, getting together or talking on the phone every day, sharing their dreams and aspirations.

There was one passion, however, that Viktor had never shared with Karla, and he wanted to tell her now. She knew he spent time at the gym, but he hadn't explained what he did there. "I'm taking my black belt test next week. Would you like to come?"

"Black belt?" Karla sounded surprised. "You're a black belt?"

"Taekwondo. It's a Korean form of karate. I'll be a black belt when I pass the test. People often bring their family and friends to watch."

"That sounds exciting. When is it?"

"Wednesday evening. It's at a gym close to Prague Castle."

"I'd love to. Is the testing hard? Are you nervous?"

"I used to be nervous when I tested for lower-level belts, but not anymore. It's just a matter of demonstrating what I've practiced."

Viktor's thoughts drifted back six years to the terrible day on the streets of Prague with Delia. That day he had been helpless against those men, and he never wanted to experience that again. When he started Taekwondo, the moves came easily to him, even though his non-functioning eye proved to be a challenge. His limited vision, however, was offset by the strength of his newly acquired sensitivity to emotions. He realized he could detect his opponent's intentions almost before they did, making his defensive reflexes lightning fast. If anyone ever threatened Viktor today, he knew he could defend himself.

Karla's voice brought him back to the present. "I can't wait to see you do your karate stuff."

Viktor heard the faint sound of a second female voice talking to Karla.

"My aunt just arrived. I gotta go. See you in school Friday."

Ending the call, Viktor hopped off the bed and knocked on the door before walking into his parents' room.

His mother turned to greet him. "You get taller every day, and better looking, too. I'm glad you could join us."

Viktor plopped in an overstuffed chair and faced the television. "I'm packed, and it's boring sitting in my room."

"Make yourself comfortable," his father said with a chuckle. "Did you lose your razor?"

"It's the five o'clock shadow look, Father. Women love it."

Magda rubbed Eduard's cheek. "Not this woman. Too scratchy." She turned back to her son. "How does Karla like it?"

"She thinks I'm hot."

His father poured drinks, dark Alhambra lager for himself and Viktor, and a glass of Àn Tinto wine for Magda. "We have something to celebrate."

They all raised their glasses.

Eduard offered a toast. "To our son. Two years. No tumors."

Viktor took a drink, savoring the flavor, and set his glass on the coffee table. "No more tests. No more doctors."

His mother smiled. "It's a good idea to go for testing every five years or so, just to be sure."

Viktor was a keen observer of body language. His mother's smile was broad and genuine, showcasing her pearly white teeth. Her eyes were radiant. But he also sensed her emotions, something she didn't show on her face. "You're worried about my brain waves. The EEG results."

"I can't hide anything from you," said his mother. "Even though you appear to be healthy, I worry. The doctor might be right. Your brain uses so much energy, it could be harming you."

"You mean my headaches, don't you?"

Eduard set his glass on the nightstand. "I'm no doctor, and I can see it. Those aren't normal headaches."

Viktor worried about it, too. Sometimes he got so dizzy he nearly passed out. "It only happens when I get upset. I've learned to control it." There were also things he hadn't told his parents, like how his vision often suffered — objects became blurry, and sometimes he saw double. The thought of losing sight in his only healthy eye was frightening.

His mother nodded. "I hope you're right."

Viktor looked at his father. "What is it? I can tell something's bothering you."

"That's the problem. You can tell. You know too much about other peoples' thoughts." Eduard reached out and held Magda's hand. "You can't let anyone know what you're capable of."

"I don't care what the EEG shows." Viktor tugged nervously at the edge of his eye patch. "I can't read minds."

Magda looked at her son. "We never said you could read minds. But sensing someone else's emotions is unusual."

His father shook his head. "This is serious. Do you want people to be afraid of you? You scare the wrong people, and you could be locked up — or worse."

Viktor didn't share his father's concern about sensing feelings. He stood up and scratched his scar. "I'm going to bed. What time is our flight tomorrow?"

"Eleven o'clock," said his father. "But we need to catch the seven o'clock commuter train to Madrid. It's a short walk to the train station, but we have to leave early."

"Do they serve breakfast on the train?"

"We can get something at the station — maybe juice or a pastry. When we get to the airport, we'll have time to eat a real meal."

Magda took her husband's hand. "Remember. We have a dinner date tomorrow night."

"Oh, that's right," said Viktor. "March eleventh. Happy Anniversary in advance."

****

In the early morning, Viktor shoved his gloved left hand into the pocket of his winter coat as he pulled his luggage with the other. Alcalá Station was only a hundred meters away.

His father wrapped one arm around Magda as he pulled their bag with the other. "You'll warm up once we get inside the station."

"I know." Magda wore a cashmere coat, with a scarf wrapped around most of her face. "Which train are we looking for?"

"There are a lot of trains to Madrid. We're going to the same station we used yesterday on our way here — Atocha."

Warm air welcomed them when they entered and headed toward the lighted board displaying train schedules. Viktor was still learning how to cope with his sensitivity to emotions. The man to his right was excited, but the woman with him was worried, and she held the hand of a young girl who was confused. Their emotions, as well as the emotions of everyone else within a ten-meter circle, assaulted his mind from all directions, as though everyone was yelling at once.

He recognized the 'emotional signatures' of his parents, but the feelings of the strangers around him seemed to blend together. All except for one person whose emotions screamed for attention.

Hatred. He sensed intense feelings coming from someone in front of him. He studied the people until he was fairly certain he knew who it was.

He looked at his father and pointed ahead to the left, about two meters away. "The man with the blue hoodie is angry at everyone. More hate than I've ever felt before. And he's struggling with a heavy gym bag."

"He probably doesn't like crowds. Keep moving. Tell me when you see which platform our train leaves on."

"You don't understand, Father. I've gotta stop him."

Viktor's sensitivity to feelings often proved to be an advantage, but it would be of no use in stopping this dangerous person. He'd have to intrude into the man's emotions – another ability he acquired from his illegal medical treatment. It wouldn't be easy. And then there were the headaches.

The man in the hoodie was close, but moving away. Viktor had to act fast. He focused on the strong hateful emotion, then he amplified the intensity and projected it back. He could sense the increase in hatred coming back from this man. It worked. Viktor had control.

He shifted the emotion from hate to fear and then terror. He concentrated on strengthening it as much as possible. Suddenly, pain struck Viktor like a hammer, right in the center of his forehead. It was the headache that always came, punishing him for his strong emotions. *My curse.* He wasn't even sure if his efforts paid off.

Fortunately, they did. The man he targeted let out a scream, dropped his bag, and clutched his head with both hands.

Viktor's eye moved from the man to the bag on the floor. Two wires, red and green, hung out of the side. Ignoring the pain in his head, he shoved the suspicious satchel out of the man's reach with his foot, and yelled. "¡*Bomba*!"

He sensed his mother's fear, and saw it in her face. His mind must have affected her as well, but not as much as the man with the bomb.

Screams erupted from the crowd. Everyone tried to get away.

Eduard grabbed Magda by the arm and yelled, "Let's get out of here. Now!"

Viktor sensed the fear from his parents and the people nearby. *I did this. Caused their fear.* He concentrated on calming himself. As he did, his headache began to subside.

The man in the hoodie must have recovered as well. He leaned over and reached for the bag.

The bomb! Viktor raised his right knee, pivoted toward the man, and delivered a round kick to the elbow. *He won't pick it up now.* Momentum sent the man to the ground, falling on his injured arm.

Eduard grabbed Viktor. "Let's move!"

The shrill sound of a whistle announced the arrival of two police officers. One of them ran over to the man lying on the ground. The other one inspected the fallen gym bag.

Viktor's vision blurred and he felt dizzy. Nevertheless, he did his best to follow his parents as they moved away from the officers.

His father pointed to the overhead board. "There's ours — Atocha Station on platform two."

As they waited in line to access the platform, an official closed the gate.

"*Atención! Atención!*" a man's voice bellowed over the public-address system. "Alcalá de Henares Security orders everyone to leave the station immediately. All trains have been cancelled. Repeat. Everyone leave the station immediately."

Angry voices erupted throughout the station. Men and women turned toward the exits, pulling their children with them.

As Eduard approached the exit, he leaned close to Viktor and kept his voice low. "Did you make him drop the bag?"

Viktor thought his father was unaware of this part of his ability. "I had to. I'm sure he had a bomb." He ignored the weakness that followed his headaches. Fortunately, his vision began to clear.

They exited the station and his father pressed him further. "How'd you do it?"

He knows. Mother must know, too. Viktor had no idea how to explain it. "With my mind. Something else I have to keep secret."

"Whatever you did, it affected me, too."

"*Atención! Atención!*" The announcement was repeated.

"What do we do now," asked Magda. "We'll miss our flight."

Viktor heard someone mention *bomb*, but he didn't hear any explosion. He pulled out his phone and searched for news. "Holy shit!" He looked up at his parents' concerned faces. "Bombs exploded on trains all over Madrid. They hit Atocha Station. A lot of people died ... dozens."

"Atocha Station?" said his father. "That was our stop! We would have been there if we hadn't missed our train."

****

Eduard sat in front of a desk in their hotel. "If you can't get me two rooms, one will do. Just get us some place to stay for the night." All trains and flights were cancelled, and there was no telling how soon travel restrictions would lift.

"Yes, Mr. Prazsky." The hotel concierge nodded and picked up his phone.

Magda tugged on Eduard's arm. She pointed toward the bar. "The TV ... uh ... look at it."

A large crowd gathered around the bar, staring at the news report on the large screen. The banner on the newscast read *Terrorist Attack in Madrid.* Eduard couldn't hear the announcer, but he saw videos of destruction in the background. Train cars with gaping holes. Torn metal, all kinds of debris, and what appeared to be bodies were scattered everywhere.

All three of them rushed toward the bar, struggling to get close to the TV. As they approached, Eduard heard the news report.

Ten bombs exploded simultaneously on four commuter trains in Madrid during morning rush hour today. Officials report at least one hundred people died and hundreds more were injured. This is the deadliest terrorist attack in Spanish history.

Authorities blamed the Spanish separatist group ETA, but our sources say it was the work of Muslim—

Eduard strained to hear every detail. If not for Viktor — his special ability — the three of us would be dead.

Béziers, France

Over six hundred kilometers north of Alcalá, a man stood in a richly appointed room next to an immense stone fireplace. His neatly trimmed beard revealed a hint of gray, and his stern expression conveyed the arrogance and authority you'd expect from the grand master of a secret international society. When he had been selected to lead Arcadian Spear, he chose the moniker Perseus.

His attention was riveted to the same newscast the Prazskys were watching in Spain.

... separatist group ETA, but our sources say it was the work of Muslim terrorists.

Spanish Prime Minister José María Aznar said, 'March 11 now has its place in the history of infamy.' The government declared a three-day mourning period, all parties have called off their campaign events, but the general election will proceed Sunday as scheduled.

A man was apprehended in Alcalá station carrying an explosive device, which police neutralized.

Perseus looked at his aide. "Excellent work, Brother Girard. Other than the bomber they stopped in Alcalá, the Madrid attack was a success."

"Thank you, Your Grace." Girard, a muscular man in his late forties with closely cropped hair, nearly two meters in height, was the personal assistant to the grand master, a man fifteen years his senior.

Perseus grasped the body of a carved ivory dragon mounted on the handle of his antique Greek cane, and raised it in the air toward five large computer screens hanging on the walls. Each screen showed graphs of selected investments, updated in real-time. "The stock market is plummeting, as we planned, but our security and defense investments will move up." He looked up at Girard. "Our partners are pleased."

Girard bowed slightly. "Several groups are organizing protests. I'm not sure which party will benefit in the election."

"I don't give a damn about Spanish politics. It's the rest of Europe and America that matter."

"Every Western government has made public statements of support," said Gerard. "I'm sure they intend to increase spending on security."

"As they should. But, we can't leave it to chance. Make sure Germany immediately calls for a European Union security meeting while tempers remain high. Make sure our man Huber is engaged."

"I've spoken to Huber. He expects the chancellor to be receptive."

"Good. But we need to keep up the pressure."

"Yes, Your Grace. We have everything in place for the attack on the high-speed line — three weeks from today."

Reign of Terror

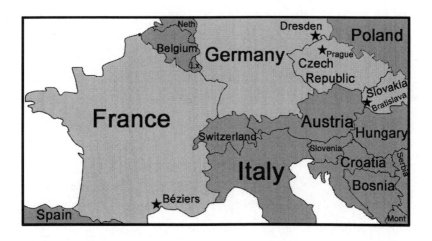

Dresden
Chapter 4

2017 - Dresden, Germany

"Father." Viktor waved as he approached the speakers' platform in front of Frauenkirche, a towering Baroque stone church in New Market Square. The mid-morning sun challenged the chill from the autumn air.

Eduard, the interior minister of the Czech Republic, returned the wave. He stood next to a spectacled man with curly gray hair — Gerhardt Huber, the German interior minister. The man was a full head shorter than Eduard.

As Viktor approached, Huber reached out and shook his hand. "*Guten Morgen.* You must be Major Prazsky. It's a pleasure to meet you." A broad smile graced his face, but his gaze remained focused on Viktor's eye patch.

Like his father, Viktor was fluent in German. His mind sensed Huber's emotions, insecure and condescending, betraying the insincerity of the man's outward smile and friendly greeting. These conflicting signals told Viktor the man couldn't be trusted. Despite this assessment, he returned the compliment with the respect this man didn't deserve. "It's a pleasure to meet you as well, Minister."

Huber released his handshake. "The story of your heroism in Kabul is well-known across Europe."

The mention of Kabul brought Viktor back to that day at the embassy, five years ago. He was with Military Intelligence, a captain at the time, when an Afghani man approached the gate. As soon as Viktor sensed the emotions of this suicide bomber, he used his mind to distract the man, and then his Taekwondo expertise to take him down.

Eduard smiled. "My son was awarded the Medal of Heroism. And now he is a member of the European Parliament."

One of the men on the security team, wearing a traditional dark suit, stepped up and whispered in Huber's ear. The minister made his excuses and left.

Once they were alone, Viktor hugged his father. "I'm glad I came to Dresden to see you. We're both on the road so much."

"I'm happy you came." Eduard stepped back to look at his son. "Did you enjoy the EU parliament meeting in Leipzig?"

"It was a special assembly. I met representatives from Arab states, too. Now my delegation's planning a trip to Tunis."

Eduard glanced at a group of people walking toward the platform. "It looks like the mayor invited a lot of borough officials, plus half the city council. And they each brought their spouses."

"You don't think much of Huber, do you, Father?"

Eduard raised his eyebrow. "No sense in hiding anything from you when you can practically read my mind."

"Just your emotions, Father. Not your mind."

"I know. It doesn't matter whether I like the minister or not. Close Czech-German relations are important. He's my counterpart and we have to work together."

Viktor nodded. "I saw some skinheads gathering on the south side of the square. Did you expect a demonstration?"

"That's Aryan Reich. They don't like Huber and they plan to march as a protest."

"You're worried. Do you think they'll start something?"

"We've been watching Aryan Reich closely for quite some time. I told Huber there's a good chance the demonstration will become violent, but he won't reschedule the speech."

Viktor saw another member of the security team approaching, a wire running to one ear. "I think they want you on stage. I'm going to find a spot near the news vans. See you later."

"Be careful. Stay away from those rabble-rousers."

As Viktor walked away, he heard the man speak to his father. "*Guten Morgen*, Herr Minister. Please follow me to your seat."

****

From his vantage point on the platform, Eduard had a clear view of people gathering in front of the stage. He looked south over the heads of the crowd, searching the area where Viktor had seen the skinheads.

There they were at the edge of the square, a group of neo-Nazis dressed in black uniforms. *Sonofabitch*! He counted about a dozen, heads shaved, chanting something unintelligible.

More skinheads appeared. Dozens more. Riot police rushed toward the intruders. *This is getting ugly fast.*

He spotted Viktor. *There you are. Be careful.*

The mayor of Dresden walked up to the microphone, shielded by bulletproof glass. All of Germany wanted to know what their government was going to do about the violent neo-Nazi attacks last month.

Eduard turned to listen to His Honor's opening remarks.

"*Guten Morgen meine Damen und Herren.*"

As the mayor spoke, Eduard turned to look at Huber in the seat next to him. He leaned over and whispered. "They've arrived, Gerhardt. At least thirty of them so far, heading into the crowd. The police haven't tried to stop their march."

Despite the cool weather, Huber's hair was wringing wet with sweat, causing his glasses to slide forward. He adjusted his spectacles to sit higher on the bridge of his nose. "I've had enough of their bullshit," said the minister, his voice shaking despite his bluster. "It's time we teach them a lesson."

"The people," said Eduard. "Innocent people could be hurt."

The police director walked over to Huber. "Aryan Reich is on the move. We have control of the situation, Herr Minister."

Huber nodded. "Keep a lid on them if you can, but don't take any shit."

The mayor was finishing his remarks. "Now, I am pleased to present our esteemed interior minister, Gerhardt Huber."

The crowd cheered when the minister rose and waved as he walked up to the microphone and stood on the special step he requested. The kind of step used by a vain man, insecure about his short stature. Huber smiled and slowly shifted his gaze above the crowd. He waited for the cheering to subside.

"Today is November ninth — a day we should always remember. Seventy-nine years ago, during Kristallnacht, the Nazis destroyed synagogues, businesses and homes across our country, setting fires and smashing windows. They murdered dozens of people. It was a sad day for Germany, for Europe, and for the world."

A scuffle broke out at the edge of the square. Police marched toward the area with riot shields and clubs to push back the skinheads.

Huber's face was pale and glistening with sweat. He gripped the lectern and glanced at Eduard before facing his audience. "Semper Synagogue was the largest in Germany, standing proudly for a century before the Nazis destroyed it. Today, New Synagogue stands on that very site, only a few blocks from here. It is an inspiration to us all. It is a reminder of the strength of unified Germany, and a defiant condemnation of the horrors brought on by the National Socialists."

Eduard looked at the people directly in front of them, mostly supporters, hanging on the minister's every word. Behind them, the reckless mob of neo-Nazi skinheads, perhaps fifty or more, forced their way toward the podium. Both federal and Saxony police encircled the mob, separating them from the crowd. More officers were positioned to intervene if the confrontation escalated.

Huber took a drink of water. "Today, Aryan Reich, a hateful neo-Nazi group, wants to return us to this shameful past." He raised his hand and made a fist. "We will not allow it!" He slammed his fist on the lectern with a loud thud. "We will crush them before their hatred—"

The blaring sound of an air horn erupted from somewhere across the square, stopping Minister Huber mid-sentence.

Eduard spotted the skinheads attacking police as well as the people in the crowd. Yells and screams broke out. Police wielded riot shields and clubs, hitting people indiscriminately.

Although a few spectators joined in the fighting, most clamored to escape the mob, running into vendor tents, knocking over tables.

A security guard stepped in close to Huber and held his hand over the mike. "We need to move you to safety. Now!"

Eduard reached for Huber's arm, but the minister pulled away and refused to leave.

The mayor and city officials led their spouses off the stage.

Riot control trucks and police entered the square, moving toward the skinheads. Officers on foot pushed the crowd aside to make way for the trucks. Pandemonium broke out as people tried to get away. Police fired tear gas grenades and pepperball rounds at the neo-Nazis. Fire hoses unleashed strong streams of water, knocking people off their feet. The wind blew away the tear gas, and the skinheads kept coming.

Huber turned to the head of security, his voice shaking as he screamed, "Wilhelm! Give 'em everything we got! They asked for it. Show 'em no mercy!"

Wilhelm switched off the microphone and forcefully pulled Huber away from the stand. "Your mike was live," he told the minister. "Everyone heard that."

Huber's eyes went wide. "Shit!" Then, in a voice barely louder than a whisper, he said, "Let's get out of here."

The security team led the way down a short set of steps as police held the crowd back for their safety. They headed into their hotel adjacent to the platform.

Eduard followed the team upstairs to their conference room. Huber took charge, phone to one ear, barking orders to his police force outside and to the four security guards in the room. Eduard felt powerless, a mere visitor from a neighboring country. *I'm glad Magda stayed in Prague. I hope Viktor's okay.*

****

Viktor had been listening to the speeches and studying the people around him in the minutes before the air horn. From his position near the news van, nearly fifteen meters away, he could sense the feelings rising from within the crowd. *Excitement. Anxiety. Hate.* They were all there, but a bit too jumbled to identify which emotions came from which individual. Those around him truly admired the mayor, but many disliked Huber.

He was surprised that many were irritated when Huber talked about the synagogues. *They have no sympathy for the Jews.* Still, most were enthusiastic when he promised to crush the skinheads.

He flinched when the airhorn blasted. The crowd's enthusiasm turned to fear and confusion. His father was moving away, following Huber and the security team.

- 34 -

Viktor pushed against the moving sea of people heading toward the exits of the square. He turned sideways and inserted an arm or a shoulder into every gap he could find. For every two steps forward, he was pushed back a step by the men and women carrying him the other way. Their screaming assaulted his ears as their panic and anger assaulted his senses. Much of their anger was directed at him for being in their way.

As he fought his way through the crowd, he almost bumped heads with a strange man heading to the edge of the square. It wasn't the man's appearance that got Viktor's attention, it was something he sensed. While everyone else was in a panic, this man was excited ... actually happy.

Viktor's phone rang. He recognized the caller. "Father! Where are you?"

****

Eduard stood by the fourth-floor window, phone at his ear, talking to his son, as events unfolded on the square. "I'm upstairs in a conference room of our hotel. You can't come up. Security won't allow it."

Viktor assured his father he would stay away from the action.

By the time Eduard ended the call, the scene below had escalated. Police fired rubber shotgun pellets and launched stun grenades. Flash. Bang. Each round brighter and louder. Skinheads swung clubs at the police and batted the grenades away. Many of these grenades flew into nearby restaurants. Patrons ran to escape the fires. Smoke and tear gas reduced visibility.

Flames erupted from several restaurants and ground level shops. Police continued to direct their water cannons on the crowd, apparently unaware of the fires. By the time they turned the hoses on the buildings, flames had reached the upper floors.

Eduard spotted skinheads approaching their hotel. A smoking grenade flew toward the entrance below. His mind flashed back to an incident with his boyhood friends, Daniel and Albert, and the fire at his school in Prague. *This is bad — very bad.*

Eduard grabbed Huber by the arm. "We've got to get out of the building ... *now!*"

The minister ignored him and continued talking on the phone. The four security guards seemed frozen by fear. None of them attempted to interrupt Huber.

The fire alarm wailed. The sound galvanized the security guards into action. "Minister Huber!" demanded one guard. He grabbed Huber and pulled him toward the exit.

Eduard ran to the door. He used the back of his hand to test for heat. *Still cool.*

He opened the door cautiously. White smoke flowed from the hallway into the room and rose to the ceiling. It came from the right side of the hallway. "Quick! Turn left to the stairs. Stay low."

All five men followed his lead.

Eduard checked the stairway door and then opened it. Smoke rose in the stairwell, hugging the ceiling, leaving the air below clear enough to see and breathe. *We gotta take a chance.* He started down.

Smoke and water escaped under the door on the second floor. *The sprinklers must have gone off.* "Don't touch the door! Down the stairs. Watch out. Wet floor."

Huber and the four security guards moved downward past Eduard. Once he accounted for all of them, he followed.

As they emerged from the building, police and security personnel rushed over and ushered them away.

Behind him, Eduard heard screams from the hotel. He spun around to see a young couple on the third floor frantically waving from their balcony window. *Gotta save 'em. Daniel and Albert died waiting for help. It never came.*

Looking around, he saw no firefighters nearby. Flames engulfed several buildings in other parts of the square. He looked back toward the couple at the window. *No one's going to help.*

Without a second thought, he ran back into the building. He heard people behind him yell, "No!" He ran faster.

****

Viktor watched in horror as smoke poured from his father's hotel. More buildings were burning. *Where is he?*

He spotted Huber with four men, all of them covered with soot, soaking wet. *Where's Father?*

As he rushed toward the minister, one of the wet security guards stepped in the way and held out his hand. "*Halt!*"

"I'm Viktor Prazsky. My father is Minister Prazsky. I'm looking for him. Do you know where he is?"

Huber nodded to the guard who stopped Viktor. "Your father helped us out of the building." He shook his head. "Then he ran back inside."

"Ran back? Why did he do that?"

The man pointed to the young couple on the third floor. "He must be trying to save them."

Viktor studied the couple. He memorized the location of their room. "Which door did he enter?"

The man pointed.

Viktor sprinted into the building and ran up the stairs, two at a time. At the second floor, smoke and water poured into the stairwell. The wail of the fire alarm made it impossible to listen for the sounds of people. He checked the third-floor door. Warm, but not hot enough to suggest flames on the other side.

He forced it open against the water pushing against it. It was dark, and ceiling sprinklers sprayed water everywhere — on the floor and in his face. A thick blanket of dark smoke hugged the ceiling. Viktor ran hunched over toward the area where he thought the couple were located. He heard coughing, and sensed the emotions of three people. One of them was familiar.

Hope and worry rushed through Viktor. "Father!"

Shapes of people appeared in the distance. They were hunched over as they moved toward him.

"Viktor?"

He was relieved to hear his father's voice. "We have to get out of here — *now!*"

His father rushed to him, followed by two people who clung together. All three were soaking wet and coughing.

Viktor grabbed his father's arm and yelled, "We don't have much time. Follow me." He turned and ran toward the stairway.

His father barked orders to the others. "This way. Gotta move — *fast*. Stay low. Watch your step." He pushed ahead of Viktor. "I'll lead. Make sure these two keep moving."

"Go ahead. Be careful."

From behind, a woman shouted. "We're with you."

Then a man's voice called out. "Let's get outta here."

His father touched the door. "It's warm, but we have no other options. Stay with me." He opened the door. The smoke was thick, the air hot. He headed downstairs.

Viktor tried to avoid breathing the thickest of the smoke. He heard coughing coming from behind, and he sensed the couple following.

"Almost there," said his father. "One floor to go. Down the stairs! Out the door — *quick!*"

Eduard grabbed his son and shoved him forward. "Don't stop."

The others followed Viktor on their way to the exit door.

Three of them escaped the building as a loud bang and a blast of heat and flames shot from the door they had just passed. Eduard's limp form tumbled down the stairs and stopped at Viktor's feet.

Arcadian Spear
Chapter 5

Béziers, France

Late that afternoon, Brother Girard approached a one-story country home in the south of France. This deceptively modest-looking home, located in the shadows of the thirteenth century Cathedral of Saint-Nazaire, was the home of Perseus, Grand Master of Arcadian Spear.

Girard faced the security camera by the door and waited for the system to recognize his face. A small green light blinked and the lock clicked. He went inside.

An elegantly framed painting of the fifteenth century Scottish Rosslyn Chapel dominated the opposing wall of the foyer. To the left was the dining room. Girard was drawn to Perseus' shrill voice coming from the room on the right. "Huber's an idiot!"

Girard, weary of the grand master's outbursts, took a deep breath and presented his most calm and concerned face. He stepped into the office and watched as his mentor swung a cane in the air, poking at the large flat-screen monitors hanging from the walls.

"It's been five hours since the attack, and our stock prices haven't risen at all!" The grand master lowered his cane, but not his voice. "The public is outraged at the carnage, and the media blame Huber's police for the fires. No government's going to buy riot control weapons for their police right now." He faced Girard. "Our associates are not pleased."

"Aryan Reich did everything we demanded, Your Grace. The police were supposed to be the heroes."

"Exactly. If Huber had kept his cool, this would have been blamed on the skinheads." As Perseus walked slowly to his chair, his breathing became labored. "But Huber had to scream to the world, 'show no mercy'. Now he's the villain." He dropped heavily into his seat and leaned his cane against the chair. Then he grabbed his handkerchief and held it over his nose and mouth with two hands. He hacked and wheezed. His entire body shook.

Girard stood ... waiting. He hated these coughing fits which had become more frequent in recent months. He felt the urge to clear his own throat. If it continued, Perseus would expect him to bring the rescue inhaler kept inside his desk drawer. The coughing subsided.

"I worry about you, Your Grace." The man's great wealth and access to the best health care was the only reason he was alive today. "That coughing can't be good for you."

"You let my doctors worry about my health. Your job is to carry out my orders." The old man leaned back in his chair and tossed his handkerchief onto the table. "So, what have you learned?"

"I talked to our friends with the Saxony police," said Girard. "The fires killed at least thirty people ... entire families died. Grieving family members are talking on the news networks."

Perseus interrupted, pointing at the live news broadcast on one of the screens. "Why are you telling me this? Don't you think I follow the news? We planned this riot and paid good money for results. Have you forgotten what business we're in?"

Girard took a slow breath and forced his lips into a smile. "I'm explaining why the police cannot afford to cooperate with us fully, Your Grace. They intend to do a thorough investigation. Huber will be questioned."

"I don't trust that idiot. He can't be allowed to talk." Sitting back in his chair, the old man reached for his always-present snifter of cognac. He swirled it and took a sip. "Take care of Huber — tonight."

"As you wish, Your Grace."

"Now we need someone to replace him. Someone who can inspire the people and their governments." The grand master set down his glass. "What do you know about this Czech minister? The one who saved those people from the fire. And his son. They're both heroes."

"His name is Eduard Prazsky. He's the Czech interior minister. The press is promoting his story — a tall, good-looking guy, a politically powerful man, running back into a burning building to save complete strangers. And his son, Viktor, ran back in to save his father."

"We could use this hero. The people will listen to him. I want to know everything about him."

"He's well liked in his country. I'll have more information for you next week."

The old man frowned and raised an eyebrow. "Next week?"

Girard nodded. "Tomorrow, Your Grace. I'll give you a full briefing tomorrow."

"That's more like it." Perseus leaned forward. "We also have to deal with our investors. Plan for another incident. Something we can do quickly to make up for our revenue shortfall." He sipped his cognac. "Somewhere in the Czech Republic. Get the Prazskys involved."

"Certainly," said Girard. He paused before making a recommendation. "Perhaps this is the time to do something on a larger scale."

Perseus gripped the handle of his cane. "I make the decisions here. I bring in the cash and control the key power centers. I won't allow you to escalate the violence beyond our control. No Al-Qaida, no Islamic State ... and nothing nuclear. Is that clear?"

Glorified bean counter. That's all you are. Successful investor — sure. But the last bold action you authorized was the Madrid train bombing. "Perfectly clear, Your Grace. We are fortunate to have you as our leader."

Perseus raised his cane and pointed it at Girard. "As long as I'm in charge, we do it my way."

"As you wish, Your Grace." *As long as you're in charge — and not a minute longer.*

Dresden, Germany

At ten o'clock that evening, Constable Becker, a stocky, middle-aged patrolman who lived in Dresden all his life, received a dispatch in his patrol car. "Unit thirty-three, respond to Taschenberg Palace immediately."

His younger partner, Gregor, drove, so Becker reached for the microphone. "This is thirty-three. What's the situation?"

"See the front desk clerk. You are expected."

Becker looked at Gregor, a tall Nordic type who probably didn't shave more than once a month. "Let's move — Taschenberg Palace is right next to Dresden Castle. No details from dispatch. Something's going on." He keyed the mike. "Thirty-three responding."

Gregor turned on the siren and headed north. Ten minutes later, he pulled up to the entrance and parked the car.

Becker had never seen this ultra-luxury hotel up close, reported to be a faithful restoration of the original eighteenth century baroque palace. As they approached, he marveled at the iron gate with cherubs atop stone columns at the entrance, brightly lit even at this hour. A palace, indeed.

Inside, they passed a few guests and a bellboy on the way through the lobby. They walked up to the only person behind the registration desk, a young man wearing a blue vest and a gold tie. Becker handed him their credentials. "Dispatch said you're expecting us. Why did you call the police?"

The clerk studied their IDs and returned them. He glanced left and right, then leaned forward and spoke in a whisper. "The man upstairs, uh ... Faust, called the police. He told me to expect you and to send you right up."

Becker exchanged a look with his partner, then asked the clerk, "What's this about?"

The man's eyes searched the room, and he continued in a whisper. "Faust only told me it is a sensitive situation." Then he handed Becker a key and gave them directions to the Crown Prince Suite.

The constable and his partner entered the elevator and used the key to access a restricted floor.

When the door opened, a frail-looking young man with closely cropped black hair greeted them. His dark-gray suit was soaked with sweat.

Becker glanced through the double doors, but saw nothing unusual. "I'm Constable Becker and this is Constable Gregor. What's your name, and what's this all about?"

"I called right away!" The man shuffled his feet. "I'm Hans ... Hans Faust."

"Tell me what happened," said Becker.

Faust tugged at his collar, his voice shaking. "He's dead! In the bathtub!"

A body? Someone could've told me. "Who's dead?"

"Gerhardt Huber," said Faust. "The interior minister."

Holy shit! The minister? He exchanged a brief look with Gregor.

They followed Faust into the room, or more precisely, the foyer *This is huge.* Becker stepped closer to the man who greeted them. "Is this the minister's suite?"

"Yes ... yes, it is."

"Were you here when he died?"

Faust shook his head. "Oh, no. I collect his correspondence every evening. That's when I found him. I called the police right away."

"Take us to the body."

Becker and Gregor followed him down the hall and through the master bedroom. The luxurious furniture and wall hangings impressed the constable. *Huber knew how to live it up — until tonight.*

The other side of the bedroom led to the huge master bath. As Becker entered the room, his eyes were drawn to the blood — lots of blood.

The minister lay in a tub of red bath water. His head dangled to the side over the edge of the tub. His neck stretched more easily because of the deep slash, gaping open like a second mouth. A bright red stain on the wall reminded Becker of those ink blot tests psychologists use — a bat maybe, but not symmetric. More blood covered a shelf that held a nearly empty bottle of absinthe next to a glass half-filled with the green liquid.

A drip from the faucet struck the calm water. A bloody butcher knife laying on the minister's right leg appeared to quiver as the ripples passed it.

Gregor sat on a chair near the door, his head down, breathing heavily. "I don't feel so good." He wiped sweat off his forehead.

Becker felt horrified, too — but not sick. The scene appeared oddly clinical, like something you'd see in a movie. He pulled out his phone and walked over to his partner. "Don't barf here. Forensics will have your ass."

Pale and sweaty, Gregor managed to force a smile. "Calling the inspector?"

"You know Falk. He'd have my head if I didn't call." Becker used speed-dial.

After three rings, Falk answered the phone.

"Becker here, Inspector. There's a body at Hotel Taschenberg Palace — in the Crown Prince Suite."

Falk didn't respond immediately. Then he asked, "Crown Prince Suite?"

"Yes, sir. It's—"

"The minister?"

"Yes, sir."

"I'll be right there."

Becker turned to Faust. "Have you told anyone how he died?"

"Not a soul."

"Let's keep it that way."

While Becker walked around and took photos from different angles, he sent Gregor to the lobby to wait for the inspector. Twenty minutes later, Gregor and Falk entered the suite.

The inspector was tall and powerfully built, with closely cropped gray hair. Rumor had it, no one had ever seen him smile, and tonight would likely be no different. "What have we got, Constable?"

Becker laid out the facts and guided him to the bathroom.

Falk inspected and photographed every detail of Huber, the tub, the blood, the knife and the absinthe, before talking to Becker. "I see Huber committed suicide. He blamed himself for the deaths in the square."

"Suicide, sir?" Becker wasn't sure if the inspector was stupid or dangerous. "His neck was slashed from ear to ear. No one could do that to himself."

The inspector walked up to Becker, only a few centimeters between their faces. "Constable. This is a suicide."

"Yes, sir!" Becker stepped back. *This man can ruin me. Hurt my family.*

"The public does not need to know the minister slit his own throat," Falk added. "All they need to know is it was a suicide. Is that clear?"

"Perfectly clear, sir!"

Fist of Freedom
Chapter 6

Dresden, Germany

Eduard lay in a private room at Frederick Augustus Hospital in Dresden. An IV dripped clear liquid into his arm. Bandages covered his left side, and his face was wet with ointment. He didn't remember how he got here. All he recalled was the hot door at his back, and then waking up in the hospital a few hours ago in pain. Burns and a concussion. That's what they told him.

Out of the corner of his eye, he saw a woman enter the room. *Magda*. He turned his head and greeted her with a smile. Following closely behind, nearly a head taller and wearing an eye patch, was his son, Viktor, a younger version of himself — broad shoulders and dark, curly hair.

Magda leaned over to kiss Eduard. Tears escaped from the corners of her deep blue eyes. "I love you, dear, but what were you thinking?" Her brown hair fell over the shoulders of her perfectly pressed, beige pant suit. She reached into her purse, pulled out a tissue and dabbed her face.

Eduard hated seeing his wife upset. He knew there was little he could say to make her feel better. "I love you, too. And I'm sorry I gave you such a scare." His turned his head toward Viktor. "They tell me you saved my life. I ... uh ..." No words seemed adequate.

Viktor smiled. "Father, I do believe this is the first time I've ever seen you speechless."

His son's levity lightened the moment, or perhaps Viktor used his mental 'gift'. Whatever the cause, Eduard suddenly felt at ease. Changing the subject, he asked Magda, "Didn't you schedule a surgical procedure for today in Prague?"

She nodded. "Looks like that bump on the head didn't affect your memory. I was scheduled to perform an angioplasty, but another surgeon is covering for me. Our new chauffeur drove me here. He made good time — just two hours."

"Your colleagues are great, always willing to help." Then Eduard thought about his own job. He wasn't used to lying around for hours without someone calling him. "Do you know where my phone is?"

Magda pointed to the table next to his bed. "Right here." She moved it closer. "But I don't expect you'll get many calls for a while. Tomas asked me to tell you not to push your recovery. Just contact him when you're ready to get back to work."

"Why would the prime minister call you instead of me?"

"Actually, it was his wife who called. Jana wants to invite us to dinner as soon as you're feeling up to it. Tomas told her you should focus on getting better."

"I'll call him when I get home," said Eduard. "They tell me I have to stay overnight. I guess they want to watch me sleep."

"You have a concussion, dear, and you inhaled a lot of smoke, but I'm sure you'll be fine. Your oxygen level is normal, and nothing alarming showed up in the blood work. You were lucky. If your burns had been worse, you'd be looking at a much longer recovery."

Eduard had heard the hospital staff discussing the riots in the square and the shocking news of Minister Huber's suicide, but he hadn't read any news reports. "Tell me about the fires. How many people died this morning?"

"At least thirty," said Viktor. "The press blames the police for overreacting and starting the fires."

Hearing the death toll made it seem more real. "It was tragic. I know the police responded recklessly, but the skinheads are to blame." Eduard looked at his son. "Did you manage to stay away from the riot?"

"I was close to the stage, away from the worst of it." Viktor scratched the scar on his temple. "But I saw—"

Eduard placed a finger to his lips to stop Viktor from talking. He didn't know if it was safe to discuss this in the hospital room. For all he knew, German authorities might hold Viktor as an eyewitness. This was one time he was happy for his son's special ability. He knew Viktor could sense his concern.

Lowering his finger, he winked before speaking. "I'm upset about the deaths, Viktor." Another wink to Magda. "I'll feel more like talking about it in a few days." He changed the subject. "I'll be glad to get home. No doctors or nurses fussing over me."

Magda put her hand on Eduard's shoulder. "You'll need to get used to people fussing over you. The news channels are calling you a hero — Viktor, too. Not only here, but also back in Prague."

"I'm not a hero. A lot of people died in those fires. Not only that, but my stupid actions risked your life." He looked at Viktor and his emotions overwhelmed him. He took a deep breath. "You could have died because of me."

"Father." Viktor moved closer to him. "You're a hero, period. Two people would have died if you hadn't gone in. You did the right thing." He nodded at his mother. "You might as well tell him."

Eduard took Magda's hand. "Tell me what?"

"You know how newspapers are." Magda sat in the chair by the bed, still holding his hand. "I received a call from a reporter. He's writing a story about the two of you, so he dug into your family's past. He learned about your tie to the Czech royal family, and he's going to include it in his article."

"Shit." Eduard shook his head. "My father always told me to keep our family history a secret. The Czech people don't remember the Habsburgs with fondness."

Viktor shook his head. "That doesn't matter. Premysl kings were loved for centuries before the Habsburgs came along."

"Do you think people understand the difference? Our ancestors didn't follow any constitution."

Magda ran her fingers through her husband's hair. "Times have changed, dear. The Czechs are proud of their history, and their royal family. They'll be proud of you, too."

****

An hour later, Eduard heard a knock and saw Josef Filipek, Director of Czech Security Information Services, standing in the open doorway.

Josef walked into the room. "Glad to see you're doing well." He looked at Magda then Viktor. "It's good to see you, too. I just wish it didn't have to be in a hospital room."

Eduard placed his finger to his lips and waved his arm around in a circle. "Thank you for coming to Dresden."

Josef nodded and continued talking. He pulled a small wand-shaped antenna out of his briefcase and checked his phone to verify the link. "I couldn't pass up the opportunity to visit. Looks like you'll do just about anything to get attention."

Eduard laughed as he watched Josef close the door and begin scanning the room for electronic bugs. "I can always count on you for sympathy. Don't let the bandages fool you, I'm doing fine."

Slowly, Josef walked around the room, waving the wand along the walls, the bed, the furniture — everything. As he walked, he watched his phone for any indication of suspicious transmissions. "You're a tough one. But you're damn lucky." After a pause, he added, "The room's clean."

"Thanks, Josef." Eduard turned to Viktor. "We want to know what you saw in the square, but I don't want German police to hold you here as a material witness. We—"

Magda interrupted. "Can they do that? Viktor didn't do anything wrong."

"Josef and I won't let that happen." Eduard looked at his son. "Just don't tell anyone what you saw — anyone but us. We'll make sure the police get the information anonymously."

Viktor nodded. "So that's the reason for all the spy stuff."

Eduard looked at Josef. "Viktor started to tell me he saw something in the crowd this morning. I interrupted him before he could go into the details."

Josef pointed to his phone. "I'm going to record this, Viktor. What did you see?"

"I was near the press section when the air horn sounded. I heard Minister Huber shouting from the stage, and people around me began to yell and push, trying to leave the area." Viktor paused. "I tried to watch Father. They led him off the stage. That's when I saw a man who acted suspicious. He was about my height, wearing a black leather jacket and dark jeans. I think—"

Eduard interrupted. "Did you see his face?"

"I didn't see him right away. He came up on my left side." Viktor pointed to his patch. "He wore a black wool cap and sunglasses. He moved toward the edge of the square, in the opposite direction of the crowd, pushing people aside — men, women, everyone. He didn't seem to care if he hurt them." Viktor looked at his father and wrinkled his brow.

Eduard figured Viktor must have used his mental 'gift', but Josef could not be told. "What do you think he was doing?"

"He had a club, or maybe a bottle, in his hand. And he headed toward the New Market Cafe. I saw the restaurant later and the entire building in flames. I think he started one of the fires."

Magda drew a hand up to her mouth. "Arson? All those people? They could have killed both of you. Who would do this on purpose?"

Eduard reached out and took her hand. "If it was arson, I'm sure the German police will find the bastards and arrest them."

After a few more questions, Josef asked Viktor to meet him in the morning to look through mug shots.

Magda stood. "Viktor and I should get something to eat." She glanced at her son and he nodded. Turning to Josef, she added, "I know you two have a lot to talk about."

"I don't want to chase you away," said Josef.

Viktor smiled and put an arm around his mother's shoulders. "We haven't had anything to eat since this morning." He turned serious. "I hope you and Father get those skinheads before they disappear."

Josef stepped back and raised an eyebrow. "This isn't the Czech Republic. We're willing to offer whatever assistance we can to the German authorities. I'm sure they'll hunt those skinheads down." He looked at Magda. "The Elbe Valley Café is less than a block away. They have a fabulous menu."

Magda grabbed her purse. "Thanks, but we'll go back to the hotel and eat there." She and Viktor said their goodbyes, leaving the two men alone.

Josef watched them leave before speaking. "Viktor always makes me nervous. It's like he can read my mind."

Eduard was used to comments like that. A little bit of the truth usually worked for most curious people. "Viktor's very good at picking up on body language. Never lie to him, it won't work."

"I'll try to remember. His observations during the riot should be taken seriously, too. We could use Viktor in Czech Intelligence, or—"

Eduard changed the subject. Can't risk exposing Viktor's 'gift', not even to Josef. "I'll be heading home tomorrow. I won't be in the office for a while, but I'll be working out of the house."

"I understand. I scheduled a security meeting at four. If you're feeling well enough, you could join us by videoconference."

"I should be able to make it, unless Tomas has a higher priority assignment for me. Now, tell me what you know about the riot."

Josef sat next to the bed. "I'll start with the casualties. German authorities confirmed thirty-three people died. Several of the critically injured will likely add to the death toll over the next few days. At least fifty people went to local hospitals with injuries related to the fires and the riot."

Eduard's eyes narrowed. He adjusted his pillow with his good hand. "How many died in the fires?"

"The majority of injuries and all the deaths were from the fires. No one died as a result of the riot itself. Three multi-story buildings burned to the ground, including your hotel."

"Did the flash bangs cause the fires?"

"The press reports it that way. The police should never have used pyrotechnics in a crowd. Skinheads used bats and clubs to knock the grenades into several restaurants along the square. They started fires in the restaurants, which spread through the apartments on the upper floors."

"But they didn't cause the building fires?"

"It's too early to confirm, but we believe it was arson. The stun grenades probably couldn't have done much damage. The skinheads set the fires on purpose. If they used an accelerant, the investigators will identify it. But if they were smart, they'd use something found in a restaurant, like cooking oil. The police were supposed to take the blame."

"Sonofabitch!" Eduard clenched his fist. "Viktor was right."

"I agree. The man he saw probably did set the New Market Café on fire."

"Did they arrest the damn skinheads?"

"The police arrested forty-seven men. Most of them were Aryan Reich 'soldiers'. They didn't bring in any of the leaders. Three of those arrested were simply caught up in the melee, and they've been released."

Eduard pounded his good hand on the bed. "Damn German laws tie up the government and render it impotent. And it's not just Germany. Too many laws protect the criminals. This is why I created the Fist of Freedom. Only the best and the brightest."

Josef nodded. "The Fist will get the job done. We'll bend or ignore any law that gets in our way. We always do."

"Give German authorities the information we have. They don't need to know how we obtained it."

Josef searched for something on his phone, then looked at Eduard. "We have the names of five men they haven't arrested, and we can point to evidence that'll make those arrests stick. We suspect three of them are leaders."

Eduard reached for Josef's arm. "Did Huber really commit suicide?"

"That's the official line from the federal police. I haven't been able to get any details so far, but my sources should tell me more."

"Damn Huber!" Eduard waved with his one good hand. "We gave him the names months ago. Either he was afraid of someone, or he was part of the conspiracy. The first deputy minister is in charge now. Let's see if he'll do what Huber wouldn't. If Germany won't arrest them, The Fist will make them disappear."

"You got it." Josef looked at his phone. "That leaves the firebombers and any other conspirators we haven't identified."

"We know what German police will do. They'll look through all the video available, but they can't legally use any phone data. If they bring in any suspects, they'll read them their rights and get them a lawyer."

Josef nodded. "I'll get The Fist's analysts on it. They won't follow Germany's rules."

"Damn right," said Eduard. "Within a week, we'll put Aryan Reich out of business."

Briefing
Chapter 7

Béziers, France

Brother Girard worked most of the night and all morning preparing for the meeting. Now he stood by the entrance to Perseus's room, fidgeting, while the grand master finished eating lunch.

The last thing Perseus ate was a slice of apple, something he usually did after finishing his Roquefort. Not just any blue cheese for him, it had to come from the Cambalou caves north of Béziers. He looked up from his meal at a tall man with a youthful appearance, wearing a white vest and apron over checked pants. "That will be all, Marcel."

"Very well, sir." Marcel bowed ever so slightly. Holding a white napkin across one forearm, he picked up the tray with the other hand and turned smartly before walking to a set of double doors at the far wall.

Marcel stood still while a security camera scanned his face. The dark wooden doors opened, revealing a large elevator. He entered and the doors closed behind him.

Girard remained by the entrance. He was amused. An elevator in a single-story home — the only clue to the existence of the sprawling complex located below, carved out of sandstone two centuries ago.

Perseus looked at Girard and waved his hand. "Come here and—" He started one of his coughing fits and grabbed a handkerchief. After wiping his mouth, he looked up. "So, what do you hear from the police?"

Girard stood before the grand master. "Inspector Falk announced Huber's death as a suicide, but declined to release the autopsy report, 'out of respect for the family's privacy'. Cremation is scheduled immediately following the closed coffin ceremony."

"Excellent. That leads us to the issue of a successor."

"The first deputy is now the acting interior minister. Should I bring him up to speed on our needs?"

"Absolutely not. We need the chancellor to select a new minister — soon."

"I can brief you on three members of parliament who would work with us." Girard knew he would have another sleepless night, preparing a briefing on each candidate.

"Perfect. Tomorrow we can discuss each of them. Tell the chancellor we will be suggesting a replacement."

Girard nodded. He had more to tell Perseus, and it wasn't good news. "The police managed to identify the Aryan Reich leader. Actually, they don't know Tripp is the leader, but a video camera captured an image of his face when he blew the horn. They know he's a key player, and they issued an 'arrest on sight' order. They haven't located him yet."

"Stupid idiot! It's time for him to disappear — no trace." Perseus brought his handkerchief to his face. One short cough and he put it away. "Make sure Tripp's disappearance doesn't adversely impact our plans for the Czech attack."

"Shouldn't be a problem. The number two man, Stuber, is anxious to lead. He'll be pleased to step up."

"Excellent." The grand master sat back in his chair. "Help yourself to a drink. I want to hear how our hero's doing. Will he be back to work soon?"

Girard went to the refrigerator, opened a bottle and returned. "Eduard Prazsky's injuries are minor. He's heading back to Prague today. His son, Viktor, pulled him out of the building."

Girard took a seat in the straight-backed, leather chair next to Perseus, where they could both view the large flat screen on the wall. He reached to the side of his chair and swiveled a tray above his lap, placing his tablet on top. He located the presentation and selected it. The name 'Eduard Prazsky' appeared on the screen below the man's picture.

Perseus sipped his cognac and focused on the screen. With a wave of his hand, he urged Girard to proceed.

Another touch on the tablet and a bullet-point list appeared. Girard started at the top, elaborating on each tersely written topic. "Eduard Prazsky is sixty-one years old. He's been a popular interior minister, and the reports of his heroism will certainly attract more admirers. Prime Minister Duris has asked him to accept other cabinet positions, but he refused, apparently preferring his current role."

Girard selected the next slide. "Prazsky's parents were wealthy, and kept their link to the Premysl dynasty a secret ... until the press discovered it yesterday."

Perseus set his glass down and leaned forward. "Is it true?"

"Eduard is descended from the Czech royal family, but historians believe the royal line of Premysl kings died out over seven hundred years ago, so Eduard is most likely descended from a junior branch. Nevertheless, he has royal blood."

"Interesting." The grand master swirled his cognac and took another sip. "I don't understand how they kept their money and low profile all those years."

"Eduard's ancestors successfully hid their assets. His father helped fund Václav Havel in 1989, during the Velvet Revolution. That appears to have bought him influence and privacy."

"What happened to Eduard's parents?"

Girard took a drink from his water bottle. "They died together twenty-two years ago in the Paris metro bombing."

Perseus raised an eyebrow. "I remember the operation well. I learned a lot from my predecessor."

"That bombing seems to be the basis of Eduard's strong stance against terrorism."

"We can use his intensity to our advantage."

Girard projected the next image. "Eduard was their sole heir. He was thirty-eight when he inherited about one billion crowns ... the equivalent of thirteen million euros at that time."

"Over twenty-two years ... it must have tripled in value by now, possibly more."

Girard pointed to the screen. "He invested well. His current net worth is approximately ninety million euros."

"Where's his money today?"

"He owns a brewery and a law firm, plus real estate in Prague and land in southern France." Another image appeared on the screen. "Eduard's wife, Magda, is a cardiac surgeon at Otakar Hospital. Their only son, Viktor, a member of the European Parliament, is being hailed as a hero for saving his father. When Viktor was younger, he was nearly killed during a riot in Prague. He and Eduard dropped out of the public eye for a few years while the boy recovered."

Perseus covered his mouth with a handkerchief and coughed. Small red blotches appeared on the white cloth. "What is your recommendation? How do we engage Prazsky?"

Girard studied the image on the screen. "After twelve years in government, he's developed a reputation as a smart, honest security hawk. He doesn't live lavishly. Despite his passion for security, he appears to have no personal ambition for power."

The grand master pointed a shaky finger at Girard. "I asked for your recommendation."

Girard wanted to grab the old man's finger and break it off. Instead, he answered in a calm voice. "You cannot deal with him like Huber. Money and power won't work. The only way you'll get his support is to convince him his country and Europe are under attack. He'll use his considerable influence to beef up security."

"We'll try your approach for now. Have Aryan Reich attack a target in Prague. Let's see how Eduard reacts."

****

Girard had been unable to reach Stuber or his other contacts with Aryan Reich. He called his contact inside the German police on the speakerphone, while the grand master listened. "What? They arrested everyone?"

Inspector Falk's voice responded over the speaker. "Every member of Aryan Reich, except for Tripp. He's missing."

Girard gave a knowing nod to Perseus. Tripp would never be found. He directed his attention back to Falk. "How the hell did you let this happen?"

"Orders came down from the first deputy minister. He had names and everything."

"Make sure Stuber doesn't talk. We'll send a lawyer right away."

"He won't talk, you can be—"

"That will be all, Inspector." Girard ended the call.

Perseus slammed his glass on the table. "Aryan Reich is done! Through! What a waste. I still expect an attack in Prague to make up for the debacle in Dresden."

"I'll work with Salafi Brotherhood. They're well organized. They consider Jews, Christians and even other 'less righteous' Muslims to be valid targets. You'll—"

Perseus' fist pounded the end table and stopped Girard mid-sentence.

"No! I need a group that will follow our orders. I won't hand those crazies a gun when I don't know where they'll point it. They're no better than the Islamic State or Al-Qaida."

"Very well, I have another plan. We'll engage a reliable regional group. Western Jihad operates out of Europe. They're hungry for support. They'll do whatever we tell them."

"You'd better be right. I don't expect this change of plans to mean a long delay. It must be done before the end of winter — four months, no more. No screw-ups. No excuses this time."

Tunis
Chapter 8

Tunis, Tunisia

Victor poured a glass of Berber Blonde into a mug while he waited for his call to connect. Within a minute, the phones negotiated a secure link. "Hello, Father. I'm in my hotel room. I swept the place for listening devices and it's clean."

"I was just thinking about you, Viktor. How's Tunis?"

"I got in last night, and we had meetings this morning. No chance to see the city yet, but I'm heading out soon."

Eduard laughed. "Sounds like a typical government junket. You go to exotic places and spend all your time in meetings."

"Right. The exciting life of a road warrior. But, I'm more interested in how you're doing" When Viktor left for Tunis his father had still been in a lot of pain from his burns.

"I feel all right, even though it's difficult doing everything left-handed."

Viktor tasted his beer. *Too sweet.* "Is Mother getting tired of changing your bandages?"

"She says my hand's looking good. I should be able to take it out of wraps and use it soon."

"That's good news, coming from Doctor Mom." Viktor knew his father often understated his own personal challenges, while his mother treated health issues seriously.

"How are the meetings going? More exciting than Brussels?"

"I don't know, Father. I thought it would be interesting being a Member of the European Parliament — we call ourselves MEPs — but I'm losing patience with the bureaucracy and the petty arguments. Maybe I'm not cut out for this job."

"Your mother and I are proud of you. When I was your age, I seldom had a chance to leave the country. This is a terrific opportunity, especially if you use your unique abilities wisely."

"You mean I should observe peoples' emotions, but don't let anyone know." *Father doesn't understand.* Anyone could close their eyes if they didn't want to see, but Viktor couldn't close his mind. He felt peoples' emotions all the time. "I observe a lot, including your conversations with Josef."

"Josef? What do you mean?"

"I know you two are hiding something. I'm sure you helped take down Aryan Reich."

His father didn't respond right away. "That was the German police. They didn't ask for our help."

"You realize if we were in the same room, I could sense whether you tried to mislead me."

His father laughed. "It's comforting to know my mind is safe on the phone. Seriously, though, you realize I can't share everything with you."

"Yeah, Father. Security."

"I'd like to hear what you learn from your meetings this week. It's important to know our European colleagues' true feelings."

"I have a pretty good sense for the EU delegates. Tomorrow I'll meet with representatives from Arab countries."

"Why don't you come over for dinner when you return? We'll have a chance to talk business after the meal."

"Sounds good. But, right now, I have to get downstairs. I'm meeting someone for dinner."

"Anyone you want to tell me about?"

"I'm thirty-one years old, Father. I meet a lot of people. Someday I'll meet the right woman, and I'll be sure to introduce her." He checked his watch. "It's good to know you're recovering so well. Give my love to Mother and take care of yourself."

"We love you, too. Have a good evening."

On his way out, Viktor stopped at the mirror. He wanted to look good, but not overdressed. His light gray eyepatch matched the vest and pants, and the light-blue, open-collar shirt gave him a casual look. His curly hair was just long enough to cover the scar on his temple, yet not long enough to be unruly. He put on his blue blazer and glanced at the mirror once more before heading out the door.

Viktor stepped into the elevator and pressed the button for the lobby. As it descended, he thought about Louise Pouilin, a French MEP attending the same meetings. She was smart and friendly — and so beautiful. Short and athletic, nicely rounded breasts that moved freely but didn't sag, tight butt, killer legs, and the sexiest blonde curls he had ever seen.

Whenever she was close, he could sense her feelings — her attraction to him. His mental gift was essentially an emotion receiver. Other women had expressed strong attractions toward him in the past, and he had a few romantic relationships. Now he was unattached, and Louise was someone special.

The elevator stopped, and a young couple with their pre-teen son stepped inside on their way to the lobby. As the door closed, the boy gawked at Viktor despite his parents attempts to distract him. Strangers often stared at his eyepatch, and he couldn't blame the boy for being curious, but it made him self-conscious. Sometimes he felt as though everyone was staring at his patch and his scar. Everyone except Louise.

The elevator opened and he moved his head to the right and then left to compensate for his poor peripheral vision. He searched across the lobby and smiled when he spotted her. She smiled back as he made his way across the room.

He walked over to meet the elegant, professional businesswoman from the EU meetings who now stood before him as a stunning beauty, dressed for a date. Tailored black slacks covered her long legs, with a blouse that matched her powder-blue eyes. He was mesmerized.

"Louise." He smiled and leaned over, giving her a peck on the cheek. He wanted more, sensing her desire as well. Unfortunately, this wasn't the time or place. Since she didn't know Czech, he spoke in her language. "*Vous êtes très belle.*"

"I'm flattered, but I believe I'm with the most handsome man in the place." She reached out for his hand. "Are you ready to venture out, or would you rather sit and have a drink first?"

Viktor glanced at her empty glass. "Let's go. Was there anything special you wanted to see?"

"I thought it would be fun to see the medina." She pointed to the bartender. "Rashad said it's an eighth-century walled city, only a few blocks from here. He said we shouldn't visit Tunis without walking through its souks — the shops in the medina."

"Sounds like fun. Let's go."

Louise wrapped a silk scarf around her hair and grabbed her jacket and purse. "How do I look? I don't want to offend the Tunisian men."

"You look beautiful. You could dress in a flour sack and still be the most attractive woman in the room." He offered his arm.

"You're sweet." She winked. "I'm ready."

They walked toward the medina entrance, identified by two large stone arches in a medieval castle wall, and ventured in.

The strong aroma of coffee from a nearby café competed with the smells of bread and spices. The narrow, winding street, rimmed with shops, was crowded with European tourists mingling with local men and women, most in Western dress, and others in flowing robes and colorful headwear. The atmosphere was electric with the energy and dialects of the people darting in and out of the busy souks. Louise window-shopped at a few places selling clothing and jewelry.

Viktor guided her away from the commotion. "Are you getting hungry?"

She wrinkled her nose. "I'm hungry, but I didn't see any place here I'd like to eat."

"I heard of a fabulous French restaurant a few kilometers north of here. We can take a taxi."

"Sounds great." She reached out and held his hand. "I suppose we'll have to follow bread crumbs to get out of the souks first."

They worked their way through the crowd, hailed a taxi, and travelled to Restaurant Carthage, where they were seated immediately and provided with menus.

"I see alcohol on the menu here, and they served it at our hotel bar, too," said Louise. "I didn't expect this in a Muslim country."

"It's a progressive place. They cater to tourists in the more exclusive restaurants."

"Do you know any good Tunisian wines?"

"I've heard Salammbo is good, especially their Cuvee Prestige Blanc or the Rouge. Not quite champagne, although it's good nevertheless. I'm going to try their local beer, Celtia."

Louise looked at the menu. "The Blanc sounds good. I'm hungry for seafood, if it's fresh. Do you know what's native to the area?"

"How about the grouper? Did you see the confit?"

After they ordered, Louise looked at Viktor. "Have you attended many of these special assembly meetings?"

"Only one — in Leipzig. How about you?"

"Last year I attended a trade council meeting in Strasbourg. The delegates were European. Here we're going to meet people outside of the EU." She flipped an errant curl out of her face. "I'm curious. What do you think of our colleagues?"

"Most of the MEPs are friendly. I talked to the German delegate. He appears angry all the time."

"That's because he only speaks German."

Viktor knew better, but he couldn't tell her how he knew. "Oh, he understands French well enough, but he doesn't want anyone to know. Any idea that's not German isn't welcome."

"He's jealous of you as well. Many of the MEPs are interested in your opinion. I certainly am." She twirled her hair and smiled. "Perhaps it's your self-confidence or your father's celebrity, or maybe because you have good instincts."

Viktor reached for her hand. "My father's a great man, but I'm not him. When people respect my opinions, I prefer to believe it's because of my compelling arguments."

They talked throughout dinner, followed by Maltese oranges and cheese, and finally espresso. Louise discussed her life as the daughter of a French diplomat and the years she lived in Morocco. Viktor talked about his life as the son of a prominent figure in the Czech Republic. He told her about his injury and the reason for the eye patch.

It was dark when they stepped outside to hail a taxi. After waiting ten minutes, one arrived. Louise asked the driver, "*Fransawia?*"

The man nodded, "*Oui.*"

Viktor smiled at Louise. "You speak Arabic?"

"Actually, it's Berber. Something I picked up in Morocco. Anyway, this guy speaks French."

Viktor talked to the driver who motioned them to get in. The man looked friendly enough, but his emotions, both envious and tense, betrayed him. Viktor held Louise's hand firmly. "Let's wait for another taxi. I don't trust this guy."

Louise reached for the car door. "I'm tired of waiting. We'll be fine."

Viktor didn't let go. "There's something about him I don't like. We should wait for the next taxi."

"We don't have much choice," she said. "We waited quite a while for this one, and it's dark already. We should take it." She smiled and nudged Viktor toward the taxi.

He's desperate ... perhaps not dangerous. "Okay. Maybe I'm being paranoid." They got in.

Viktor sensed the increasing nervousness of the driver who turned down a dark alley. No lights shone from any of the houses. The streets were deserted.

"Where are you taking us?"

The driver answered in broken French. "Go to hotel."

Trouble. Viktor knew the man lied. "If you don't drive us directly to our hotel, I'll call the police."

Louise looked concerned. "What are you doing?"

From the front seat he heard, "No police. Hotel."

Viktor took Louise's hand and spoke quietly. "Just being cautious."

The driver slowed to pass a dumpster, then he quickly set the brake, turned around, and pointed a gun at them. "Give me phone ... money ... now."

Slowly and reluctantly, Viktor pulled out his phone and wallet and offered them to the driver. He thought about that time, thirteen years ago, when he stopped the bomber in Madrid. And there were other times when he used his mind to affect people. Sometimes it was subtle, calming someone who was angry. A few times, he hurt people, but when he did, he always hurt himself as well. Right now, he knew he had to stop this man, but he had to be careful not to harm Louise.

He focused on the man's nervousness and synchronized his emotions to match. Then he increased the intensity. *It worked.* He felt the man's emotions responding to his. Viktor knew he had control. Then he concentrated on instilling fear, and he amplified it as much as possible.

The driver's eyes bulged wide and his gun hand went limp. *It's now or never.* Viktor's Taekwondo training kicked in. He dropped his phone and wallet and delivered a throat strike with one hand, then he grabbed the gun with the other and smashed it against the side of the driver's head. The man slumped over in his seat.

Louise screamed, "Oh, my God!" Her trembling hand reached for Viktor.

He put his arm around her, just as a crushing headache struck him in the temple and bright light blinded him. *Can't see!* This was the punishment he experienced whenever he became aggressive with his mind. *My curse.*

He wanted to scream out, but he held Louise tightly instead, trying to calm her while also using her body to brace himself.

The light dimmed and he saw the blurry shape of Louise. No movement from the front seat. *Did I hurt her*? He held his breath. "Are you all right?" *Please be okay*!

Louise's voice was weak. "He … he was going to shoot us."

She's okay. Viktor let out his breath. Relief rushed through his veins. A strong wave of fear still poured from Louise. Some of her fear must have been real, caused by the threat from the driver, but Viktor was certain he amplified it.

His head continued to throb, but his vision began to clear. He pointed the gun at the driver, even though the man wasn't moving. "You're right. He wanted to shoot us. I'm calling the police."

Viktor called the embassy, explained the situation, and did his best to describe their location. They assured him the police were on their way.

Louise sat silently next to him, too unsettled to be comforted.

She stopped shaking and Viktor sensed her relief. "Do you want to get out of the taxi?"

She shook her head.

As they waited in the back seat, Viktor thought about his dangerous 'gift' — controlling other people's emotions. But it came with a cost. He wasn't sorry for the driver who planned to rob them, or worse. His gift saved them. It also terrified Louise, and temporarily blinded Viktor.

Would he go blind permanently one day when he used his gift? Could he hurt someone by accident? *Like Louise*. What if he got angry, or drank too much? The more he thought about it, the more he worried.

A police car showed up with two French-speaking officers. Viktor handed the gun to one of them. The officer verified who called and who was driving while his partner held a gun on the slumped-over driver.

The officer with the gun asked, "What happened?"

"He pointed a gun at us," said Viktor. "We were sure he was going to kill us. I grabbed his gun and hit him."

"Has he moved since you hit him?" one officer asked.

"No, he hasn't."

The second officer opened the driver's door, and checked for a pulse. "He's dead."

Louise's eyes bulged as she stared at the officer. "Dead? Oh, my God!"

Viktor put his arm around her and looked at the officer. "I hit him. But I didn't want to kill him."

A smile appeared on the officer's face. "Five tourists have been robbed by a taxi driver in the last week. If this is the man, you won't be in trouble. You'll be a hero."

Aryan Reich
Chapter 9

Prague, Czech Republic

Viktor returned from Tunis two weeks later. He joined his parents at Kramar's Villa, home of the prime minister, located a short distance from Prague Castle.

After ascending an elaborate staircase, strolling along several well-appointed hallways, and turning right and left numerous times, he felt like he was walking through an elegant maze.

Prime Minister Tomas Duris and his wife, Jana, led the Prazsky family to the gold lounge. The early afternoon sun shone through floor-to-ceiling windows, bathing the room in bright light. Five plush French Provincial chairs, arranged neatly around a matching, ornate glass-topped table, caught his eye.

Viktor was still taking in the splendor of the room when his mother spoke to Jana. "I swear you take us to a different room every time we visit, each more beautiful than the one before. Especially now, with the Christmas decorations."

Jana smiled. "This mansion has fifty-six rooms — many more than we could ever use. But the Czechs expect their prime minister to live here. They hire decorators to prepare government buildings for the holidays. They do a fabulous job."

Tomas invited everyone to take a seat while the butler placed a tray with coffee on the table. Eduard picked up a cup and raised it to Tomas. "We appreciate your assistance in getting Viktor out of Tunis."

"I can't thank you enough," said Viktor "The ambassador and his staff made my stay comfortable, but I was pleased to leave the embassy."

Despite his gratitude toward Tomas and the ambassador, Viktor's experience had changed his views on government service. It wasn't right for the EU to abandon him to the Tunisian legal system. Why should he keep working for a bunch of politicians who treated him like the hired help?

It wasn't all bad, though. He smiled as he thought about the time he spent with Louise. He hoped to see her again soon. "The Tunisian judge was satisfied with my testimony, especially since I agreed to submit to video interviews later, if asked."

Tomas set his cup on the table. "They treated you like a murder suspect. The police knew the driver robbed other visitors, but they were embarrassed they hadn't caught him. I believe the *Spy Magazine* article was more influential in your release than my request."

Jana laughed. "The magazine called you the most eligible bachelor in Prague."

This discussion embarrassed Viktor. He tugged at his eye patch. "It's the Premysl bloodline thing."

"Speaking of the Premysls," said Tomas. "Have you heard about the research project at St. Vitus Cathedral? They're studying the bones of the ancient kings buried there. Probably your ancestors."

Eduard waved his hand dismissively. "Heard of them? They want me to send a DNA sample. I received a kit in the mail."

"I hope you consider it." Tomas reached for his coffee. "They're searching for people who might be related to 'Good King Wenceslas' and the Otakars. So far no one's matched ... maybe you'll be the first."

Viktor shook his head. "I sure hope not. Father and I already get too much attention."

Dresden, Germany

Hans Stuber, one of the leaders of Aryan Reich, lay on a bench in the weight room of Dresden Penitentiary, his arms fully extended with ninety kilograms of weight on the bar. Other prisoners stood by, cheering him on to break his personal record.

At his head, one of the prisoners acted as a spotter, ready to catch the weight if Stuber lost control. Two men stood on the left side of the bench and two on the right. They counted in unison, "six ... seven ... eight—"

As he extended his arms for the ninth time, he saw movement from a man on the right. It was Gunter, a large, muscular ex-wrestler serving a life sentence. This man, who had pretended to be a friend, raised a crudely formed knife above Stuber's chest.

Years of martial arts training had served Stuber well throughout his violent life. His body reacted instinctively to the threat. He pushed the weight away from his head.

His left hand grabbed the knife, fingers wrapped around the blade which sliced into his palm. Determined, he ignored the pain and grabbed Gunter's wrist with his right hand.

As the big man leaned forward, pressing down with all his weight, Stuber dug his thumb into the radial nerve of Gunter's wrist, loosening his grip on the knife. With both hands, Stuber managed to twist the point of the blade up and pull his left hand off the blade. Gunter fell forward on the knife, his weight nearly crushing Stuber and covering his chest with warm, sticky blood.

A shrill alarm pierced the air. Four guards brandished their clubs and rushed to the bench as additional security personnel, overlooking the scene from above, brought their weapons to the ready. Two guards pulled Gunter's lifeless body away from the bench, and two more grabbed Stuber. The remaining guards ordered the prisoners to line up in formation and return to their cells.

Prague, Czech Republic

A week later, Eduard invited Josef into his office at the headquarters building of the Czech Ministry of the Interior. He directed him to a small seating area in the corner. "Have you identified any more of the skinheads?"

"Seven more. Two right away, and the rest this past week. We analyzed video, phone records and cell tower data from the incident in Dresden, and correlated them to each known Aryan Reich member talking on the phone. From this, we discovered additional collaborators communicating from other points in the square."

Eduard couldn't believe the leaders would be that careless. "Why wouldn't they use throw-away phones?"

"They *did* use prepaid phones, and they threw them away after the riot. Our analysts identified the suspects from video and call traffic alone. These guys communicated using coded keywords, so the voice recordings weren't helpful."

"Bring me up to speed on the interrogations."

Josef picked up his tablet computer. "They're going much better since the attempt on Stuber's life. He hadn't given us a thing before that. Now he's playing for our team. His hand was a mess, took over a hundred stitches. He wants revenge."

"What's he telling you?"

"Stuber was the head of operations — second in line to Tripp, their leader."

"Tripp? He blew the horn to start the riot, right? Did you find him?"

Josef shook his head. "We can't find him, and neither can the German police. According to Stuber, Tripp disappeared the night of the riot. Either he's in hiding or he's dead."

"Damn." Eduard sat back in his chair. "So, what else do you have?"

"In addition to Stuber, we interrogated the heads of tech and finance. I doubt we'll learn anything from the muscle guys, but we'll talk to them, too."

"Who's calling the shots?"

Josef shook his head. "They don't know. Hard to believe, but it's true. They were contacted on the Internet using an anonymous message board, and they received instructions via encrypted anonymous email."

Eduard shifted uncomfortably in his chair. "Who pays them? Where does the money come from?"

"Are you familiar with the hawala system?"

"I've heard of it," said Eduard. "An informal system to transfer money. Is that how they get paid?"

"They use a broker, a hawaladar. Each time their mysterious benefactor decides to send money, he forwards instructions via anonymous email, and Aryan Reich sends a courier to the hawaladar identified. Once the courier gives the proper password, he receives the cash. Clients never identify themselves. The password is the only thing that ties the sender to the recipient."

"Wait. We regulate those systems here, at least the legal ones. So does Germany. We can track them down. Where's the hawaladar?"

"That's the problem, Eduard. They always go to Bratislava. We'll have to get the Slovak Republic to investigate."

"Damn. Even if they agree to help, and even if they get information from the hawaladar, the mysterious 'puppet master' will divert the money elsewhere before we can intervene."

Josef spoke, a look of resignation on his face. "The people behind this are smart. I'm sure they've severed all links by now."

He held up a hand. "There's something else our financial analysts noticed."

Eduard looked up from his notes. "What is it?"

"They found suspicious stock trading with two companies that supply riot gear and weapon systems to European police organizations–including German federal and Saxony police departments."

"Suspicious?"

"The stocks of *Protection Systems* and *State Guardian* fell precipitously one week before the riot in Dresden. Several anonymous sources posted phony negative 'insider information' about both companies. Their stocks lost half their value. Then a few investors bought up much of their stock the evening before the Dresden riots, at rock bottom prices. After the attack, both stocks rose in value significantly."

Eduard felt a chill. *Sonofabitch!* "This 'puppet master' knew about the attack! He planned it! Who bought the stock?"

Josef's face said it all. "We don't know. They broke the trades into pieces, each one below the reporting thresholds. They also used fictitious names to open multiple overseas brokerage accounts and create multiple shell corporations. They sold their shares at the market close, and liquidated the shell companies."

"Holy shit! We have to find this puppet master. He's pulling the strings, using these fanatics. This isn't about the Nazi cause. It's all about manipulating stocks for profit. Aryan Reich was doing his dirty work, but now that they've gone to ground, he'll be looking for a different group to do his bidding."

Royal Blood
Chapter 10

2018 - Prague, Czech Republic

Viktor stood on his balcony, cell phone at his ear, watching couples and families stroll down Wenceslas Square in the heart of Prague. "I saw the news, Father. Does this mean we've heard the last of Aryan Reich?"

"They're out of business. When we identified Tripp's body, that clinched it. All their leaders are dead or in prison."

Viktor saw Louise walking toward the building. His heart beat faster at the sight of her. She waved and he waved back. The incident three months ago in Tunis could have driven her away, but it seemed quite the opposite. *She's the one. How lucky can I be*?

His father's voice interrupted his thoughts. "I wish this ended terrorism in Europe, but other groups are always looking to strike."

"That's for sure." Viktor walked inside and closed the French doors. "I have to go, Father. Louise is here." He headed toward the front door in anticipation.

"Don't forget, you promised to bring her over to meet us soon. Have a great evening."

The doorbell rang and Viktor opened the door.

Louise stepped in and he caught a whiff of lavender, evoking memories of their time in Tunis. Her soft, blue eyes appeared even bluer when complemented by the delicate aquamarine necklace he'd bought her in Paris. He could sense her happiness, love, and sexual desire.

Louise brushed a lock of curly hair from her eyes. "I'm inside, silly. Maybe you should shut the door."

"I'm sorry." He closed it and turned the deadbolt. "I couldn't stop admiring you."

She wrapped her arms around his neck. He pulled her closer and brought his lips to hers. The bulge in his pants pressed against her and she lifted her leg to meet it. They shared a probing kiss, trading turns with their tongues. He loved her taste, her smell, her touch. His sensitivity to emotions heightened everything. He felt her passion as well as his own. It took all his willpower to withdraw his tongue and move his head away.

Louise smiled and puffed her lips in a sexy pout. "What's wrong, sweetheart? I know you want me."

"More than anything." He stepped back. "Can we save it for dessert? I don't often cook, and I want tonight to be special."

"You're cooking? What are you making?"

"Chicken cordon bleu. Should be done in about ten minutes. I have vegetables to cut up."

"That's sweet. I didn't know you could cook." She kissed him again.

"I found the recipe in a French cookbook and it sounded simple enough."

"Let me help with the vegetables."

While preparing dinner, the subject turned to Viktor's family. "Remember I told you Father had his DNA tested?"

"I do. Did anything come of it?"

"It sure did. You'd think Father would be proud, but he seems embarrassed."

"Why? What did they find?"

"His DNA matched a Premysl king. *Twenty-Four News* is broadcasting the segment at seven o'clock."

"Let's watch it."

"There must be hundreds ... maybe thousands of Premysl descendants out there. I don't know why he's so worried."

****

After dinner, Viktor and Louise curled up together on the sofa facing the TV. The program covered world and national news, then broadcast a teaser before going to commercial. "Did the royal bloodline of Bohemian kings die out? The answer when we return."

Louise squeezed his hand. "Here comes the story."

Back from commercial, the anchorman repeated, "Did the royal bloodline of Bohemian kings die out? At Prague Castle, a team of scientists have spent more than a decade studying the remains of medieval kings located in the crypts below St. Vitus Cathedral. They have recently achieved a breakthrough."

The young newscaster appeared on the left side of the split screen. He wore a dark suit and spoke in the clear, authoritative tone common for his profession. On the right was a middle-aged man wearing a green sweater. His dark hair was thin, with a long strand of his comb-over snagged on the top of his wire-rimmed glasses.

The newsman faced the camera. "Dr. Dominik Vavrek, the project director of the Ancient Bones Project, is here to explain."

The older man smiled at the camera, sweat beading on his forehead.

"Dr. Vavrek. Thank you for joining us this evening."

"I'm glad to be here."

"Ancient bones and Bohemian kings. Sounds exciting. What can you tell us about your project?"

"The royal crypt of St. Vitus holds the remains of royalty and saints. Some of the bones date from the tenth century."

"Tenth century? Truly ancient."

"The Premysls ruled Bohemia for more than four centuries. History tells us the royal bloodline ended in 1306 when the king died and his son was murdered."

"So what has your team been studying?"

"We've been analyzing DNA from these bones, using the male Y chromosome to follow the royal bloodline of kings. We discovered two Premysl kings and one duke with the same Y-DNA markers."

"The same markers? Does that mean the two younger men are direct descendants of the older one?"

"That could be the case, but brothers would also have the same gene markers." Vavrek pushed at the bridge of his glasses. "Premysl Ottokar the First and Ottokar the Second are the kings. They're descendants of Václav the Good."

"Václav? You mean Good King Wenceslas?"

"Yes. He died in 935. He was actually a duke, but most people prefer the 'Good King' title."

"Are there any direct descendants?"

"There are thousands of Premysl descendants alive today, but we've never found any men with Y-DNA matching the royal line of kings ... until Monday. Interior Minister Eduard Prazsky's DNA is a match. As far as we know, he's the only person alive from the royal line of kings — he and his children."

Louise squeezed Viktor's hand. Her eyes remained riveted to the screen.

The announcer glanced to his left, then focused on the camera. "Minister Prazsky has a son ... Viktor. Would he be in the line of kings as well?"

Dr. Vavrek nodded. "We haven't tested his DNA, but certainly Eduard's son would be a descendant as well."

Viktor grabbed the remote.

Louise took his hand and kissed it. "Wait."

The announcer got in the last word. "Eduard and Viktor Prazsky. The new Premysl dynasty." Recent photographs of Viktor and his father appeared on the screen before they went to a commercial.

This wasn't a welcome development. How would Viktor's fellow MEPs react — not Louise — the others. *The election's a year away.* Maybe it was time to consider resigning from the European Parliament.

"You can turn it off now, Prince Viktor." Louise looked at him as though star-struck, then she winked.

He frowned. "It's not funny. The Czechs and the rest of Europe threw the Habsburgs out a century ago. Czechs don't like royalty. My father and I will be vilified in the press."

"Habsburgs? I thought you were a Premysl."

"The Habsburgs and Luxembourgs married into the Premysls in the thirteenth century."

"You've always told me the Czech people are proud of their Bohemian past. They're going to be proud of you, too." She touched his cheek and kissed him gently. "Frankly, I think your royal blood is kinda hot." She kissed him again and leaned back on the sofa, pulling him on top of her.

Her tongue darted quickly into his mouth and then back, beckoning his to follow. They fumbled, groped and tugged at each other's clothes. Viktor lifted her blouse and pulled at her bra, freeing one breast and sucking it hungrily. She arched her back as his tongue caressed her nipple.

He pulled his shirt over his head and she helped him. Undressing each other, they touched and kissed in every way possible. They knew what pleased each other, and nothing about sex was awkward between them. She was on top when he was ready to climax. Viktor sensed her excitement building at the same time. They shuddered and moaned in unison before she collapsed on his chest.

Sweaty and exhausted, Louise lifted her head and looked at Viktor. "I always thought it was rare to have orgasms together, but we always do. It's as if our feelings are always in sync. We have something special."

Viktor brushed the hair out of her eyes, and smiled. "I've never loved anyone as much as you."

They untangled their bodies and sat up. He kissed her gently. "I have something to tell you that I've never shared with anyone before. If it doesn't scare you away, I'd like to marry you."

She shook her head. "I'd love to marry you, sweetheart. Nothing you say could ever scare me away."

"I hope you still think so after I tell you." He cleared his throat and scratched at his scar. "I can't explain why, but I can sense other people's emotions — not only yours."

"You can read minds?"

"No, I can't read minds. But I can sense when someone is happy, sad, angry ... their feelings. Even when people try to hide their feelings, I know their true emotions. I can even tell when they lie."

"You do understand people better than I do."

"That's not all." He looked away briefly. "I can also control the emotions of others — both good and bad."

"Control emotions?" Louise licked her lips slowly, seductively. "That explains our perfectly timed orgasms."

"I've tried hard not to use my mind to affect your emotions, but orgasms are beyond my control."

"I'm not complaining, Viktor. I love you."

"I love you, too." After a brief kiss, his expression turned serious. "I have the most powerful effect on people when using negative emotions. It scares me sometimes."

Louise paused for a moment, "Like the taxi driver in Tunis?"

"Yes ... this has to be our secret."

Ploughman's Oasis
Chapter 11

Prague, Czech Republic

Viktor had never introduced Louise to his family. His father's responsibilities with the government, and his mother's schedule at the hospital made scheduling difficult. There never seemed to be a convenient time when Louise was in Prague.

By early spring, Viktor was tired of all the excuses. On a beautiful Saturday afternoon, he invited the three most important people in his life to lunch at New Town Café.

Viktor spoke French, since Louise was still learning Czech. He squeezed her hand as he smiled at his mother. "We love the trout. It's their fresh catch." He pointed at her menu. "I think you'd like it, too."

His father looked up from the menu. "They brew their own pilsner here. I'll try it with the pork."

After ordering their meal, Eduard turned to Louise. "I've heard a lot about your episode in Tunis. Is that where you met?"

"We attended the same EU parliament meetings." Louise put her hand on Viktor's arm. "Tunis is a fascinating place and we enjoyed seeing it together. I only wish we had taken a different cab."

Viktor locked eyes with Louise and smiled. "I was afraid she'd never want to see me again after that." His mind drifted to the embassy in Tunis, where they became lovers.

Magda cleared her throat and drew her son back to the present. "Louise. Viktor tells us you live in France."

"I have a home in Carcassonne, near my parents."

"That's a beautiful place," said Magda. "I love strolling through the walled city. It's like stepping into medieval times, but with shops and restaurants."

Viktor turned to his mother. "Louise's father was in foreign affairs. Her family moved around when she was younger."

"I grew up in Morocco when father was the ambassador." Louise glanced at Viktor and smiled. Her head nodded ever so slightly.

He stood and looked at his parents, who sat silently waiting for him to speak. "I know you haven't gotten to know Louise as well as I have, but you'll be seeing a lot more of her from now on." He knew he shouldn't be nervous, but he was. "Louise and I are engaged to be married."

His father stood and shook his hand. "Congratulations." Then, in an unusual display of emotion, he hugged Viktor.

Magda smiled at Louise. "Congratulations to you both." She looked at her son. "Have you picked a date?"

He laughed and exchanged a knowing glance with his fiancée. "One decision at a time. We just decided to get engaged. Give us some time to think about a date."

Despite the smiles, Viktor sensed wariness from his parents.

He realized what it was, so he sat down and spoke in a low voice. "Louise is aware of the unusual way my mind works. She knows everything."

****

The following evening, Viktor took Louise to a popular disco near the Charles Bridge in Prague, a kilometer from his apartment. He thought a bit of exercise would offset their alcohol consumption from the previous night.

Walking north on Wenceslas Square, Viktor sensed he was the focus of peoples' attention. Louise was right, the media reporting on his royal bloodline turned the Prazskys into celebrities. His picture, including the conspicuous eye patch, appeared in all the papers and magazines. As they left the square, the crowds finally thinned out, giving them a few minutes of anonymity.

Viktor took Louise's hand. "The river's straight ahead."

"This is a long walk. We're taking a taxi home, aren't we?"

"Of course." Viktor put his arm around her. "I wouldn't want to wear you out."

"Too late. You wore me out before we left the apartment." She smiled. "I'm not complaining."

As they turned the corner, Viktor pointed ahead. "There's the disco, only two more blocks."

"Is it the building with the clock tower?"

"It's the one to the right. Ploughman's Oasis is a multi-story disco."

"Ploughman. You said he was the first king of Bohemia, right?"

"Not exactly. But legends do say the first Premysl was a ploughman." He took Louise's hand. You're going to love the disco."

A line had formed in front of the building as people passed through security before paying the cover charge. Viktor and Louise walked toward the end of the line, passing couples and groups of young men and women. His special 'gift' detected confusion and lust — lots of horny drunks.

As they approached the end, Viktor sensed strong negative emotions coming from someone in front of them. Most likely, it was the short brunette with long hair, wearing a clingy blue dress with a plunging neckline and a skirt cut well above the knees. She stood stiffly erect, balanced precariously on high stiletto heels. The outfit was not unusual for this club, but the woman was alone, and despite her smile, he sensed her embarrassment.

Viktor focused on her emotions. *She's smiling, but nervous. Concentrating. Softly chanting. Like she's in church.*

"It's weird," he whispered to Louise, "but I think the woman in front of us is praying."

Louise moved to get a better view. She whispered to Viktor, "Her smile seems forced. She doesn't want to be here." The line moved forward. "And it's obvious she's not used to walking in those heels."

As they approached the door, they saw a man at the entrance. He was tall and muscular, wearing a gold shirt and slacks, his outfit matching two other men standing nearby. The unhappy woman in heels instantly transformed into a salacious flirt. She strutted slowly up to the man, licked her lips with the tip of her tongue and gave him a sexy smile. "Are you the bouncer?"

"Just the doorman," he replied. "I need to look in your purse."

She giggled as she offered him the tiny Neiman Marcus clutch purse she carried. "Sure, have a look."

Viktor moved closer to get a better view of the purse, while the man opened it to reveal a phone, lipstick, a compact, an ID or a credit card, and keys.

"You're good," the man said. "Go on in."

She smiled, tossed her hair back, and walked to the open door.

Viktor stared at her as she disappeared inside. *What the hell? Scared and praying. Nervous. But nothing in her purse ... I'm being paranoid.*

****

Inside, loud music and flashing lights assaulted Nasim Shabir's senses. She was relieved that her prayers were answered. A devout Muslim, her clothes usually covered most of her body, but Falak, her husband, insisted she dress like other patrons, and to act like them, too. She was embarrassed to be dressed like this. She felt like a slut.

Walking slowly down the hallway, she entered the main dance area. The lights on the ceiling and the dance floor made it difficult to orient herself. Another distraction was the dancing flames from candles on all the tables.

Off to the right, she found what she was looking for. Falak had told her to find the bar near the stairway. Men and women stood three-deep at the bar, others sat at high top tables. More people walked up the stairs leading to the dance floors above.

A tall woman, probably the hostess, walked over and yelled loud enough to be heard over the music. "Seat at the bar?"

Nasim shook her head and asked in a loud voice, "Toilet?"

Following the hostess' directions, she headed toward the sign. Inside, she entered a stall and sat on the seat. She opened her clutch and pulled out the phone and the earbud. Her 'phone' was filled with fifty grams of explosives prepared by Falak. The earbud served as a timer that initiated the explosive. The studs on the purse would add to the shrapnel. She plugged the earbud into the phone, put them both back into her purse, and returned to the disco.

Nasim headed toward the bar at the stairs she had spotted earlier. She saw a young man sitting at a table, smiling at her. She smiled and pranced slowly toward him.

He jumped up and nearly fell over in the process. Then he leaned in and whispered. "Buy you a drink?"

She nodded, smiled, and lightly touched his arm, as she sat down on a cheap plastic chair covered with an even cheaper cushion. "Whatever you're having."

He got the waitress' attention and ordered two hurricanes.

She reached into her clutch and twisted the earbud. "I need to go to the toilet." She reached over and touched his arm, then leaned forward, giving him an unobstructed view of her breasts.

Falak had said this was necessary to distract a man. "I'll be right back."

As his eyes were focused on her exposed flesh, she slid the clutch onto her seat and stood up to walk away. The timer would go off in two minutes.

****

Viktor ordered two drinks, handed one to Louise, and looked around for a place to sit. He pointed toward the toilets. "Look. That woman. Didn't we see her outside? The one who stood in front of us."

The woman stopped, looked around and walked in their direction.

"I think so," said Louise. "She looks confused."

As she approached, Viktor sensed her unique 'thought signature'. "That's the one. And she's afraid of something."

Louise turned as the woman approached. "Are you looking for a seat?"

Fear in her eyes, she ignored Louise and pushed her way through the crowd toward the door.

Observing with all his senses, Viktor drew a conclusion. "Something's wrong. She's in a panic—"

Near the stairway, a bright flash and a loud bang drew everyone's attention. Furniture splintered and people were thrown from the blast.

Viktor pushed Louise down to the floor and covered her with his body. "Are you all right?"

She looked around. "I'm okay. What was that?"

They both managed to stand. Men and women lay on the floor bleeding, many covered with broken tables and chairs. Small fires broke out at the tables. Those who could stand were screaming and pushing as they fled the room. Flames spread quickly and dark smoke rose. *Cheap plastic! Toxic smoke.*

Viktor grabbed Louise's hand. "This place is a fire trap. Stay low. Away from the smoke." He knew they had to get out of there quickly, but injured people lay on the floor in front of them. *Can't help everyone.*

The fire grew rapidly. An alarm screamed for their attention. Smoke darkened the room and cold water sprayed from the ceiling. Viktor reached for an unconscious woman, head surrounded by a dark liquid. *Blood?*

He knew his 'gift' should sense something from the woman — unless she was dead. *Nothing I can do for her.*

He didn't have much time. He pushed thoughts of the dead woman aside and reached for the man next to her. Viktor sensed the man's pain. *He's alive.*

He reached under the man's armpits and turned to Louise, who was soaked from the sprinklers. "Push your way to the exit so I can follow you."

A large piece of glass was lodged in the man's leg, but Viktor knew he couldn't stay there to tend the wound. "He's coming with us."

Emergency responders took the injured man from Viktor as soon as he emerged from the building.

Louise was wet and dirty but appeared unharmed. As they embraced, Viktor replayed everything in his mind. *That woman ... she did it!*

Béziers, France

The following afternoon, Girard entered the grand master's office. After the success in Prague, he expected praise. Actually, he hoped for praise but didn't really expect it.

Perseus stood to greet his aide. "The disco attack went exactly as I planned. All of Europe is outraged. Our investors will do very well, and so will we."

All Girard heard was the old man taking credit for success. He paused to take a breath before responding. "Yes, Your Grace. Just as we planned."

Perseus started coughing, wheezing and shaking. He pulled out a handkerchief and held it to his mouth. With his other hand, he pointed at Girard, then the table. His convulsions continued.

Girard wanted to watch this asshole cough himself to death. Instead, he went to the table and opened the drawer. He picked up the rescue inhaler, looked at it, and checked out the label. *This could be just what I need. It could work.*

The old man's wheezing interrupted his thoughts.

After removing the cap and shaking the inhaler, Girard gave the device to Perseus, who exhaled and thrust the mouthpiece between his lips before pressing the canister and taking a deep breath.

"Stop staring at me!" Perseus held out the inhaler. "Put this back in the drawer."

Girard hated this ungrateful old man. Nevertheless, he dutifully followed orders. If things went well, the bastard always took credit. If they went poorly, all the blame was laid at Girard's feet. The abusive tirades were unbearable. Girard was certain he could lead Arcadian Spear more effectively than this piece of shit. *It's time I did something about it.*

Perseus reached for a cognac and sat back in his chair. "Give me an update."

Girard nodded. *You're the boss — for now.* "The Czech report was picked up by other news agencies and bloggers. It's all over the internet."

"Read it to me."

Girard located it on his tablet computer. "Western Jihad, a Muslim extremist group, bombed a busy discotheque in Prague, killing eleven patrons and injuring forty others. Three members of the group were apprehended four kilometers away in a house in Žižkov, along with bomb-making materials."

"Excellent." Perseus set down his drink.

"The National Freedom website in Germany published the report. They cited this attack as part of a Muslim plan to kill Christians. Their post received twenty thousand hits in the first hour. Then Twitter spread the story. The hashtag #*muslimbomb* hit the top of the trends list."

Perseus nodded his head in approval. "What about retaliation?"

"We're all set. I got a well-known blogger to call for a 'flash mob' at five o'clock. Once everyone shows up at the Bohemian Mosque, our folks will throw rocks and Molotov cocktails. They know how to stir up anger in a crowd. One person brought the head of a pig to throw into the flames."

"This should inspire copycat attacks in Berlin and Paris."

Girard bowed slightly. "Prazsky will certainly go after Western Jihad, and I expect he'll solicit help from Germany and France."

"That's what we want. More spending on security equipment and services. The Czech people will rally around the recommendations of Prazsky. We need him to fan the flames of anti-Muslim hatred. But we need to go further. We need him to become the charismatic leader uniting Europe in opposition to Islam."

"Shouldn't that leader be the pope?"

"The pope? He's soft on Muslims. No, we need to focus on Prazsky. We need to strengthen the credentials of his bloodline. It's time to introduce the world to the Christian royal family."

"You mean the Desposyni?"

"Exactly. When Travers releases her new book, it will raise public awareness of the Desposyni. We need to connect the dots for Christians around the world."

"What happens if we raise Prazsky's profile, but he doesn't take a firm stance against Muslims?"

"When Western Jihad takes the next step, Prazsky *will* take it personally."

Desposyni
Chapter 12

Prague, Czech Republic

Last night, Eduard rushed to the scene of the deadly bombing at Ploughman's Oasis and learned Viktor had been inside during the attack.

He spent the following morning talking to the press, and ensuring the police and security teams had the resources they needed for the investigation. He reserved the last meeting of the day for an update from Viktor and Josef. The three of them sat in a small conference room adjacent to his office, studying the face of a young, Middle Eastern woman projected on a large screen.

Eduard broke the silence. "Is she the bomber?"

Josef nodded. "Her name is Nasim Shabir. She's a member of Western Jihad. Viktor identified her from the club, and the security camera video supports our suspicions."

Viktor added, "I first saw her in the line outside, and then again shortly before the bomb went off."

Eduard leaned forward. "Pull up the club video."

Josef selected the first clip. "You can see the time in the lower right corner, and I've highlighted her face in all the clips. Here's the first one. You can see her in the line outside, in front of Viktor. The camera didn't pick up anything unusual."

Viktor looked at his father. "She was all by herself. She looked confused and afraid."

Eduard realized his son wasn't guessing about her emotions, he was stating a fact.

Josef ran a second video, this one taken inside the club. "She didn't appear on video from cameras at the bar or in any place restricted to employees. She only showed up in the area around the lower level dance floor. Here she's heading to the toilet ... this is three minutes later as she's coming out ... and this one shows her sitting at a table — the one where the bomb exploded a few minutes later."

When the video switched to another scene, Eduard interrupted. "Don't you have any more video at the table? She must have planted the bomb there."

Josef paused the video. "That camera follows a predefined path around the dance floor, repeating the cycle all night. Five minutes before and after this shot, she wasn't there." He pressed play and the video continued. "Here she walks toward the toilet, but then turns and walks away. Ninety seconds later, the bomb detonated."

"We saw her," said Viktor. "Louise thought the woman might be lost and offered to help, but she ignored us and forcefully pushed through the crowd, like she had to leave in a hurry. A few seconds later, the bomb went off."

A few seconds. Eduard thought about how close Viktor came to death. A lump formed in his throat as he faced his son. "We could have lost you."

Viktor scratched the scar by his eyepatch. "This woman could have killed Louise, too. I want to help you get her."

"You already have. It would have taken Josef's team a long time to identify the bomber without your help."

"I'd like to do more. I want to continue to work on the investigation with you."

"You already have a job," said Eduard. "You're in the European Parliament."

"You're the politician in the family, Father, not me. Four years of stuffy meetings is enough. I plan to resign." Viktor turned to Josef. "Couldn't you use someone like me on your team?"

Josef raised an eyebrow, but said nothing.

Eduard faced his son. "I had no idea how you felt about the Parliament. I'll support you with whatever decision you make, but things aren't that simple." He glanced briefly at Josef before continuing. "You're a material witness, not a member of the investigative team. I promise we'll talk more about this later. Right now, Josef and I need to go over the details of the case."

Viktor stood. "I'm serious about resigning." He walked a few steps toward the door and turned around. "And I know I can help."

When Viktor left, Eduard turned to Josef. "I didn't expect him to ask you for a job."

"Frankly, I'd love to hire him. Better yet, bring him into our Rapid Deployment Unit. He's a war hero, he's in great physical shape, and he has good instincts." Josef set his tablet down. "You know he'd be a terrific addition to the Fist of Freedom, too."

This discussion made Eduard uncomfortable. He always expected Viktor to be a politician — maybe prime minister one day. But right now, he had a more pressing issue — the terrorists behind this attack.

He waved his hand dismissively. "Let's get back to the investigation."

Eduard studied the video of the carnage inside the club, and the photographs taken by the investigation team. It was clear that the explosion and fire originated from the table where Nasim was seen earlier on video.

It was difficult to review the data without reacting to the horrific human toll. Eduard poked his finger toward Josef. "How did you miss this attack? We had a deep-cover agent inside Western Jihad for more than a year. What's he been doing?"

"It takes time to establish trust. This group wasn't a priority before the bombing. They operate in small cells, and our man only knows people in the cell he's infiltrated."

"They're our top priority now. Get everything you can from our inside man. It's time to take out his cell leader and set up our guy to take his place."

"We'll contact him and get this rolling."

"What about the people picked up with explosive materials in the guest house?" Eduard sat back in his chair.

"They gave us the name of their recruiter, but we aren't even sure it's his real name. I think all three of them were set up. Someone made sure we found them."

"Do we know where to find Nasim Shabir?"

"Our inside man has a pretty good idea. I'll have more information this evening."

"As soon as you find her, we'll arrest her."

Josef crossed his arms over his chest. "Let's not move too fast. I suggest we hold off on the arrest."

Eduard pounded the desk. "Why the hell not? She killed eleven people. Almost killed Viktor. She could kill again."

"We need to identify other members. The Fist of Freedom can put her house under surveillance. We can also bug her phone with our newest software, so every time the phone gets within six meters of another, it'll wirelessly spread the infection with the same software. Within a few days, we can eavesdrop on quite a few phones."

"Don't let her get away. We can't let her kill again."

****

An hour later, Eduard arrived at home and walked into the living room, where Magda sat in her overstuffed chair by the fireplace. As he approached, she looked up from her book and smiled.

He leaned over and kissed her. "You're the highlight of my day."

"You make my day pretty special, too." She closed her book and set it on the end table. "Do you have any late meetings tonight?"

"Not a one. I'm ready to relax."

"Fix us a drink?"

Eduard poured a glass of Riesling for his wife and a mug of pilsner for himself, then sat in the chair next to her.

Magda reached for the TV remote control. "There's something you need to watch. I kept the recording."

"Oh?"

"Jana told me you were mentioned on Patricia White's talk show, so I watched it."

"Oh, no. What did she say?"

"One of her guests said you might be related to Jesus."

"What?" Eduard slammed down his glass. "Where do people come up with this crap?"

"Calm down. You need to watch it."

"Okay. Let's see what they're saying." Eduard leaned back in his chair.

Magda selected the *Patricia White Show* from the recordings. She fast-forwarded, glancing at her husband. "Julie Travers is promoting a new book. As soon as I spot her, I'll slow it down." A thin, fortyish woman with long red hair walked onto the stage. "There she is." Magda pressed *play*.

Applause filled the room and Magda lowered the volume. A beautiful young woman with short brown hair stood and faced the camera. "This morning, I'm happy to introduce the successful author of five popular historical novels, here to discuss her latest — *Merovingian Affair*. Please welcome Julie Travers."

Julie hugged Patricia and sat on a couch.

As the applause died down, the host began, "Thank you for coming, Julie. We're excited to talk about your new novel. I just read it, and had a hard time putting it down."

"I'm glad you liked it."

"For those in the audience who haven't read it," Patricia said, "this novel is set in France during the early sixth century, when Clovis the First became the Frankish king." The camera switched views as Patricia faced the author. "Let me ask you, Julie. How much of the book is based upon historical fact?"

"Everything about the political and religious leaders is accurate, with literary license to fit in the romance between Bernard and Amelia."

Eduard fidgeted in his chair as he glanced at his wife. He thought of a hundred things he would rather watch. *She's just pushing her book.*

On TV, Patricia seemed interested in Julie's comments. "Their forbidden affair was exciting! So, even though Bernard was a bastard, his bloodline made him a contender for the throne."

"Absolutely. Royal bastards were often recognized and granted status in those days — especially if their father was a Desposyni."

"Let me ask the question on many of your readers' minds. Did Desposyni actually exist?"

Eduard shrugged his shoulders. His mind began to drift to his earlier conversation with Josef. He wasn't sure it was a good idea to allow her to walk around freely. *That woman's dangerous.*

Julie's laugh brought Eduard's attention back to the screen. The camera zoomed in for a close-up. "This is the most controversial part of the book. Everyone asks me about it."

She looked directly at the camera. "After the death of Jesus, a Jewish Christian movement began. James, the brother of Jesus, was the first leader. He was the first in a royal bloodline called the Desposyni. For many years, the families of James and his siblings were recognized as royalty."

"Does this mean Jesus himself was married and had children?"

Eduard heard these theories before. *Another one of those books.*

Julie continued. "That idea was featured in several popular books, but was never proven. The Desposyni have nothing to do with that theory."

"Is there any evidence to support their existence?" asked Patricia.

"Until recently, I would have said no. A few papers reference a meeting between Pope Sylvester and a group of Desposyni, although nothing could be corroborated. Then, last year they found new documents at the Nicomedia dig site in Turkey, where Emperor Constantine died."

"What did they find?"

"One letter was from 325 AD during the Council of Nicaea. Sylvester, the Bishop of Rome at the time, sent two legates with a letter. It described a meeting with people he called Desposyni. There was no doubt Sylvester recognized their royal status."

"That's interesting. What ever happened to them?"

"In the early fifth century, Faramond, a Desposyni, became the first Frankish king. His descendants were the Merovingians."

"Don't some scholars believe Clovis and other Merovingians came from Jesus himself? And the Habsburgs, too?"

"It's a popular belief, although no records exist from that time. The Habsburgs married into every important dynastic family, and some people claim they come from Merovingian blood."

"How about the Czech royal family — the Prazskys?"

Eduard gripped the arms of his chair.

"The Premysls were the Bohemian royal family. Eduard and Viktor Prazsky are modern descendants. I never investigated any link. There are about a hundred years between the last Merovingian and the first Premysl," said Julie. "But that's an interesting question."

Magda turned off the TV. "The rest is about her book."

Eduard stood up and paced the floor. "Now the press is going to say Viktor and I are descendants of Jesus' family." He looked at his wife. "We'll never have any privacy again."

Surveillance
Chapter 13

Prague, Czech Republic

A white van, with the name Karlín Heating and Cooling painted on the door, was parked across the street from the largest indoor gun range in Prague. Inside the van, Viktor kept an eye on three video screens. One camera pointed to the entrance to the range, and the others pointed east and west. No one was walking along the street, but cars were parked solid on both sides.

Viktor shoved a pizza box toward his partner on this stakeout. "There's still one slice left. Help yourself."

Rashad, a young man from Jordan dressed in jeans and a flannel shirt, shook his head. "Don't you ever get tired of pizza? Tomorrow I'll buy lunch. Burgers — anything but pizza. Especially cold pizza."

"Maybe we'll get lucky and our bomber will show up today. She needs to keep shooting to maintain her skill."

Nasim Shabir had vanished from sight immediately after the disco bombing. When the Fist learned she was married to an explosives expert named Falak, they scanned every video feed available for both of their faces. Two weeks ago, Nasim's image showed up on a video from this gun range, and they hoped she'd return.

Rashad closed the pizza box. "I don't understand why we don't arrest her when she shows."

"Josef was clear about it. We're after the money man — the puppet master. He thinks if we follow her, she'll lead us to someone higher up the organization."

"Okay, if that's what he wants," said Rashad. "You know, she might decide to go shooting at one of the other ranges. Maybe she left Prague. She might never return."

"Well, that's a cheery thought."

"You getting tired of surveillance? Do you miss the excitement of your political life?"

"You don't know how boring politics can be. I'm here to find Nasim and the rest of those killers." Viktor glanced at his laptop and pointed to the screen. "Look, that man just walked past us and we picked up his cell phone information."

"How come a politician like you knows so much about this equipment?"

"I was in intelligence in Kabul. We monitored everything that generated radio waves. Of course, things have changed a lot in five years, but I do my best to keep current."

"Did they have cell phones in Afghanistan?"

Viktor nodded. "They did, but not many people used them. Here it's different. Seems like everyone in Prague has a phone. Fortunately, each one needs to reach out to the nearest cell towers."

Rashad nodded toward a tool pouch on his right. "And we happen to carry our own little cell tower with us."

"You get that interceptor unit close to Nasim, and I'll do the rest."

"If she shows up, I'll get her number." Rashad pointed at the screen on the right. "We have some customers coming from the east. The range hasn't even opened its doors."

"They're all guys. None of them are short enough."

"More coming from the west. One's short. Could be her." Rashad grabbed his tool bag and left the van.

Viktor studied the video. *Nasim? Maybe.* Rashad appeared on the screen. He looked like an air conditioning repair man on a service call. He walked closer to his target as she approached the front door of the shooting range. Then he scratched his right ear.

It's her! A cell phone number popped up on Viktor's laptop, then another. He grabbed his phone and speed-dialed the command center. "Target at site one. Unaware. Repeat, target at site one."

A voice came back from the command center. "Acknowledged. Site one."

Five numbers now showed on his laptop. Viktor uploaded custom spying software to each of the phones. Once the uploads were complete, he had total control of the microphones, cameras and everything stored on the phones. He immediately downloaded contacts, pictures, text messages and call logs. Then he contacted the command center and gave them the numbers. They'd gather the call history from the phone companies.

Rashad entered the van. "Team Three arrived. They've got eyes on Nasim." He sat down next to Viktor. "What have you got?"

"I copied everything to your laptop. Here's the first one. Everything's in Arabic. Why don't you check it out?"

Rashad studied the data. "She's only got one contact — Falak."

"That's definitely hers." Viktor turned geotracking on her phone, then her camera. The video was dark. *Probably inside her purse.* He muted the volume control inside the van before turning on her microphone. When he slowly raised the volume, all he heard was noisy gunfire drowning out other sounds from the phone. *Stupid shooting range.* He turned down the volume.

Rashad called the command center and gave Falak's number to them, then he sat behind the wheel. He would drive today while Viktor operated the equipment

An hour later, Nasim stepped outside and walked to the west. When she was out of sight, Rashad pulled out, relying on Viktor to navigate using the tracking data from her phone.

A message from Team Two appeared on the laptop. Viktor read it to his partner. "She's in a dark blue Škoda hatchback."

Three teams were pre-positioned in different locations about a kilometer away, each one watching and listening to the transmissions from Nasim's phone. As planned, each team would take turns approaching Nasim close enough to get eyes on her, but then would drive out of sight.

When the tracking slowed to a stop, Team Three sent a message. "Olsany Manor. In the parking garage."

Viktor searched for information on the building and displayed it on his laptop. It was a large six-story concrete apartment complex, covering an entire block. A historical building with no elevators. The apartments on each floor were so close together, it would be difficult to identify where she went.

Team Two was assigned to locate her. Geotracking wasn't accurate enough to pinpoint her position, so the team followed her phone's signal like a beacon.

Viktor listened to the sound transmitted from her phone. He heard steps in a stairwell. When she opened a door, all he heard was an annoying hiss. *Sounds like a noise generator.* Something spies and assassins use to render audio bugs useless.

The video sent from her phone changed from total darkness to a brief flash of her face. Then she powered it off.

Team Two sent a message, "Lost her signal." This meant they'd have to go door-to-door with a small directional microphone and listen to each apartment. It was time-consuming, but they'd find her.

****

Once Team Two identified her apartment on the third floor — made easier because of the noise generator — Viktor spoke to the apartment manager. He was in luck. Viktor and Rashad moved into the third-floor apartment next to Nasim Shabir the following day.

The noise generator successfully concealed her conversations, but it also muffled the sounds of Viktor slowly drilling a hole through the wall into the upper corner of her living room.

Rashad looked through the eyepiece of a borescope camera while holding the end of a long optic fiber. "It works, but it looks weird."

"That tiny ball on the end is a fisheye lens. It'll give us a wider view inside." Viktor climbed to the top of a ladder against the wall. "Give it to me." He took the thin fiber and slowly fed it through the new hole.

"Stop," said Rashad. "It just broke through."

Viktor climbed down the ladder and connected the camera to a large monitor. On the screen appeared the image of a nearly empty room — only the bare essentials. One sofa, one chair and a small dining table next to a basic kitchen. Not even a TV. All the way to the right was an open door to another room where Nasim sat in a chair. She appeared to be talking to a man in the bed, but the audio simply picked up the hiss of the noise generator.

"Must be Falak," said Rashad. "That explains why no video cameras have captured his image. It looks like he's sick — or injured."

"He wouldn't be the first bomb-maker who injured himself. I wonder how serious."

For the next two weeks, Viktor and Rashad spent their days on surveillance. Falak never moved. Nasim only left the apartment to buy food and go to the pharmacy. Surveillance teams followed her each time. The only medicine she ever bought was morphine.

Rashad pushed his chair away from the monitor. "It's hard to see Falak from here. I believe Nasim is preparing for her husband's death."

"I'm not sure this surveillance is worth the effort," said Viktor. "We aren't learning a thing. Even if she didn't use those audio jammers, these two aren't talking. I don't think Falak can hear."

"Why do you say that?"

"It doesn't look like she's talking to him. If he injured himself making a bomb, he could well have ruined his hearing." Viktor looked at the last two pieces of pizza. "I don't think I'll miss anything while I'm gone."

"Going anywhere interesting?"

"We're spending a few days in Paris. Louise wants me to meet her parents."

"I think I'd rather face terrorists than meet my future in-laws."

****

Josef filled in for Viktor in his absence. After two uneventful days, Josef considered ending the surveillance and arresting her. But if he did, they might never be able to identify the puppet master funding Western Jihad.

Rashad pointed to the screen. "It's almost one o'clock. That's when she turns her phone on — every day at one, for about half an hour."

Josef watched as Nasim turned on the phone. The hiss of audio jamming came across the speakers.

Nasim walked over to comfort Falak. Then the phone rang.

Rashad jumped. "It never rang before."

Josef looked at the laptop monitoring her phone. The incoming number appeared, and he wrote it down.

Inside her apartment, Nasim looked at the number and wrote it down, too. It rang three more times, but she didn't answer. Then she cleared the call log and turned off the phone.

Josef sent the incoming number to the command center, then spoke to Rashad. "It's a prepaid calling card. Whoever it was, turned off their phone. This call let Nasim know the number. I'm sure she'll use it soon."

She spread out her prayer rug and began the same ritual she repeated five times each day.

Rashad shook his head. "Something's wrong."

"What do you mean?" Josef wrinkled his brow. "You've reported her praying every day like clockwork."

"This isn't her normal schedule. She prayed just one hour ago, and now she's praying again."

When Nasim completed her ritual, she rose and reached for the morphine. She emptied all the pills from the bottle onto a plate and crushed them to powder.

Josef leaned forward, straining to see what she was doing on the video. "That's a lot of morphine. This can't be good."

Nasim poured a hot cup of tea, emptied the medicine into the cup and stirred it. She carried the cup to her husband. It was difficult to see what she was doing because of the camera angle.

Rashad shook his head. "I guess he drank it."

When Nasim returned to the living area, she turned on her phone and made a call. This number was different, and Josef passed it along to the command center.

Even though everything was recorded, Rashad listened to both sides of the call. Nasim spoke in Arabic, so Rashad translated for Josef. "She said her husband can't supply what she needs. Then she asked, 'Can I count on you?' ... The man on the other end of the line said, 'thirty minutes', then he hung up."

Josef was still on the line with the command center. "Another prepaid phone. Geolocation was Prague, eastern Žižkov district, but now the phone is off. Not enough time to triangulate more accurately."

Back in her apartment, Nasim threw her clothes into an oversized purse and headed out the door.

Josef called the command center with the approximate geolocation in Žižkov. "Pre-position two teams at that point."

"She left her phone on," said Rashad. "She does that whenever she leaves."

Josef closed the laptop and tucked it under his arm. "Let's follow her. She's not coming back."

Rashad drove while Josef monitored the phone's location and forwarded the tracking data and audio to the other teams.

The phone stopped moving outside another large concrete block of apartments, similar to Olsany Manor. The audio played the sound of a car door, footsteps and the echo of her feet in a stairwell.

Rashad parked fifty meters away. When they got out of the van, Rashad listened to the audio as he walked briskly next to Josef, who used a signal finder to follow Nasim's phone.

While they walked, Rashad translated what he heard. "She asked someone if it was ready ... A man said, 'One kilo. Detonator, too.' ... She wants a second detonator."

Josef and Rashad entered the stairwell and headed upstairs.

Rashad continued to follow Nasim's conversation. "I think he gave her the detonator ... He yelled — angry."

A loud bang — an explosion — came from above. Loud enough to hurt Josef's ears. Something slammed hard. *A door?*

Dirt, dust and pieces of wall and ceiling flew forcefully down the stairs toward him. He crouched low and grabbed the stair rail.

"Are you okay?" he asked Rashad, who crouched next to him.

"Yeah ... yeah." Rashad shook his head. "What the hell did she do? The phone's dead, too."

"You think she did this — on purpose?"

"I know the man was pissed off — right before the explosion."

Intelligence
Chapter 14

Prague, Czech Republic

"Explosion?" Eduard shouted into the phone. "So, where's the woman?"

Josef answered in a slow, even voice. "We had her under constant surveillance. She led us to a bomb-maker and it looks like she set off an explosion."

"She set it off? Did it kill her?"

"Nasim isn't there. The bomb-maker is dead. I think she killed him on purpose."

"She got away from you?" Eduard paced in front of his fireplace. "You're tracking her, aren't you?"

"I'm afraid she left her phone at the scene, burned in the fire. We lost her."

Eduard stopped pacing. "You told me not to worry! You let her walk around freely for two months. She almost killed Viktor. This surveillance is over. We're shutting down Western Jihad right now. Just like Aryan Reich."

"Uh … one more thing … It looked like the man was making Semtex, but the explosion was only PETN and RDX."

"I'm not an explosives expert, Josef. What are you telling me?"

"We believe Nasim took the Semtex … maybe a kilogram or more."

"Find that woman! Find her now!"

****

Two hours later, in a small hotel room near Prague's Pavlova Station, Oleg Baros, a man in his mid-thirties, sat in a chair next to the TV.

Gustav, a young man with a hard look about him, punctuated by a large scar directly under his right eye, sat on the bed. He held up a photograph. "I was thinking about the new guy — Ludvik. Do you think we can trust him? I just had a feeling, like maybe he's a cop."

Oleg wondered if this man held the same suspicions about everyone. "I figured the same thing."

The door burst open. Five men in SWAT gear rushed in, guns trained on Gustav. "Hands in the air — now!"

Gustav leapt out of the chair. "What the hell?" His gaze darted between the intruders. "Who the fuck are you? What's going on?"

One man shoved his gun into Gustav's chest. "Hands up, scumbag!"

Raising his hands, he glanced at Oleg, who sat there calmly watching. "You're a cop? You piece of *shit*!"

"That's right, asshole." Oleg stood and poked his finger at the terrorist leader. "You're busted."

One of the men stepped closer to Gustav. "Shut up. Don't try anything you'll regret."

Staring with contempt at the man he had trusted, Gustav stood still while two men grabbed him roughly. Another poured chloroform on a cloth and held it tightly over Gustav's mouth and nose. He struggled, but it didn't help. After a few gasps, he went limp. One of the men pulled out a syringe and plunged it into Gustav's arm.

****

Eduard met Josef at a warehouse near Florenc Station, not far from the hotel. The Fist of Freedom often used this place.

With Nasim on the loose, they had to extract information quickly.

Josef led Eduard to a seat in a small office. "You don't have to be here, you know."

"Nasim killed eleven people. Almost killed my son. We've got to find her before she kills again." Eduard took a seat at the table that supported three large, flat-screen monitors plus a desktop computer and a printer.

Two of the monitors displayed moving lines, like something you'd see in a hospital. The other displayed the live image of a man, chained and sitting at a table, head down as though he was trying to sleep. He was naked, except for a headset and a band on his arm. He was shaking. Two men in heavy jackets stood behind him. One chair sat on the opposite side of the table. A toilet sat in the corner.

Josef pointed to the video. "The prisoner's name is Gustav. We believe he's the head of Western Jihad. He's in a frozen meat locker we modified for interrogations. You probably saw the door on your way in. You'll meet the men with him, Oleg and 'Doc'. The other monitors show his brain waves and pulse."

"Did you learn anything when you grabbed him?"

"The handgun we found in his room was untraceable and the passport is fake. His prepaid phone is the one that called Nasim today. There's no personal data, and the call log was empty. We checked phone company records. It only made that one short call to Nasim's phone — ten seconds — just long enough to pass along the caller ID to her. Later, after he was sedated, the phone rang."

"Was it her?"

"Not sure. We monitored the call while one of our guys answered it. Nothing but dead air for a few seconds, then the call ended. We suspect she was waiting for some code word.

Now the caller — probably Nasim — knows the phone is compromised. She'll assume Gustav was grabbed."

"We don't have much to go on."

"We have Oleg, the young man standing next to Gustav. While undercover, Oleg used specially designed glasses to take pictures of everyone he met." Josef pulled out a handful of photos. "When we show them to Gustav, he'll have a tough time disguising his reaction to the photos — especially since we shot him full of scopolamine and he's being monitored by all this equipment."

"Better than a lie detector?"

"Definitely. The drug is often called a truth serum, but some people can resist it. I wonder if he could get away with lying to Viktor."

Eduard knew the answer — no one could fool his son. But he didn't want to bring Viktor into this dirty business. "Hard to say." He turned to the screen and watched an older man walk away from Gustav and Oleg. A few seconds later, Eduard turned to see the man enter the office.

Josef motioned toward the door, where the man removed his jacket. "That's Doc. He'll monitor everything during the interrogation."

Doc nodded briefly and took a seat. "I'm ready when you are."

Josef stood up, grabbed a briefcase and jacket, and walked to the door. Before leaving, he turned to Eduard. "Oleg and I will handle the interrogation. You and Doc can watch us from here. If you want to communicate with me, let Doc know."

When Eduard settled in the chair, he spotted Josef on the screen, taking a seat across the table from Gustav. Josef set his briefcase on the floor and adjusted his earbud.

Doc leaned forward. "If you hear me, nod your head."

On the screen, Eduard saw Josef nod, then unholster his Taser and jam it into the prisoner's lower abdomen, using it like a stun gun.

The naked man lurched and screamed, but his restraints held him to the chair. His eyes were wide open. "Where am I? What is this? Who the hell are you?" He kept pulling at his chains.

"I'm the one asking the questions," Josef said in a voice that made it clear who was in charge. "You *will* give me the answers one way or another. Do you understand?"

"You don't scare me." Gustav strained at the chains and tried to stand. "I want my lawyer."

Oleg glared at the prisoner, their faces only a few centimeters apart. "No bullshit, asshole. If you don't cooperate, we'll turn you into a crippled eunuch."

The naked man, still shaking, sat straight and defiant. "I know my rights. I told you, I want my lawyer."

Josef pulled Oleg away and pointed his finger in Gustav's face. "When you bombed the disco and killed those people, you gave up your rights. No one knows you're here. We can do anything we like. Anything at all."

Gustav's eyes opened wide. He shook against his bonds.

"I'm going to ask you a question." Josef tapped on his Taser. "I suggest you tell the truth. Who is the leader of Western Jihad?"

Gustav's eyes darted around the room. "I don't know."

Back in the office, Doc spoke into the microphone. "He's lying."

"Lying comes with consequences." Josef jammed the Taser into Gustav's abdomen, holding it there while the prisoner screamed and strained against his shackles.

Josef withdrew the Taser and remained silent.

The chains held the man tightly while he continued to struggle. When he regained his composure, he sat up straight and defiant once more. "You're fucking crazy! I want my lawyer."

"One more time. It gets worse if you lie. Who is the leader?"

"I don't know. I don't know nothin'."

Doc confirmed the lie.

Josef shook his head. "I'll have to punish you now." He grabbed his briefcase, set it flat on the table and opened it. Inside were knives, picks, shears, and other instruments of torture. He pointed to the prisoner's hands, attached firmly to wooden blocks on the table, fingers spread. "We'll start with your left hand. You don't use it much."

Gustav's eyes widened. He screamed when he saw Josef take a sharp chisel in one hand and a wooden hammer in the other.

"Your little finger first." Josef held the chisel on the second knuckle and struck it sharply with the hammer. The prisoner's finger separated from his hand with a crisp crunch, like a carrot being chopped. Gustav screamed, struggled and pissed on the floor. Josef removed the severed piece and wrapped the stump in a rag.

Eduard nearly jumped out of his chair, eyes fixed to the screen. "What the hell?"

"Josef thought you might react like this," said Doc. "He told me to remind you what this scum did. The people in the disco."

Eduard turned his attention back to the screen. He knew Viktor could extract information from the man without resorting to torture. But his son was still new to the job, not yet ready for clandestine interrogations.

It took a few minutes before Gustav said anything coherent. "*Čuráku!* My fuckin' finger! You cut off my fuckin' finger!"

"That's right." Josef held it up and waved it in the man's face. "Smells like raw meat, huh?" He set it on the table in front of the bloody rag. "You've got nine more and ten toes. If you continue to resist, you'll lose them all ... one at a time." He moved his face closer to his prisoner. "Then I'll turn you into a girl."

Gustav shook and struggled. He rocked his head forward and back.

"You can stop me any time you want. All you have to do is cooperate. If not, this day will get a lot worse." Josef folded his arms across his chest. "Who is your leader?"

"I don't know."

"You disappoint me." Out came the chisel. "Time for another finger."

Doc spoke into the mike. "His pulse rate is off the charts. He's ready."

Eduard smiled. "I hope you're right."

Doc pointed at the screen. "Watch the master at work."

Josef put the chisel away. "Shit! I don't have time for this." He grabbed a large butcher knife. "You're too stubborn. It's time for a gelding." He turned the chair, exposing the prisoner's genitals.

"Wait!" Gustav screamed. "Wait!"

Josef smiled and rested the knife on the table, "Why should I wait? So, you can lie to me again?"

"No!" The prisoner shook his head quickly. "I'll tell you anything you want!"

Josef turned the prisoner's chair back toward the table. He held up a water bottle, "Drink?"

The man nodded.

After squirting water into the prisoner's mouth, Josef began. "Who is the leader of Western Jihad?"

Gustav's head dropped to his chest. In a barely audible voice he responded, "I am."

Doc smiled. "Truth! You've got him." Turning to Eduard he added, "We should start getting answers now."

"I hope you're right."

On the screen, a smile spread across Josef's face. "That wasn't so bad." He waved a stack of photos at Gustav. "Now you need to identify each of these people. We know the identity of several of them, so we can tell if you're lying." He put one hand on the butcher knife.

One by one, Josef showed him the photos. The computer analyzed his brainwaves and facial microexpressions to identify which answers were truthful.

Josef held up the final photo.

Gustav studied it. "Nasim Shabir."

"I'm going to ask you an important question. One you will not want to answer honestly. But remember what happens if you lie." Josef held Nasim's photo closer to the man's face. "What does this woman do for you?"

The naked man's eyes widened, then closed. When he opened them, he responded softly. "She handles bombs."

"Do you mean she uses bombs to kill people?"

Gustav didn't respond right away, but finally relented. "Sometimes."

"Where is Nasim right now?"

Looking directly at Josef, he responded, "I don't know." He narrowed his eyes before adding, "I really don't know."

Doc looked at the instruments. "He's telling the truth."

"He's lying." Eduard pounded his fist on the table.

Doc shook his head. "I believe he doesn't know. Give Josef a chance to learn what he can."

Josef pulled out a pair of pruning shears and jabbed it toward the man's genitals. "This is your moment of truth. I want to know where she'll attack. No clever answers."

"I don't know where she is."

"That's not what I asked. Where is she going to attack? Tell me *now*." Josef held the shears with both hands, opened the blades in front of Gustav's face and slammed them shut with force. "You think it'll hurt when I cut it off, but the real pain comes when I cauterize it."

"The *castle*!" Gustav strained against his chains as he yelled. "Prague Castle!"

His head drooped as he answered each of Josef's follow-up questions. The target was St. Vitus Cathedral, in the heart of the sprawling castle grounds.

"When does she attack?"

Gustav looked up. "Saturday."

"How do you contact her?"

"I don't. She contacts me after she finishes the job."

Doc watched the monitors through the exchange. "He's telling the truth."

Eduard stood. "Thank you very much, Doc, and please thank Josef. I have to prepare the team to stop this attack." At the door, he turned. "And tell him to find out who's funding them."

Western Jihad
Chapter 15

Prague, Czech Republic

Eduard dodged another puddle as he walked along the castle grounds on his way to St. Vitus. It was Saturday morning, several hours before sunrise, when he entered a gray tour bus parked nearby. The bus was a custom-designed mobile command center filled with monitors and communication equipment.

Major Sedlak, a former college wrestler, stood to greet him. "Minister Prazsky, I didn't expect you to join us."

Eduard glanced briefly from one end of the bus to the other. Several of the operators stopped what they were doing to see what he wanted. "I'm here to observe, Major. This is your command. Your region's police force. I won't interfere."

"Thank you, Minister. Please take a seat." He pointed to the one next to his own.

One of the operators brought a cup of coffee. "Cream? Sugar?"

"Thank you, Sergeant. I drink it black." Eduard swiveled in his chair back to Sedlak. "This operation's personal, Major. My son was in the disco. This bomber could have killed him. We've got to stop her before she kills again."

"That's why we're here." The major pointed to a map. "The castle grounds open at five, just before sunrise, but St. Vitus doesn't open 'til nine."

Eduard sipped his coffee. *Nice and hot.* "I asked the president to shut down the castle tours today, but he refused.

He feels we can't shut it down every time we receive a threat — especially on the opening day of the new Ancient Kings exhibit. People are coming from all over Europe for this."

Sedlak looked at the minister. "Are we sure no VIPs will be here?"

"All government leaders agreed to avoid the castle tomorrow. I had originally planned to speak at the opening, so sent out a press release announcing a change of plans."

An operator at the far end of the bus announced. "Eagle eye system in place and tested."

"Very good." The major turned to Eduard. "Our facial recognition system will identify Nasim Shabir when she walks through any of the entrances or past the cameras anywhere on the grounds."

"She would be stupid to enter without some kind of disguise."

"The system is not fooled by a disguise. We'll deny entrance to anyone who refuses to uncover their face."

Eduard leaned forward. "Does it pick her out immediately? Can we arrest her at the gate?"

"It takes about two minutes from the time the image is captured. We can't stop her at the gate, but once we identify her, we'll locate her with camera drones." Sedlak pointed to one of the screens. "One of our drones is approaching St. Vitus now, using infrared. At daylight, they switch to the visible spectrum."

"Command center tests successful and operational," announced another operator.

"Crab team operational," said a different voice.

Sedlak explained. "Crabs — that's the bomb squad."

Another voice announced, "Cuckoo's nest operational."

Eduard raised an eyebrow. "Cuckoo?"

"It's the sniper team. They've prepared their 'nests' before guests arrive. Once Nasim is located, they have standing orders to take the shot — if they have an opportunity that doesn't put visitors in jeopardy. It's too risky to try to apprehend a known bomber in the middle of a crowd." Sedlak nodded at one of the screens. "Our pre-action checklist is complete. All we have to do now is wait for the doors to open."

****

Early that afternoon the rain stopped and the sun came out. Viktor led Louise and her parents to the Ancient Kings exhibit in Prague Castle. They originally planned to spend all week at Louise's home in Paris, but changed their plans at the last minute to come to this grand opening event. Monsieur and Madame Pouilin had never visited the castle before.

After walking through the exhibit in the Theresian Wing of the Royal Palace, Viktor led them outside. "Do you want to see where the kings are buried?"

Monsieur Pouilin looked at St. Vitus Cathedral. "Absolutely. That's why we came."

They walked to the large brass doors at the western entry and stepped into the neo-Gothic section. Magnificent stained-glass windows shone colored shafts of light into the cathedral. Large columns flanked the central nave and led up to an impressive vaulted ceiling.

Louise hugged Viktor's arm. "Beautiful. It reminds me of Notre Dame."

Viktor had been here often. He was proud to share the experience with Louise and her parents. As they walked down the narrow aisle on the side of the nave, they passed several small chapels, ornately decorated with gilded statues. But it was St. Wenceslas' Chapel that drew their attention. "That's his tomb — from the tenth century."

Monsieur Pouilin looked at Viktor. "He was your ancestor? Your blood relative?"

Viktor nodded. "He's one of the most revered men in Czech history. I'm very proud of my family." He led them back to the western entry, occasionally stopping to admire mosaics and statues.

"Thank you, Viktor." Louise's father smiled as he stepped out of the church. "This castle is immense. We're not prepared to see it all today."

"Of course, Monsieur Pouilin. Shall we head for the car?" Viktor led the way toward the gate leading into Courtyard Two.

As they walked under the archway, two guards quickly erected portable barriers at the gate they just went through, effectively blocking off access to that part of the castle. Both guards appeared nervous. Viktor sensed tension and fear in the guard nearest to them. *Something's wrong.*

Suddenly, a shrill, wailing sound erupted from loudspeakers. Louise and her parents looked to Viktor, but he had no idea what was happening. Then a calm woman's voice made an announcement in Czech. "Attention. Attention. For your safety, we ask all guests to leave Courtyard Two immediately and proceed to the main gate. We apologize for the inconvenience." The announcement was repeated in German, English, and Russian. The entire message was repeated several more times.

People stopped and looked around. They all talked at once, then began moving out of the courtyard.

"This way." Viktor led Louise and her family toward the gate leading to Courtyard One. To their right, a woman walked away from the gate.

Louise pulled Viktor toward the woman. "She doesn't know what's happening. We need to help her. Maybe she couldn't understand the announcements."

As they approached, Viktor sensed a familiar mind. *Ploughman's Oasis. The woman. Nervous, praying. Sudden calm.* He saw her reach into her purse. *It's Nasim! Shit!*

Viktor focused his mind on this woman's emotions alone — like radar locking onto its target. He sensed her anxiety and amplified it. If he maintained his focus, Louise and her parents should not sense it. At least he hoped it worked that way.

The woman stopped her praying, turned and glared at him.

Viktor had control of her emotions. He projected terror and rage.

Her eyes widened and he turned up the emotional intensity as high as he could.

****

Back in the command center, Eduard stared at the screen. A camera drone had been tracking the bomber since they identified her, and the snipers were watching for an opportunity to take a shot.

Then Eduard recognized the image of his son standing next to Nasim. *He was in Paris. What's he doing here?* "That's Viktor! That's my son!"

The major watched the screen. "She's looking directly at him ... She dropped her purse."

Eduard was on his feet, his pulse racing. "Take the shot!"

The image on the screen zoomed in closer to Nasim. Suddenly her head snapped back, blood sprayed behind her, and she collapsed.

Eduard stared morbidly at the image. The remains of her head lay in a puddle of blood — and the puddle was growing larger. *She's dead. It's over. Where's Viktor?*

Sedlak looked around the command center. "Clean hit. I want cameras all around the area." Five screens displayed the scene, each from a different vantage point.

Eduard looked frantically from one screen to another until he saw Viktor pushing Louise and two older people away from the woman. He gasped. He'd been holding his breath without realizing it. After several large gulps of air, his breathing slowed.

Sedlak looked at Eduard. "No explosion. No innocents injured." Then he barked orders to his team. "Crabs. Freeze it"

A short robot on tractor treads approached the dead woman. Sedlak pointed to a screen. "That's the camera on the robot."

Eduard saw the image of her purse and camera case. The robot extended an arm and opened the purse, then the case, transmitting video of the contents. The only suspicious item was a large telephoto lens.

"What's that?" Eduard watched the screen as the robot moved a small cylinder next to the suspicious lens.

"Trained honeybees." The major turned to Eduard and smiled. "They sniff better than dogs. We'll know if it's a bomb when they get close enough."

"Explosives confirmed," said an operator. "Probably Semtex."

The robot poured liquid nitrogen on everything, a precaution meant to freeze the power supply of any potential ignition device. In a calm, inhuman manner, the robot grabbed the purse and camera case, and dropped them into a containment vessel.

A man in a large protective suit pushed a wheeled blast shield as he walked up to the robot and the dead woman. He would inspect and dispose of the explosives.

Brother Girard
Chapter 16

Béziers, France

The attack on St. Vitus had failed. Girard stood before Perseus, talking to their contact in Prague on speakerphone. "Is she dead?"

The grand master sat silently in his chair, his frown telegraphing disapproval. Even though they both planned the attack, Girard knew the old man blamed him for the failure.

A voice responded on the speakerphone. "I watched the video. She's dead. There's no doubt."

"Anyone else injured? Any damage to the cathedral?"

"Explosive ordnance neutralized the bomb."

"Send a full report tonight." Girard ended the call.

The old man pounded his fist on the table. "You said don't worry. You told me the bomber would slip through their defenses."

Girard's jaw tightened. Nothing was ever the fault of the grand master.

Perseus pointed to one of the computer screens. "Important people made *trades* based on a successful attack. *We* made trades. Do you think those stocks will rise after this failure?"

Girard's pulse throbbed at his temple. He hated criticism. He didn't tolerate it from anyone except this old geezer. *I should be in charge — not him.*

Rubbing his neck, he forced a smile. "Prazsky's men showed the world the value of his riot equipment. European governments will invest, just as we forecast."

"Are you *stupid*? You haven't learned a thing! No people *died*. The public was *not* outraged. They have no incentive to spend." Perseus covered his mouth with his handkerchief and coughed. "Tell me why you failed."

Girard imagined his hands around Perseus's scrawny neck. His fingers tightening. The old man's eyes bugging, his feeble arms waving in desperation as he drew in his last breath. One day, someday, but for now he looked the grand master in the eye and responded in a cold, professional voice. "The police infiltrated Western Jihad, Your Grace. They were prepared for the attack."

Perseus gave a dismissive wave. "You recommended this group. You recommended Aryan Reich, too." The grand master's voice weakened. His breath was labored. He signaled for assistance.

Girard retrieved the emergency inhaler and studied it. It felt about half empty, but otherwise looked identical to a new one. *If I don't give it to you, will you die? ... Too risky.* He offered it to Perseus.

He watched the man struggling to breathe, enjoying his vulnerability. *Just die, old man. Save me the trouble of killing you.* As the personal assistant to the grand master, Girard was also the heir-apparent in the event of the old man's death. *Perhaps it's time for a change.*

Perseus tossed his bloody handkerchief in the trash. "What are you going to do to make up for your failure?"

Girard played the loyal servant — for now. "Prazsky's team stopped the attack. Should I eliminate him, Your Grace?"

"Absolutely not! Minister—" Another coughing fit interrupted him, but he recovered quickly. "Minister Prazsky's reputation is growing. If this had been successful, I'm certain he would have inspired his peers to increase security. When we strike our next target, he will prove valuable."

"Perhaps now is the time to strike Turkey. I believe—"

"No! We strike Prague." Out came a fresh handkerchief to cover more coughing. "I want another attack. Make it personal for Prazsky. This time I expect the public to rise up in anger."

"As you wish, Your Grace." *You'll never live to see the attack!*

****

On Rue d'Arcole in Béziers, Girard sat across the table from an old Frenchman. They were alone in the back room of a small café with bars on the windows. "You can call me Henri," said Girard. "And I will call you René."

"Let me see it." René held out his hand. Girard unwrapped the inhaler he just purchased at a nearby pharmacy and dropped it into the man's hand.

"What do you think? Can you modify it?"

"*Mais oui*, Henri." He turned it slowly in his hand and studied it. "Does he always put it directly in his mouth?"

"Yes, he does." Girard's eye twitched. "What's your concern?"

"If any of the spray escapes, you will need to keep your distance for a few minutes. There is not enough toxin to kill others in the room, but you would not want to take any chances."

"I'll be careful."

"And be sure he does not prime it."

"He only asks me to prime new ones — the first time." Girard worried about the risk he would be taking, but his hatred for the grand master was stronger.

René set the inhaler on the table. "Any questions?"

"I thought botulism was something you got from bad food. Why not use ricin or some other poison?"

"Botulinum toxin is one of the most poisonous biological substances known. I selected it because the symptoms are similar to a stroke, and it's seldom suspected if there's no contaminated food. Also, it's not contagious."

"I never heard of anyone getting botulism from breathing it. How do you know it'll work?"

"It's true. You don't usually get botulism from the air, but there was an incident in a lab in Germany. All over the news." René smiled and raised an eyebrow. "I also know it'll work because I have three satisfied clients ... none of them came back for a refund."

Gerard was intrigued with this deadly toxin and its potential. "Could this be deployed on a larger scale?"

"I wish I could offer you encouragement, but my experience is limited to individuals inhaling it in concentrated form."

So, botulism wouldn't be effective as a weapon of terror. But Girard could use it for a single murder. "All right. Back to the matter at hand. How long does it take after he inhales it?"

"Symptoms usually begin within twelve to thirty-six hours. Everyone is different. It might happen in four hours, or not for eight days." René held up a vial. "Without this antitoxin, death is certain."

"You said it's like a stroke, but people survive strokes."

"This is a neurotoxin. It paralyzes muscles, including those used for breathing. For anyone with the respiratory problems you described, breathing will become progressively more difficult."

It would be risky, but Girard recalled the humiliating meeting after the St. Vitus failure. "How soon will the modified inhaler be ready?"

"It'll take two weeks."

"Can't you rush it?"

"If you are willing to pay double, it will take a week. Triple, and I can have it ready by tomorrow morning."

"I'll be back tomorrow." He paid in cash. "I need it to be half-full."

Girard stepped outside and stood at the doorway, staring blankly across the street. He'd have to slip the tainted inhaler to his master, and then put the good one back after the botulism had done its work. And he had to make sure he didn't touch the toxin.

He would return here in the morning to pick it up on his way to the grand master's home. *Sleep well, old man. Tomorrow you die.*

Power Play
Chapter 17

Béziers, France

Brother Girard stood before Perseus. "Strahov Stadium in Prague is expecting an audience of over a hundred thousand people, two weeks from now. It's a fundraiser. Three major rock groups will perform."

The grand master set his cognac down. "Who will you engage for this? Someone more reliable than Western Jihad?"

"Let me engage Salafi Brotherhood, Your Grace. They—"

"You don't listen! I've told you before. I don't trust those crazies, and I'm losing my trust in you."

Don't trust me? Girard touched his jacket pocket, feeling the lump where he kept the poisoned inhaler. If only the opportunity presented itself. "No Salafi Brotherhood, as you wish. You can trust—"

Perseus rose from his chair, brandishing his cane at his aide. "You're an *idiot*! You think you're ready to take my place?" He began coughing. "You have a lot to learn!" He coughed again and wheezed before dropping back into his chair. As the coughing continued, he waved his hand at Girard.

It's time to end this. Girard nodded, walked to the table and stood with his back to Perseus. He opened the drawer with one hand, while his other hand removed the modified inhaler from his jacket pocket. He reached into the drawer, pulse racing, and pretended to remove the unmodified device. Then he waited to hear another cough before turning around with the deadly inhaler, removing the cap and shaking it.

When the old man reached out, Girard handed him the device containing botulinum toxin, hoping he wouldn't prime it. His palms were sweating. *Can he tell it's different?*

The grand master exhaled. He brought the inhaler near his face and paused. He looked at it. Stared. Turned it. His eyes narrowed.

Did he sense a difference? Heavier? Lighter? Did it feel different?

Then Perseus coughed. Softly at first, then more violently. He put down the inhaler and raised a handkerchief to his face. When the aftereffects of the coughing subsided, he dropped the cloth and again picked up the inhaler. This time he didn't hesitate, he took it straight to mouth. His lips caressed the sleeve used to draw in its precious contents — what he expected to be the precious contents. After he removed it from his mouth, he held it out and examined the device. A few seconds later, he offered it to his aide.

Girard used a handkerchief as he reached for the inhaler. He didn't want to touch it.

"What's with the hankie?" demanded the old man.

"Blood." Girard pointed to his own mouth. "You have blood on your lips."

Perseus wiped the blood from his mouth while Girard walked to the table. He pretended to replace the inhaler in the drawer. Instead, he slipped the deadly device, still wrapped in the handkerchief, into his jacket pocket. He turned and faced Perseus.

The old man poked his finger at Girard. "You think you're *smart.*"

"Your Grace?" *Does he suspect? He can't know!*

"You think you can do my job better than me, but you can't. I trusted your judgement and you *failed.*"

"I will use a different group, Your Grace. Mukhtar Battalion is—"

"This is what you'll do." The old man pounded his fist on the end table. "Tomorrow, I want you to present the plan for Strahov Stadium. No Brotherhood."

"I won't disappoint—"

"Tomorrow."

Girard nodded. *You're a dead man. You just don't know it.*

****

It was ten o'clock at night. Girard sat in the study of his home in Béziers, working on plans. How long did he have to suck up to the old sonofabitch? *Four hours to eight days.* That's how long René said it would take. *Without the anti-toxin, death was certain.*

The old man would die, that's for sure. Would anyone realize it was murder? *The doctors won't give him anti-toxin unless they suspect botulism. If they have any suspicions, they'll check the food in the kitchen — but they won't find a thing.*

René said it would look like a stroke. Stroke victims usually show early symptoms. Girard looked up the medical contact number for the old man. What should he say? *I'm worried about him, Doctor. He seems even weaker than normal today, and he's acting confused.*

That sounds believable. *I wasn't sure if I should call. Please don't tell him. You know how he is.*

He replayed the script in his head until he believed it himself. Then he called the number and acted like the concerned assistant.

****

Early the next morning, Brother Girard rushed to the Béziers Central Hospital emergency room. Julien Martel had called him because his father, the grand master, listed Girard as his primary business contact. It was unlikely the son knew about his father's 'business'.

Julien was in the waiting room. "Mister Girard?" He walked over and extended his hand.

"You must be Mr. Martel," he responded, shaking his hand. "No one would tell me what happened to your father. I pray it's not serious." *I hope he's not talking.*

Julien's well-coiffed, light brown hair and expensive dark suit added to his stuffy, arrogant demeanor. He looked to be in his late forties, maybe fifty. "Perhaps we should go to the cafeteria to talk."

As they walked, Julien said his father had suffered a massive stroke. He didn't seem as upset as Girard expected. The man didn't appear to suspect a thing.

They sat at a table away from everyone else. "You work with my father," said Julien. "He always insisted I contact you in the event of an emergency."

"I'm glad you called."

"My father is dying. He can't breathe on his own. Without those machines, he would already be dead."

"I'm so sorry," feigned Girard. "I can only imagine how you and the family feel. If there's anything I can do, please let me know."

Emotion finally showed on Julien's face — but not much. "Thank you. I was his only family. He's made sure I won't need help from anyone." He reached into his jacket pocket, pulled out an envelope, and handed it to Girard. "He left this for you."

****

The envelope contained the combination to the grand master's safe. This gave Girard enough information to carry on business.

For two weeks, he led the organization in his master's absence. Every time he received a call from someone in the inner circle, he held his breath. He was sure he covered his tracks, but it would take only a single mistake to expose him.

After Julien Martel called with the news of his father's death, Girard convened a meeting of the Arcadian Spear inner circle to name a replacement, as required in the bylaws. When Girard was selected, he knew his worries were over. Following tradition, he selected a new name — Ajax. Then he moved into the grand master's home in Béziers. The power of the office was now his.

Girard selected Brother Legrand, a former colleague from their investment banking days, to serve as his aide. Although the same age, Legrand looked like an aging accountant compared to the more youthful, athletic Girard. The two of them had joined Arcadian Spear together and had moved up the ranks rapidly.

Legrand had never seen the inside of this house, so Girard gave him a brief tour of the study and the other rooms. He explained the computer screens, and how they were used to track investments.

"Very impressive," said Legrand. "I've been handling operations, so I never understood where the money came from."

"I'm sure you realize operations influence stock prices." Ajax pointed to the screen displaying income and expenses. "Properly timed trades drive a substantial portion of our revenues."

"I understand."

Ajax marched over to the place his former master used to sit and settled into the chair. The old man's cane rested against the arm, expensive and ornate. A symbol of power. He grasped it in his hand. *The power is mine.*

Motioning for Legrand to sit, Ajax continued the education of his assistant. "As many of our brothers know, power and money are the keys to continue our legacy. We use money to achieve the power we require, and we use power to make sure the money flows."

"Of course."

"But the key to sustaining this cycle is to inject conflict and chaos. When there is conflict, participants desire strong leaders. We select those leaders and many of their key officers. They also need arms and support. We supply all this and more, making our friends rich and happy while we enjoy our share."

Legrand looked surprised. "I've been deeply involved in the funding of our terrorist network. Are you saying we supply America and Europe as well?"

"Yes, that's exactly what I'm saying. When a separatist group fights their government, we make our money supplying arms, intelligence, and support to both sides. We use this money to influence leaders and their subjects. The same concept works for wars and terrorism."

Legrand opened his tablet. "My contacts in Europe should be helpful."

"The European groups are not working out. Western Jihad's failure in Prague was a disaster. We lost money, and our associates lost money. It's time for a change."

"What do you have in mind?"

"My predecessor's focus was too limited. We'll be dealing with Middle Eastern organizations."

"I have some experience in that area of the world."

"Interesting." Ajax grabbed the handle of his newly acquired cane and squeezed it. *Time to think big.* "How familiar are you with Pakistan? Especially their nuclear program?"

"I know a few men involved with weapon design, but they never deal directly with nuclear material."

"Talk to your contacts. I plan to obtain the expertise and materials to build a warhead." Ajax knew this would be a formidable task. No terrorists have ever created or obtained a nuclear weapon. But, as grand master, with all the resources at his command, he might be able to do the impossible.

Legrand raised an eyebrow and tugged on his ear. "I have to be honest with you." He shifted in his chair. "I'll develop a plan, but it'll be expensive and risky. I can't promise results will come quickly."

Ajax sat silently, watching his new aide sweat. "You and I will work well together, Brother Legrand. I need you to tell me the truth all the time — even when the news is not what I want to hear." Then he smiled. "I'll expect regular updates on your plan for a nuclear weapon. At the same time, we need to keep the cash flowing with a conventional attack. One that will devastate Turkey. I intend to keep you busy."

"As you wish, Your Grace."

Your Grace. He always hated saying that to the old man, but he loved the sound of it now. *The king is dead — long live the king.*

Escalation

Ankara
Chapter 18

Prague, Czech Republic

Eduard invited Josef into his office at the Czech Ministry of the Interior and directed him to a corner with three chairs around a coffee table. "Thanks for coming. Please sit down. You said this was important."

Josef sank into a chair and pulled out his tablet. "I'm glad you could squeeze me into your schedule. We haven't seen stock manipulation like this in months. Four months, to be precise. Ever since we shut down Western Jihad."

Eduard leaned forward. "Are you sure it's the same pattern?"

"Exactly the same as we saw before the incidents in Dresden, the disco in Prague, and the Castle." Josef turned his tablet around so Eduard could see the charts. "This time, the targeted companies specialize in nuclear disaster cleanup. Radco stock dropped over sixty percent after reports that union negotiations broke down. Same thing for Kleener. These are companies that worked on Fukushima and Chernobyl — removal, treatment, storage, and other services."

Eduard stood and raked his fingers through his hair. "*Nuclear*? We have to alert our allies immediately. What do you expect?"

"The timing matches increased chatter among Kurdish militants. This suggests a potential attack."

"But where?" asked Eduard. "Kurds are spread out across four countries."

A short buzz came from Eduard's desk. He walked over and pressed a button on the intercom. "Yes?"

"The prime minister is calling," announced the voice of Eduard's secretary.

"Put him through." He answered it on the first ring. "Hello. Prazsky here."

"Eduard," Tomas Duris, the Czech prime minister, responded. "I'm in Ankara."

"Tomas, I hope you're enjoying Turkey. I wish I could've traveled with you for this meeting."

"I know, but they need you in Prague. Simon travelled with me. He's in a meeting with the Turkish foreign minister."

Eduard strained to understand Tomas over the background noise. "How can I help you?"

"I'm about to go into session at the Turkish parliament. They plan to discuss the EU accession. I wanted to ask you about their support for anti-terrorist funding."

"Are you close to traffic? I'm having a hard time understanding you."

"Sorry, Eduard. I just stepped out of the limo. We're heading toward the Assembly Building." Tomas' voice became muffled and impossible to hear, then he continued. "Wait a minute. There's some kind of fuss here. Police arguing with the driver of a truck. I guess I'll have to call you—"

Eduard heard a loud bang on the phone, then sudden silence. *Did he hang up?*

When he called back, all he got was voice mail. *Come on, Tomas.*

He called again without success. He asked Josef to join him at his desk. "Something's wrong." Eduard showed him the number. "Keep trying this number. If you get through, give me the phone."

Josef called the number. "I thought you were talking to the prime minister. What happened?" He shook his head. "Goes right to voice mail." Josef hung up and prepared to call again.

Eduard nodded. "I was disconnected. There was a loud bang. Like an explosion." He placed a call to Simon Cerny, the Czech foreign minister.

"Explosion?" Josef jerked his head up, his brows knit with concern. "Are you sure?"

Eduard held up his hand before talking on the phone. "Simon. Are you with Tomas?" He walked to the other side of the office.

The foreign minister spoke in a hushed tone. "No, he's still on his way here. But, something happened. There's been a bomb threat. No one's allowed in or out of the parliament building."

Eduard's heart pounded. "I was talking to Tomas. He was outside. I heard something — sounded like a bomb. He might be hurt."

"What? Tomas—" Simon's voice became garbled for a moment, then he spoke clearly. "Gotta go. Priority call from Prague."

Another buzz from his secretary.

He punched the button. "What is it?"

"The deputy prime minister needs you to come to Straka's Academy right away. He's convening an emergency cabinet meeting."

Shit! This is serious. "What's this about?"

"He didn't say. Gotta make more calls."

"I'll be there in twenty minutes." He hung up and walked back to Josef. "Sorry I had to take that call."

"I haven't had any luck reaching Tomas."

"Keep trying. I've been called to an emergency meeting."

****

Eduard entered the conference hall in Straka's Academy, seat of the Czech government, and stood by the chair next to the deputy minister, who barked out orders from the front of the room. "Put Minister Cerny on the speaker as soon as he calls. He's now en route to the embassy." He turned to Eduard. "Glad you got here so quickly. The news is bad."

"Tomas?" Eduard's voice shook. He held his breath waiting to hear about his friend.

"Let me tell everyone at once." He faced the members of the cabinet. "May I have everyone's attention, please?"

Silence fell across the room as all eyes faced front.

"It is my somber responsibility to announce that Prime Minister Tomas Duris ..." his voice shook. He took a drink of water. "Tomas was killed less than an hour ago in Ankara."

Eduard felt sick to his stomach. He looked around the room, hoping someone would say it wasn't true. All he saw were blank stares and gaping jaws.

"Cerny here." The voice of the foreign minister on the loudspeaker brought Eduard's attention back to the meeting.

The deputy minister faced the others in attendance. "Minister Cerny, we have the cabinet assembled, and I have informed them of Tomas' death. Please tell us what happened this morning in Ankara."

Minister Cerny cleared his throat. "This has been a terrible day. A truck bomb exploded outside the parliament building around ten o'clock this morning — nine o'clock in Prague. It looks like the work of a suicide bomber. At least forty people died. Tomas was outside near the truck when it exploded. They tell me he died instantly." The foreign minister's voice wavered. He stopped talking.

Several cabinet members whispered private comments while waiting.

Cerny continued, stopping to catch his breath every few words. "Two men on Tomas' security team died ... Two are in the hospital ... I don't have their names." His voice grew stronger. "I was inside the parliament building when it happened. We went into lockdown. Emergency personnel searched the building. No casualties. I couldn't use the front entrance to leave for the embassy because of high radiation readings."

Radiation? The word electrified the room. Startled the members of the cabinet voiced their anger.

The deputy minister rapped his gavel. "Gentlemen. Our colleague is still speaking."

Cerny sounded calmer as he went through a few more details. "Emergency responders detected high levels of radiation in the immediate area. Now they're taking measurements in the surrounding neighborhoods, at the Parliament and the mosque. Turkish officials are treating this as a dirty bomb attack. They may decide to relocate the seat of government to Istanbul until the area can be declared safe. They told me to leave — to return to our embassy."

The deputy minister asked, "Are you safe, Simon?"

"They said we're safe for now. I plan to go wherever the Turkish government goes. If that's Istanbul, I'll follow them there."

The defense minister spoke up. "Unless the radiation levels are unusually high, it could take two or three days at ground zero before you have to worry for your health. Just stay away from the area and leave when you can."

"I appreciate the advice ... oh, one more thing. Most of the casualties were Muslims who came to worship at the Mosque of the Grand National Assembly."

Eduard's phone vibrated. It was the president's office. He excused himself and stepped into the hallway to call back.

"Prazsky here."

The man on the other end of the phone spoke in a calm voice, introducing himself as a member of the president's staff. "I've been directed to summon you to Lumbe's Villa."

"I'm to come to his home? Now?"

"That's right. The president wishes to discuss a replacement for Prime Minister Duris."

Fallout
Chapter 19

Prague, Czech Republic

Eduard glanced through the French doors of his home in northern Prague. The leaves had fallen from the linden trees. Two bikers rode along the river in front of the setting sun. If only life could be this idyllic all the time.

Eduard shifted in his chair, his hand balled tightly into a fist. "Those bastards killed Tomas." He glanced at Josef on the other side of the fireplace. "They're crazy murderers, not religious martyrs."

Josef nodded. "This is a terrible time for our country."

Eduard clicked the button on his remote control, closing the curtains. "I spent all day with the deputy prime minister."

"He's got quite a responsibility, filling in for Prime Minister Duris."

"Only until they select his successor." Eduard clicked another button. Two oak panels slid open exposing a large monitor in the center of the opposite wall. "The president intends to appoint me. But first, he wants to be sure the Chamber of Deputies will support his selection."

The screen came to life and displayed STAND BY.

Josef's jaw dropped. "Really, Eduard? You're going to be prime minister?"

The screen changed to READY.

"You can't repeat this until it becomes official. When it does, I'll need to form a new government and select the members of my cabinet."

"I'll stay on top of things with the Fist of Freedom. If there's anything you need, just let me know."

"Thank you, Josef." Eduard reached to his left and swung a tray up to his lap. A keyboard, trackball and hand scanner were attached. "Let's see what the Fist found out so far."

He placed his left hand on the scanner and tapped a few keys to log in. Then he looked up and verified the cameras and microphones were active.

The face of Director Togan from Turkish intelligence appeared on the left side of the screen. The man ran his fingers through his closely cropped silver hair, as his smile rearranged the wrinkles on his ruggedly handsome face.

Below the image of Togan appeared the faces of two other men. Then the images of Eduard and Josef popped up on the right. A few more faces were added as others logged in.

Eduard pressed a button and his image enlarged and moved to the center of the screen. He spoke in English because it was the only language all attendees understood. "It's good to see everyone join the conference on such short notice. We're going to find out who did this, and they're going to pay. I'd like to ask Director Togan to brief us on the latest information."

The Turkish intelligence director's image replaced Eduard's in the center of the screen. "Yesterday's suicide attack was carried out using a truck bomb containing approximately one thousand five hundred kilograms of fuel oil and ammonium nitrate fertilizer. They arranged the barrels of explosive along a curved plate of steel to direct the blast toward their target."

Josef asked for clarification. "Didn't you say it was a dirty bomb?"

"Yes, it was," continued the director. "They inserted a cylinder containing five kilograms of radioactive strontium 90 into the bomb. We believe they planned to drive the truck closer to the parliament before detonating, but the bollards and the security team did not allow it. The driver set off the bomb while arguing with the security team, so the focus of the blast was directed more toward the mosque than the parliament building."

Eduard had been so upset about Tomas, he hadn't truly appreciated the full scope of horror from the attack. "Tell us about the casualties."

"Forty-three dead and at least a hundred twenty-five injured." The security director paused briefly to drink some water. "The dead were mostly visitors to the mosque and the parliament, plus residents of the buildings to the east. Damage to the parliament complex and the mosque was limited, due to the distance, the barriers, and blast protection. None of the members of parliament were injured. The president was at his residence, so he was safe. As I'm sure you know, the Czech prime minister was visiting Ankara, and was killed, along with two of his bodyguards."

Eduard tried to contain his emotions for this meeting, but the reference to Tomas' death brought all those feelings rushing to the surface again. He could mourn later. He took a deep breath and pressed on with the meeting. "What about radiation?"

"The levels are too low to harm survivors in the blast area — at least not immediately. But, anyone remaining there for two or three days may get radiation poisoning. Strontium 90 has a half-life of twenty-nine years, so it's going to be an expensive cleanup operation. Two hours after the explosion, the Turkish president announced the government was moving temporarily to Istanbul — where I am now."

"How's the public reacting? Are the reports of riots true?"

"Ankara is in chaos. People leaving town have created traffic gridlock. Those remaining are fighting to protect their homes from roving gangs, intent on looting and burning."

"Who's behind the attack?" asked Josef. "What do we know?"

"The press believes this is the work of a Kurdish separatist group, although it could be a Salafi Sunni faction from Iraq. The truck was destroyed, but there were security cameras. We identified Tardu Farhi as the suicide bomber using images captured on video before the blast. He had no known links to any extremist group. He rented the moving van near his home in the Balgat neighborhood, not far from his target. His family is poor, so he couldn't afford to rent a van without assistance."

Director Blum of EU intelligence added more detail. "We believe the strontium came from a radiothermal generator. Disposal of these RTGs is regulated in most countries, but is known to be lax in Russia and Kazakhstan. It would be difficult to disassemble an RTG and re-package the strontium in downtown Ankara, so we assume this was done in one of their training camps — most likely in the mountainous areas — perhaps in Syria or Iraq."

After a lengthy discussion, Eduard summarized. "We have two actions to take. First, we must identify the groups responsible, including those supplying the strontium. Second, it's time for the Fist of Freedom to discourage these suicide bombers — starting with the mullahs who glorify martyrs, and the families who encourage their children to sacrifice their lives."

Béziers, France

In the south of France, Ajax, the new grand master, faced Brother Legrand. "No one in the Turkish Council of Ministers was injured in Ankara. Now we must force the changes we require. The people must be convinced this happened because of weak leadership — either the president or the Council of Ministers. The Turkish public must demand to know who let this happen. We need to back the president into a corner."

"I'll get our media contacts on it, Your Grace."

"I'll make it clear to the Turkish president that he must blame the ministers or face impeachment. He'll make the changes we demand."

Legrand nodded. "It seems the Czech prime minister was killed in the attack."

"Yes," responded Ajax. "This is fortunate, since my sources tell me the Czech president wants Prazsky to replace him. Make sure this happens."

"I will," said Legrand. "By the way, EU intelligence has learned quite a bit about the operation. Do we have some damage control to do here?"

"I appreciate your concern, but we have this covered. Our people will make sure the official estimate includes opposing views, and identifies flaws in the current analysis. No effective actions will be taken based upon the intelligence presented so far."

"That's good to hear." Legrand turned to leave.

"Not so fast." Ajax held up his cognac and swirled the brown liquid. "It's been four months. Give me an update on the nuclear warhead project."

Legrand turned and faced him. "I'm working on a plan, Your Grace. I've identified an engineer from Pakistan who builds nuclear weapons. We need him to steal the design documents and come work for us. Once he agrees, we face two major decision points — obtaining the nuclear core and delivering the weapon to your target."

"Let me simplify the delivery issue. I'm not looking for a missile — just a warhead we can deliver by transport ship."

"That does simplify things. As far as nuclear material, the Pakistani design requires plutonium. I'm looking into possible sources."

Prague, Czech Republic

Two weeks later, Eduard invited Josef to a private meeting in the old cabinet room at Kramář's Villa, the official home of the prime minister. "Quite a view, isn't it?"

Josef took a sip of pilsner and looked beyond the balcony to the gardens below and the castle in the distance. "I guess you'll be spending a lot of time here."

"Pretty much. But I promised Magda we'll still spend time in our home." Eduard waved his glass toward the fireplace. "Let's sit over there. I want to hear your ideas about the people who fund these attacks." He turned on the television and put the sound on mute. "Ankara coverage should be on soon."

Josef took a seat next to Eduard. "Two weeks ago, I told you about the negative reports on Radco and Kleener stock. Well, someone bought large blocks of their stock at rock bottom prices the day before the attack. Then they sold it after the stock rose the next day, more than doubling their money."

"Both of those companies got contracts to clean up the radiation in Ankara. Do we know who bought the stock?"

Josef shook his head. "They used fictitious names to open overseas brokerage accounts. The same pattern as Dresden and the two attacks in Prague. We should assume one person or group directs and funds them all. That means intelligence from Aryan Reich and Western Jihad should give us clues to the money behind the Ankara attack."

Eduard set his beer down. "So, this is the same puppet master?

"It sounds likely to me."

"Hey ... It's on." Eduard turned up the volume on the TV. A banner ran across the bottom of the screen on the American TV newscast.

ANKARA BOMBER'S MADRASA.

The anchorman introduced a young woman standing before the camera holding a microphone. "We have Konca Osman from our Turkish affiliate. Konca, what are you seeing in Ankara right now?"

"I'm standing in front of a building where a large crowd has gathered. This is the madrasa Tardu Farhi attended. He was the suicide bomber who killed forty-three people and injured a hundred forty-seven. Many Muslims come here to listen to Mullah Kiraz."

The network anchor spoke next. "Many of the victims of the bombing came to worship at the Mosque of the Grand National Assembly. Muslim worshippers represent thirty-five of the fatalities and eighty-three of the injured. The mosque was damaged in the explosion, and is now contaminated with radiation." He turned his gaze to the scene at the madrasa. "Konca, I see a large crowd behind you. Can you tell us what they're doing?"

"The crowd is furious with Mullah Kiraz, whose fiery speeches are said to encourage martyrs against the secular Turkish government. They are also angry with Farhi's parents, who are rumored to have received money from extremist groups as a reward for his martyrdom. The crowd has not yet resorted to violence, but community leaders fear an escalation. Back to you."

"Thank you, Konca. Please stand by while we talk to our panel of experts."

The Turkish reporter's image remained on the screen behind several network news commentators who discussed their viewpoints.

Near the scene of the madrasa, three shots rang out. Screaming erupted and the people in the crowd scattered. Those inside the building ran away as though the devil was chasing them.

The camera lurched wildly and then settled on the reporter who had ducked behind the news van. She seemed to regain her composure when she spotted a young man in Western dress, wearing a white cap, running from the madrasa. She shouted a question to him in Turkish.

The young man slowed enough to answer without stopping.

Then the reporter turned to the camera and spoke in English. "Mullah Kiraz and Tardu Farhi's parents have been shot. That man said all three are dead!"

Eduard turned from the TV to Josef. "Perhaps this will cause parents to think twice before making martyrs out of their children."

Diplomacy
Chapter 20

Prague, Czech Republic

Eduard stood at the podium in Thun Palace, speaking to the Chamber of Deputies, the lower house of the Czech parliament. He had been a member for twenty years, but this morning he spoke as their prime minister. "Muslim extremists are the biggest threat to our security, and the security of the NATO alliance."

He scanned the sea of faces, friends and a few opponents. He suppressed a smile when he spotted Viktor standing by the double door at the entrance — the newest member of his personal protection team.

Tomas had been a great prime minister. Eduard knew he couldn't truly replace him, but he couldn't think of anyone else who could do better. He glanced at his notes. "When Western Jihad brought terrorism to Prague, Czech intelligence and police worked together to hunt them down and end the violence."

This triggered a round of applause from all corners of the chamber.

Eduard hoped they would continue to support him when he took a stand on a controversial issue. "Salafi Brotherhood has brought terrorism to Turkey. Is this simply a Turkish problem? One that Turkey should fight alone?" He knew many of them held that opinion. "This fight threatens us all. Salafi Brotherhood operates throughout the Middle East, establishing new cells in Europe. And, let's not forget. They killed Tomas Duris, our prime minister and my dear friend."

Murmurs filled the chamber.

After Eduard laid out his plan for multinational cooperation against terrorism, he yielded the floor.

The Chairman of the Chamber of Deputies recognized the Minister of Defense, Pavel Franko, who stepped up to the podium. "I whole-heartedly agree with Prime Minister Prazsky. But I believe the problem extends beyond the actions of small extremist groups. Islam is an intolerant religion. They call for the massive slaughter of infidels — which includes most of the citizens of our country. We can only stop terrorism by opposing the Muslim countries supporting it."

Franko expanded on his views with eloquence and passion, eliciting applause from a small group of members.

The chairman then allowed Eduard to further clarify his position. "I agree with my colleague about the danger of terrorism. But, I must disagree with his use of a broad brush to smear more than a billion Muslims. This same brush could have been used to smear all Christians during the Irish violence in the twentieth century. We should focus on the extremists terrorizing our homeland and all of Europe."

Most of the deputies looked at their papers or whispered to their colleagues. Even his allies refused to look at him. Nevertheless, he continued. "I remind you, many of our allies have a large Muslim population. Turkey and Albania are NATO partners. For years, Saudi Arabia and other Arab states have fought terrorism with us."

There was little applause. The discussion went on two more hours. It seemed clear no minds were changed.

****

After lunch, Viktor and the rest of the prime minister's protection team escorted Eduard to the foreign ministry in

Czernin Palace. The discussion in parliament this morning was still fresh in Viktor's mind. *Father trusts people too much. Franco is right. We can't trust any Muslim leader.*

They walked upstairs to the Oriental Lounge, where the Saudi ambassador, a prince in the royal family, would be waiting with Minister Cerny. Two security officers led Eduard down the hallway, while Viktor and another officer followed.

Outside the meeting room, two officers stood guard and opened the door as they approached. When Eduard and his entourage entered, everyone in the room rose. Viktor took his position to the right of the door before it closed behind them.

Minister Cerny approached Eduard, accompanied by a man in flowing white robes, wearing a red and white checkered scarf fastened by a black headband. "Prime Minister Prazsky, I would like to introduce you to His Excellency, Ambassador Shahid bin Abdulaziz al Saud."

"It is a pleasure to meet you, Your Excellency." Eduard extended his hand.

"My pleasure as well." The ambassador accepted the prime minister's hand and shook it firmly. "Is Prime Minister Prazsky the proper way to address you, or is there a more appropriate title for your position in the royal family?"

"I'm impressed with your knowledge of our local news, Your Excellency. The Premysl kings left power in the thirteenth century, and we've had no royalty here since the early twentieth century. The press makes more of my bloodline than is merited."

"Thank you for the clarification." The ambassador nodded briefly.

As a security officer, Viktor continually scanned the room, looking for any potential risks. At the same time, he was close enough to observe the exchange, and also sense the emotions of the ambassador.

When everyone took their seats, Viktor continued to pay attention with all his senses while his father discussed a wide range of subjects with the Saudi prince, from trade to foreign policy.

Eduard steered the conversation to his highest priority. "Terrorism is a threat to both our countries. We need to work together closely to root it out."

The ambassador folded his arms across his chest. "We have been sharing intelligence and coordinating operations with NATO for many years. Is there an issue?"

Viktor detected a hint of condescension in his voice and realized the ambassador was annoyed. *He believes Father's inexperienced and easily misled.*

Eduard placed his hands on the table. "We appreciate your cooperation with our fight against Al Qaida and the Islamic State, but our biggest threat comes from a different group. We have no intelligence on Salafi Brotherhood. Can you help us?"

"We do not recognize any Islamic State. Those terrorists do not represent Islam. They are a danger to all Muslims. They are Daesh."

Wow! Viktor had not expected his intensity. *The ambassador hates ISIL.*

"We agree with your view of ... Daesh." Eduard leaned forward. "We also appreciate the tough position you're in, Your Excellency. Many of your religious leaders preach support for Salafi extremism. They also preach hatred and violence against Westerners. Nevertheless, I'm asking for information on Salafi Brotherhood."

"Prime Minister Prazsky. Our king does not control what mullahs teach in our country or anywhere in the world. Your country also has leaders who preach hatred and violence. We are not that different."

Viktor took it all in. *The Saudis will never do anything to piss off the radical mullahs. We'll get nothing but lip service from him.*

The smile on Eduard's face disappeared, replaced by a menacing stare. "Will you share the information you have about Salafi Brotherhood?"

The ambassador swiveled his chair slowly to the right and then back. "I have no information about that group, but I will talk to our intelligence team. Whatever we have, we will share."

Viktor couldn't believe the blatant lie. *That piece of shit! He knows something. He's protecting terrorists!* Viktor would pass this information on to his father as soon as practical.

****

At home, Viktor sat with Louise on the love seat. This should have been their time to relax, but he was upset about the meetings today. "Father doesn't understand. We won't be safe until every Muslim is dead." As soon as he said it, Viktor wanted to take it back. He reached out and put his hand on her arm.

She flinched at his touch and responded with uncommon anger. "You really mean that?" Her shock and disgust flooded his brain.

Gotta control my anger. Especially around Louise. Slowly, he reached for her arm again. "I was pissed off and said something I didn't mean. I must sound like a monster."

"You really did, Viktor. You know there are over a billion and a half Muslims in the world. Kill them all?"

"I didn't mean it literally." He turned and held both her hands. "It's just that Father believes most Muslims are peaceful, and only a few extremists are dangerous." *She's not happy. Tread lightly.*

Louise spoke softly and clearly. "The Muslims I grew up with in Morocco were friendly."

"I understand what you're saying. I just don't trust them."

Béziers, France

In the south of France, Legrand stood before his leader. "The press is pushing hard to find out who to blame — who dropped the ball and who allowed the attack to succeed."

From the comfort of his seat, Ajax dictated his requirements. "Find out who riled up the Turkish Muslim population against the suicide bomber."

"I'll talk to my sources. I think it's the same group that sent in the assassin. It's not easy to put a perfect shot into the heads of three targets, and then slip out in the melee."

Ajax pounded his fist on the arm of his chair. "The people seem happy with this vigilante justice. We can't allow vigilantes to become heroes for the people every time a terrorist strikes."

Legrand stood silently, waiting to learn what was next on his master's agenda.

Slowly sipping his cognac, Ajax asked, "What news do you have from Prague?"

"Minister Franko just sent an update." Legrand consulted the notes on his tablet computer. "Prazsky's telling the members of parliament that Muslims are not evil — only the extremists. He's also emphasizing his support for Turkey and Saudi Arabia."

"It's time to change Prazsky's attitude. Time to hit him where it hurts."

Strasbourg
Chapter 21

Strasbourg, France

Viktor held Louise's hand. He smiled at his parents. This was their first family dinner together since his father became prime minister two months ago. "You're quite the celebrity, Father. Place Kléber's the largest square in the city. Security is expecting record crowds for your afternoon speech."

Eduard nodded. "I'm pleased the European people show this much interest in our position on terrorism. We'll need their support to get action from the leaders who represent them." He glanced at Louise. "I'm afraid your colleagues seem more interested in petty politics than the security of their people."

Louise set down her champagne glass to respond, but remained quiet when the waiter approached with their soup.

Viktor sipped his drink — an earthy Bière de Garde. He had just completed a full day as part of the advanced security team, preparing for his father's entourage to fly in from Prague, then escorting the motorcade from the airport to the Crossroads Hotel. He looked around the private dining room, searching for threats, then reminded himself he was officially off-duty.

After the waiter left, Louise spoke up. "I agree with you, Mister Prazsky—"

Eduard raised his hand. "Please, we're family. Call me Eduard ... or Father. And I didn't mean to pick on you. I was referring to many of your colleagues."

A smile spread on her face. "Father ... I prefer that." She reached for her spoon. "I meant to agree with you. Some of us

EU Parliament members fight for the people, but too many are more concerned with their own careers and power."

Magda lightly touched Louise's hand. "Enough of politics. Let's talk about your wedding. June is only seven months away, you know. Have you picked a venue?"

Viktor had been avoiding the subject, but he saw Louise nod. Now was the time to come clean. "Mother. Ever since the Premysl bloodline was revealed, the press hasn't left us alone. Louise and I thought it would be better to have a small family wedding — out of the public eye."

His mother looked like someone sucked the life out of her. She glanced at Eduard, but he simply shrugged his shoulders.

Louise spoke softly. "I'm sure this is a surprise. We can talk about it again in a few days." She paused. "We have more news. Viktor and I have decided to go to Cyprus for our honeymoon."

****

The sun was nearly overhead when the motorcade stopped at Strasbourg's Monument to the Dead. Viktor stepped out of an armored limousine, joining another Czech security officer and six French guards. They formed a corridor for Eduard, who stepped out of a chauffeured car and walked toward the statue.

As his father approached, Viktor nodded. "Excellent speech."

Eduard had spoken to the EU Parliament this morning. The semi-circular assembly room was immense, with hundreds of seats for parliament members like Louise, and hundreds more for visitors. Eduard smiled at Viktor. "I don't know how many minds I changed. I'll have a more receptive audience when we go to the square."

A handful of reporters, pre-vetted by security, interviewed Eduard and took pictures while he honored the Strasbourg soldiers who died in two world wars plus Algeria and Vietnam. Then it was time to head to the square, one kilometer away.

Eduard insisted on walking, rather than riding in the motorcade. He and Magda took the lead, followed by Louise. Two columns of security officers flanked them, with Viktor taking a position near his father.

The senior French guard stepped out of line and approached Eduard. Although the officer appeared calm, his emotions screamed like a beacon to Viktor. Not rage, not anger — he was not a threat. It was anxiety and fear.

Viktor listened carefully while the man spoke to his father.

"Prime Minister Prazsky, I'm Commandant Pascal of VIP services. I want to warn you that anti-NATO activists are expected to attend this event. They may be disruptive, but our team is will deal with them."

Eduard nodded and Pascal stepped back into line.

****

On the platform, Viktor was on duty, but he sat with his family — between Louise and his father, who sat next to his mother.

When the EU president finished his remarks, he introduced Eduard. The crowd cheered when he rose from his seat and waved.

After a minute, Eduard held up his hand as a request to stop cheering. "Thank you for such a wonderful introduction, Mr. Dressler. It's a pleasure to be in Strasbourg, a city with a rich history going back more than two millennia. I'm especially fortunate to be here in time to see this magnificent Christmas tree. I understand it was delivered from the Vosges Mountains."

Viktor's eyes were drawn to the enormous tree — over thirty meters high. Every year, a tree was brought here to be the centerpiece of the Christmas market celebrated since the sixteenth century.

"Strasbourg is also a city of diversity and tolerance," continued Eduard. "In a community with multiple religions and languages, you are free to worship as you wish and to speak the tongues of your family and friends."

Viktor sensed his father's anxiety. He was about to change the subject, and wasn't sure how the people would react.

Eduard spoke forcefully. "Many Muslim extremists have a different view. They kill people who don't share their beliefs and don't follow their strict interpretation of religious laws. Seventeen years ago, Al Qaida tried to attack Strasbourg Cathedral only a few blocks from here."

Viktor sensed the commandant behind him experiencing a heightened level of fear. The emotion was strong. He turned and saw Pascal edging slowly closer to the podium, exchanging glances with other security personnel.

"Security has become a major issue throughout Europe," his father continued. "Terror attacks have increased in frequency and scope. In Dresden, Prague, and now in Ankara. The EU and each member country must invest in security and intelligence. The EU must take the lead in coordinating these efforts."

Eduard laid out the details of his plan for the Czech Republic, and continued to appeal for support from the EU and other nations. As he started to wrap up his speech, he thanked several people and organizations for their contributions.

He reached out to Magda as she rose to stand next to him. "I especially want to thank my lovely wife, Magda—"

Suddenly, Viktor felt a spike in emotions — fear — coming from the commandant behind him. Then his mother screamed and spun toward his father. Blood stained her shoulder and trickled down her blouse. A loud boom rang out in the square. A banner fell behind them. People screamed. So many that Viktor didn't know if they were yells of support or shrieks of horror.

"*No!*" yelled Viktor, as he pushed Louise down. A French security guard grabbed his father and pushed him to the platform. His mother collapsed.

In his peripheral vision, Viktor saw the commandant's head explode. Blood and brains sprayed people nearby. The officer crumpled to the floor. The screams from the crowd were so loud, Viktor couldn't tell if any more shots were fired.

Louise appeared unharmed, so Viktor hurried to his mother. She was lying on the floor. Blood spurting from her shoulder. "Help her," he shouted. He squeezed her arm, searching for a pressure point. The flow of blood slowed, but continued oozing between his fingers.

Medical responders pushed Viktor aside and tended to his mother.

His father was lying on the floor shielded from any potential attack by a security guard.

"Are you hit?" Viktor shouted.

"Get off me," Eduard hollered, pushing at the guard who had him pinned. "My wife's been shot. Get off me *now!*"

"She's bleeding," said Viktor. "They're working on her."

Eduard closed his eyes. "I'll never forgive myself for this. That shot was meant for me."

Viktor put his hand on his father's shoulder. "It's not your fault. It's the sonofabitch with the gun. We'll get 'em."

He turned to see how Louise was doing. She looked scared, not hurt. "Are you okay?"

"I'm fine. Don't worry about me. Stay with your mother."

Viktor felt angry — too angry. He sensed others reacting to his emotions. *I've got to calm myself.* With effort, he relaxed and focused on his mother, who lay there moaning. "You're going to be fine, Mother." *She's gotta be okay.*

A French security officer with an ear bud pressed a button on his lapel and spoke loudly into a microphone, "Sniper on the upper floors of Hotel Isle Grande. Respond *now*!"

Viktor looked where the officer pointed. A tall building was visible a few blocks away. He stared intently at the upper floors, searching for any sign of an open window. At this distance, he couldn't see a thing.

Salafi Brotherhood
Chapter 22

Strasbourg, France

Eduard had been waiting for hours at Strasbourg University Hospital, when a security guard opened the door to allow a young doctor wearing blue scrubs to enter the room. Eduard stood immediately, followed by Viktor and Louise.

The doctor smiled when he approached. "Prime Minister Prazsky, I'm Doctor Ebner. Your wife's surgery went well, but she won't be able to talk to you until tomorrow." He turned to Viktor. "I understand you saved your mother's life."

Eduard grabbed his son, squeezed him hard and sobbed, while Viktor buried his head in his father's shoulder. After a few moments, Eduard let go. He struggled to regain his composure and turned to the surgeon. "I have both you and my son to thank."

The doctor nodded. "A bullet severed her brachial artery. She would have bled to death if your son hadn't maintained pressure to slow the bleeding."

Viktor dabbed his eyes with a handkerchief. "The blood kept coming. I was afraid it wasn't going to stop. I was relieved when the medical team arrived."

Louise reached out and held Viktor's hand.

Eduard felt a wave of relief for the first time since she was shot. "Is my wife out of danger?"

"She's in recovery now. The bullet travelled completely through her arm, just below the shoulder joint, missing her humerus, the upper arm bone, by less than a centimeter."

"Will she have full use of her arm?"

"She will require more surgeries." The doctor's voice was flat. He sounded like he was reading a script. "Right now, I can't predict how well it will heal."

"What is it, Doctor? Is there something wrong?"

"Although the bullet only penetrated soft tissue, it damaged several nerves and muscles. I can't guarantee she'll regain full use of her left arm."

Eduard gave Viktor a worried glance. "If this means the end of her surgical career, she'll have a hard time accepting that."

"She's alive, Father. The rest pales by comparison."

Doctor Ebner explained the next steps in her recovery and the surgical procedures ahead.

After the doctor left, two security guards escorted them to Magda's recovery room, where more guards stood at her door. Inside, an IV bag hung overhead, delivering dark red blood into her arm. A monitor beeped and wiggly lines moved across the screen. They stood silently at her bedside.

A lump formed in Eduard's throat. "I'm so glad you were there for your mother. I couldn't bear losing her."

"I'm glad I was there, too, Father. Even so, this was the worst day of my life."

Eduard grabbed the side of Magda's bed. He almost lost her today. And twenty years earlier, they almost lost their son.

Viktor pulled his phone from his pocket and glanced at it. "Josef just landed. He's heading to the hotel. Should be there in less than an hour. Wants to talk to both of us." Turning to Louise, he added, "Sorry, but I'll—"

"No need to apologize. Help them catch the shooter." She wrapped her arms around his neck and kissed him. "Give me a call after your meeting. No matter how late it is."

****

Eduard opened the door of his hotel room and invited his security director inside, accompanied by two Czech guards. He extended his hand. "Great to see you, Josef. I want to thank you for coming on such short notice. I know it's late. Viktor's here."

Josef shook his hand. "I got here as soon as I could. I wish we were meeting under happier circumstances." He nodded at Viktor, who stood by the wet bar, then turned to one of the guards. "You guys can stand outside. I'll assume responsibility for the prime minister."

Once the officers left, Eduard and Josef took a seat at the coffee table in the living room.

Viktor brought three bottles of water from the refrigerator, set them on the table and took a seat.

Josef reached for a bottle and turned to Eduard. "How's Magda doing?"

She almost died. Her career could be over. Eduard inhaled slowly then let it out. This was not the time to deal with those emotions. "She's out of danger. The surgery was successful. Right now, she needs rest."

"That's good to hear."

Eduard leaned forward. "What about the shooter?"

"We haven't identified him yet." Josef took a swig of water. "Here's what we know. Immediately after the first shot, police in the square looked in the direction where the sound seemed to originate. Seconds later, the flash from the next shot pinpointed a window on the twelfth floor of the Hotel Isle Grande. Police secured the building within ten min—"

Viktor interrupted. "Did they get him?"

"They stormed the room. No one was there. An HK417 sniper rifle was leaning against the window. A pair of thirty-aught-six shell casings lay on the floor. No prints anywhere. Police questioned everyone on the twelfth floor. Several hotel guests reported hearing two loud bangs, a few seconds apart. One guy peeked out his door after he heard the shots and noticed the stairway door closing. No one stood out as suspicious."

He got away. Frustrated, Eduard focused on the clues. "Whose room was it?"

"It was reserved on-line three days ago, using a stolen credit card number. The man — it was a male name — checked in during the busiest time of the day using fraudulent credentials. The clerk didn't recall any details. No one saw anyone enter or leave the room."

"How about video?"

"At check-in, the camera captured an image of a man — we think it was a man — of average height and weight, wearing a dark hoodie. The face was not visible to the camera. Similar images were captured in the hallways. He must have known where the cameras were located."

"So, we don't have any usable images? This was a professional. Do you have any leads?"

"We have one lead. It concerns the French officer killed in the attack. He was the one in charge of VIP services — your security."

Viktor slammed his bottle on the table. "Commandant Pascal! Was he in on it?"

Eduard's head snapped toward his son. *He knows something.*

Josef continued. "Yes, we believe he was. After the death of the commandant, the captain took charge of the team. He asked his lieutenants one key question. Which members of the counter-sniper team were assigned surveillance of the Hotel Isle Grande? None of them knew. It turned out no one was assigned. The commandant made the decision."

"What are you saying?" asked Eduard. "Was this a conspiracy?"

"I'm afraid so. We discovered the commandant had money problems until one week ago. That's when fifty thousand euros were wired into his bank account from the Cayman Islands. Whoever planned the shooting could not allow him to live and talk."

"They said it was a Muslim terrorist attack."

"It was. Within minutes of the shooting, Salafi Brotherhood claimed responsibility and posted a message on a jihadist website — in Arabic, French, German and English.

"I heard that, but didn't get any details."

"The messages attack you personally. Here's the French version." He located it on his tablet and handed it to Eduard.

"It looks like a police photo of Nasim Shabir's body." He showed it to Viktor.

Josef nodded. "It is. They call her a hero, and say you executed her at Prague Castle."

Viktor jumped to his feet. "That's bullshit, Father. You saved lives. You saved my life ... Louise, too. That woman killed eleven people in the discotheque, and could have killed dozens more at the castle."

Shaking his head, Eduard tried to concentrate on the words from the website. "It's extremely long, and it rambles quite a bit. What are they saying?"

"It says you direct your followers to kill Muslims, and you spread lies about Islam."

Eduard slammed his fist on the chair. "Bullshit! I'm against *all* terrorists, Muslim or not." His face was hot and sweaty.

"I know. They're twisting your words." Josef pointed to a spot on his tablet. "You need to read this part."

Eduard read the highlighted section out loud:

He will die. So will his followers. In our war against the infidels, Islam recognizes no distinction between leaders, armies, and civilians. No infidel is innocent. No man, woman or child.

He stared at Viktor. "They're not just threatening me. They're threatening my family. It doesn't make sense."

"I agree. They never planned to kill you."

"What?" Eduard stopped pacing and turned. "I don't understand. Of course, they planned to kill me. They hired a sniper to do it."

"Think about it. How could an experienced sniper miss you, injuring your wife instead — and then put a bullet directly through the brain of the commandant three seconds later?"

"Sonofabitch!" Eduard wanted to throw something or hit someone. It wouldn't help. "You mean they tried to kill Magda on purpose? Is she a target right now?"

Josef held up his hand. "The guards won't let anyone get to her. And, I don't believe she's a target anymore."

"You're not sure?" He looked at Viktor, who was breathing slowly, deliberately. Eduard had seen his son act like this before. *He's upset. Controlling his emotions.* "Let's sit and listen to what Josef has to say."

Viktor took his seat. He stared at the floor, saying nothing.

Josef ignored Viktor. "They wanted to make it look like an attempt on your life. The sniper could have killed you or Magda if he wanted."

Exhausted from the stress of the day, Eduard wasn't thinking clearly. "Why would they do it? If they didn't want to kill me, what did they want?"

"They received the publicity they sought without killing you. Their message was repeated on hundreds of websites today. Many imams and mullahs have already spread the word. You're a symbol they can use to spread hatred."

"They shot Magda on purpose? This is crazy." Eduard paced the floor. "They're crazy."

"That's what we believe. I suggest we tell no one what we suspect. Not even Magda."

Eduard nodded. "You're right." He reached over to his son. "Are you okay?"

"It's been a long day, Father." His head down, gazing at his feet. "I need time to think." Then he raised his head and locked eyes with Eduard. "Let's hunt these bastards down and kill them all."

Daijal
Chapter 23

Strasbourg, France

Eduard began his day in his wife's hospital room. Despite the bandages and monitor, her face lit up when he approached.

He reached out and held her hand. "It's wonderful to see you awake, my love. Is there anything I can do for you?"

Magda's voice was weak and hoarse. She cleared her throat. "Good morning, dear."

Eduard reached for the plastic bottle by her bed. "Take this." He held the straw to her lips and waited while she took a sip and swallowed.

She pushed the bottle away. "You always brighten my day."

He leaned over and carefully kissed her. "How are you feeling? Are you in any pain?"

"They're keeping me comfortable." She winked. "They must be good drugs."

"They treat you special because you're a doctor. I guess it's like a private club."

Her eyes closed tightly, then she opened them. "I've been lucky. Things could have been much worse." Tears ran down her cheeks. His wife almost never cried. "You know our son saved my life."

"I know. Doctor Ebner told me. I'm so glad Viktor was there. I couldn't bear losing you." Eduard grabbed a tissue and wiped her face. "Did you talk to the doctors? Did they answer your questions?"

"You know me so well. They gave me the details — surgeon to surgeon. I have more operations to look forward to — as the patient."

"They said you need more surgery."

"Yes, I do. You know I'm always honest with my patients, so I'm being honest with myself as well. Depending on how things go, it may be time for me to retire — or practice medicine from behind a desk."

A lump formed in Eduard's throat. He leaned over to kiss her again. "I'm so sorry. It's my fault."

Magda didn't wait for the kiss. "No! You're not to blame. You weren't the one who shot me. It was the man with the gun."

He reminded himself to be careful what he said. "The entire Muslim world hates me and wants me dead. That puts you in danger, too."

"You're the prime minister. You have people who protect us."

Eduard shook his head. "They should have protected you this time. We relied too much on French security. I won't let that happen again." His hand tightened into a fist. "We'll be surrounded by Czech security as long as I'm a target."

She gave him a wink. "A bit of diplomacy might help to change Muslim minds."

"Diplomacy indeed. I've set up meetings with several leaders of Muslim countries. Perhaps it'll work." *I doubt it will mean a damn thing.*

Béziers, France

Legrand stood before Ajax. "We have eliminated all evidence tying us to the commandant. The police know about the money transfer, but there's no way to identify the source." He held his breath waiting for his master's response.

"And the shooter?"

"He disappeared after completing the job. The police continue to search. So far they can't find him."

Ajax smiled. "Excellent job, Brother Legrand. Our arms and security revenues are up in NATO countries across Europe — also in the major militant organizations of the Middle East."

Legrand wasn't used to receiving praise. He responded with a brief nod. "Salafi Brotherhood has been a good partner. But we have a minor problem. The Saudis told Murat Bayik, the leader of the Brotherhood, he must move his operations out of the Kingdom."

Ajax leaned forward. "Will the royal family leak his location? Do we need to intervene?"

"They would never give up the Brotherhood. Bayik is moving operations to Bosnia — to Sarajevo. One of the few Muslim countries in Europe."

"Keep me informed." Ajax swirled the cognac in his glass and took a sip. "What's the status on the nuclear warhead?"

Legrand was reluctant to give the grand master too many details. The more Ajax knew about a project, the more he expected. "I've identified a site in Madrak, India for our Pakistani engineer to work. He says the most difficult component to build, aside from the nuclear core, is the explosive lens that surrounds the plutonium. He's using a well-proven design, but it will require several underground tests — just the lens, no plutonium. And I have to find a source for some special detonators."

"How soon will the warhead be ready?"

"I can't give you a timeline until I have a solid plan for the plutonium pit. Pakistan is the best source. I plan to identify and compromise the right people at one of their storage facilities."

"Interesting. The engineer and plutonium both come from a Muslim country." Ajax's yellowed teeth peeked through his smile. "This is perfect."

Prague, Czech Republic

Eduard took a seat in a television studio, next to the desk of Basil Marwan. The prime minister was expected to participate in live interviews, and Eduard would have to get used to it. He turned to his host. "It's a pleasure to meet you. I respect your even-handed, intelligent reporting."

Marwan, a syndicated columnist whose weekly editorials appeared in newspapers throughout the world, was also a regular contributor to an American cable news network. If anything in the Middle East was newsworthy, he covered it. A green screen was behind them, but Eduard knew the viewers would see a background of Prague at night with the castle in the distance.

The reporter glanced at the papers on his desk before facing the camera. "Thank you for taking time to join us. I want to express my sympathies for the attack on your family. How is your wife doing?"

"Thank you. Magda's out of the hospital. She faces more surgery. Her overall condition is improving, although she still has challenges with her arm."

"I'm so sorry. I wish the best for her recovery."

"Thank you."

The reporter leaned back in his chair. "Prime Minister Prazsky, you've been in office for three months now, following the death of your predecessor. What's it like being prime minister of the Czech Republic?"

"I was fortunate to work closely with Minister Duris for many years. He was my mentor. He delegated many details to the members of his cabinet. I plan to do the same."

Marwan's next questions probed more deeply into Czech politics and the challenges of forming a new government. Then the conversation shifted to the assassination attempt.

"I know this is a sensitive topic, but I have to ask how you feel about the media coverage since the attack."

"The media focuses on the negative and the sensational. I'm shocked by the hatred directed toward me. I believe the press is fanning the flames. The media portrays me as someone who hates all Muslims."

"This interview could be an effective way to get your message out. What do you want to tell the people?"

"I have always spoken out against terrorists. Evil people killing innocents, Muslim or not. I remain fiercely opposed to these killers. Since this attack, I've come to realize their support is wider than most people understand. I've learned extremists are passively supported by many moderate Muslims."

"You've never mentioned this *passive support* issue before. Does this mean you've changed your position?"

"Yes, I have changed my position," said the prime minister. "Western security is threatened by extremists. It's also threatened by many so-called moderates. I no longer trust any Muslim leaders who refuse to speak out against people who kill in the name of their religion."

****

The following morning, Viktor came to Kramář's Villa early, before the first meetings on his father's calendar. As they sat in the study, he saw the paper on the table, opened to the editorial:

EDUARD PRAZSKY
THE ANTICHRIST OR JESUS' DESCENDENT?
by Basil Marwan

In the last few months, Czech Prime Minister Eduard Prazsky has been transformed from a European celebrity to a lightning rod for believers of two major religions. His notoriety has spread throughout Europe and the

Americas, primarily with Christians, after scholars suggested he could be a blood relative of Jesus.

Prazsky's firm stance against terrorists has inspired Salafi Brotherhood to single him out as an enemy. They claimed responsibility for his attempted assassination, and they continue to call for his death. They name him Dajjal — the false messiah described in the Koran.

Throughout the Muslim world, Prazsky is considered a dangerous leader, slandering the followers of Islam.

Many Christians see Prazsky as a strong world leader in the fight against Muslim terrorism. Others see him leading in the fight against the spread of Islam. Some fear he is the Antichrist.

Prazsky's influence extends beyond the borders of his country. When he speaks, his admirers and opponents listen. When his followers speak, their leaders listen, or risk losing popular support.

Viktor couldn't stay in his seat. "A Muslim shoots Mother — actually, the world believes he tried to kill you, yet the press calls you the Antichrist?" He started to pace. He learned how to minimize the effect of his anger on others, but it took concentration.

His father remained seated. "I don't like it any more than you do. I thought the interview went well, but sensational reporting sells."

Viktor grabbed the back of a chair. "If I could kill that sniper with my bare hands, I would." He slammed his fist on the chair.

"I feel the same way, Viktor. But the way to catch these killers is to understand them. Josef was right."

"Right? About what?"

"The attack wasn't intended to kill me, or your mother. They wanted to use me to spread hatred. Look at the editorial. Pitting Christians against Muslims."

Viktor sat down and tried to make sense of it all. "Someone wants to start a religious war? A modern Crusade?" He scratched the scar on his temple. "Who would do that?"

"The same people behind the attacks in Ankara, Prague Castle, the disco and even Dresden. If they can make money from terrorist attacks, imagine how much they can make from a world war."

Pursuit
Chapter 24

2019 - Béziers, France

Legrand projected a graph of revenues on the large screen in front of Ajax. "Anti-Muslim sentiment has driven security expenditures up significantly in France and Belgium. The rest of the EU is up as well."

Ajax smiled. "Excellent job, Brother Legrand." He jabbed his cane toward the lowest line. "But our American revenues are flat."

Legrand nodded. "Their president requested an increase in defense spending, but Congress refused to authorize it. The American public feels they shouldn't pay for a 'European problem'."

"It seems America needs motivation." Ajax pointed to another line on the chart. "Our revenues in Turkey are rising, primarily for decontamination, cleanup and rebuilding in

Ankara. The public supports their leaders, blaming Western countries for their problems."

Legrand shifted his focus to match those of his mentor. "The Turkish president works well with Muslim leaders, especially the Grand Muftis of Istanbul and Ankara. Turkey is becoming less secular. They're returning to their Islamic traditions and distancing themselves from the West. The EU can forget about Turkey as a potential member."

That brought a smile to Ajax's face. "We must drive them out of NATO." His smile didn't last. "Have we learned anything about those vigilantes in Ankara? It's difficult to enlist suicide bombers when their families are targeted for assassination."

"None of my contacts know anything about them. They must be unsanctioned renegades."

Ajax picked up his cognac and swirled it slowly. "It's time to deal with the Americans and their NATO alliance." He took a sip and stared at the dark liquid. "Incirlik Air Base — NATO airmen are stationed there. Develop plans for a spectacular attack."

"As you wish, Your Grace."

"Make that two plans. Anyone who interferes will pay steep a price."

Prague, Czech Republic

Viktor shifted in his chair while he waited to attend his first videoconference with The Fist of Freedom. He'd always known his father kept secrets, but Eduard opened up after Magda's shooting and the public anti-Muslim backlash. *We'll get the bastards who shot Mother — killed Tomas.*

Eduard set up the call in the den of his home. This was necessary because the official prime minister's residence was configured to support official government communication, not secret communication with The Fist.

Before they connected, Eduard gave his son some advice. "No need to hold back. Everyone is an equal here. Josef has briefed them on your intuitive ability to detect people being deceptive — with the commandant, the Saudi ambassador and the woman in Prague. Just don't mention brain waves."

"Don't worry." Viktor tugged at his eye patch. "Will Josef be here?"

"He'll join from his home."

The screen showed the face of each member as he joined the conference. They were all men. Each of them appeared at least a decade older than Viktor. Some were in uniform. Josef was the only person he knew.

Eduard opened the meeting in English. "My son, Viktor, is joining for the first time. As you're aware, he'll be assisting with interrogations."

Josef spoke up. "I'm looking forward to working with him."

Eduard glanced down at his papers, then up at the camera. "I know several of you missed the last meeting due to the holidays, so I'll start with background information on Salafi Brotherhood. You might not realize the significance of the name. Salafists represent an extreme fundamentalist sect of Sunni Muslims. The Brotherhood is every bit as violent as Al Qaida and Daesh. They recognize Daesh as the Islamic State."

A man in a khaki uniform spoke with a British accent. "Are they a splinter group of ISIL — or rather Daesh?"

"The Salafi Brotherhood originated in Iran, where they fought Shia Muslims decades before the rise of Daesh. Over time, the group expanded through Iraq, Turkey, and most recently into Bosnia."

A gray-haired man wearing a dark business suit spoke up. His accent sounded Hungarian. "It's this latest move that concerns me the most, since Bosnia's applied to join the EU. Even today, Bosnians have easier entrance to the EU than other visitors. A passport is all one of these terrorists needs to enter Hungary or Slovenia. Once there, they move freely throughout the 'no borders' Schengen countries of Europe.

Eduard nodded. "Soon, Croatia will join the Schengen region, giving Bosnians another entry point." Setting down his papers, he added, "Which is why intelligence is so important. I'll turn the briefing over to Director Filipek."

Josef's image filled the middle of the screen, replacing Eduard. "Murat Bayik is the leader of Salafi Brotherhood. He's moved his base of operations to Sarajevo, somewhere near Mount Igman. We're not sure how to find Bavik, but our Bosnian Serb sources led us to a Brotherhood training camp on Vlašić Mountain. We obtained satellite images of the camp near Travnik. One—"

The Englishman interrupted. "Shouldn't we take this to the Bosnian government?"

Eduard answered. "Sarajevo will not help. They consistently deny the presence of any terrorist groups, especially in the Federation District, which is Muslim."

Viktor couldn't believe Sarajevo would behave that way. He had to ask. "But if we show them the evidence, will they take action?"

Eduard responded. "Their government turns a blind eye to Salafi Sunnis, even terrorist groups. A large section of their country is sympathetic to these fundamentalist groups. More importantly, they're frightened of reprisals from the Brotherhood and Daesh."

The Englishman smiled. "Will they agree to look the other way if we go in?"

Eduard shook his head. "We believe they'll share everything we tell them with Bavik."

Viktor realized the Bosnian government was dysfunctional — half were Muslim, half Christian — but he hadn't understood the full extent. *Our ally helping terrorists?*

"Gentlemen." Josef took control of the meeting once again. "We deployed a small team to gather intelligence at the training camp." He smiled. "We conveniently forgot to ask the Bosnian government."

All right! Viktor understood why they needed The Fist. None of their governments would approve the surveillance.

Josef continued. "We inserted our team covertly using a repair van that was officially dispatched to service a nearby antenna farm. Let me show you what they found."

A video filled the center of the screen.

"It starts with this clear view of Paljenik, the iconic building and tower located atop Vlašić Mountain," said Josef. "Everyone in Bosnia recognizes this site. Now the camera is panning along the terrain from the tower to the camp. Anyone familiar with the area would be able to identify the location. Those numbers are GPS coordinates added to the video."

The Hungarian spoke up. "The picture isn't very clear."

"The camp is quite a distance away, taken using a long zoom lens. They used a parabolic microphone to pick up the sound, but the low frequencies aren't quite right because of the distance. The trainers are barking orders in Arabic. They're teaching lethal hand-to-hand combat. Now you see the images switched to later in the day, taken during rifle practice."

When the video ended, Eduard's face filled the center of the screen. "This evidence makes it hard to deny. If this went public, I believe Bosnia would need to respond." He raised one finger. "Better yet, we can release this to the public anonymously. And we can be sure the media sees it ... do we agree?"

The attendees unanimously approved. Josef posted the video to several web sites five minutes later.

Brussels, Belgium

Two weeks later, Eduard stood before the European Council, speaking his native Czech, while interpreters in soundproof booths translated his comments into twenty-two other languages. "It's time we focused on the threat closer to home."

The members of the Council, mostly heads of state, sat around the large oval table in Brussels, listening through their headsets. Most of the attendees had their eyes firmly fixed on Eduard, since a vocal majority of the people of Europe considered him a celebrity and paid close attention to his views on security.

Eduard sipped his water then began speaking. "Salafi Brotherhood is in Bosnia! On our doorstep. Everyone's seen the video. And what does our 'good partner' say? Their prime minister says the video is a fake. Fabricated by the rebellious Serbs, seeking to split his country in half."

Eduard continued, confident that most of the leaders felt a sense of outrage at this. "Who will take action to stop them from entering Europe? Not Bosnia. Not NATO. The American president doesn't think Europe is a priority. We're on our own."

He faced the European Council president. "I recommend we immediately take steps to limit travel from Bosnia to the Schengen countries of Europe. First, we must require a visa for entry. Second, we must stop all plans to bring Bosnia into the EU."

Heads nodded. *So far, so good.* "Finally, we need to take the fight to Salafi Brotherhood. We are each responsible for the security of our own countries. If Bosnia and NATO won't do anything, we must take action on our own. We cannot allow sanctuaries for terrorists. We must pursue them no matter where they hide."

At this suggestion, Council members began to shuffle papers and look around the room. Nevertheless, Eduard pressed on. "This council has direct control of the EU rapid response battalions. If this doesn't call for rapid action, I don't know what does. All these battalions do today is train and support peace-keeping missions."

Eduard knew this last recommendation went too far for most of the leaders. He would have to settle for restricting travel and blocking Bosnia's entrance into the EU for now. Later, after drumming up public support for stronger action, he would bring it up again.

Béziers, France

Legrand projected a French news article on the screen. The headline read:

Czech PM Demands—Keep Bosnia out of the EU

He faced the grand master. "Prazsky has the support of a significant percentage of Europeans."

Ajax nodded. "That video did it. Have you discovered where it came from?"

"We can't track the video to the source. We have no information about who managed to record it. They could be the same vigilantes who killed the mullah in Ankara."

"Perhaps they are." Ajax sipped his cognac. "But whoever it is, they handed us a gift."

"What do you have in mind, Your Grace?"

"We'll use this to ramp up tensions in Bosnia." Ajax pointed to a screen with the map of Europe. "Tension is already high between Christian Serbs in the north and Muslim Bosniaks in the heart of the country. That training camp could be the flashpoint we need. This will pit the religions against each other inside Europe."

Legrand shook his head. "Do we support the Christians or the Muslims?"

Ajax stared at his aide as if the man was exceptionally stupid. "I thought you understood. We support both sides."

"Sorry, Your Grace. I understand."

Travnik
Chapter 25

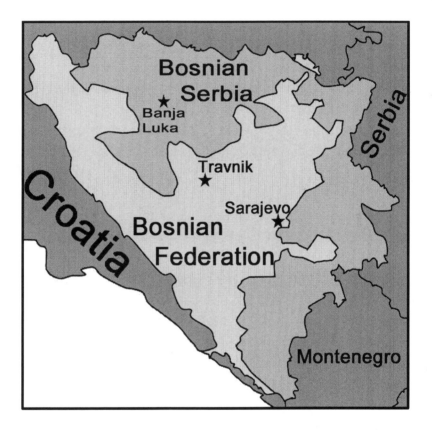

Banja Luka, Bosnia

At an air base in Banja Luka, Sergeant Novak of the Bosnian Serb Army sat facing his captain's desk. "Take out the training camp? Are you serious?" Novak didn't know what to think of his new leader, a man too young for his rank and too bold for his age.

"Deadly serious, Sergeant." He pointed to a chair next to his own. "Sit here, I want to show you something." The captain turned his computer screen while Novak moved closer. "Check out this video."

Novak saw the tower on Vlašić Mountain. "I've seen this before."

"You haven't seen this one."

The views of the camp were crystal clear, and Novak could see individual buildings. A man's voice described the images with military precision. "Where did this come from?"

"We sent a recon team to gather intelligence. They've been recording activities for three days." The video stopped.

Novak turned to his captain. "Do you seriously plan to go after them?" His team had trained together for four years, but the only action they'd seen recently was guarding a mosque during street protests. As a Christian, it was hard to be enthusiastic about protecting Muslims in the capital of the Bosnian Serb Republic. *I'd rather kill them.*

The captain leaned forward. "The prime minister would never sanction the attack. That's why you cannot mention this to anyone outside the mission — especially the Bosniak Battalion." He paused briefly. "To answer your question, I want you to destroy the camp ... completely."

Novak never trusted Bosniaks — or *any* Muslims. "No way I'd talk to them. They'd warn the terrorists. What happens if we're discovered?"

"Sarajevo will respond against your team with force. After all, this is a military attack on Bosnian soil." The captain tapped his pen on the desk. "Get in and out — quickly."

Novak's mind shifted into planning mode. "My men can do it, if you give us the equipment and support we require."

The captain leaned back and smiled. "Tell me what you need and you'll have it. But ... we have to make this look like a rogue military operation. No hi-tech weapons. No drones. No laser-guided missiles. Only weapons used by the Bosnian Army."

"What good is that? Anything I want — as long as it's the same old crap."

"How about an M79 Wasp rocket launcher? ... I'll throw in all the rockets you can carry. Not an old one. A new one, right from the factory in Croatia."

"My team's been trained on the weapon, but not with live rockets. We'll need to practice with live ammo before the mission."

"Whatever you need."

"I'm amazed, Captain. Whenever I've asked for anything before, you've told me it's not in the budget."

"This is a special project, and budget decisions are way above your pay grade — mine, too. You have three days to prepare. I lined up a Huey crew for transport. And, before you ask, it's the only aircraft available for this operation."

"Three days! No way we can be ready that soon."

"Three days from tonight. End of discussion."

Leaving for Travnik, Bosnia

Novak and his men were energized. They were going to take out terrorists — Muslim terrorists. When they weren't studying the reconnaissance videos, the six-man crew hollered out questions to each other, testing their recall of the target site and the layout. They practiced in their white winter gear because the mountain was covered in snow.

The captain had surprised Novak with one piece of hi-tech gear — a battery-operated parabolic microphone system with a sophisticated sound processor. "Be sure to bring this back."

Novak designated call signs for each man on the team. His sign was Wolf Three. "Wolf Two, you've got the rocket launcher.

Wolf Five, the sound unit. The rest of us will each carry two rockets."

He pointed to the M72 light machine guns. "Everyone check out your piece before we board. Make sure your night vision goggles are working."

Thirty minutes later, they loaded everything into the Huey, a UH-1 Iroquois helicopter. The flight crew and the assault team went through their checklists. At zero one hundred hours, they lifted off. It took over half an hour to cover the one hundred kilometers to their landing area atop Vlašić Mountain, flying the last thirty kilometers barely above tree level. After landing, the men jumped out with their gear. The Huey departed for a more secure location to stand by for extraction.

Under cover of darkness, the team navigated their way in stealth five kilometers to the chosen site. They set up on high ground, about three hundred meters from the camp, in a small grove of scruffy pine trees. Novak adjusted his night vision goggles for a tight fit and focused on the camp. Five buildings came into view. *Just like the video.*

Wolf One used his goggles to begin a grid-based search of the surrounding area. Wolf Five set up the microphone system and aimed it for the best reception of sound. Even with a hi-tech microphone and sound processor, it would be difficult to hear anything useful at this distance over the noise.

Novak donned a headset and listened to the faint sounds of footsteps on gravel as the guard walked his rounds. He heard no voices. Given their inexperience at night warfare, they would wait for early dawn. That would make it easier to identify targets, aim and assess the results.

Wolf Two set up the Wasp rocket launcher and checked out the target area through its sight. Wolf Six gathered all eight rockets to prepare for loading. He inserted one from the rear.

The others checked their weapons and watched the target area. They were ready.

Dawn arrived slowly. Morning sounds of the camp reached Novak. He made a soft sound of a wolf pup to get his team's attention. *Showtime!* He held up his fist.

Wolf Two scanned each building through the Wasp sight.

A door opened in one of the buildings below. People stepped outside. Novak said, "Go."

****

Corporal Kasun, Wolf Two, held his aim on the building where the men emerged. He slowly squeezed the trigger. Flames shot out the back of the launcher. Kasun watched the rocket speed toward the target. Two seconds later, the building erupted in flames. Another second, and he heard a loud boom.

Kasun smiled. Perfect shot. Then he saw men running ... no, staggering away from the fire. Reality set in. These were people, and he'd just killed a lot of them.

Private Zorić, Wolf Six loaded another round.

Kasun chose a building with a cluster of men standing outside. *No time to think about death. Focus on the mission.* He fired another rocket, destroying the building. After reloading, he went on to building three.

Some of the men in the camp fired their rifles in his direction. *It's my rocket launcher. They're shooting at me.* The sergeant had told him Bosnian rifles couldn't hit anyone from that distance, but bullets often had a mind of their own.

To his right, Novak was on the radio, calling the Huey for extraction.

A flash appeared next to one of the buildings, followed by a loud bang. *What the hell?*

Kasun moved his sights in the direction of the flash. A grenade landed fifty meters from the team, spraying fragments.

This is getting close. He took aim and eliminated the man with the grenade launcher.

He fired seven of the eight rockets, making solid kills with each one, but he saved number eight in reserve for any emergency that might arise before extraction.

Finally, they could hear the Huey arriving. *Hurry up. Get us out of here.*

A thundering boom came from the camp, and then another one. It wasn't a rifle — it was a big gun. The barrel extended above the roof of the buildings. *Where the hell was it hiding all this time?*

He aimed at the anti-aircraft gun, but it was too late. The Huey was hit. It spun like a top, tilted to one side, and smashed into the ground. The fuel ignited, turning the copter into a fireball. No one on board could have survived. Incoming gunfire was getting closer.

We're fucked! Despite the danger, Kasun had to take out that gun. He aimed and fired their last rocket. *Direct hit.*

Then he heard the roar of an approaching jet. Searching the sky, he spotted it heading directly toward them.

Who's plane? Not ours … Shit! … Huey's burning. Can't stay here.

Kasun abandoned the launcher, grabbed his rifle and ran toward the team. There was no cover. Bullets ripped up the ground in front of him and tore into Sergeant Novak. His riddled body collapsed. *Oh, my God! He's dead!*

The plane roared overhead, as the rest of the men scattered in all directions away from the sergeant's body. *Wide open. No cover.*

Kasun ran toward the distant tower.

The plane turned and made a second pass over their position. Once again, bullets tore up the ground, this time hitting three men. *Only me and Zorić, now.*

The plane made another pass. Kasun watched the pattern of bullets tear through the only other survivor of his team.

Alone now, he ran frantically, trying to escape the plane. *Jump*! His foot landed on a rock, his ankle twisted, and he went down. Something slammed him in the leg — hard. Kasun never felt the second bullet, or the third.

Brussels
Chapter 26

Brussels, Belgium

A week later, Eduard attended a special EU Council meeting in Brussels to discuss the Serbian attack in Bosnia. Most of the leaders had attended the summit meeting last month, but this crisis brought them back.

The French Prime Minister presented his position, one that did not sit well with most of his peers. "It was a blatant, unprovoked attack by Bosnian Serbs against other Bosnian citizens. To make it worse, the Serbs are calling for secession. They have denounced the Dayton Agreement and recalled Serbian military and security units to Banja Luka. They also ordered Federation units and personnel to leave Banja Luka immediately."

Eduard had no patience for this blowhard. He glared at the Frenchman across the large oval table, waiting for other leaders to listen to the translation before standing to be recognized. "This was a goddamn terrorist training camp. These people tried to kill me. They shot my wife. They bombed Ankara and God knows where else. I'm glad the Serbs attacked the camp. I wish they'd gotten away safely."

Undeterred, the French Prime Minister responded. "All of Bosnia is subject to the office of the High Representative, including the Bosnian Serbs. They're not a separate country. We must not allow them to secede. We must denounce this act and oppose the breakup of the country."

Eduard turned to face him. "This is all about politics to you. The only reason you defend the Federation is because your country holds the position of High Representative this year. The Bosnian government is a forced marriage between people who hate each other. This very council is opposed to it. Isn't that right, Mr. Dressler?"

"You're right, Mr. Prazsky," said the council president. "We won't accept Bosnia as an EU member as long as they continue to have a divided government."

"Serbs are Christian." Eduard extended his right arm and paused. "Bosniaks are Muslim." He extended his left arm. "And this Muslim government provides a safe haven for terrorists." Leaning forward on both palms, he added, "I call for the EU to support Serb secession."

****

Two hours later, Viktor stepped out onto the balcony of the fifteenth-century gothic town hall, and approached the microphone. His gloves and double-breasted coat kept him warm on this sunny February afternoon. He looked across Grand Place, Brussels' enormous central square, where the shadow of the church stretched across thousands of people below, assembled to hear the European Council's response to the situation in Bosnia.

His father decided to take his message directly to the European people, and he'd asked his son to join him. Since the public was fascinated with the Prazsky bloodline, they would use their celebrity status to enlist popular support.

Viktor nodded to the EU Council president and spoke to the assembled crowd in French. "*Merci*, Monsieur Dressler, for that glowing introduction." He faced the crowd and greeted them with, "*Bonjour*." He added one of the few Flemish words he knew, "*Goedemiddag*."

To his delight, the people cheered.

When the crowd noise subsided, he continued in French. "It's a beautiful day in Brussels, the sister city of my hometown, Prague." He paused to gaze across the mass of people. "Belgium suffered mightily through two world wars, as did my homeland. Here in Brussels, over seventy years ago, Western Europe made the decision to form an alliance, one that blossomed into NATO. Belgium is also a founding member of the European Union."

He glanced at the government officials on the balcony, all smiling at the compliment. Then he turned back to the crowd. "My homeland suffered decades of oppression behind the Iron Curtain, but we managed to win our freedom and join with our European partners. Last year I had the honor to serve as a representative for united Europe."

Polite applause came from the crowd.

"Europeans need to stick together. These are challenging times. In November, Salafi Brotherhood sent an assassin to kill my father. By good fortune, he missed. But by bad fortune, he nearly killed my mother. Today, her surgical career is ended."

Angry voices spread through the crowd.

"The assassin has not been found, but some of those who planned it were discovered in Bosnia."

At the back of the square more people crowded in to listen.

"A good European partner would go after these terrorists. Instead, the Bosnian government harbors them."

The crowd noises became louder.

"Government forces defended the terrorists when Christian Serbs from their own country sought justice. Bosnia is *not* a good partner for Europe. Their support for these murderers identifies them as a terrorist state."

The crowd began to chant, becoming louder as others joined in. "Viktor! Viktor!" Their voices grew more insistent. "Viktor! Viktor! Viktor!"

He held up his hands and the crowd cheered even louder. He nodded politely and waited for it to subside.

When he could make his voice heard, he continued. "Thank you very much for your support. I now have the privilege to present one of the leaders of the European Council."

By now, people filled every corner of the square.

"Let me introduce a man I have admired all my life, the Prime Minister of the Czech Republic, my father, Eduard Prazsky."

Cheers filled the air when Eduard approached the microphone.

Viktor shook his father's hand, then raised their joined hands high above their heads, like a referee declaring the winner of a boxing match.

The crowd went wild. "Prazsky! Prazsky!"

Prague, Czech Republic

Viktor returned home the following day. The place felt empty without Louise, who was in Switzerland for a conference. Funny how quickly she had become an essential part of his life. A bell rang, interrupting his thoughts.

He opened the door. "Come in, Josef. Did you have any trouble finding my place?"

"No trouble at all." Josef used his familiar wand-shaped antenna to electronically scan for bugs at the entrance area. Neither man said anything to acknowledge these actions. Instead, they spoke as if nothing was unusual. "My wife and I know Wenceslas Square very well, especially near the museum. This is a nice apartment, a bit more modern than your father's place."

"It's much smaller, but it's perfect for me. Would you like a quick tour?"

Josef followed Viktor around, making small talk while he continued to scan each room. He put the antenna in his pocket when he finished. "It's clean. We'll send in a team to set up your videoconferencing system next week."

"Thank you." Viktor motioned toward the living room chairs. "Please have a seat. Can I get you a beer?"

"I'd love one." Josef smiled. "You're just like your father. Beer goes with everything."

Viktor selected two slender, tapered pilsner glasses, designed to show off the light color, clarity, and head. He poured the drinks, set one in front of Josef, and took a seat across from him. "My father loves his breweries and his beer. After all, this is Bohemia."

The director took his first sip. "Ah, an excellent pilsner." He sat back and looked at Viktor. "But we're here to talk about the Fist of Freedom."

"I'm excited to be a member of the group. I learned a lot on the conference call. The world needs people who aren't afraid to take bold action against cold-blooded killers."

"Your father told me you want to get actively involved, and you want to help us with witness interrogations. He said you're exceptionally observant, and you have an uncanny way of telling when someone's lying."

"Father's right. Of course, I'm sure you'll have to see for yourself. Just give me an opportunity."

"You may get your chance soon."

"I'm looking forward to it." Viktor sipped his beer and focused on keeping his emotions even. "But what I really want is ... can you tell me about the sniper? The one who shot Mother."

Josef set his glass down. "We believe we have identified him."

"You did?" Viktor jumped out of his seat. His heart raced. "Who is he? Where is he?"

"Sit down. Please. You're making me nervous. I'll tell you everything."

"Sorry." Victor returned to his chair. *Can't let my emotions affect Josef. Need to remain calm.*

"Let me start with what we know." Josef sat back in his chair. "We scoured videos using our facial recognition system. In one video, two days before the Strasbourg shooting, we singled out a man named Hatim Kader at the Frankfurt airport."

"I've heard the name before."

"I'm sure you have. He's responsible for several assassinations in Germany and France over the past four years. We identified photos of him taken in Strasbourg airport. It was a few hours after we spotted him on video in Frankfurt. He arrived the same day that someone checked into the hotel room used by the sniper."

"Do we know if he's the one who checked in?"

"The hotel has no video with his image. But we saw pictures of Kader's face taken by two separate bank cameras on the day the sniper shot your mother. One in Place Kléber and one near the Hotel Isle Grande."

The evidence was compelling. A known assassin at the square and near the hotel. Viktor took a deep breath in an attempt to control his emotions. "That has to be the guy. Where is he?"

"We spotted him yesterday in Frankfurt, and we sent in a surveillance team. We located his hotel and bugged his room." Josef paused a moment. "We have no jurisdiction in Germany."

"Is that it? If he stays in Germany we can't touch him?"

"I didn't say that. I have a plan."

Extraordinary Rendition
Chapter 27

Frankfurt, Germany

Franz Berger stood in a room of the East Francia Hotel, dressed completely in black, phone at his ear. "All set, Josef. We're monitoring Hatim Kader from an adjoining room and we're about to go in. I'll call you with an update when we're on the road."

Fifteen minutes earlier, Kader, the man who'd shot Magda, had called an escort service. Berger had intercepted the call and dispatched a hooker who frequently assisted the Federal Police.

Berger put down the phone and turned to face his three-man team. Each member wore identical dark clothes. "Has Lisa arrived?"

Leon, his second in command, gave a thumb's up. "She's a talker. Sounds like she's already naked and starting to remove his clothes."

This morning, while the assassin had been out, the team planted bugs. They replaced the deadbolt on the adjoining room door, so even when Kader locked it from his side, Berger could unlock it magnetically from the other. He inserted his earbud to listen, and the men donned their ski-masks, waiting for her signal.

Through the earbud, they could hear Lisa teasing him. "Let me see what you're hiding in there." A few moments later, she gave the signal. "My, that's a big one!"

The men burst through the door. Berger took the lead, Taser at the ready. The other three held their silenced pistols with both hands. Lisa dropped to the floor.

The assassin was a tall, clean-shaven Middle Eastern man with curly black hair. He was in his mid-forties, naked, with the build of a man fifteen years younger.

Berger, flanked by two men holding pistols, centered his aim on Kader's naked chest.

Leon checked out the bathroom and closet.

Berger spotted the gun on the nightstand just before Kader dove for it. Before the assassin could reach it, two men jumped on top of him — one on his legs, one on his back. Leon pulled the man's head up by the hair and forced a chloroform-soaked rag over his mouth and nose.

Kader struggled for a few seconds, then went limp. He would remain unconscious for a while, but they'd need to sedate him again.

Berger handed the hooker a thick envelope filled with cash. "Thanks, Lisa. You're the best."

She took it and got dressed without counting the money.

He watched her leave. "Okay, Leon. Get the cart from the other room. Bring it around to the hallway door and knock."

Leon left through the adjoining door and closed it behind him.

Berger took the assassin's gun, phone and passports, while the others removed the bugs they had installed earlier.

A few minutes later, Leon knocked on the hallway door and they let him in. He entered wearing hotel worker's clothes, rolling a laundry cart. The men helped Leon remove the laundry while Berger gave the assassin another dose of chloroform.

"Damn!" Said one of the men. "Where'd you find these clothes? They smell like someone shit in a locker room."

Leon turned up his nose. "The smellier the better. Can you imagine anyone who would voluntarily dig through that pile, even if they're suspicious?"

The four of them lifted the still-naked man into the cart. Then they tossed the laundry on top. Next, the team searched the room thoroughly, finding no papers and no computer. They gathered his clothes and adjusted the bedding to make it look like only one person slept there. They ran the shower and prepared the room to give it the 'lived in' look.

"We'll meet you downstairs," said Berger.

Leon rolled the cart out the door to the service elevator. The remaining men returned to the adjoining room, changed into street clothes, and packed their gear in suitcases. They left the room at one-minute intervals, and headed down the stairwell. Berger was the last to leave.

At the loading dock, they rolled the cart up a ramp into a boxy, white laundry truck. Two of the men jumped in and drove to a warehouse two blocks away. The others followed in a rented car.

Inside the warehouse, they dressed in black again and covered their faces with masks. They strapped the naked Kader into a chair with his feet secured to stirrups, covered his mouth with duct tape, and waited for him to regain consciousness. An enema bucket sat beneath the seat.

Leon handed each of his men a bottle of water. "He's waking up."

Berger splashed water on the assassin's face.

Kader opened his eyes wide and struggled against the restraints. His eyes darted frantically. Muted screams were silenced by the tape.

"Time to flush him out," said Berger. "I don't want him taking a shit on the trip."

Leon lubricated the enema tube and inserted it into the struggling man before starting the flow of water. "Damn, I hate this part of the job."

Twenty minutes into the enema, the discharge running out of Kader looked like tap water. Leon stopped the flow and yanked out the tube.

Berger injected Kader with fentanyl. "Time for a nap."

They put an adult diaper on the assassin, dressed him in a black jumpsuit, loaded him into the trunk of a new full-size Škoda sedan, and started a fentanyl drip to keep him sedated. An oxygen tank lay nearby, attached to a mask on his face.

They loaded the car onto a trailer with nine other Škodas. To avoid suspicion at autobahn weigh stations, Kader's car had a small engine and no spare, reducing the weight.

Once they finished loading, they headed out pulling the trailer. It took five hours to reach Pilsen in the Czech Republic, stopping four times along the way to check the fentanyl drip.

When they arrived in Pilsen, they pulled into the employee garage of a brewery, unloaded the cars, and parked them in assigned spaces. The brewery's customer service team was expecting this delivery of new cars in the morning. Berger parked Kader's car in another section of the garage. They removed the assassin from the trunk and strapped him into a wheelchair.

The city of Pilsen was riddled with tunnels created centuries ago. They'd become a fascination for tourists in modern times. The tunnel Leon wheeled Kadar through, however, was not open to the public. This one led to only one place, a special cell in Pilsen Prison. The extraordinary rendition was successful.

He would become a ghost detainee. No information would be recorded about his internment. As far as the world was concerned, Hatim Kader was last seen in Frankfurt.

Pilsen
Chapter 28

Pilsen, Czech Republic

Viktor rode in the passenger seat of a black Mercedes on his way to interrogate the sniper who shot his mother.

Josef drove past the famous double arch entry of the Pilsner Urquell Brewery, home of the original pilsner beer, and approached a smaller brewery, one kilometer away. He pressed a remote control, opening the garage door. When he drove inside the large warehouse, the door closed behind him as he parked.

Viktor stepped out of the car and looked around. Pallets of beer, grains and hops lined the walls. "Why isn't anyone here?"

"They called an employee meeting to ensure our privacy. We need to enter the tunnels quickly."

Josef pressed the remote in his hand. A small door opened in the wall at the back. The smell of mold was strong, mixing with the warehouse's odor of stale beer. Once they stepped inside, the door closed behind them. A series of bulbs in wire cages dotted the distance ahead, the light sneaking and hiding as it crossed the face of the stone walls and bumped along the arched ceiling.

Viktor stepped into a pool of water deep enough to wet the toe of his shoe. His next stride carried him back to dry stone.

Josef walked confidently toward the next light, and then the one that followed, down one ancient tunnel, then a narrower one to the left, this one with a lower ceiling.

Viktor followed, avoiding puddles of water whenever possible. His foot slipped, but he caught himself. They turned into several more tunnels, some narrower, some wider. Most went to Viktor's left, but enough went to the right to make the way back unclear.

Josef aimed his remote at a section of the wall. A concealed panel slid to one side. They now faced a sturdy metal door.

"We're here." Josef placed his thumb on a panel by the door and it opened, exposing a dark room. When they entered, the lights came on. The door closed behind them.

Viktor felt like he stepped from the fourteenth century into a well-lighted modern bank or corporate headquarters. Three flat-screen monitors sat on a table, chairs in front of each. At the end of the table sat a desktop computer and a printer.

One screen showed the live image of a dimly lit prison cell, with a naked man in chains sitting at a gray metal table. His head was down, his body shaking. Dozens of wires led from a cloth hat and a black armband on his left bicep to a small gray box on the floor.

Two hard, empty metal chairs faced the slumped man. A metal sink and toilet sat in the corner.

Josef pointed to the screen. "That's Hatim Kader. His cell is next door. We're monitoring his pulse and brain waves. This room is soundproofed. We can speak freely."

Viktor nodded. "So, this is what they call a 'dark site'. No one will find this place without your help."

Josef held up his tablet computer. "A little background on Kader. His family came from the small town of Maheen, near Homs, Syria. We believe the Syrian Army killed his wife and all the men in his family. He had a sister. Her whereabouts are unknown."

"Hard life. But what was he doing in Frankfurt?"

"We think he's between jobs, laying low after Strasbourg. Didn't have many personal items in the room, and none of them were traceable to anyone else. We got his prepaid phone, but it was clean. Never been used to call anyone, but it did receive one short call two days ago from Zugdidi, Georgia, along the Black Sea."

"So, we've got almost nothing. I guess it comes down to interrogation."

Josef took his eyes from the monitor. "That's right. Here's how we'll do it. I'll conduct the interrogation while you sit here, and—"

Viktor rubbed his finger over the scar on his temple. "I hate to be a problem, but I can't gauge his responses using a monitor. I need to sit in there with you."

Josef didn't respond right away.

Breaking the silence, Viktor spoke first. "I promise to watch and listen. I won't say a thing."

The security director studied Viktor's face, as if he was looking into his soul.

Viktor sat upright in his seat, emoting confidence and sincerity — emotions that often had a positive effect on people nearby but never seemed to provoke the headaches or vision problems.

"All right," said the director. "But you must remain quiet and let me control this. Understand?"

"Absolutely! You're the expert. I'll take notes and share them with you."

Josef glanced at the screen. "Kader doesn't know where he is, and he doesn't speak Czech. He's fluent in French, so that's what we'll use. We've injected him with scopolamine — a kind of truth serum. It's not like the movies, but it loosens him up a bit. And, for your information, if he doesn't cooperate today, he'll have a bad day tomorrow. That's when the gloves come off. I can't allow you to attend that session."

"I understand. I hope we extract what we need today."

"I'll be switching subjects quickly with my questions during the interrogation. I'll start with a few simple ones to get him comfortable, then I'll shift to the attack, and then to his contacts. After a while, the guard will come in and whisper something to me. I'll appear interested and excuse myself. This usually makes them worry about why I have to leave the room."

Viktor smiled. "You must have done this before."

"You'll want your coat."

Viktor nodded. "I'm ready."

Josef stood. "The guards don't know the prisoner's name, so never mention it while they're in the room." He opened a door, not the one they entered through. The smells of sweat and urine rushed in with the frigid air. They stepped into a short stone hallway with one heavy iron door on each side. An armed guard immediately snapped to attention. Josef walked up to him. "We're ready to talk to the prisoner."

The guard opened the cell door, walked in, shook the prisoner, and forced him into an upright sitting position. Josef and Viktor took seats across the table from Kader, who looked exhausted. Viktor sensed the killer's contempt, but not a bit of fear. He also thought it odd for this Muslim man to shave his beard.

After the guard left, Josef addressed Kader by his first name. "It's good to see you again, Hatim. I brought one of my colleagues here to observe."

The prisoner glanced furtively at Viktor.

Poker face can't fool me. He knows who I am. Viktor made his first entry on the notepad.

Kader wasn't talking, so Josef continued. "I presume no one has done anything to harm you since you've been here."

The prisoner stared at Josef, but said nothing.

Viktor sensed the man's anger. *If he had a weapon, we'd be dead.*

Josef grabbed Kader by the chin. "Yesterday, we told you it's important to answer our questions. Remember?"

The prisoner nodded his head and responded softly, "Yes."

Defiant, but resigned to submission.

Josef released the man's chin. "Let us start by talking about your struggle with Assad, and what happened to your family."

"There's nothing to tell. Assad, the filthy pig, killed everyone in my family."

Lie. Someone in his family is alive. Maybe his sister. He made another note for Josef.

After a few more questions about his family, Josef switched topics. "What were you doing in Frankfurt?"

"I'm retired. Frankfurt is a great city to visit."

Another lie. You're an assassin.

"Were you ever in Strasburg?"

Kader's eyes moved to the right, a sign he was creating a story, then he focused on Josef. "A few times."

"Where were you on November fifteenth? The day someone took a shot at Minister Prazsky?"

"I don't know. That was four months ago. You think I took the shot?" He shook his head. "You got the wrong guy."

He's the assassin. The one who shot Mother. Viktor forced himself to contain his emotions. *Josef's in the room. I must be careful.*

"Have you ever stayed at Hotel Isle Grande?"

"I can't remember every place I stay."

Lie.

"Were you hired to shoot Minister Prazsky?"

"Of course not."

He told the truth. This asshole wasn't supposed to kill Father. Mother was his target. Viktor took a few slow, deep breaths.

The questioning went on for another thirty minutes. Josef looked over to Viktor and pointed to his notes.

With a nod, Viktor slid them over.

Josef glanced at the notes, then looked at the prisoner. "Your sister married your cousin in Homs and her husband was killed. Where's your sister now?"

Kader's eyes narrowed, and his voice hardened. "I have no idea. I hope she left Syria."

Wow. He doesn't want us talking about her. He knows where she lives. This has him worried.

Changing the subject, Josef asked, "What business do you have in Zugdidi, Georgia?"

Kader's eyes moved sharply to the right, but he maintained his poker face.

That took him by surprise. He's afraid we're onto something.

"Never heard of the place."

"Is there any reason someone in Georgia would call your cell phone?"

"Perhaps they called the wrong number."

Lie.

"Let me ask it a different way. Do you know who called your phone?"

"I have no idea."

He really doesn't know. Why not? Viktor wrote another note.

As Josef had planned, the cell door opened and a guard asked him to step out of the room.

Viktor was now alone with the man who shot his mother. He no longer needed to control his emotions. He promised Josef he would only listen. Now he wished he'd never made the promise.

Kader looked at Viktor and winked.

He's taunting me ... Stay calm. "You know who I am," he said to the prisoner. "You shot my mother."

Kader's eyes didn't move, but a defiant smirk appeared on his face. His emotions expressed anger — nothing more.

He doesn't understand fear. It's time he learned. "We're going to find your sister. I'll bet she sleeps with many men."

A g*limmer of fear. Not enough.* Viktor reminded himself of his promise to Josef — just listen. But this man shot his mother. *He'll pay!* Throwing caution to the wind, Viktor focused on Kader's fear and paranoia, raising the intensity.

Kader looked uncomfortable and started to sweat. His breathing became heavier. His legs shook.

Viktor didn't hold back. "When we find her, we'll bring her here. We know how to hurt people. The guards enjoy having sex with women prisoners. Sometimes they let the *dogs* fuck 'em, too." He unleashed the most intense emotions he could.

Kader shook so hard his chair rocked from testing his restraints. His pupils dilated. His irises nearly disappeared. He slammed his head on the table.

He won't forget that lesson. Viktor ended his onslaught of negative emotions and began meditating to calm himself. Then he braced himself for the headache he knew would come.

The cell door opened and a guard rushed over to Kader, grabbed the man's shoulders and shook him.

Suddenly, intense pain slammed into Viktor's head. *My curse.* This headache was more intense than he'd ever experienced before. Bright light blinded him for a second before his vision faded into darkness. *Pain. Can't see!* Holding the side of his head near the scar from his injury, he refused to scream. *Can't let anyone know.*

Josef's strong hand held his shoulder. "Are you all right?"

Viktor turned toward Josef's voice. His blurry shape coming into focus. He ignored the searing pain. "I'm fine."

The guard interrupted. "I can't feel a pulse. This man isn't breathing. I summoned assistance."

Viktor could make out the shapes of Kader and the guard.

"Release his restraints," demanded Josef.

Two more men rushed inside the cell, carrying equipment. Viktor strained to make sense of the blurry images moving about. The men moved Kader to the floor.

Josef clipped something onto Viktor's finger. "They can take care of the prisoner. I'm checking your pulse and oxygen."

Viktor's head pounded, not letting up. His vision remained poor. But he had to hide his symptoms, like he did his entire adult life. "I feel a bit woozy, Josef. Let me sit here a while. Why don't you check on the prisoner?"

Three men huddled around Kader. It was difficult to determine what they were doing. One of them said, "Clear." Everyone stepped back.

Josef removed the clip from Viktor's finger. "Your pulse is a bit elevated, but not to a dangerous level. You'll be okay." He turned to the medical team. "How's our subject doing?"

One of the men answered. "So far, CPR and defib aren't working, but we aren't giving up."

Part of Viktor wanted the man to die. He deserved death. But Viktor was also terrified that the power of his mind might actually be able to kill someone. *What kind of monster am I?*

The medical team delivered another shock to Kader, then took turns performing CPR. They shocked him once more. More CPR.

Despite their efforts, Kader died.

Debrief
Chapter 29

Prague, Czech Republic

Early the next morning, Viktor waited outside his father's office. He had managed to get on the calendar for a few minutes between two of the prime minister's meetings.

Viktor hadn't slept well. He should be happy, his wedding only two months away. Instead, all he could think about was the interrogation in Pilsen. He had killed that sonofabitch! He didn't just hurt the man. He killed him. He wasn't sorry Hatim died. The man deserved it. *I killed him — using brainwaves!*

I'm dangerous. I could lose my temper. Lose control. Josef's pissed. I made a promise. But, I screwed up — big time.

The door to his father's office opened, and Pavel Franko stepped out. Viktor sensed the defense minister's disappointment and anger, despite the man's phony smile. "Viktor, how good to see you."

"It's good to see you, Minister." Viktor glanced into the office where his father waited. "The prime minister is expecting me." He walked past Franko and closed the door. *I don't like that man.*

"Viktor. Come in and have a seat." Eduard waved him over. "We have a few minutes before the foreign minister arrives."

"Thanks, Father." Viktor sat in front of the prime minister's desk and brushed his hand through his hair. "The man who shot Mother is dead."

Eduard's face went slack. "What? How do you know?"

Viktor tightened his grip on the chair. "Josef asked me to brief you." He rubbed his neck and continued. "The Fist of Freedom nabbed the guy. I assisted with the interrogation."

"Who was he? Who hired him?"

"Hatim Kader, a wanted Syrian assassin. They found him in Frankfurt. We don't know who hired him. I don't think he knew either. Our only lead is a caller trying to reach him from Zugdidi, Georgia."

"How did he die?"

Viktor took a deep breath. He couldn't tell his father the truth. He couldn't tell anyone. "Kader must have had a heart attack during the interrogation." He leaned forward. "You're right. He wasn't supposed to kill you. He shot Mother on purpose."

Viktor sensed his father's anger behind the calm exterior.

Eduard sat still and nodded. "Well, I don't feel sorry for the bastard, but I wish we could have learned more about the people who hired him. I don't believe your mother or I are any safer since he died. Whoever hired him could send another assassin. We've got to find the people pulling the strings."

"Josef is coming over to my place this afternoon to review what we learned." Viktor shifted in his chair. "He suspects something about my abilities."

The phone on the prime minister's desk beeped. Eduard pressed the speaker button. "Yes, Eva?"

"The foreign minister is here."

"Send him in." Eduard turned to his son. "Thanks for letting me know. We'll talk later."

As Viktor stood to leave, his father stopped him. "One more thing ... I trust Josef with my life. You can, too."

****

"Come in, Josef." Viktor directed him to a seat in the living room. "We can talk. My apartment is secure, I checked for bugs an hour ago."

Josef smiled. "You're getting good at this."

Viktor headed toward the kitchen. "Can I interest you in a pilsner?"

"We have our best conversations with beer."

Viktor returned with the drinks and took a seat.

Josef raised his glass. "I want to thank you for your assistance with Hatim Kader. You have quite a talent."

Thank me? Viktor raised his glass and tried to look relaxed. "I'm glad I could supply my feedback. Did you get enough information before he died?"

"We were monitoring his pulse and brainwaves, and we used a computer to analyze videos of his facial responses. Often this helps us determine if the subject is telling the truth." He set his beer on a coaster and his smile faded. "I read through your notes from the interview. Every time our instruments indicated whether he lied or told the truth, your feedback agreed."

"I've always had a knack for that."

"Kader was trained to resist interrogation. We couldn't always figure him out, but you did. And we believe your assessments. We've seen other people with your abilities, but not as accurate."

Viktor shifted in his chair. *He knows!*

"Our equipment detected the frequency of Kader's brainwaves. They tended to fall in the ranges associated with relaxation, stress reduction and pain suppression. He learned how to control his feelings."

"Like bio-feedback training?" asked Viktor. "Maybe he practiced yoga or meditation."

"Very possible, which is why it's so surprising his brainwave patterns shifted when I left the room. His heart rate rose at the same time."

Viktor took a breath and looked at Josef. "I got angry listening to him. Couldn't keep quiet. I must have upset him. I didn't expect him to die."

Josef waved his hand in dismissal. "His death was no loss. We weren't going to get any more out of him."

He's nervous. Josef is never nervous.

"Frankly, Viktor, I believe *your* brainwaves affected *his*."

This was Viktor's closest secret, but Father said to trust Josef. "Is that even possible?"

"It's called entrainment. We usually do it with sound or pulses of light, using frequencies close to the subject's brainwaves. Once their brain synchronizes with our signal, we slowly change it. The subject's brainwaves often shift with it."

"There wasn't any sound or light equipment in the interrogation room."

"Right. Something else caused the change in his brain wave patterns. It wasn't our equipment, and you were the only person in the room with him."

So, that's how I do it. Maybe if I don't deny it, he'll let the subject drop.

Josef continued. "We think Kader experienced a headache, like an intense migraine. His heartbeat became irregular, and he pissed himself. He died of a heart attack, but an autopsy showed no signs of heart disease. A burst of adrenaline probably flooded his body, causing ventricular fibrillation."

He'll never let me near another interrogation. "I don't know what to say."

"I do," said Josef. "I'd like to bring you into more operations."

Viktor had been holding his breath. He let it out. He felt his right hand tighten into a fist. "I have to think about this. It's a lot to take in."

"You're an exceptional man, Viktor. The Fist needs you."

Early Warning
Chapter 30

Prague, Czech Republic

After dinner with his parents, Viktor stood and tugged at his belt. "I ate too much." He followed his father into the den for their meeting with the Fist of Freedom. "I'm glad to get out of my apartment for the night. I love Louise, but a night with her sister and the bridesmaids would be too much."

"Your life's about to change more than you know." His father poured beer into two mugs and handed one to Viktor. "Are you leaving for Cyprus right after the reception?"

"We'll fly to Vienna and stay there the first night. The next day, we'll fly nonstop to Paphos." Viktor lifted his mug and admired the dark color. "Something new from the brewmaster?" He tasted it. "A nice black lager — strong. It's quite good."

"They're testing it in a few pubs in Prague."

"It's got my vote." Viktor set his mug down. "Did you see the news today?"

"The demonstration in Germany?" Eduard began the login process to join a videoconference, and put the microphone on mute. "What a bunch of crazies."

Viktor grinned. "They want you to be king of Europe, and lead the armies against the damn Muslims."

"Like I said, they're nuts. We spend more time at council meetings talking about news reports than real issues."

The videoconference screen appeared and Josef Filipek's face popped up along the side of the screen, followed by other members of the group.

Eduard turned on the microphone and opened the meeting. "We have new intelligence relating to Salafi Brotherhood. Director Filipek has prepared a briefing for us."

Josef's face moved to the center of the screen. "Thank you, Minister Prazsky. A known associate of Murat Bayik, leader of Salafi Brotherhood, picked up 250,000 lira from a cash broker in Turkey. That's about sixty-five thousand euros."

Director Togan from Turkish intelligence asked, "Hawala broker? Do you have a specific location? Where did this man take the money?"

Josef projected a map onto the screen. "He got the money from a hawala broker near Gercus, located in a remote mountainous area — no cameras. Fortunately, this is one of the sites where we installed surveillance. When our facial recognition system identified him, there was no time to reposition a satellite or deploy a drone to follow him."

A British intelligence officer asked, "Don't these money brokers scan for bugs?"

Josef nodded. "These are smart bugs. They listen and analyze silently for two weeks, only recording when motion is detected. When they transmit the stored video, they use frequencies and times that present the lowest risk of detection. Plus, they're low power, sending to a nearby relay."

"Why did you bug this Turkish hawala broker?" asked Togan. "I thought we were focused on Zugdidi, Georgia."

"We planted bugs at ten locations, including the one in Georgia. The only transaction related to known terrorists occurred near Gercus. We also set up an intelligence trigger to capture information on Bayik and his associates."

"Gentlemen," said Eduard. "These bugs appear to be effective. I suggest we deploy additional devices in more locations. Since we know Salafi Brotherhood has a lot of money in southeastern Turkey burning a hole in their pockets, we need to focus on intelligence from that region."

Béziers, France

Legrand stood before Ajax, delivering an update on the nuclear project. "My man in India tells me final integration testing of the explosive lens was successful. The engineer is completing the rest of the warhead now. All we need is the plutonium pit."

"Have you found a source in Pakistan?"

"General Shaheen is the official in charge of the Khushab nuclear reactor. He's become a wealthy man, selling controlled documents and chemicals to the highest bidder. I believe we can make a deal with him."

An uncommon smile appeared on Ajax's lips. "Work out the timeline to move the finished warhead to a container ship — destination Rotterdam."

Rotterdam! Legrand had vacationed there. He remembered the people he met and the places he visited. This would kill them all and destroy the city. Killing people was his business, but this was wholesale slaughter. *Tens of thousands — maybe more? Can I do this?*

Ajax picked up his glass. "Any questions?"

"No questions, Your Grace. I'll update you again in two weeks."

"Now, tell me about your trip to Washington, D.C."

Legrand shook off his thoughts of the death they were bringing to the Netherlands. "The American president has nominated our man, Hatcher, to replace his defense secretary, but the Senate opposes him."

Ajax stood facing his computer screens. He waved his hand dismissively. "American politics! Find out which senators are blocking his appointment and fix this."

"I will, Your Grace." Legrand had already compromised the most senior senator opposing the nomination. He recorded a video of the man enjoying himself with two hookers. Something his wife and constituents would find offensive.

Ajax settled into his chair. "Europe is easier to control. Prazsky's keeping the Bosnian civil war alive, driving up our revenues. But Serbia's still reluctant to step in."

"They're afraid NATO will interfere."

"Is Salafi Brotherhood ready for Incirlik?" Ajax reached for his cognac. "That should take NATO's attention away from Bosnia, and drive a wedge between America and Turkey."

"We can pull the trigger in a couple of weeks. Everything will be in place."

"If those vigilantes from Ankara try to interfere, we'll be ready for them."

Prague, Czech Republic

Two weeks later, Eduard invited his security director into the office. "Have a seat, Josef. Can I get you something to drink?"

"No thank you. We should convene the Fist of Freedom, but I need to brief you first."

"Let's have it."

"Remember the money transfer to Turkey? The 250,000 lira?"

"Of course. Do we know where the money went?"

"No, but we believe Captain Karga, a Turkish Air Force officer stationed at Incirlik Air Base, has been recruited to kill top-ranking NATO command officers."

Eduard was stunned. Not only was this a NATO air base, but Magda's brother, Patrik, was stationed there, along with his family. "Has the base commander been informed?"

"Leadership has been thoroughly briefed." Josef looked at his tablet computer. "America's NSA noticed increased chatter between suspected Salafi Brotherhood leaders and Captain Karga. Our intelligence also discovered several cryptic messages in known, shared email boxes that Karga accessed."

"Have they detained him?"

"Not yet — because of politics. The NATO commander is American, and the suspect is Turkish. The commander has scheduled a meeting with the Turkish Air Force colonel for tomorrow, but it isn't certain he'll be able to convince the colonel without more compelling evidence."

Eduard slammed his fist on the chair. "These wimps have no balls! They'll sit around debating and attending meetings while this guy takes out our officers."

"We expect the attack to take place within the next few days."

"Damn politicians! They'll never get approval to detain him. We can't wait."

Josef shook his head slowly. "Turkey has always been skeptical of European intelligence."

"What do we know about this Turkish captain? How can we get to him?"

"As with most officers working at Incirlik, he and his wife live on base."

"They must go to town occasionally."

"His parents live in the northern part of Adana, not far from the base. He visits them often."

Eduard had an idea. "I want a team in Adana right away. As soon as he visits his parents, we move in."

"It might be difficult to grab him on the road without being seen."

"Then send the team to their house. We can't afford to be gentle."

"Are you suggesting we invade his parents' home?" asked Josef.

"That's exactly what I mean. Use all force necessary to get the information we need."

"What about his family?"

Eduard thought about Magda's brother, and about the thousands of Americans at the base. "Perhaps a threat to his family members will make him more cooperative. After that, eliminate him."

Adana
Chapter 31

Adana, Turkey

The next day, a delivery truck drove along the road just outside the double chain-link security fence at Incirlik Air Base, heading to the area known as The Alley. It stopped in front of a carpet store. The driver verified they were expecting the shipment, then unloaded two rolls of carpet from the truck. Each roll formed a tight fifteen-centimeter cylinder, two meters in length. He carried them inside, waited for a signature, and drove away.

The man who signed for the delivery carried the packages to the top floor. The outside of each roll was made from rug material, but inside each roll was a weapon. One false carpet roll contained a disposable rocket launcher. The second contained a 105 mm thermobaric warhead. He inspected them and assembled the launcher.

He rested the launcher on the window sill and looked through the optical sight, searching for a specific building across the street. When he located his target, he adjusted the scope to bring it into clear view.

He smiled, then moved the launcher into a closet.

A few blocks north, the truck made another delivery to a private home along the border of the air base.

****

Major Patrik Moravec read the newspaper each morning while drinking his coffee, before driving to the Patriot defense command center operated by his Czech unit. He was responsible to protect Adana and the air base from incoming ballistic missile attacks.

The phone rang and he answered, recognizing the voice of his brother-in-law. "It's good to hear from you. Is there anything wrong?"

Eduard Prazsky's voice was calm and reassuring. "Everything's fine here. Your sister's doing well — enjoying the life of leisure. Somehow the hospital manages to save lives without her."

"Sorry to sound alarmed, but Magda's usually the one who calls." An awkward silence followed. "That didn't come out right. I guess it's the shooting. I worry about my sister, and I'm happy to hear she's adjusted to retirement."

"We're fine ... really. Is everything okay at your end? Has NATO command increased base security?"

Patrik smiled. Eduard was always on top of security issues inside or outside the Czech Republic. "The base newspaper and radio have warned Americans to be alert. They canceled most social events this week. We often receive warnings like this. It's not a big deal ... or is it? Do you know something?"

"Command knows what they're doing. But tell me, do you deal directly with anyone in the Turkish Air Force?"

"Okay, stop. Enough. What's going on?"

"It would be a good idea if you and the family stayed away from anyone in the Turkish Air Force for the rest of the day. I wish I could say more, but you know how it is."

Patrik was accustomed to danger. But threats to his family were different. "What are you saying, Eduard? Should I take the kids out of school?"

"No, no. Just take precautions."

"I'll make sure the kids come home directly after school. We'll stay around the house as much as possible."

"I have to go. Be cautious."

Patrik thought about the warning. *'The rest of the day'.* *Very specific. Must be serious.*

****

Shortly after sunset, a few kilometers north of the base, Pete Morgan sat inside a blue, late-model Toyota Corolla parked in a residential area. He and the three men with him looked like brothers, but they weren't from the same family. Each had a short haircut and wore dark clothing over a tight, muscular build that screamed military.

Pete, the team leader, sat in the passenger seat, phone at his ear. "Roger that." He hung up and turned to the driver. "Subjects are five minutes out, approaching from the east."

Using binoculars, Pete watched Captain Karga pull into his parents' driveway and walk with his wife to the front door.

Karga rang the bell. The door opened, bathing the couple in light. The silhouette of a short woman appeared, inviting them in.

Pete had studied the family and the layout of the home. He knew no one in the family owned any weapons. The only security at the house was a dead bolt on the front door.

The men screwed silencers on the barrels of their handguns and donned ski masks. They disabled the car's interior light and stepped out. In the evening darkness, they walked quietly around to the back of the house.

A nod from Pete started their movement, smooth and deliberate. One person cut a hole in the outer pane of the sliding glass door. He cut a smaller hole in the inner pane. Then he reached through, unlocked the door and quietly slid it open.

They moved inside silently through the kitchen, stopping twice when sudden sounds came from further inside the house. One of Pete's men slowly opened the door to the dining area. It was clear, with no one immediately on the other side. Two of them rushed in, their guns held in front of them. Pete came in last watching the side doors as he walked toward the living room.

Karga knocked over the coffee table as he leapt to his feet. "What is this?" He didn't move toward the men invading his home. His family remained seated. "What is this?" he repeated. "Who are you?"

His wife clutched at his arm and screamed. The older couple sat on the sofa and hugged each other.

Pete moved into the living room. His men fanned out on each side of him "Shut up. Sit down. Hands in the air." He moved forward, pushing his silencer against Karga's forehead. His team pointed their guns at the others.

Karga raised his hands. "If you want money, we'll give it to you."

"Yes," said the older man. "I'll give you whatever you want." His hands shook, and so did his voice.

The old woman clung to her husband, sobbing uncontrollably. "Please, please, leave us alone."

Pete swung his gun away from Karga to point it at the older woman. "I told you to sit still and be quiet!"

The captain looked at her and motioned downward with his hands.

While the older woman continued to sob and shake, Pete shoved his gun in her face. "Stop making noise, now."

Her husband held her chin and talked to her softly. "Please be quiet, dear. It'll be better for all of us."

She hugged him hard and stopped crying.

Pete looked at his team. He pointed to the family members. "Tie up those three and gag 'em. Then tie the captain to the chair. Don't gag him. We have things to talk about."

He motioned the hostages to their feet. The older couple rose slowly. The captain's wife remained close to her husband.

Once they were bound and gagged, Pete pointed. "Take 'em to the bedrooms. I'll stay here with the captain."

Karga spoke calmly to his wife. "Do as they say. Everything will be okay."

One of the team members led her away. She kept looking back at her husband, sobbing.

As soon as Pete was alone with Karga, he sat down, his nose only centimeters from the man's face. "I know you plan to kill officers at Incirlik. I need you to give me the details right now."

The color drained from the captain's face. "I have no idea what you're talking about! You have the wrong man."

Pete was unconvinced. *This man plans to kill NATO officers. He deserves no sympathy.*

After two more unresponsive efforts, Pete decided to escalate. He gagged Karga and unsheathed a black knife with a blade as long as his hand. He cut deeply into the man's right cheek, close to his eye.

Blood ran down the captain's face onto his shirt. He struggled, his scream muted.

After Karga stopped thrashing about, Pete removed the gag and questioned him again. No progress.

He replaced the gag and held the man's left hand tightly, slowly bending the little finger until it broke. Karga shook and strained against his bonds, his screams absorbed by the gag. Pete grabbed the ring finger. Karga stiffened and tried to make a fist. Pete snapped Karga's ring finger.

After the captain stopped struggling, Pete removed the gag. Captain Karga again denied any knowledge of Murat Bayik or Salafi Brotherhood.

Pete raised his voice. "Bring his wife out here."

One man brought Mrs. Karga into the room and pushed her onto a chair. Her eyes widened and her hand went to her mouth

Noble Phoenix   Mark A Pryor

when she looked at her husband's bloody face and his mangled hand.

Pete removed the gag and Karga pleaded, "*Please*, leave her alone. She knows nothing. I would tell you *everything* if I could, but I don't know *anything* you're asking."

When his phone rang, Pete answered and listened for a few seconds. "Understood." Putting his phone away, he turned to the others in his team. "We have to leave. We'll soon have company."

He grabbed his knife, yanked Karga's head backward, and slit the man's throat. Blood gushed, and an unearthly wheeze came from the hole in the captain's neck as he shook violently. Death came within seconds.

Mrs. Karga's screams were muffled and weak despite the strain of her effort. Her eyes bulged. Her brows up. Her forehead wet. Her body sagged and her head drooped to her chest. Her husband was dead. She knew it.

Pete's orders were to kill Karga, not innocent family members. He pointed, and the team quickly moved outside to the car. The sound of sirens was advancing from the east. The tires on their Toyota spun on the pavement as they accelerated to the west.

"Someone called the police," said Pete. "I got nothing out of him, but his killing days are over. We saved lives tonight."

****

Patrik read the frightening headline in the morning paper, then called Jon, his security officer. "What the hell's happening? We go on alert, and then an officer is murdered. We're not even safe in our homes." *Is this what Eduard was worried about*?

His kids complained yesterday afternoon and evening. His wife was grumpy, too. No one liked being confined to the house. Now he was afraid to let them out.

"Calm down, Patrik. The Turkish officer was visiting his parents. He wasn't on base. No one's going to invade your home."

"Did this have anything to do with the security alert?"

"You know I can't share any information ... but I expect the alert to be reduced later today."

"Reduced?"

"I say again, I can't talk about it. See you Monday."

Patrik hung up the phone and thought about the call from Eduard — and the murder, and what Jon had said, which wasn't much — hell it was nothing. Then he heard his wife, Běla, come downstairs.

It was Saturday and the kids usually slept late. That made no difference to Běla. She would stop in the kitchen to pour her ritual cup of coffee. He heard her mug hit the hard counter, then the carafe go back in the coffee machine. He wasn't in the kitchen, but he knew the routine. Seconds later, the slurp of her first sip. "Turkish coffee is the best."

"Nothing's too good for you." He stood and gave her a quick kiss.

Běla set down her cup. "Is the good major going to allow his wife to leave the house today?"

"You make me sound like an ogre. Is there any reason you need to go out?"

"Well, I always go to the commissary after payday. It's kind of a tradition here. Besides, we're low on milk and eggs."

If he asked Běla to skip shopping, she'd know how worried he was. Perhaps he was being too protective. The base was a safe place, and she was only going to the commissary.

"I'll be the good husband and watch the kids while you're shopping."

****

On the top floor of the carpet store, a man removed a hand-held rocket launcher from the closet and carried it to the roof. He rested it on the low wall at the edge of the roof and took careful aim through the optical sight. At the agreed time, he fired the rocket. He watched through the sight as it sped toward the Incirlik base hospital windows. The stabilizers kept it on target. When the thermobaric warhead burst through a window, it detonated. The initial explosion rapidly consumed all the oxygen within a thirty-meter radius. A few milliseconds later, a thunderous blast and an enormous fireball destroyed half the building.

He left the weapon where it was and ran downstairs to blend in with the crowd.

His partner fired a second rocket with the same type of warhead at the base commissary. Běla was right. It was a tradition for many families to go shopping after payday.

Prague, Czech Republic

Eduard picked up his phone. He didn't have a chance to speak before Josef's voice announced, "There's been another strike."

"What? Where? ... How bad?"

"Two rocket attacks on Incirlik Air Base. The first hit the hospital. The second the commissary."

"How bad?"

"Hundreds, we've been told. Nothing's final."

"Christ! All those innocent people."

"I'm afraid it gets worse."

"How? What could be worse?"

Josef spoke low, in a monotone. "Our intelligence before the attack. It was bogus. We were played. I don't believe the officer ever planned to attack anyone."

"Our team killed an innocent man?"

"It's possible. To make matters worse, a video of our team leaving the home in Adana was posted on the Internet. It was night-vision, not something your average suburban neighbor would have handy. You can't see any faces, but they look like a well-trained military team departing in a hurry. Turkey will blame the West."

"Yeah. It won't take much to drive them away from Europe."

"Gotta run, Eduard."

"Get back to me when you have more."

Eduard's phone rang. It was Magda. "Hello, dear."

His wife was hysterical. He tried to calm her down. "What is it? ... Patrik? ... Oh, my God — Běla?"

Paphos
Chapter 32

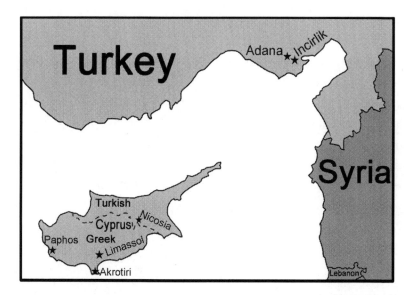

Paphos, Cyprus

At the Sea Goddess Resort, three hundred fifty kilometers southwest of Incirlik, Viktor watched the gentle waves of the Mediterranean break on the pristine beach below his rooftop patio. To his right was a harbor filled with boats, large and small. Beyond was the iconic, boxy shape of a medieval castle.

He turned to admire Louise, lying on a lounge chair, soaking up the sun on every part of her stunning body. Like many European women, she preferred to sunbathe in the nude.

She opened her eyes and looked at Viktor with a satisfied smile. "I know what you're thinking, sweetheart." She raised herself up on her elbows. "Don't you ever get tired? You're the best lover in the world, but right now I'd like to take a dip in the pool."

Viktor made an exaggerated sad face to show his disappointment, then he slowly changed it to a smile. "I'd love a dip in the pool. But, we need more lotion before we go." He gave her a naughty wink. Applying the lotion led to more lovemaking.

As they lay next to each other, pleasantly exhausted, Viktor turned to his new bride. "My love, I can't believe how incredibly lucky I am. I wish this moment could last forever."

Louise sat up. "I love you, too, sweetheart. But I still want to take a dip in the pool."

They put on their swimsuits and cover-ups, grabbed two towels, and headed down the glass-enclosed elevator. During the slow descent, they watched couples below walking arm-in-arm. On the ground floor, they strolled past clothing and jewelry shops, restaurants specializing in Greek and French cuisine, and a spacious lounge surrounding a sunken bar with five flat-screen TVs, each one showing a different sporting event.

Stepping outside was like entering paradise. Palm trees were everywhere. The pool looked like a sprawling lake, complete with islands and bridges. Some vacationers enjoyed the water, while others lay on lounge chairs.

"Over there." Louise pointed to a spot away from the crowd. They dropped their towels and cover-ups on two lounge chairs.

She reached for the hook on her bikini top. "I see topless women here, so it must be acceptable." She removed it as Viktor smiled with approval.

They stepped into the pool, swam under a bridge, and sat at the swim-up bar.

A lovely brunette in a tiny pink bikini stopped cleaning glasses and walked over to them. "*Yasou.*"

Although Viktor was good with languages, Greek wasn't one of them. "Do you speak English?"

"Of course," she said. "Most of us do. So, what will you have?"

Viktor had looked through their extensive wine and beer lists earlier. He knew exactly what to order. "White Commandaria for my wife, and I'll have an Aphrodite's Rock ESB."

They sat on the underwater bar stools sipping their drinks and made small talk with the bartender. Then they got out of the pool.

Back on their lounge chairs, they relaxed and enjoyed the sun. As Viktor admired his bride's body, he noticed three young men a few chairs over staring at her. With a woman as stunning as Louise, it was not unusual for men to take notice, but these guys were leering, poking at each other and laughing. Then she noticed them.

Viktor stood and walked toward the snickering threesome. He sensed their lust and daring, but also nervousness. He could confront them, but that might turn into a fight. He could use his mind, but he'd have to be careful. He'd killed a man in Pilsen, and nearly blinded himself doing it.

The men seemed oblivious until Viktor projected a light touch of fear. They stopped laughing, looked at each other, then stood and left.

Viktor smiled as he slowly returned to Louise, and tried to ignore the low-level pain of his headache.

"You're my white knight. They were creepy."

A warbling alarm interrupted them — not excessively loud or annoying, but easily heard throughout the pool area. It came from speakers installed all over the resort. The employees dropped what they were doing and headed toward the lobby. The bartender started closing the bar.

When one of the servers walked by, Viktor asked, "What's going on?"

She slowed and spoke over her shoulder. "Not sure. We need to report in when the emergency system goes off."

Viktor turned to Louise. "Let's go to the lobby and see what the emergency is."

They grabbed their cover-ups and towels before heading inside.

People in the lounge gathered in front of the TVs, each one tuned to the same American news network. A video showed two large army tanks in front of the entrance to a military base. Police cars parked nearby. Viktor and Louise walked closer. The next video was a long shot across a field to a chain-link fence, where smoke billowed from behind a dozen emergency vehicles.

Viktor could hear the TV. The reporter spoke English, and his voice became clearer as they approached.

> *... Incirlik and Izmir air bases are in lockdown.*
>
> *Last night in a separate incident, terrorists broke into a private home north of Adana and killed a Turkish officer. An anonymous night-vision video was posted on the Internet, showing four people dressed as commandos leaving the home before police arrived.*
>
> *The Turkish Diyanet insists the commandos are NATO special forces. The Grand Muftis of Istanbul and Ankara are encouraging their followers to protest. Muslims are marching through the streets in Istanbul, Izmir and Adana chanting, "Death to America, Death to NATO."*
>
> *The American State Department has requested their citizens leave Turkey immediately. Several*

*European governments have requested the
same from their citizens.*

*More on this breaking story as it becomes
available.*

Viktor looked at a young man, perhaps English, sitting near him. He tapped the man on the shoulder and asked, "Excuse me. What did I miss?"

"Terrorists killed a lot of people at a military base in Turkey this morning. Last night, commandos broke into a home and killed a Turkish officer."

Louise grabbed Viktor's arm. "I can't believe it. First Ankara, and now this."

Viktor dragged his fingers through his hair. "Let's go to our room. I need to call someone who knows more."

As they started to leave, the reporter began again.

*To repeat, we have breaking news out of
Turkey.*

*At ten o'clock this morning, local time, two
rockets were fired at Incirlik Air Base in Adana,
seriously damaging the base hospital and the
commissary, killing and injuring hundreds of
military personnel and civilians. The assailants
remain at-large.*

*Authorities did not disclose information about
the suspects, and they have not released official
casualty figures.*

*All Turkish, American and other NATO military
personnel have been told to report to their units.
Incirlik and Izmir bases are in lockdown.*

In a separate incident ...

Viktor whispered in Louise's ear. "We heard this part. Let's go upstairs."

She nodded. "This is terrible ... but I'm confused. Why did our hotel use the emergency system? We're not in Turkey. We're in Cyprus."

Her question made Viktor think. "Northern Cyprus is Turkish. Good thing we're in the Greek part of the island."

They rode the elevator to the penthouse. Inside their suite, Viktor made a secure call to Josef.

After the phones exchanged codes and synced up, Josef answered. "Where are you?"

"We're in Cyprus on our honeymoon. What the hell happened today?"

"Cyprus! What city?"

"Paphos. In the south. What's going on?"

"Turkish Muslims are demonstrating, forming mobs and who knows what else. Riots are reported in Northern Cyprus, too."

"Are we safe in the Greek section?"

"The Turks are angry at everyone from the West. Mobs are demonstrating in the north. The UK has territory north of you. Border guards stopped a truck with two Turks in Nicosia carrying small arms and rocket launchers. They're trying to take the fight into the Greek section."

"We're planning to stay here five more days. Are we in danger?"

"Yes." After a brief pause, he added, "There's a small airport to your west, but there's little security there. I'd prefer you go to RAF Akrotiri, about eighty kilometers east of you. It's inside another UK territory. The base is protected by the British. Pack quickly. Leave now. I'll make a call to let them know you're coming."

"Okay. We'll get moving right away."

"One more thing. The group that attacked Incirlik was Salafi Brotherhood, but it hasn't yet been made public."

****

They rolled their own luggage through the hotel to the valet. When their silver Mercedes arrived, they tossed their things in the trunk and hopped into the car.

Police sirens wailed in the distance while people on the street dashed by.

"What's going on?" Viktor asked the valet.

"Someone threw a fire bomb at a mosque. It's only a few blocks that way." He pointed to the west.

Viktor saw smoke rising in the distance. He set the GPS for RAF Akrotiri and turned to Louise. "Let's go."

Heading northeast through town, they passed crowds waving signs. Viktor had learned the Greek alphabet in school. He could often understand words by sounding them phonetically. "I see something pronounced *TOOR-koy* on many of the signs. I think it's Turkey ... or Turks."

Louise looked at Viktor, panic in her eyes. "Please hurry"

Traffic moved slowly. Demonstrators rushed toward the car. Viktor sensed the anger and excitement of the crowd, determined to attack the Mercedes. He honked and drove aggressively, but was forced to stop when five young men joined hands in front of their vehicle and refused to move out of the way. More people swarmed around the car, pounding on the hood, doors and windows.

"They're going to break in!" shouted Louise. She jerked away from her door when someone kicked it.

Viktor couldn't fight them off physically, and he wasn't prepared to use the car as a lethal weapon. The only option available was to use his mind, but this wasn't just three guys at the pool. A light touch wouldn't work.

"Hang on!" Viktor grabbed Louise by the arm. This was not the time to focus on the emotions of any single person. He decided to radiate fear to everyone around him. This was dangerous to Louise and the people outside — and to himself. He looked at her. "I have no choice. You're going to be scared." He focused on fear, then terror.

Louise's eyes opened wide. Her hands covered her mouth and nose. She took one hand away and grabbed him. "Oh, my God." Her breathing became erratic. She began to shake.

Viktor squeezed her arm, but he maintained his focus. "Your fear. It's not real. I'm doing it."

Demonstrators closest to the vehicle stopped pounding and looked at each other. Then they turned away from the car and pushed forcefully against the mass of people. Slowly, an opening formed in front of the Mercedes as Viktor's mind compelled them to flee.

Louise screamed, "Go!"

Viktor eased on the gas and moved steadily forward. The headache came suddenly — like someone driving a spike into his eye. Tears welled up and his vision blurred. He saw shapes well enough to avoid people and large objects. At least he hoped so. He had to calm his mind. For both their sakes.

"Go faster," said Louise. "They could come back."

"I can't ... I can't see. Not well enough to drive." Despite concentrating on calming emotions, the effects from his aggressive actions did not abate quickly. "It's my curse. My head ... the pain. Help me."

Louise placed her hand on his leg. "How can I help?"

"Be my eyes. Help me steer. Turn the wheel if you have to. Tell me what you see."

"There's a parking lot ahead on the right. Go straight until I tell you to turn."

It seemed like forever, but he managed to drive into the lot and park. The pain in his head became unbearable.

Louise got out, went around the car, and opened the driver's door. "Move over. I'll drive."

Viktor unfastened his seat belt, then twisted and struggled his way over the console to the passenger seat and leaned his head on the window — but not for long. He opened the door and threw up on the pavement. He didn't have much in his stomach, but it all came out.

Louise opened her door and walked around to Viktor. "Are you feeling better? I've got a bottle of water."

He took the water and rinsed out his mouth. "I'll be all right." He managed a weak smile. "You'd better get back in the car and drive us to Akrotiri before we encounter another mob."

Viktor leaned against the door while Louise made her way through the city. He closed his eyes and tried to relax. He dozed off until light shone into the car when they emerged from a tunnel. "Where are we?"

"We're on the main east-west highway, about six kilometers from our next turn." Louise reached out and held his hand. "Are you okay, sweetheart? How are you doing?"

"My headache's died down, but my vision's still blurred. I'm feeling better, but I don't want to drive." *Will my sight come back? Will I lose it completely some day?*

Neither of them spoke while she continued along the highway. She took the exit toward the airbase, which led them through several small towns.

The secure phone rang. Viktor picked it up and waited for the connection to complete.

On the other end, Josef asked, "Where are you? Are you near Limassol? The Great Mosque there is under attack by Greeks. They're throwing Molotov cocktails."

"We're near Kolossi Castle, heading south to the base."

"You should be all right."

"Someone attacked a mosque near our hotel, and demonstrators got aggressive with our car."

"I'm glad you made it out. Riot police are fighting mobs throughout the hotel region. Keep driving down the peninsula to the base."

Viktor hung up.

Louise drove along the salt lake until the airport tower appeared on the horizon. She placed her hand on his arm and squeezed gently. "Thank you, sweetheart. No telling what would have happened if you hadn't chased those thugs away from the car. I only wish your special gift didn't come with a curse."

As she pulled up to the gate, a soldier held out his hand and demanded, "ID."

He took their passports and looked closely at their faces before returning them. "We've been expecting you. Please park next to the Land Rover. Corporal Comstock will take care of everything."

They parked next to the corporal, who moved their luggage to the Land Rover. "We'll handle the arrangements with the car and your hotel, sir ... ma'am. I imagine you're famished. You'll have time for a quick bite before your plane leaves."

Viktor exchanged a look with Louise. "Thank you, Corporal. Our plane?"

"Yes, sir. You leave for Prague in an hour."

All the pent-up tension from the ride drained out of him. He embraced Louise. The strength of her grip surprised Viktor.

Even as relief rushed over him, his thoughts turned to the future. *We've got to nail these terrorists. But I can't risk my health. I don't want to go blind.*

Funding
Chapter 33

Prague, Czech Republic

Magda wished her brother, Patrik, had time to mourn. Incirlik was no place for his children right now. Lucie would be starting high school next year and Daniel was about to begin his final year. As summer vacation approached, their lives had turned upside down.

"How are the children doing, Patrik?"

When he spoke, his voice was full of anger. "They're pissed off. Someone killed their mother, and I can't stay home to talk with them. We're on full alert."

Magda wanted to reach out and hug her younger brother, but she had to get him to focus on the children. "Is anyone with them? A friend? A neighbor?"

"Every family has their own grief to deal with. We don't even know how many of our neighbors lost someone. Two hundred forty-three people died — out of five thousand on this base. Everyone's mourning."

"Eduard told me they're evacuating the families ... we want the children to come here."

All she heard was Patrik breathing, and then, "Běla's gone. They're all I have."

Magda remained quiet, giving her brother time to think about the situation. The silence went on long enough to become uncomfortable.

Finally, Patrik spoke. "You're right ... and I'm grateful. I'll specify your address for their evacuation."

"Will you be safe?"

"I think so. But it feels like we're under siege, along with the Americans and the British."

Earlier this morning, Magda had listened to Eduard explaining the situation, but she still didn't understand. "Why do the Turks blame you, Patrik? Do they believe Europeans or Americans did this?"

"They're convinced Western special forces broke into a private home and executed Captain Karga. Frankly, so am I. Plus, many Turks hate NATO and want them out of the country. They believe this attack, and the one in Ankara, happened because their government let infidels into the country."

"They're fighting in Cyprus, too," said Magda. "Viktor was there on his honeymoon." No one had told Magda her son was in danger until after he flew home last night. "He told us the Turks were protesting violently in Greek territory. He and Louise could have been killed."

"I'm glad they got out of there. The Turkish people don't want any Westerners on their land. They think they own Cyprus, too."

"It's a dangerous situation. Can't you come to Prague for a few days?"

"I'm afraid not. We're confined to base—"

A garbled voice in the background interrupted Patrik.

"Gotta go, Magda. Duty calls."

****

Eduard felt the enormous burden of leadership. The Turkish president insisted NATO stop using Incirlik immediately — to leave the country within thirty days. The Czech Republic and other European countries were also sorting out their positions with Cyprus. In the middle of all this, he had to deal with Běla's death, and extracting Viktor and Louise from danger.

After dinner, Eduard sat alone in his den. Viktor, Josef and other members of the Fist of Freedom joined him remotely via videoconference.

Director Togan ran through the current situation and gave his closing remarks. "The most urgent problem is the tense standoff at Incirlik, especially because of American nuclear weapons."

Josef's image replaced Togan's in the center of the screen. "Thank you for the briefing, Director. Do your sources believe America could be forced to abandon their nuclear warheads?"

"Of course not. I'm sure Turkish leaders understand America won't allow it. In my opinion, those warheads will move to another NATO country — perhaps Romania."

Josef pressed further. "Aren't your country's leaders worried about their defense? Giving up their nuclear deterrent."

Togan shook his head. "In the Muslim world, Pakistan is the nuclear power. This would open up an opportunity for them to take on a greater role. Other Arab countries, including the Saudi Kingdom, talk with Pakistani nuclear scientists and purchase military equipment from them — including missiles."

"Thank you, Director."

Eduard spoke. "Next topic is covert operations. I've listened to each of you express your lack of confidence in our decisions, especially after the debacle with Captain Karga and his family. I agree we should put a hold on these operations until we have a chance to improve our intelligence." Sitting back, Eduard added, "But there's no reason to stop our intelligence gathering, so let's see what Director Filipek has to tell us."

"Thank you, Minister Prazsky." Josef glanced at the papers in front of him before proceeding. "Turkish police are searching for our Adana team. They're no longer in Turkey, and we believe they left no trail to follow. Director Togan will let us know if any clues surface."

Togan nodded.

Josef projected a street map on the screen. "Several residents outside Incirlik reported a fast-moving object headed toward the air base immediately before the explosions. Police discovered an RPG-7 rocket launcher on the roof of two different buildings marked on the map. Both had been fired. The roofs had damage and residue consistent with rocket backfire. No video coverage was available in those areas, so we have nothing to add. Fortunately, Director Togan can keep us informed while the investigation proceeds."

Eduard took control of the meeting. "I doubt we'll be able to trace the weapons back to the people who planned it. If anyone discovers a new video source, satellite imagery, or any leads, please let Director Filipek know. Now, let's move on to the source of their funding."

Josef projected another map on the screen. He pointed to a small town just north of Turkey on the Black Sea. "Evidence points to Zugdidi, Georgia, as the source of terrorist money for the three attacks we've been tracking. We suspect it will prove to be the source of this latest attack as well."

He moved the pointer to a town in southeastern Turkey. "Hawala broker records in Gercus show several small money transfers from Zugdidi before the bombing in Ankara." He moved his pointer to western Slovakia. "Bratislava received money from Zugdidi before the riot in Dresden and also before the bombing in Prague."

Viktor interrupted. "The man who shot my mother received a call from Zugdidi."

"That's right," said Josef. "This town is the key. Which brings us to the latest attack. Our facial recognition system identified an associate of Murat Bayik, leader of Salafi Brotherhood, in Gercus. Director Togan has requested access to the broker's records prior to the attack on Incirlik. What can you tell us, Director?"

"This is the same broker who opened his informal, coded books and answered our questions about the Ankara bombing. We should receive the information we require."

Eduard heard enough. This Georgian town had been well-known for decades as a haven for smuggling and money laundering. It could be the breakthrough they were looking for. Up until now, their efforts to follow the money were going nowhere. "We investigated banks in Zugdidi ... about fifteen years ago. I know people who still do that work. I'll make some discreet inquiries."

Béziers, France

One week later, Brother Legrand brought urgent news to Ajax. "We have to shut down Zugdidi."

Ajax set his cognac on the table. "What's our exposure?"

"Right now, virtually none. All inquiries went through our man at the bank. He deflected them."

"Shut it down right away," said Ajax. "Is Moldova operational yet? Can we move funds through there instead?"

Legrand located the information on his tablet. "Very soon. I'll push up the schedule and we'll start diverting funds to Moldova as soon as possible."

"Who's behind the inquiries?"

Bracing himself for his master's response, Legrand answered. "Minister Prazsky."

"Prazsky!" Ajax knocked his glass off the table, spilling cognac across the floor. "He's been good for our business, even though he didn't know it. But it seems our efforts to manipulate him have backfired."

"My sources are insistent. It was Prazsky." Legrand poured cognac into a fresh glass.

Ajax slammed his fist on the table. "He's outlived his usefulness."

"As you wish, Your Grace." Legrand considered methods of assassinating Prazsky. It would be difficult with the tight security around him.

"On second thought..." Ajax leaned forward and pointed at Legrand. "It's time for the direct approach with Prazsky. Tell him to leave our banks alone. Make sure he knows it's not a request."

Confrontation

Special Delivery
Chapter 34

Prague, Czech Republic

The summer sun illuminated the sky as Viktor jogged south along the Vltava River in Prague. In a few hours, it would be too hot. It used to be a daily routine. Now the only morning he ran regularly was Saturday. He smiled, thinking of Louise still asleep at home.

As he approached the railway bridge, an alleyway allowed sunlight to spill through the solid wall of buildings on his left. He stopped running and climbed the stairs to the pedestrian walkway. At the top, he resumed jogging, enjoying the view of the sun's rays reflecting off the water.

Wide enough for three or four people abreast, the walkway had railings on both sides. Ahead, midway across the bridge, Viktor spotted three men walking toward him. He shifted closer to the railing.

The men blocked his path. Viktor slowed to a stop and jogged in place. One man pointed a gun at him and stepped forward. "Place your hands behind your back and turn around."

Viktor stopped. If all three had been unarmed, he could defend himself, but the gun changed everything. He had to use his mind, no matter the consequences.

He locked onto the emotions of the gunman. *Nervous.* Amplifying the man's emotions, he shifted them to fear and then terror.

The man's eyes widened. He shook from head to foot. Then he dropped the gun.

Viktor delivered a sharp kick to the gunman's groin and drove a knee into the man's face, dropping him to the walkway.

The headache that always followed Viktor's strong emotions struck before he could confront the others. The pain instinctively made him close his eyes. When he opened them, his good eye didn't respond to the morning sun. His head throbbed. He couldn't see. Yet he stood before the men who threatened him as he prepared to defend himself.

He sensed the emotions of two men — not three. The man with the gun was unconscious or dead. Ignoring the pain in his head, he stood straight. Pitch darkness faded as two blurry shapes appeared before him. There was no telling how his body would react if he attacked them with his mind, but he had no choice.

One of the men bent over and picked up the gun. The other one shouted, "We have your wife!"

What? He's telling the truth!

The same voice spoke again. "We've got Louise."

His vision improved, but he decided not to fight — not yet. "Where is she?"

The taller man spoke. "If you don't cooperate, you'll never see her again. Turn around. Hands behind your back."

Viktor detected some deception that time. *Empty threat?* He refused to submit. "You don't have her." He saw the men a bit more clearly even though his vision remained fuzzy.

The taller man pointed a gun at Viktor. "Are you willing to take a chance? They'll kill her. And they'll take their time."

Something wasn't right, but if he resisted, Louise could be hurt — or killed. *You win.*

The man stepped close and jammed his gun into Viktor's gut. "Do as we say or your wife dies. Turn around."

Viktor spoke while he turned. "Is she all right? Did anyone hurt her?"

Arms wrapped around Viktor from behind, holding him motionless in a bear hug. "She is being treated well — for now."

Lie! He doesn't know where she is!

A hand held a wet cloth over his mouth and nose.

Chloroform. Viktor lost consciousness.

****

Eduard carried his coffee into the study in Kramar's Villa. One advantage of being the prime minister was waking up a few meters from the office. Of course, it was a disadvantage as well.

Josef was there, as were Simon and Pavel, ministers of state and defense. The others would arrive soon for the morning security briefing. Everyone took a pastry and sat down.

Eduard's secretary knocked at the doorway.

"What is it, Eva?"

"Your daughter-in-law needs to speak to you."

"Tell her I'll call her after the meeting."

"She sounds upset. Says it's urgent."

He didn't like the sound of that. He glanced at his watch. "I'll take it in my office." He turned to the others and announced, "Be right back."

He picked up the phone. "Louise. Is everything all right?"

Her voice shook. "Viktor's gone ... missing!"

Eduard hadn't spent much time with Louise. His son never shared intimate details of their relationship. Did she and Viktor have a fight? Was something really wrong? He spoke in a calm, even tone. "Tell me what happened. Why are you worried?"

"He went jogging over two hours ago. He's never been gone this long."

"Did he take his phone with him?"

"He always does." She paused, her breath fast and shallow. "But he didn't answer."

"You know he could be out of cell range, or his battery could have died. There are many reasons he wouldn't answer." When she didn't respond, he added, "But I know you're worried. I'll have someone look into it. Do you know where he jogs?"

"He always runs along the river and across the railway bridge. He takes Charles Bridge on the way back."

"Let me handle this. I'll get back to you."

After the call, Eduard asked Josef to track Viktor down. Then he returned to the study.

When the meeting ended, Eduard headed toward his office. Eva glanced up from her desk. It seemed like she wanted something.

"Not now, Eva. Tell Josef to join me right away."

Eduard sat at his desk and waited. *Viktor's okay ... I hope.* The instant Josef entered, Eduard asked, "Did you find Viktor?"

"Not yet." Josef took a seat. "We're still searching, but I'm concerned."

"Why?"

"Viktor's phone track led to the railway bridge. At 5:47, it stopped communicating with the towers. It never contacted any tower on the other side of the river."

"You mean his phone last worked near the bridge?"

"That's right. Two officers searched the area along his route. There was no sign of Viktor or his cell. No one in the neighborhood saw anything."

"So, his phone could have died. Keep searching."

Josef stared at the window as if captivated by the view, then turned to face Eduard. "We found a few drops of fresh blood — not Viktor's blood type."

"Where? How fresh?"

"On the walkway of the bridge. Only a few hours old."

"Are they searching the river?"

Josef nodded. "The team should be there by now. I'll keep on top of it."

Eduard spoke into the intercom. "Eva, cancel my meetings for the rest of the morning."

"Right away. And, someone left a note for you. The envelope's marked *Personal*. I'll bring it in."

"Maybe later ... wait. Who gave it to you?"

"I don't know. It was on the floor by my desk."

Josef shouted at the intercom. "Don't open it."

He grabbed Eduard's arm and pulled him from the chair. "Gotta leave. No telling what's in the envelope." Barking orders to security personnel while he passed through the outer office, Josef motioned for Eva to follow.

****

Eduard sat behind a desk in a small, windowless room, twenty meters beneath the Saint Václav Hotel. He had visited this secret bunker years ago as the interior minister. Now he used it for its intended purpose, protection of Czech government leadership.

Eva set a sandwich and a cup of coffee on the desk. "You should eat before Josef arrives. I know you won't take time once he's here." When he didn't respond, she walked away.

He picked at his lunch. Earlier, he had received word the police found a man's body downriver from the railway bridge. It wasn't Viktor. The coroner would investigate the cause of death, but officers on site determined he died from a blow to the face.

The sound of a buzzer announced Josef's entrance into the bunker, a piece of paper in his hand. Eduard looked up. "What have you got?"

"This is a copy. They're still analyzing the original."

"They said the note was safe. No bomb, no chemicals."

Josef took a seat. "There were no fingerprints on the note, and only Eva's fingerprints on the envelope. The security video near her desk didn't cover the area of the floor where it was found. They used a common Windows font to print everything using a popular inkjet printer. Unless we learn something from the paper, this is untraceable. We need to find out who delivered it."

Eduard turned to Eva. "Make a list of names. Everyone in your office this morning before you found the note."

"I'll list everyone who had an appointment. It was a busy morning. Some people came in without an appointment. I'll review the security video to jog my memory."

"Thank you." He turned to Josef. "What did the note say?"

"The envelope said 'Prazsky, Personal'. Inside is a website address plus two words." He handed it to Eduard.

`http://screamingmime.com` – Left Eye

This was a weird way to communicate. "Screaming mime?" The following words confirmed Eduard's worst fear. "This is about Viktor. The patch on his left eye."

Josef turned his tablet computer to face Eduard. "Screaming mime is a website designed for anonymous postings – used by drug addicts, beaten wives and terrorists. There was a single entry under the title 'Left Eye'. Here it is."

> *Your son is embarrassed. He doesn't want you talking to the bank.*
> *He is deathly afraid.*
> *If you stop talking to the bank, he will come home.*

Eduard read it again. "They have Viktor."

"They want you to stop investigating the bank in Zugdidi. These are the people who fund the terrorists. It's got to be from the same puppet master we've been pursuing."

Eduard stared at the words.

> *Deathly afraid ... stop talking to the bank.*

"I have to put the investigation on hold until we find Viktor." His heart raced. "Otherwise they'll kill him."

Extortion
Chapter 35

Prague, Czech Republic

When Security declared it safe, Eduard moved from the bunker to his study in Kramar's Villa. A few weeks earlier, he had asked two former colleagues to investigate suspicious banking transactions in Zugdidi, Georgia. Today, he called each of them to say thanks, telling them he had all the information he needed. Each man offered to keep digging, but Eduard assured them it was not necessary.

He stared at Josef. "We both know kidnappers seldom release their hostages alive."

Josef turned his tablet computer on. "Don't focus on the things you can't control. You did what they demanded and we're doing everything we can to find Viktor."

"How will they know I called off the investigation?"

"I posted a response on the 'screaming mime' web page." He turned his tablet to Eduard.

All is forgiven. Please come home

Eduard's brain processed the meaning of the message, while his mind returned to the call to Magda about Viktor's kidnapping. She was already grieving for Běla and taking care of the children. He should be with his wife right now, but locating his son took priority.

Then there was the call to Louise. She thought he was calling to deliver good news. It felt cruel, telling her what they knew.

He had to lie to them — both of them. He said the kidnapper insisted no one speak about it publicly. In fact, Eduard feared the publicity would help the kidnappers more than Viktor.

Josef interrupted his thoughts. "Do you want me to come back later?"

"No." Eduard took a breath and sat back in his chair. "Are we making any progress?"

"We reviewed every available security video near the bridge. One of them shows a man we believe to be Viktor, slumped between two unidentified men walking off the railway bridge. He appears drugged or unconscious, with one man supporting him on each side."

The words hit Eduard hard. "Why do you think it's him?"

"It's the right time and place, and he's wearing the jogging clothes Louise described."

Eduard ran his fingers through his hair. "The body in the river and the blood on the bridge could mean Viktor put up a fight." He looked at Josef. "At least you have a lead."

"The video of the men was too grainy and pixelated to see the faces clearly. Still, we can judge height and weight. There weren't many cars on the road that early, so we suspect the white Škoda hatchback captured on video nearby belonged to the kidnappers. Other security cameras captured photos of the same car along a route heading to the Žižkov district. The license plate was covered with dirt — unreadable. We couldn't track it to its final destination because we lost camera coverage."

"Not many cameras in Žižkov." Eduard figured they'd park the car in a garage or a warehouse. Maybe someone saw it.

"We've deployed federal and city police, and a rapid response unit. They have pictures of Viktor, the Škoda, the men carrying him off the bridge, and the body we pulled from the river."

"Have we identified the man in the river?"

"There was no ID. A fingerprint search came up empty. We hope to match his face using images from security cameras in Prague and elsewhere." Josef held up an envelope. "This is the message Eva found. The reason we couldn't lift fingerprints is because they used liquid skin — the stuff used to seal cuts."

"The 'delivery boy' didn't wear gloves. Either we saw him, or he thought we might."

"Right. We have a mole." Josef pointed to his tablet. "We're checking out everyone on Eva's list." He looked at his tablet again and poked at the screen.

"What is it?"

"About an hour ago, we received a new message on the *screaming mime* web page. All it contained was GPS coordinates for a location in Podvini Park. We sent a team out there."

"What did they find?"

"They just sent me the photos. I'm pulling it up now. They found a small box at the base of a tree. After checking for explosives and other chemicals, they opened it." He turned his phone to Eduard. "Here's what they found."

It was an eye patch. The same kind Viktor usually wore. Eduard's pulse raced. "Do they have a photo of the other side? The inside?"

Josef pulled up another picture. "What's that?" He zoomed into a small mark at the bottom.

"VP." Eduard slumped in his chair. "Viktor monograms the back."

****

Viktor awoke in a cool room on a hard bed with railings on both sides. His wrists were cuffed to the rail on the right. Still groggy, he searched for any sign of injury. *None.*

A burly man with closely cropped hair sat near the bed, a gun in tucked into his shoulder holster. He held a magazine in his hand but wasn't looking at it. Viktor recognized the face. *One of the men from the bridge.*

There didn't appear to be any furniture in the room, except for the bed and the chair. Beyond the man was a metal door with bars. A toilet sat in the far corner.

It wouldn't help to incapacitate the man in the chair by altering his emotions. He couldn't risk anything while his wrists were attached to the bed. Even if he could escape, Louise would still be in danger. This would require all of his senses.

The man was sweating. His nervous tension radiated to Viktor's sensitive brain. *Gotta calm this guy down.*

Viktor concentrated on overcoming the man's tension by sending out soothing emotions and feelings of trust and sympathy. Then he acted drowsy and spoke with a calm voice. "Where am I? Who are you?"

"Awake? Finally. Ivan will be pleased."

"Who's Ivan."

"You will meet him soon enough."

"What do you want from me? Where's Louise?"

"Ivan will ask the questions. He knows about your wife."

He's telling the truth. Might as well wait.

Viktor heard footsteps outside, coming closer. He sensed someone — aggressive and arrogant.

The guard opened the door. A tall man strutted into the room, his pasty-white face framed by wild graying hair. He wore a dark business suit with a gun bulge under his jacket. *This is Ivan.* Viktor sensed fear from his guard and contempt from the older man.

Ivan walked over to the side of the bed and waved his hand at the guard. "Leave us, Miloš."

Viktor could see their faces and he knew their first names. If they ever released him, he could identify his captors. *They don't care. Dead men can't identify their captors.* He needed to escape ... but first, he had to make sure Louise was safe.

He projected feelings of calm, trust and sympathy to his captor, "What do you want? Where's Louise?"

Ivan smiled, or rather smirked. "Your wife is tied up at the moment. She is rather chilly without her clothes."

The man lied. None of this is true. But he expects a reaction. Viktor pulled at his handcuffs, trying unsuccessfully to sit up. "Where is she? Let her go."

"We will do whatever we want. She is a pretty woman."

"Let me see her. Is she here?"

"She is nearby. If you cooperate, you will see her." Despite Ivan's words, his emotions betrayed the lie.

"You don't have her!"

"Enough of your questions. Now you will answer mine." Ivan pulled a notepad from his coat pocket and flipped a few pages. "You are in politics, like your father. Do you talk about work?"

"I'm no longer in politics."

"Certainly, you discuss the important things — terrorism, the European Union, banking? Tell me what I want and your wife will be released."

The man's anxiety spiked at the word 'banking'. *This is about banking? They're going to kill me. Louise, too. Gotta do something.*

"Okay ... you win ... I'll tell you everything I know if you release Louise." Viktor squirmed in his bed. "But I have to take a piss first."

Annoyance showed on Ivan's face. "Hold it in. I want answers now."

Viktor squirmed and moved his legs as much as the constraints would allow. "It's hard to think when my bladder's ready to burst."

Ivan pulled a gun and some keys from his jacket and walked over to Viktor. "Make it quick. Don't try anything smart. Your wife will suffer." He unlocked one cuff, freeing Viktor from the bed rail, allowing him to stand and look around. He braced himself, feeling the gun pressed hard into his back.

Viktor locked onto the man's emotions. He amplified Ivan's nervousness, then transformed it to terror and increased the intensity. The man gasped. The pressure from the gun eased, followed by the sound of a thud against the floor.

Spinning around, he spotted the gun at the man's feet.

Ivan's eyes darted in all directions, like a madman. He trembled and collapsed.

Viktor picked up the gun and hit the man on the side of his head — hard. Blood ran along the floor toward a ring with three keys. He reached for them just as the headache arrived. A sharp pain struck behind his eyes and a brilliant light filled his vision. *My curse. Can't see!* He got down on his knees, blindly groping on the floor. *Wet. Blood.* His little finger bumped something. It jingled. He grabbed the keys.

Even though he couldn't see, he sensed Ivan — alive and unconscious. The stabbing pain didn't let up. He felt for the keyhole in his handcuff, then he inserted the smallest key and turned it. It worked, freeing his wrist. A search of the man's pockets revealed no phone.

Blurry shadows formed slowly. Viktor could identify Ivan, the bed and the toilet. He scratched the scar on his temple and noticed his eyepatch was missing. Why did they do that?

No time to worry about it. He had to get out of the room and find a phone. First, he had to make sure Ivan couldn't move or yell if he woke up. Viktor removed the man's coat and shirt, then hauled him onto the bed and handcuffed both of his wrists around the rail. He used Ivan's shirt as a gag.

Viktor's vision improved, and he found the door. It was locked and none of the keys fit. He looked around. How could he get the guard to come here? *The toilet.*

He removed the top from the tank, carried it across the room and threw it against the wall. The porcelain shattered on the floor.

He stood at the side of the door with his back to the wall, holding Ivan's gun in his hand. He heard another door open in the distance.

Heavy footsteps, getting louder ... closer. A familiar voice — the guard, Miloš — called out, "Ivan!"

Viktor sensed worry and fear from the approaching guard. Surely, the man could look through the barred window and see Ivan handcuffed and gagged on the bed. Viktor held his breath.

At the sound of a key unlocking the door, Viktor raised his gun above his head. The door opened, swinging outward, toward Miloš. The barrel of a handgun appeared, followed by a wrist. Viktor swung his gun down like a hammer onto the guard's wrist, knocking the man's gun to the floor.

Viktor rotated on one foot into a fighting stance, confronting Miloš, who was bent over holding his hand. The guard looked up, fear in his eyes. Viktor drove the heel of his palm into the man's chin, then smashed the gun against his head. Miloš collapsed into the room. Viktor propped him against the open door and took his gun, keys and phone. *At last — a phone.*

Viktor couldn't risk the door closing and locking him inside, so he removed Miloš's shoes and used them as doorstops. Then he removed the man's shirt and dragged him next to Ivan. He unlocked one cuff from Ivan and snapped it onto the guard, attaching them both to the rail.

Once the men were gagged and secure, Viktor ventured out of the room, spotting a door at the end of a long hallway. He approached, gun at the ready.

He peered through the barred window on the door to an unfinished basement with a stairway leading up. A man sat in front of a television. No telling if there were any others.

Viktor glanced at the phone — no signal. He walked back toward the farthest end of the hallway, looking for a stronger signal. When he got one bar, he placed a call.

A welcome voice answered. "Minister Prazsky."

He whispered into the phone. "Father. I need your help. Can you find me?"

"Viktor? Is that you? Where are you? Are you all right?"

"I don't know where I am. There's someone between me and the exit." He took a breath. "I need you to locate this phone."

"Josef is joining the call. I'm having a tough time hearing you."

"Eduard, what do you need?" It was Josef's voice.

"Find my phone," said Viktor. "Get me out of here."

"Viktor! ... Right away. Stay on this line."

"Father ... Do you know where Louise is? Is she safe?"

"Louise? She's with your mother right now. She's the one who told us you were missing."

A wave of relief swept through Viktor. *I was right! It was all a lie.* He stayed close to the wall, his eyes glued on the far end of the hall.

His father's voice interrupted Viktor's thoughts. "Are you still there?"

Viktor told him everything that happened.

When he finished the story, Josef spoke. "Don't worry, we'll get you out of there."

"Did you locate me?" Viktor walked back toward the doorway to check on the remaining guard. As he got closer, his reception got worse.

"You're in Žižkov. Sergeant Laska's rapid response unit is nearby. They're triangulating from the cell tower signals. Once they get close, they'll use phone transmissions to pinpoint your position. I have the sergeant on the line."

"We identified your location," said Laska. "It's a pub called the Red Underground. We're approaching the alley at the back—"

Viktor looked at the phone — no signal. He peeked through the barred window and spotted the guard in front of the TV.

The man turned his head and yelled, "Miloš. What are you doing?" He stood and walked toward the door.

Viktor ducked below the opening in the bars.

Footsteps approached. "Miloš, come on. Don't take all day." Keys jingled and fit into the lock.

Viktor grabbed the handle on the door and hung on, bracing himself against the wall. Someone pulled on the door, but Viktor held it shut.

"*Kurva*! The door—"

A loud blast came from the other room. Another bang, followed by the sound of heavy boots racing down wooden cellar steps. "Police! Drop your weapons!"

Viktor dropped to the floor.

Two gunshots. Three. The sound of footsteps and the banging of large objects hitting the walls. "Don't move."

Then silence.

Two more gunshots. Someone yelled, "Clear!"

Laska's voice followed. "Lone gunman down ... Where are you, Viktor?"

"Just inside the door."

"Stay back. I'm going to blow it."

Viktor ran back into the room with the bed.

A loud explosion was followed by a metallic bang. Dust flew down the hallway into the room.

Bootsteps rushed toward Viktor. Laska entered the room and spotted the two men attached to the bed. He looked at Viktor, smiled and gave him a thumbs-up.

Josef arrived within minutes of the assault. He spoke to Laska before walking over to Viktor. "I'm so glad you're safe." Then he winked. "I'll make sure the report doesn't reflect anything unusual."

"Thank you, Josef."

"Oh … your father told me to give this to you." In his hand, he held an eye patch.

Defiance
Chapter 36

Prague, Czech Republic

It was a warm August afternoon in Letná Park when Viktor jogged with Louise along the river. Their shadows ran ahead of them while the sun sank lower in the sky.

Louise glanced at him and smiled. Viktor loved her natural blonde hair, but today a brown wig covered those curls. News of the kidnapping brought them more unwanted attention, so they concealed their identities whenever they ventured out. Sunglasses hid her powder-blue eyes. Nevertheless, her beauty shone through the disguise.

A playful thought occurred to Viktor. He tugged subconsciously at his own wig and whispered his fantasy to Louise. "I've never made love to a brunette before, but I have a strong urge to come over to the dark side."

Her smile was a mixture of seduction and mischief. "Mmmm ... those blond locks of yours turn me on. Maybe we could slip behind that clump of trees and do the deed right here."

Viktor smiled. "I'll bet you'd do it, too. What about our bodyguards?"

She glanced at the man five meters ahead, dressed as a jogger, wearing an earpiece. "Oh, he and his partner can watch if they want. Maybe if we asked, he'd even take pictures."

Viktor liked the teasing banter, but they couldn't afford to attract attention. "You always brighten my mood."

"Speaking of brightening your mood, I think we've earned a beer ... or two."

Up ahead, the road divided. One path descended toward the river, but they took the high road to the left. Trees lined the entrance to an outdoor beer garden filled with picnic tables. It was shady and Viktor started to remove his sunglasses — then changed his mind. He remembered he wasn't wearing an eyepatch, and he felt self-conscious without it.

After selecting a table away from the crowd, Viktor bought two beers. Their bodyguards selected a table nearby, sipping on bottled water and chatting with each other.

Sweaty and tired, Viktor admired the view of Prague across the river. His eyes drifted to Louise, then the guards. He kept his voice low and his emotions in check. "I hate this security. And I hate hiding."

Louise turned away from the river. "We can handle the paparazzi — they love you. But the terrorists scare me. Shooting your mother ... the disco ... Turkey." She reached for his hand. "They were going to kill you."

Viktor felt the guards react to her words. He looked around, verifying what his senses told him. No one else was listening. "They've killed hundreds of people. They killed Aunt Běla." He gave Louise his handkerchief. "We've got to stop them. Hunt them down and kill them."

A group of college kids, carrying mugs of beer and laughing, settled at the table next to Viktor. He and Louise exchanged polite smiles with the group. They finished their beers in silence before heading home.

****

Back in their apartment, Viktor continued the fantasy they had begun in the park. "Come here, you sexy thing. Don't take off the wig."

Louise smiled. She stood still and began to unbutton her blouse. "Sit down, sweetheart, and enjoy the show."

Viktor pulled out a dining room chair and sat facing her.

Louise licked her lips. "Have you ever had a lap dance?" She slowly removed her clothes, then removed his. They played out their roles, giving each other pleasure on the chair, the floor, and finally the bed.

Exhausted from the run and the lovemaking, Louise laid her head on Viktor's chest and wrapped her arms around him. They both fell asleep.

A few hours later, they awoke hungry and sweaty. They shared a playful shower. Viktor smiled at the thought of enjoying both an exotic brunette and his blonde wife in rapid succession.

Neither of them felt like cooking, so they ordered pizza and watched Louise's favorite movie, *Les Misérables*. After the movie, Viktor poured drinks. "Maybe we should plan a trip to see your parents. You haven't been to Paris since we got married."

"That sounds great. But don't feel guilty because I moved here to live with you." She sipped her wine. "Besides, I love my job at Foreign Affairs."

"How do you like Simon ... I mean Minister Cerny?"

"I only met him a couple of times. Not sure he knows who I am."

"He knows," said Viktor. "Simon told me he's impressed with your multi-national experience. Says you write like a native-born Czech."

Louise smiled. "I'm still learning the language, but I'm glad my writing doesn't show it."

Viktor looked at his watch.

"Time for your meeting?"

"That's right." He stood and gave her a kiss. "I have to do everything I can. The only way to get our lives back is to catch these killers."

Viktor went to the study and logged into the videoconference a few minutes early. Only one other person was on the call. "Good evening, Father. How was your day?"

"Frustrating as usual. Lots of timid politicians."

"How are Lucie and Daniel doing? Losing their mother and moving to Prague. Can't be easy."

"They're having a hard time—"

Josef joined the call, followed by other members of the Fist of Freedom. By the scheduled start time, they had a quorum.

Eduard began. "First, I'll summarize the situation in Turkey. There's no action for the Fist to take. After Turkey relented in their standoff over the nukes, America decided to shift deployment to Romania. Within the year, we believe America will pull all their nukes out of Turkey."

Turkish Intelligence Director Togan spoke. "As expected, our government is in talks with Pakistan. If they supply my country with nuclear weapons, Pakistan will gain influence throughout the Middle East." Uncharacteristically, his voice weakened and shook. "Our people want nothing to do with the West."

Josef's face moved to the center of the screen. "Let's go onto the next topic. We questioned the men involved in Viktor Prazsky's kidnapping. Ivan Kovac was the leader. The others are local tough guys who knew nothing other than what Ivan paid them to do"

That sounded right to Viktor. "What information did Ivan give you?"

Josef brought up an artist's sketch. It was a thin face of a middle-aged accountant, his nose long and narrow, supporting a small pair of wire-rimmed glasses. "Ivan received his orders and money from this man. We haven't matched his face to anyone. Minister Prazsky's secretary gave us a list of people who could've delivered the threatening note, but Ivan didn't recognize any photos we showed him."

Viktor smiled, imagining Josef's interrogation of Ivan, using his proven combination of intimidation and brutality. In addition, Ivan would have been wired up to instruments capable of revealing his emotional response to photos of people. "Did you question the people on Eva's list? The ones who could have left the note?"

"We gave lie detector tests to everyone on the list — with the exception of the ministers. Everyone passed the test."

The ministers! It must have been one of them, but it would be politically difficult to submit them to a test.

His father's face filled the center of the screen. "We made progress following the money trail."

Viktor's secure phone rang. He recognized the name of the caller and answered it. "Josef. I'm listening to Father."

"I know. So am I. I'll make this quick. Perhaps you could use your special talent to identify the minister who left the note."

"I had the same thought."

"It would really help. You can identify him without his knowledge. I just want to ask you — please — when you identify the man, do not take action. If you do, it could screw up our chances to find the puppet master."

Viktor didn't like it, but Josef was right. "I understand. Now, I've got to get back to Father's briefing." He ended the call and turned his attention to the meeting.

His father was still speaking. "... requested an official anti-terrorist funding investigation of the hawaladar in Zugdidi, Georgia."

Josef interrupted. "It's worth mentioning, this was an official investigation — not a covert action. We went through formal channels."

"That's right." Eduard continued. "The investigators identified several suspicious transactions, and our analysts compared them to similar ones in Adana and Bratislava. It reinforces our theory — Zugdidi is the common thread."

A man with a British accent interjected, "So we believe this Georgian hawaladar sent funds for all the attacks? Who gave him the money to transfer?"

"Our cameras matched faces to the transactions. It appears there are two people who move cash from the Free Georgia Bank to the hawaladar. We've asked investigators to audit the bank."

The same Brit asked, "Minister Prazsky, these people kidnapped your son and threatened you when you looked into their banking. Aren't you worried they might take drastic action?"

"Security for everyone in our family has been increased. If we don't shut this group down, we'll be living under a constant threat. Besides, it's the right thing to do."

Viktor was proud of his father. More than ever, he looked forward to catching the puppet master.

Béziers, France

Brother Legrand waited for Ajax to calm down. First, the kidnapping fell apart, then Prazsky ignored the ransom demands and began aggressive investigations in Georgia. Legrand knew what was coming next.

"Damn Prazsky!" Ajax slammed his cognac glass on the arm of the chair. Liquid flew in all directions. "If we can't intimidate him, then it's time to get rid of him."

"As you wish, Your Grace."

Mole
Chapter 37

Prague, Czech Republic

At nine o'clock, Viktor arrived at his father's office. By now, the meeting with Simon Cerny would be ending. Viktor didn't believe Simon was the mole, but he and his father had to covertly test each minister who could have left the kidnapper's note.

He walked into the reception area. "Good morning, Eva."

"Go on in," she said.

When Viktor opened the door, Simon stepped forward to greet him. "It's good to see you. I can't begin to tell you how concerned we were."

Eduard stood and walked around his desk. "We haven't found the people who ordered Viktor's kidnapping."

"I thought the case was closed." Simon raised an eyebrow.

A manila folder sat on Eduard's desk. He pulled out a sketch and handed it to Simon. "They took orders from this man. We have no idea who he is."

Viktor observed Simon throughout the exchange. The man's emotions were consistent with his reactions — surprised to hear the mastermind was at large, and curious to see the artist's sketch. The foreign minister wasn't hiding anything. He wasn't the mole.

After studying the image, Simon handed it back to Eduard. "I've never seen him either."

As they agreed in advance, Viktor said the phrase that would let his father know he could trust Simon. "I'm sure the experts will sort this out."

"I'm sure they will." Eduard set the sketch on his desk. "I don't want to keep you, Simon. Please don't share this information with anyone. Now, Viktor and I have business to discuss."

Once the minister left, Eduard led his son to the small conference area in the corner of his office. "I'm relieved to know my good friend isn't the mole."

"I was sure it wasn't Simon." Viktor sat next to his father. "But one of your trusted ministers must be. I plan to help Josef follow the traitor once we discover who he is."

"All four ministers who were in my office when the note appeared confirmed their appointments today."

"Great. And, you leave for Budapest tomorrow."

Eduard shook his head. "Not 'til Sunday. I'll meet with you and Josef tomorrow."

"If all goes well, we should have several leads by then."

"We'll get them. I believe they follow the directions of a puppet master. A powerful man, probably a man, who feels threatened because we're tracing his money back to the source."

"I've been focused on the attacks on our family, almost forgetting the same man's responsible for the deaths in Turkey and Prague."

The conversation moved to Běla, then to the larger issues in Turkey. Viktor thought about the mastermind behind this violence. *Killing people. Fanning hatred. War.* "You think the puppet master makes money from all the fighting? Selling arms?"

"Yes, I do." Eduard explained the complex path this money travelled.

"You know, Father. I don't understand the money laundering business anywhere near as well as you do. So, you say Zugdidi is the key location?"

"We believe it was, but that ended a month ago. Right after I investigated the hawaladar. All the suspected accounts in Free Georgia Bank were closed the same day. None of the owners could be identified."

"Did they move their money to a different bank?"

"That's what Josef and I believe. We developed a theory based upon bank and hawala records plus video footage. A few accounts in Free Georgia Bank received money transfers from Germany, France and Scotland. From there the cash moved out of the banks and into the hawala system."

"You know which banks supplied the money?"

"Right down to the account numbers. We've requested audits of each account."

The intercom buzzed and Eva's voice interrupted their discussion. "The defense minister is here."

"Send him in," said Eduard.

Viktor opened the door. He never liked Franko even though the man served in three successive administrations.

Looking stiff and uncomfortable, the defense minister spoke. "Viktor. I didn't know you planned to join us."

"I'm just leaving. Father and I were talking about the men who kidnapped me."

"I'm glad you escaped unharmed. No punishment is too harsh for those men."

Despite the kind words, Franko's emotions betrayed his dislike for Viktor. Of course, that didn't make him a kidnapper. If he turned out to be the mole, Viktor would have to remain calm, especially if they wanted to find the man funding everything.

Eduard stood and walked around his desk. "We haven't found the people who ordered his kidnapping."

This seemed to catch Franko off guard. "Didn't the police arrest everyone involved?"

The man's emotions were off the chart. Viktor sensed it all. Surprise, worry and fear — especially fear. And he lied. *He's part of the conspiracy!*

Eduard opened the folder on his desk and handed the sketch to Franko. "They took orders from this man. We have no idea who he is."

When the defense minister glanced at the picture, he shook his head. "I wish I could help you, but he doesn't look familiar to me."

Lie! Franko's the mole. He knows this guy. Viktor closed his eyes and took a few slow, deep breaths. He detected his father's concern. When he opened his eyes, both men were staring at him. "Sorry, I'm a bit tired." He pointed at the sketch and said the key phrase to alert his father. "We'll find him."

Eduard's face went slack for a moment, then his usual smile returned. "Well, I don't want to keep you, Viktor. Minister Franko and I have things to discuss before the emergency meeting."

A look of surprise came over Franko's face. "Emergency meeting? I didn't see it on the schedule. Will it take all morning?"

"We'll bring in lunch. You need to cancel your other appointments for the day."

****

The next morning, Eduard sat alone in his study. He joined a videoconference with Josef and Viktor. Yesterday's 'emergency meeting' was a ruse to keep Franko in the office. Two staffers had worked with him on a detailed defense proposal and kept the minister busy until the middle of the afternoon.

"Did I delay him long enough, Josef?"

"Perfect. When he left the office, he seemed nervous. Did you give him anything to worry about?"

"I told him we had a lead on the man in the sketch and expected to make an arrest within a few days. The sonofabitch looked like he was going to throw up. Franko was never alone in the office, except — did he make any calls from the men's room?"

"No, he didn't. He knows we control all government devices. We remotely updated his phone yesterday, so he's walking around with a live mike, except when he turns it off or doesn't carry it. Our guys are listening to everything he says."

"Did you wire his house?"

"We installed bugs in his home and office, and also on his computer. A complete search of the house came up empty. His computer is so clean, he must delete the history every day. If he uses email, he leaves no trace of it."

Eduard let out a sigh. "All that work and you found nothing?"

"We copied his hard drive and swapped it with the original. Hopefully, forensics will find something. His spycraft is solid. We have to act soon before his next sweep for bugs."

Eduard's heart raced. *This guy's a real spy. We've trusted him for years. He helped the man who shot Magda. The ones who grabbed Viktor. He deserves to die.*

Josef's voice interrupted Eduard's thoughts. "We placed him under continuous twenty-four-hour surveillance. We'll also check his snail mail before it's delivered to his home."

"Anything suspicious so far?" Eduard wouldn't be surprised if Franko tried to skip town.

"He turned off his phone as soon as he left the office. On the way home, he stopped at a store and bought a prepaid phone. Then he sat in his car and used it to call somewhere in southeastern France. We captured the call data but not the audio. When he stopped for gas, he removed the sim card and threw the phone in the trash."

Eduard figured Franko would flush the sim card down the toilet. "How's he going to communicate to the puppet master? If he can't lead us up the ladder—"

"He will. I'm sure he will. Last night he accessed a few web sites. I believe that's how he gets his orders. We're checking on those."

Budapest
Chapter 38

Budapest, Hungary

It was early in the afternoon in the southern wing of the Hungarian parliament building, when Eduard stepped out of the president's office and entered Munkácsy Hall. The meeting had gone well, but surveillance of Pavel Franco back in Prague was foremost in his mind. If the traitor didn't lead them to the source of terrorist money soon, Eduard would bring him in for enhanced interrogation.

Simon Cerny, the Czech foreign minister, interrupted Eduard's thoughts. "I'm pleased President Bartos is on board. It would make things more difficult if he opposed the prime minister and speaker."

"I agree," said Eduard. Simon was a trusted friend, but he didn't have a 'need to know' about Franko. "The General Assembly responded well to our proposals. Hungary will continue to be a good partner in our fight against terrorists."

Josef rose from a bench by the windows and approached them. "How did it go?"

Simon glanced at his watch. "Sorry, I've got to leave. I have a meeting at the foreign ministry."

Looking at Simon with a frown, Josef asked, "Aren't you joining us at Hero's Square? I planned to include you in the motorcade."

"I wish I could. Saint Steven's Day celebrations are enjoyable, but duty calls."

Eduard shook Simon's hand. "See you this evening, then. You can't miss the fireworks."

As the foreign minister walked away, Josef pointed to one of the plush benches along the windows. "We have a few minutes before the limousine arrives. Why don't we sit down?"

Eduard nodded and headed to the bench. "Is this your first time in the parliament building?"

"I've seen pictures, but you can't really appreciate it until you step inside. The columns and the arches are bigger than Prague Castle — and all this gold."

Eduard sat next to Josef and pointed to the immense painting that dominated the wall in front of them. "That's the most valuable piece of art in the building. It's called *The Conquest*."

"Conquest? No swords? No blood?"

"You're not the first person to mention that." Eduard looked around. "Is it safe to talk here?"

"Parliament Security assured me no one will use this hall until we leave." Josef pulled a small antenna from his vest pocket and pointed it at Eduard. "I also checked for bugs while you were meeting with the president. This hall is secure."

"What's going on with Franko. Any progress?"

"He must be worried. Last night he posted a message on a website. It said, 'Beware, Lion is hungry.' We think Lion refers to you."

"He's warning someone we're on their trail."

"That's our guess." Josef unfolded a piece of paper and handed it to Eduard. "Forensics found this on Franko's hard drive. It appears to be a list of cell numbers for prepaid phones in southern France. It was encrypted, but our folks cracked it. We also found some files he deleted ... well, he thought he deleted them. Some are old versions of that list. He deletes numbers from the top."

"So, he calls the phone number on the top of the list, then deletes it?"

"We believe so. We monitored call traffic from Prague to all the numbers on the list, and discovered one ten second call made a few minutes after Franko bought a prepaid phone. We think that's how he gives his handler the new number — now we know it, too. Whenever he makes a call or receives one, we'll get everything, including audio."

"Now we wait." Eduard hated waiting. These people — these killers — could attack anywhere. They could attack Magda or Viktor again. "But there's something that doesn't add up. The money trail doesn't include any Muslims or Muslim group? Same with the kidnapping."

Josef nodded. "I've been thinking the same thing. This isn't about Muslims. The Aryan Reich attacks weren't about the Nazi cause, either. This is all about money."

Josef's phone rang. He listened, then looked at Eduard. "Time to go."

****

Josef rode with the Hungarian Protective Service team inside the motorcade command vehicle that was responsible for the security of two identical limousines, collectively known as *the package*. Eduard sat in one of the limos. The other was a decoy.

The motorcade proceeded slowly out of the garage below the parliament building, led by Budapest police on motorcycles and in cars. A military assault van was next, followed by the decoy, then Eduard's limo and Josef's van. More assault and communication vehicles followed, along with members of the local and foreign press.

Josef scanned the video screen in front of him. "The crowds along the route appear well behaved." He spoke French to the team leader. The others in the van only spoke Hungarian. "Should be an uneventful drive."

"We wish for that, but we are prepared." The leader pointed to the screen, where twenty images were arranged in a four by five rectangle. "The images from upper floors are sniper positions. And you can see drone videos — one in front, one behind."

Everything went smoothly as they followed Vaci Street, turned right and approached the square. A large crowd filled the area in front of the Millennium Monument. In the center was the iconic column, jutting ten stories into the air, topped with a statue of Archangel Gabriel.

Josef spotted the roped off pathway through the crowd leading to a platform at the right of the column. Eduard would speak there, protected by a bulletproof shield. As the motorcade slowed, Josef stood and headed toward the door.

"You cannot leave the vehicle yet." The team leader pointed to a chair. "Please sit while Security escorts the prime minister through the crowd."

"I planned to escort him to the monument."

"Our protective service team is trained for this."

Josef watched as four armed guards flanked the door to Eduard's limo. If this were Prague, Josef might do this differently, but here the host country called the shots.

The team leader smiled at Josef. "You wonder about bullets? These men are well trained. Two carry riot guns. Rubber bullets."

Josef studied the video while Eduard stepped from the limo. Four guards formed around him, searching the crowd as they moved slowly toward the monument.

"Drone!" The shout came from an operator in the van.

"*Lő le!*" This shout from the leader. He pointed to an image of a quadcopter that looked like a kid's toy with four propellers racing toward Eduard. Glancing at Josef, he added, "They shoot it."

Josef rushed out of the van in time to see three guards knock Eduard to the ground and cover him with their bodies. The fourth swung his riot gun upward and fired at the drone. A bullet hit the small copter and drove it away from the crowd, into the intersection.

A cloud of smoke was followed by a loud bang where the drone fell. A young couple across the street yelled and dropped to the sidewalk.

"That's a grenade!" yelled Josef. "They tried to kill Eduard."

"Drone!" Another shout from the leader.

The guard who downed the first drone swung his gun around searching the sky.

Another quadcopter streaked in from the north. And still another from the south. Heading for Eduard. The guard never got off a shot before the first drone hit him. Two more clouds of smoke. Loud bangs. *More grenades.* Eduard remained buried under three guards.

Screams erupted from the crowd. People turned to run away. A dozen bodies, maybe more, surrounded Eduard and his guards, who remained on the ground, atop a growing pool of blood.

"No!" Josef ran toward the spot. The brave guards died to protect Eduard, but two grenades landed directly on top of them.

Before he could reach Eduard, the medical team arrived and began triage. They checked one of the guards and announced, "*Hallot.*"

Josef knew the Hungarian word for 'dead'.

They removed the guard's body from the pile and checked out the second guard. "*Hallot.*" After removing the body, they reached Eduard. "*Hallot.*"

Resolve
Chapter 39

Prague, Czech Republic

Viktor relaxed in his apartment, sitting in his favorite overstuffed chair with his legs on the ottoman. Through the glass French doors of his patio, he looked across Wenceslas Square, bustling with people enjoying the sunny afternoon.

He turned his attention back to his tablet computer and the latest surveillance report on Franko. No calls sent or received using the new prepaid phone. Viktor copied the address of the web page Franko used for his latest post, then opened it to take a look. *What the hell?*

It was a wildlife conservation site with a section for followers to share their thoughts and experiences. And there was the anonymous post – 'Beware, Lion is hungry.' Nothing further. No response.

The apartment door opened. He turned to face the pleasant interruption, listening for the sound of her voice.

"Are you home, Viktor?"

"In the den. How was lunch?"

Louise's bright yellow sundress complemented the blonde curls bouncing off her exposed shoulders. And those lovely legs, bare and inviting. He stood to meet her.

"We went to that new French restaurant, Cafe Josette. I liked it, and so did the other girls." She wrapped her arms around Viktor's neck and kissed him. Her tongue slipped between his lips and probed deeply.

Viktor returned the kiss, their bodies pressed together tightly. Without a word, he carried Louise to the bedroom where he pulled her sundress over her head. She kicked off her shoes.

Viktor's phone chirped.

Louise looked at him quizzically.

"That's the sound it makes for a news alert. I'll check it later."

She kissed his neck and unfastened the top button of his shirt, then the next. Her lips moved to his chest. Slowly, she undid every button, then pulled off his shirt.

The phone chirped again ... and again.

Louise looked at Viktor. "Maybe you should check. It might be important."

He grabbed the phone and glanced at the headline:

Czech PM Attacked in Budapest

His mind raced. Budapest! Father's there. He has security.

Frantic, Viktor searched for more reports on the story. No details. Every source said the same thing. Father was attacked. First Mother, now Father. Is he hurt? Who did this? Franko!

Louise fell on the bed and curled up in a ball. "Viktor! Please stop."

The sight of his wife, crying and shaking, was terrifying. I did that. My anger.

He concentrated on soothing, loving emotions as he stroked her hair. "I'm so sorry. I didn't mean it."

Viktor sensed Louise relaxing. She stopped crying. He held his breath waiting for her response.

She lowered her knees from her chest and rolled onto her back. "I'm okay, now. You really scared me. Like you did in Cyprus."

"I could never forgive myself if I harmed you."

"What happened, Viktor? Tell me."

He took a deep breath and let it out slowly. Time for self-control. "Someone attacked Father. He's probably hurt, but I don't know how bad."

Louise sat up and hugged Viktor. "You need to find out."

"If it's bad news ... I can't be near you ... not until I learn what happened."

"Go into the living room. I'll stay here."

Viktor rushed into the room and turned on an American network news channel. A headline banner appeared below the reporter.

> *Bombing Kills Dozens in Budapest. Czech Prime Minister Feared Dead.*

Dead! He dropped the remote control. *Father dead? Impossible!*

"Viktor!" Louise screamed from the bedroom. "Stop it!"

He brought his emotions under control long enough to call out to his wife. "I have to go. This is too much."

Time to focus. He had to get to his car while avoiding the security detail. Grabbing a shirt, he slipped out the door and down the stairs to the garage.

He drove directly to Letná Park, jogged along a tree-lined path to a remote spot, stopped at a fallen log, and sat. Finally, he could release all his feelings — anger, rage, sadness.

He searched the news on his phone, and his worst fears came true:

> *At least twenty-three people died and forty were injured in a drone attack at Heroes' Square in Budapest, Hungary.*
> *Czech Prime Minister Eduard Prazsky, who died in the attack, appeared to be the intended target.*

No! Viktor's heart raced. *Not Father!* He pounded on the log and released all his pent-up grief and anger. Despite the warm afternoon sun, he felt cold. Tears flowed from his eyes.

He regained his composure and forced himself to read the details of the report. Three small drones carrying hand grenades attacked his father from different directions. Security guards tried to protect him, but they died in the attempt.

Franko! That traitor! He deserves to die. Salafi Brotherhood. Muslims. They deserve to die!

Viktor let his rage take over once again. No need to hold back.

A sudden scream got his attention. A few meters down the path, he spotted a jogger bent over, holding his head. Viktor reigned in his emotions. Before long, the man stood upright, turned around and walked away.

As the man disappeared along the path, Viktor's anger took focus. *Franko! I'm going to kill the sonofabitch!*

Then he thought of his family. *Mother. She's all alone. She has Daniel and Lucie. Mother comes first.*

Running Scared
Chapter 40

Béziers, France

Legrand was excited. Today everything went as planned — well, almost everything. He arrived a few minutes early to his evening meeting with Ajax, the grand master, and had to wait while the man finished his chocolate mousse.

After Marcel cleared dinner, rolled the tray into the elevator and disappeared behind the closed door, Ajax waved his arm beckoning Legrand to approach. "The execution was performed flawlessly. I commend you."

"Thank you, Your Grace. The drone pilots blended into the crowd leaving no trail for police to follow."

Ajax nodded. "The media was very responsive. All the riots were reported as spontaneous uprisings against Muslims during the evening news cycle."

Two complements in a row. Legrand wasn't used to such praise. "Our organizers did a fabulous job, especially in Amsterdam. The firebombed mosque has become a rallying point for both pro- and anti-Muslim protesters, but I think the intensity of the response is mostly due to Prazsky. Half the people loved him, and half hated him."

"He's more helpful dead than alive. Trading has already driven up the value of our European security services stock. By tomorrow, our top ten investments should double in value."

Legrand had to admit his boss was good at his job.

Ajax reached for his glass and swirled the cognac gently below his nose. "Keep an eye on his son, Viktor. He has followers, too." He sipped the brown liquid, then set the glass down. "If he shows any interest in our banks, he'll suffer the same fate as his father."

Nodding, Legrand located a document on his tablet. "I've made progress on the nuclear weapon."

Ajax raised an eyebrow. "The plutonium core?"

"The general and the security director of the Pakistani reactor facility are with us. In two weeks, we'll have the plutonium pit we require to complete the warhead."

"Excellent. Tensions between Muslims and Christians are the highest they've been since the Crusades. The time is right for full-scale war."

"The weapon weighs over a thousand pounds," said Legrand. "And once nuclear material is reported missing, the Americans will try to track its radiation signature."

"Make sure no one reports it missing. Cover it in lead if you have to. If anyone locates it before it arrives in Rotterdam harbor, detonate it."

"As you wish."

Ajax picked up his glass. "Any questions?"

"No questions, Your Grace."

"Brief me on your progress in two days."

Legrand nodded. "We have one other issue to discuss."

"What is it?"

"Minister Franco is running scared. He thinks his cover might be blown. He wants us to protect him."

"You know what to do. Take care of it."

Budapest, Hungary

It was dark by the time Josef Filipek returned to his hotel. He hadn't eaten, but he wasn't hungry. He was exhausted and angry.

Eduard's dead. Franko works for these killers. Josef wanted to grab Franko immediately, but he knew it would be better to wait for the man's handlers to make contact. Josef was flying home in the morning. Unless Franko made contact, it was time to bring the bastard in. No arrest, no lawyers, no mercy.

Sitting at a small desk, Josef opened his laptop and initiated a secure link to the videoconference. The team awaited his update.

He logged in and heard the familiar voice of the Turkish intelligence director. "... agree. We don't need to address that today."

Josef's image filled the center of the screen. "What don't we need to address today, Director Togan?"

"Good to see you, Director Filipek. We were just discussing how to deal with Prime Minister Prazsky's death ... who should lead the Fist. We decided to postpone the decision, and simply ask you to brief us on the situation."

The mention of Eduard's death drove home the reality of the situation. Josef searched the faces on the screen, all seemed to be patiently waiting.

Togan spoke up. "We all miss the prime minister. I can only imagine how you feel."

Josef took a deep breath and exhaled slowly. "I know the news reports were confusing today. Some even said Eduard was alive, but ..." He closed his eyes briefly, then continued. "I called Prime Minister Prazsky's wife. Viktor is with her."

Miniature images of his colleagues appeared along the border of the screen. No Viktor. No Eduard. Josef looked at his notes. "I just completed a debriefing with the Hungarian Protective Service team. Three hobbyist quadcopter drones targeted Eduard from high altitude. Each carried a fragmentation grenade. Their flights went undetected until they were two hundred meters away. One officer managed to down a drone, but two hit their target."

He reported the details of the attack and the actions of the Hungarian police. "The drones had cameras, so the pilots could have been one kilometer away from the square, maybe more. The police have no leads at this time."

Togan interrupted. "You say Hungarian authorities have no leads, but what about us? How do we track down the killers?"

Josef looked up from his notes. "I'm certain the puppet master behind this attack is the same one we've been pursuing for Viktor's kidnapping, Turkey and everything else. We believe Minister Franko can lead us to him."

Prague, Czech Republic

Josef's plane landed in Prague before noon. He checked his messages. One of them came from Franko's surveillance team thirty minutes ago:

Phone turned on. No call yet.

Josef sent a staff member to retrieve the luggage. Then he headed to the car to make a secure call. "Any news?"

The team leader responded. "Ten minutes before my text, Franko read an item on the same wildlife conservation site he used before. It said, 'Listen to the hawk.' He turned on his phone. We're tracking his calls."

"Notify me if anything else happens." Josef turned on his earpiece and drove toward the office.

On the way, he assigned three more agents to monitor Franko in case the man started to move. Before he reached his destination, the phone rang once more. "News?"

"Franko just received a call and answered, saying, 'Lion's den.' The caller responded with, 'Horse market one hour,' then hung up."

"Horse market?" Josef hit the brakes and took a sharp U-turn. "That's Wenceslas Square. If he leaves, follow him. Don't lose him. Use the camera drones. I'm on my way." *Franko gets to live another day.*

Josef dispatched four snipers to the square. Once Franko arrived, they would select positions where they had a clear line-of-sight.

Reports came in from the surveillance team. Franko parked near the southeast end of the square. He walked past the statue of the saint, sat near the bus stop and pulled out a book.

Josef arrived nearby ten minutes later.

The snipers reported their positions. Two non-descript SUVs parked on opposite sides of the square. Inside each one, surveillance teams pointed directional microphones and video cameras at their subject. They also monitored the drones. If anyone showed an interest in Franko, someone would follow or shoot them.

Tourists and locals walked by. Some sat on benches. Busses dropped off passengers and picked up new ones. None of these people paid attention to Franko, who appeared absorbed in his book.

The loud crack of a powerful gun rang out. Franko's head jerked backward before he collapsed on the pavement. The doors of the SUVs opened. Agents, wearing body armor, rushed to the scene.

Someone's voice barked into Josef's headset. "Shot came from Karol Bank — upper floors. Team on its way."

Another voice announced, "Head shot. Blood. No pulse."

Josef screamed into his microphone, "We need Franko alive."

"The back of his head is missing, Director. He's dead."

Josef clenched his fists. *We'll find the people behind this. I promise you, Eduard.*

Money Trail
Chapter 41

Prague, Czech Republic

Viktor pored over the documents his mother removed from the wall safe. It felt wrong rummaging through these personal papers, but it had to be done. One folder contained confidential information compiled by the Fist of Freedom — about Franko and the terrorist money trail. That was something to study, but not until he was alone.

Magda closed the safe and covered it with the family portrait. She smiled as her gaze lingered on the picture. All three of them had posed for it two years ago, when Viktor was a member of the European Parliament. "That was a happy occasion. I'll always remember your father like he was on that day." She sat next to Viktor and took his hand. "He would want us to get on with our lives. It's been two weeks."

"You're right." Viktor faced his mother. "If only the media would let us."

"Your father was a great man." She squeezed her son's hand. "People all over Europe loved him. I wish they'd celebrate the good ..." Her voice trailed off as if her mind was somewhere else.

"I know. You don't like the angry mobs."

"I'm ashamed of them. Those people do nothing but foment hatred and violence against Muslims." Tears welled up in her eyes. "Your father wasn't like that."

"Louise agrees with you." Viktor sympathized with the anger of the people, but his mother didn't want to hear talk of revenge.

Magda reached for a folder on the coffee table and opened it. "Doctor Martin will be here soon."

Lawyers! "I don't understand why Father didn't leave everything to you."

"You know I don't understand breweries or law. All I need is our home." She handed Viktor the folder. "And what would I do with real estate in France?"

He looked through the papers. "I don't want to manage real estate either. Better to sell it."

****

After they met with the lawyer, Viktor drove home and went directly to his study. All through his life, he never worried about money. He knew his father had extensive holdings in the Czech Republic, handed down from his family. Viktor looked through the list from the lawyer — at the French assets he inherited. *Father must have been one of the wealthiest men in Narbonne. Now I am.*

The last time Viktor saw his father was when they realized Franko was a traitor. At the funeral, the casket was closed — the grenades caused too much damage. *Gotta stop these killers.*

Viktor grabbed his phone and placed a secure call to Josef, who answered after the third ring.

"Good evening, Viktor. How are you doing? How's your mother?"

"Mother's handling it well. But I won't rest until we get the bastards who killed Father." Viktor put the phone on speaker. "Do you have any leads on the drone pilots?"

"We found one of the control units behind a gas station. No prints. DNA inconclusive."

"Inconclusive? What does that mean?"

"It was in a dumpster, lots of DNA, some of it human. No matches against any database. Without a match, and without any suspects, DNA is not useful."

Two weeks without a lead. Viktor stood and paced the room. "No witnesses? How did these guys get away?"

"They could have operated the drones from inside an apartment. No one saw anyone suspicious in the area. And, before you ask, the hand grenades are the same type sold by the Russian mafia to criminals and terrorists all over Europe."

Viktor stopped pacing. "Russian mafia? They killed Father?"

"Slow down. They're simply arms suppliers. The puppet master we're after runs a highly organized group, using terrorism to manipulate stocks. He laundered his money through Zugdidi and the hawala network. Even if we shut down the Russian mafia, the terrorist attacks would continue."

That made sense, but it left them at a dead end. Viktor sat down. "Do we have anything to go on?"

"Two leads. The call Franko received came from a prepaid phone purchased in Toulouse. We couldn't identify the exact location because the caller hung up so quickly. However, we know it came from southern France."

Viktor was losing patience. "Toulouse? That's half a million people. Not much of a lead to go on."

Josef continued. "We're also following the money. Some fund transfers to Zugdidi came from a Narbonne bank. This could be significant—"

"Toulouse and Narbonne are only a hundred fifty kilometers apart. Doesn't seem like a coincidence."

"Exactly. Franko's contact and the money trail both led us to the same region. I plan to demand an audit of *Crédit de la Robine*, the bank that sent the money. But I'm afraid they'll shut down the accounts, like they did with *Free Georgia Bank* in

Zugdidi, where the account owners used fictitious names, leaving us no trail to follow."

"Wait a minute, Josef." Viktor grabbed the asset list he had received from his lawyer. There it was — *Banque Mutuel* in Narbonne. "I have an idea."

Narbonne, France

It took a week for Viktor's lawyer, Doctor Martin, to arrange the meetings in Narbonne. The president of *Banque Mutuel* organized a briefing by six senior bank officers to go over the Prazsky holdings, and to explain the services available to Viktor. When they finished their presentations, the president stood. "Mister Prazsky. Do you or Doctor Martin have any questions?"

Viktor glanced at his attorney, then rose from the chair. "You have a professional team here, and the presentations were informative. Doctor Martin and I have several issues to discuss. We'll be contacting you before the end of the week." He reached for his tablet and prepared to leave, then added, "I have to say, I was initially concerned when I heard rumors of banks in this region laundering terrorist money, but it's clear you've implemented strict controls and effective oversight."

The president walked over to Viktor. "I'm pleased we were able to demonstrate our strong support for anti-terrorist funding measures. We hope to continue our strategic business partnership with you."

While shaking hands on the way out, Viktor had one more chance to sense the emotions of these men. None of them had lied to him, and none were alarmed at the discussion of terrorist funding.

Their next stop was *Crédit de la Robine*, only two blocks away. According to Josef, someone in this bank assisted the terrorists by making money transfers to Zugdidi. No Prazsky money was deposited here, so Viktor needed to take a different approach.

The *Robine* bank president organized a briefing. He introduced each of his officers to Viktor and Doctor Martin as they gathered informally around coffee and pastries. After everyone was seated, he delivered a few opening remarks before getting down to business. "We are pleased with the opportunity to demonstrate why we should be your regional bank."

Viktor remained seated as he responded. "As I'm sure you're aware, my father and I have always supported the fight against terrorism. I've been told some banks in this region are engaged in money laundering for terrorist organizations. Before I select a bank, they will have to demonstrate what safeguards are in place to prevent this illegal activity."

Fear. Someone across the table reacted to his speech with fear.

The president nodded his agreement. "We take this seriously as well." He waved his arm toward one of the officers. "Monsieur Duval is our compliance officer. He will explain our procedures and oversight."

Viktor maintained a poker face. Whoever supported the terrorists did it without the president's knowledge.

Duval thanked his boss and walked to the front of the room.

Viktor sensed the man's emotions. *That's him.* It made sense. The compliance officer would be in the best position to hide illegal money transfers.

Monsieur Duval described the methods the bank used to prevent money laundering, but his emotions continued to betray him.

Viktor had no doubt. He reached casually into his pocket for his phone and pressed a button on the side. It rang. He acted surprised and pulled it out, offering an apologetic smile. Facing the man, he looked at the screen and pressed it, then set it on the table. "Excuse me, Monsieur Duval. My phone won't interrupt us again. Please continue."

The next step was in the hands of Josef and his surveillance team outside the bank. By now, they should have received the picture of Duval plus Viktor's voice stating the man's name.

Empty Quiver
Chapter 42

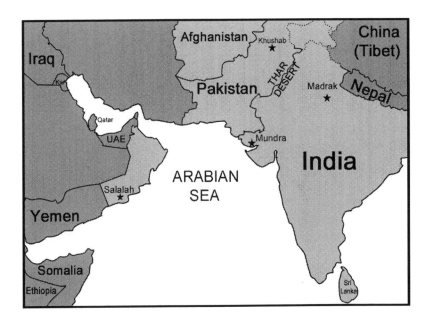

Khushab, Pakistan

Major Dewan, Director of Security at the Khushab nuclear reactor in northern Pakistan, waited outside the main gate as a white van drove toward the inspection bay. Yellow stripes with black arrows adorned the sides. Strategically located placards made it clear the vehicle carried radioactive materials.

The major's heart pounded. *Everything's going to work as planned.* General Shaheen, the official in charge of this facility, had paid the major a lot of money in the past to smuggle designs and chemicals out of the plant for his rich clients. But, today would be the biggest payday of his life.

As they waited for the vehicle to park, Captain Parwaz turned to the major. "May I ask you a question?"

Dewan nodded. "You want to know what new kind of equipment they are testing. Am I right?"

"Yes, sir. I'm curious."

"You must remind yourself. We are security officers. We are not cleared for this information."

When the van stopped, Parwaz requested the manifest and IDs from the driver and his passenger. He compared the pictures on the IDs to the faces of the people, then handed the documents to the major.

Dewan examined their papers. Doctor Ahuja, the passenger, was a nuclear scientist, and the driver was his lab assistant. The manifest listed three sealed containers of test equipment. The major nodded at the driver then turned to Parwaz. "Check the camera, Captain. I'll check the vehicle."

Dewan opened the back and checked the codes on each label against the manifest. Each yellow box was about thirty-five centimeters square and twenty centimeters in height. The radioactivity placards meant these shielded containers could not be opened safely here.

He closed the back. "Everything checks out."

The captain nodded. "Video and radiation scans are good."

Dewan and Parwaz got into their Range Rover and led the van to the plutonium reprocessing center. The blast doors swung open slowly. Both vehicles entered, parking next to the laboratory entrance before the doors closed behind them.

The major stepped out of his car and walked up to the security panel, placing his left hand on the scanner. When the light turned green, he entered the proper code on the keypad and the door opened. Lab personnel expected them. Two men in white lab coats rolled a dolly to the van.

The driver and the doctor stepped out of their vehicle, walked to the rear and opened the back. As they reached inside, a man from the lab held up his hand. "We will move them. You have been assigned a private room."

Dewan and Parwaz walked next to the dolly. The driver and Doctor Ahuja followed. They entered the laboratory where a large stainless-steel cabinet sat in the center of the room, and racks of equipment lined two of the sides. On the far wall, an odd closet with a large window jutted into the room. Two large rubber gloves with sleeves hung from holes in the window of the closet. This was the glovebox. The only place safe enough to handle radioactive material.

After the men in lab coats moved the yellow boxes onto the table and departed, the major approached Parwaz. "Plutonium pits are dangerous, Captain. There's always a risk of exposure to radiation during testing. I must remain, but you will stand guard outside the door."

"As you wish." Parwaz stepped outside, leaving the major alone with the doctor and his assistant.

Dewan reached for his phone. "Should I request the first half pit, Doctor?"

"Yes. I'll be ready." Ahuja broke the seal and opened one of the three yellow boxes, removing a Geiger counter, a scale, a block of putty, and two tubes of small lead pellets. He left the other yellow boxes unopened.

The major looked at the glovebox. He had often seen people use them, but he never understood how they worked. "How will you get the pit out of this contraption?"

The doctor pointed to the right side of the closet where his assistant stood wearing long-sleeved gloves. "He will remove it through the rubber door on the side."

Dewan shook his head. "I'm sure you know what you're doing."

Ahuja pointed to the window. "Look through the glass. There are two chambers."

Walking up to the window, the major peered inside. "The one on the left is much larger than the one on the right."

"Yes, it's the main chamber. A vacuum constantly sucks air through a filter to remove radiation. When the pit is delivered from storage, it will come through the rubber door at the back. You will hear it sucking air until the pit is inside and the door closes behind it."

"But how do you get it out of the glovebox?"

The doctor pointed to the small chamber on the right. "This is the antechamber. Anything that enters or leaves the main chamber from the right must go through this area. And it must remain in the antechamber a few minutes to allow the air to be purified."

"Like an airlock in a space station?"

Ahuja nodded. "You can think of it that way. I will push the pit through a rubber door into the antechamber. When the air is purified and pressurized, my assistant will reach through the door on the right and retrieve it."

Dewan heard the muffled sound of rushing air, announcing the arrival of a sealed case entering the main chamber. "It's here, Doctor."

Ahuja inserted his arms into the rubber sleeves hanging from the window, pushing them inside the glovebox. He fit each finger into the gloves, grabbed the case containing a half pit of plutonium, and pushed it through the rubber door into the antechamber. Once again, Dewan heard the sound of rushing air.

When the doctor gave him a nod, the assistant reached through the rubber door and grabbed the case with his gloved hands. Air rushed into the glovebox until the plutonium case was completely removed and the door slammed behind it.

The assistant carried the heavy case to the table while Ahuja removed his arms from the gloves. He grabbed the Geiger counter and waved the probe along the outside of the box.

Dewan looked at the meter, relieved to see the needle all the way to the left. "Does that mean we'll live?"

The doctor smiled. "Just being cautious. The plutonium is well shielded, and the case picked up very little radiation from the storage facility." He and his assistant lifted it onto the scale. He wrote down the weight. "Let's pack this up."

The doctor broke the seal on one of the two remaining yellow boxes and opened it. He removed a case that looked identical to the one containing plutonium. "What do you think?"

The major shook his head. "I can't tell them apart."

"Good thing, Major. I hope your equipment handlers have the same problem." He pointed to the plutonium case. "That one contains half the fissile material for a bomb — warm and radioactive. The other one contains lead — cold and boring." He placed the plutonium case into the yellow box, closed it and affixed a new seal.

The assistant lifted the lead container onto the scale. The doctor placed putty on the case, then stuck one lead pellet into it, followed by a second. After adding five large pellets and two small ones, he was satisfied. "Now it's the same weight as the plutonium. That should fool them for a while." He opened the case and stuck the putty inside before closing it.

Dewan watched as they placed the lead case back into the glovebox, then he made a call to the material handlers, notifying them it was ready to be returned to storage. He also requested another half pit. The doctor and his assistant repeated the process. They now had two half pits of plutonium, enough for a bomb.

Béziers, France

It was early evening when Brother Legrand made a secure call to General Shaheen on his satellite phone. "Did everything go smoothly today?"

"My security team escorted your engineers out of the facility with one complete pit."

Even though he planned every detail, Legrand could hardly believe it. "How long do we have before international inspectors arrive?"

"Six days until our next scheduled inspection. I plan to be gone before that, thanks to your generous retirement plan."

The general would disappear all right. Legrand had plans to make it permanent. "You earned your money. But tell me, do inspectors ever show up unannounced?"

"They could call a surprise inspection, but that's rarely done here."

"Excellent. Will the inspectors realize it's missing?"

"I'm certain they will. And missing nuclear weapon components trigger an international alert — Empty Quiver. The Americans will leave no stone unturned."

Breakthrough
Chapter 43

Narbonne, France

Viktor sprinted from his car and entered a customized tour bus parked along the Canal de la Robine in Narbonne. Inside, Josef sat on a swivel chair surrounded by communication equipment, facing five monitors.

It was a warm day in September, and the short dash to the command center bus made Viktor work up a sweat. The air-conditioning felt wonderful. "Did I miss anything? I got here as fast as I could."

Josef motioned to his left. "Have a seat. Your man from the bank is definitely involved with the puppet master."

Viktor tugged at his eyepatch. Each time they had a lead on this guy, something always happened and the trail went cold. "I knew Duval was dirty, but are you sure he's tied to the puppet master?"

"I'm sure." Josef pushed a paper in front of Viktor. "As soon as you sent us his name, we dispatched a black bag team to his home and put a keystroke recorder on his computer. When he got home, he immediately posted this entry on a wildlife conservation site." He pointed to the phrase on the top of the page.

Saw lion cub today

Viktor read the post. "That's the same way Franko communicated. Father was the lion. So, you think I'm the lion cub?"

"I believe he's telling his handler he saw you at the bank. Then this morning, another post appeared." Josef pointed to the second message.

Listen to the hawk

Viktor looked at Josef. "It's the same message used to tell Franko to turn on his phone. Did someone call Duval?"

"Yes. We don't know who it was, or what they said, but he left immediately for Les Platanes, a small restaurant, five hundred meters from here." Josef pointed to a screen playing a video taken from a high vantage point — two people at an outdoor table.

"Is that video live?"

Josef nodded. "He's the one on the left. The guy on the right just showed up."

"I can't see the faces very well."

"The camera's attached to a drone one kilometer away. Any closer and they might hear it." When Viktor raised his eyebrow, Josef continued. "We'll get a closer look shortly."

Two motorcyclists drove by the command center. Their bikes were so loud, no one spoke until they passed.

With a smile, Josef explained. "As soon as those bikers reach Les Platanes, no one will be able to hear the drone."

The men on the screen turned to glare at the approaching motorcyclists, who pulled up to a stop and began racing their engines.

Viktor's eyes were riveted to the video. He felt like he was riding on the drone as it flew closer to the men at the table. Their faces came into clear view just before the drone swerved away, continually keeping the camera aimed in their direction.

Still pictures of Duval and the other man appeared on the screen. Josef pointed to the image on the right. "Our analysts will use facial recognition to identify this man and collect intelligence."

Viktor studied the face. Something about him looked familiar. "Do you have that sketch? The one the artist made when talking to my kidnapper?"

Josef stared at the image and nodded. Then he tapped on the keyboard and projected the sketch on the screen.

The two faces side-by-side removed any doubt from Viktor's mind. "That's him! He could be the puppet master."

"Slow down, Viktor. No doubt he had something to do with your kidnapping, but we don't know who he is. He might be a middleman. We need to follow him."

The video had no sound. Viktor watched them finish their lunch, apparently oblivious to the surveillance.

As the men rose from the table and began to leave, a message popped up on one of the screens. Josef summarized what it said. "Our man is Henre Legrand, a wealthy day-trader, living in Béziers. We have his address. Our analysts are digging into his background and financial transactions."

As Legrand drove away, the drone followed, with the command center bus trailing half a kilometer behind. They travelled east to the A9 autoroute, then northeast to Béziers and north along the Orb River to a modest-looking home.

"Interesting," said Josef. "Legrand's home is several kilometers south. I wonder what he's doing here."

Béziers, France

Inside the house, Brother Legrand stood before the grand master. "Viktor Prazsky met with bank officers in Crédit de la Robine two days ago. He requested a briefing on terrorist financing."

Ajax leaned forward, grabbed his cane and pounded it on the floor. He turned to glare at Legrand. "Is he still in Narbonne? Where is he staying?"

"I'll find out, Your Grace."

"Kill him. If not here, then in Prague."

"As you wish." Legrand nodded. "I'll also close our accounts in Narbonne today, and immediately shift to the bank in Oldenburg."

The grand master eased back into his chair. "Give me some good news. How are you doing with the bomb?"

"I talked to our man in Madrak, India. He's been keeping our Pakistani engineer happy and giving him everything he needs. The bomb is assembled and tested as thoroughly as possible without the plutonium pit."

"Where is the plutonium now?"

"They just smuggled it across the border in the Thar Desert. When it arrives tomorrow, our engineer will test the pit before inserting it into the bomb. That shouldn't take long. It'll be on the ship in three days."

"Let's hope your man's right about the inspectors. The bomb needs to be at sea before the plutonium is missed."

****

Half a kilometer south, inside the command center bus, Viktor studied the live video stream of the house. For three hours, two drones had been taking turns flying over the building, capturing images in visible light and infrared, while scanning for electronic signals across a wide frequency range.

Josef silently tapped on his keyboard, while strangely colored images of the house from several different angles appeared on the monitors. "What the hell?" He zoomed closer to the back of the building.

Viktor squinted at the images. To his eye, it was an unexceptional house. "What is it?"

Waving his hand dismissively, Josef zoomed in on a window at the side of the house. "Amazing."

"So?" Viktor nearly shouted. "What's all this spy gear telling you?"

Josef stopped typing and slowly looked up, his eyebrows pinched. "Remarkable." He stroked his chin with his fingers. "I've never seen anything like it."

"Come on, Josef. What the hell's going on?"

"Well ... It's supposed to look normal. It's designed to conceal everything." He pointed to the screen. "The windows are mirrors, probably one-way. Normally, we would pick up sounds from the vibration on the windows, but all we detect is a constant hiss. They're using a white noise generator to avoid surveillance."

"What about infrared? Radio waves? They must show something."

Josef shook his head. "The only radio waves leaving the house are through the antennas on the roof, and everything's encrypted. If they have WiFi, cell phones, microwave ovens — anything — we should detect it. But there's nothing. It's like the house is shielded. Like the walls are a big Faraday cage."

"Faraday? What's that?"

"No radio waves can enter or escape."

"Does it block infrared, too?"

"No, just radio frequencies. But the entire exterior of the house is nearly a constant temperature. The walls are cool, even though they would have turned on the heat when it got cold this evening. It's clear they've installed a system designed to mask the temperature gradients inside."

Viktor was elated. "If this place is such an electronic fortress, it has to be the puppet master's home. Guess you can't send your black bag team in to wire the place."

Josef pursed his lips and shook his head. "This is going to take some planning. With all the electronic protection, we should assume the house has excellent physical protection. Even if we could plant bugs and keep them secret, they would be useless because of the Faraday cage."

"Should we engage French police or Interpol?"

"Perhaps, but we'd need compelling evidence first."

"Why?"

Josef typed on the keyboard, bringing up an image of the back of the house where two panels appeared near the base of the house. "I told you the entire house is a single temperature."

"Yeah. Some kind of cooling system."

"Well, those panels are vents, and their temperature is ten degrees warmer than the rest of the building. It can't be the heater, or the temperature would be much higher. Something inside needs to be vented — something big. Something that's not generating heat right now."

Viktor thought of the home where he grew up. "Like an emergency generator? Father had one installed at our house years ago. Some winters we lost power for hours. Without that unit, we'd be sitting in the dark, getting cold."

Josef nodded. "I think our puppet master installed one, too. Only bigger — industrial grade. The type of emergency power unit you would use for a data center. They probably have an important computer inside, one that's loaded with valuable information. We need to keep them from wiping it clean when we go in."

Fortress
Chapter 44

Béziers, France

The Fist of Freedom rented an office in downtown Béziers to serve as the command center for surveillance of the puppet master's house. Inside the office, Viktor sat next to Josef, studying the video from a drone slowly circling the targeted building. The shadow from nearby buildings extended east as the sun sank lower in the sky.

Patience wasn't Viktor's strong suit. "What the hell is Legrand doing? He spent two hours inside yesterday and he's in there again today."

Josef swiveled his chair to face Viktor. "He's the only person entering or leaving through the front of the house. We've also spotted one man and three women who use the lower level back entrance. The man is a chef and the women are maids."

Viktor tugged at his eye patch. "Legrand went home last night and returned today, so this must be where he works. Odd, he works on a Saturday."

A few taps on the keyboard and Josef displayed two houses on a split screen. "Legrand's Béziers home is worth half a million euros. He owns the one on the right, too — in Saint-Tropez. Plus, his holdings in telecom and airline stock are substantial. No one could accumulate that much wealth on the relatively meager income he reports."

"French authorities should find that interesting."

"Sure. They could arrest Legrand. But this goes beyond tax fraud. I've spoken to the French director of counterterrorism and offered to share some of our information on terrorist financing and money laundering. He's alerted the captain in charge at Béziers."

Terrorist. The word helped Viktor to focus his thoughts. *Legrand's not the target. Use your head.* "Someone lives inside this mystery house. Someone who needs maids and a chef. The puppet master lives here."

"I agree. But the man hasn't left his home — at least not since we've been watching."

Viktor tapped on a keyboard, and text appeared on one of the screens. "It says the building is owned by the Occitan Vintner Society. The owner's name is right there. What do you know about him?"

"No one with that name exists. It's a false name. This is an old house, and all the names of the owners for the last hundred and seventy years have been phony. Before that, the owners were famous Jacobin leaders — Couthon and the Nodier family."

"As in the French Revolution?"

Josef nodded.

"Okay, they use false names. Who pays their bills? Taxes, electricity?"

"It's all done with electronic fund transfers. Same banks we've been tracking for terrorist funding."

Same banks? "It's them, Josef! What are we waiting for?"

"It's not going to be easy to get inside, even with police support. And we have to do it quickly, so they won't have a chance to wipe the computer clean."

"They can't erase the data if we cut power."

"Cutting power isn't as easy as it sounds. They get electricity from two different power companies." Josef pointed to the south side of the house. "Montpellier Power comes in here." Pointing to the north side, he added, "Narbonne Electric comes in here. On top of that, I'll bet there's a bank of batteries to take over until the emergency generator kicks in."

"If we can't save the data, we might as well surround the house and break down the doors."

"That'll be dangerous without floor plans. And I suspect there are underground rooms and tunnels." Josef leaned back in his chair. "When it was built in 1784, it included a wine cellar. Construction workers were employed for years after the house was complete — until 1805, perhaps longer."

Viktor looked at the image of the building. "The river runs along the back of the house. They can't dig very deep."

"True, but this is sandstone and the land rises sharply to the east. They could dig horizontal tunnels many kilometers in any direction away from the river."

"The place is a fortress ... but everything has a weakness."

Josef glanced at a text message on his screen. "Someone inside's making a satellite phone call. It's encrypted and it's being routed to Zugdidi, Georgia. All the calls have gone there. We're pretty sure that location is used to forward calls to their ultimate destination, wherever that is."

****

Inside the house, Brother Legrand stood before Ajax and used the speaker phone to talk to his contact in Madrak, India. "Is the bomb ready for transport?"

A man answered in English. "The plutonium pit arrived yesterday. Our engineer completed assembly and testing early this morning. I've installed the satellite link to arm and trigger it. Operationally, it's ready, but remains unarmed."

"Will it be ready to load at Mundra Port tomorrow?"

"You can be sure. We have the sea container here. When it arrived, it was loaded with four temperature control units and other steel-making equipment. We hollowed out one of those units before putting the bomb inside the empty cabinet. The engineer coated it and filled the empty space with High-Z foam to shield the radiation. Only the satellite antenna cable extends from the foam."

"Has the container truck arrived?"

"It's here, filled with other cargo. We repacked a few items, put the bomb in the rear, and attached the antenna. The truck leaves in thirty minutes. We have twenty-four hours to deliver it to the port. We should be there early."

Legrand made a few notes on his tablet. "Excellent. Anything else from your end?"

"Should I eliminate the engineer after the container truck departs?"

As the grand master silently shook his head, Legrand responded. "Not at this time. We may need him." He disconnected the call and turned to Ajax. "The *Agrippina* will sail out of Mundra with our cargo tomorrow evening."

The grand master smiled. "I commend you." He sat back in his chair and reached for his cognac. "Have you located young Prazsky?"

"Only his hotel, Your Grace. He's scheduled to check out in five days, but he's not in his room right now. Our man will take him out when he returns."

A small red light flashed on the arm of Ajax's chair. He pressed the light and it went out. "That will be all for today."

Legrand bowed slightly as the elevator door opened and Marcel walked into the room, holding a serving tray with dinner for Ajax.

****

Two hours later, at the rear of his employer's home, Marcel Blanc opened the door of his Fiat Pop and squeezed behind the wheel. It was Saturday evening and he just finished cleaning the kitchen after serving duck confit to his pompous boss. There was always a lot of food left over. Enough for a poor young chef to enjoy a free dinner at work, but it was against the rules — and there were cameras. No, he would head to Jean Jaurès Square for dinner and Sauternes. Alone.

He shut the door and turned the ignition. The car struggled to life and belched a cloud of smoke. One of these days he'd have to buy another car. He drove away from the house and headed east into the narrow streets of the city.

The wail of a siren caught his attention. Looking in his rear-view mirror, he saw a police car closing in from behind, lights flashing.

Damn! I wasn't speeding. Maybe his car was smoking too much. Maybe the police just wanted to pass. Marcel spotted a place to pull over. He slowed to a stop.

Shit! The police car pulled right up behind him, both doors opened, and two officers stepped out. *Two? That's not good.* Marcel took a deep breath, let it out, and lowered the window.

One of the uniformed men walked up to the car. "Identification."

Marcel took his wallet from his pocket and surrendered his ID.

The man studied it. "Marcel Blanc?"

"Yes, officer."

"Please step out of the car."

The other officer walked up to join his partner.

Marcel thought about refusing or complaining. No, that would just make things worse. He opened the door and stepped out.

"We are taking you to the station. If you cooperate, we will not have to cuff you."

Cuff me? "Are you arresting me? What's the charge?"

"At this time, we just want to question you. If you don't cooperate, we will arrest you."

Feeling helpless, Marcel walked over to the police car and got into the back seat.

Coercion
Chapter 45

Béziers, France

Viktor stood outside the interrogation room, observing through a one-way mirror. On the other side of the mirror, three men sat around a table illuminated by a bright fluorescent light. Josef and a French prosecutor sat with their backs to Viktor, facing a young man with black curly hair and horn-rimmed glasses, who identified himself as Marcel Blanc.

Josef had insisted Viktor observe the interrogation from behind the glass, since his face was so well known in Europe. "Bear with me," Josef had said. "If all goes well, I'll invite you to join us."

From his vantage point, Viktor watched and listened to everything, but he was too far away to sense emotions.

"Marcel," said the prosecutor. "What kind of work do you do?"

The man's eyes looked nervously at Josef, then the prosecutor. "A chef ... I'm a personal chef."

"That sounds like an important job. Who do you work for?"

"Monsieur Roy." Marcel glanced down at his hands. "I don't know his full name."

Josef laid a picture of Legrand on the table facing Marcel. "Do you recognize this man?"

"Monsieur Beringer. He works for Monsieur Roy, too." The chef laced his fingers together, then pulled them apart long enough to point to the picture. "Actually, Monsieur Beringer is my boss. He works for Monsieur Roy."

Josef slapped his hand on the table, moving the photo closer to Marcel. "Don't lie to me! This is Henre Legrand. He's a terrorist and a murderer. So is Monsieur Roy. That makes you a terrorist, too."

Marcel flinched and sat back in his chair, his eyes wide. "I'm not a terrorist. I'm a chef." He gripped the arms of the chair. His eyes moved from left to right and back again as though he was looking for a way out. "I don't know what Monsieur Roy does. I just prepare his meals."

The French prosecutor nodded. "I see. Tell me, who signs your paycheck? You report your income, don't you?"

Marcel fidgeted and slumped in his chair. Sweat formed above his eyes. He wiped it away with his hand.

"Cash business is it?" The prosecutor wagged his finger at the young man. "Tax fraud. Taking cash from terrorists. They will want to speak with you in Paris."

Josef turned to the French official. "It's getting late. We should remand him to Béziers prison for tonight. We can take him to Paris in the morning."

Marcel bolted upright. "Prison? I'm only a chef ... I want to see a lawyer."

Josef shook his head. "You can talk to your lawyer tomorrow in Paris. Tonight, you go to prison."

"How can you send me to prison? You didn't arrest me."

The prosecutor folded his hands in front of him. "France takes terrorism seriously. We can hold you for questioning four days without charging you. The anti-terrorism task force in Paris will gain your cooperation, or they will arrest you. Meanwhile we must remand you to prison."

Marcel took a deep breath and placed his hands face down on the table. "I didn't do anything wrong." He clenched and released his fists. "I'll cooperate ... I'll cooperate right now. Don't send me to prison."

Josef exchanged a look with the prosecutor, who nodded. He turned to face the chef. "If you're willing to cooperate right now — fully cooperate — we can keep you out of prison."

Marcel's mouth broke into a weak smile as he nodded. "I'll tell you everything I know."

Josef set a pad and pen in front of the man. "Write down everything you know about Monsieur Roy and his house. We also need your assistance tomorrow." Josef turned to the window and waved to Viktor. "Right now, we want you to talk to one more person."

As soon as he saw the high sign, Viktor rushed to the interrogation room and opened the door.

Marcel looked up. His jaw dropped. "Viktor Prazsky? Are you really him? Wait until I tell my friends I met you."

Viktor reached out and shook the chef's hand. "I understand you're going to help us apprehend the men who killed my father. The men who killed innocent people in Turkey, Germany and my country." As he spoke, Viktor sensed Marcel's excitement. He locked onto the young man's emotions, and transformed them to trust and pride.

When a police artist joined them, the chef described Monsieur Roy in enough detail to produce a sketch on the computer. An hour and a half later, Viktor stared at the face of the mysterious puppet master. The man looked hard, probably late fifties, early sixties. Marcel, nearly two meters tall, said Monsieur Roy was almost the same height — and muscular, like a former boxer or weight lifter.

Viktor realized if Legrand used the name Beringer, then Roy must be a false name as well. The sketch wouldn't be useful for facial recognition. Perhaps it would trigger someone's memory.

Josef dismissed the artist so Marcel could describe the house — the parts he had seen.

The young chef believed Monsieur Roy worked and lived on the upper floor, a section where Marcel had limited access. The lower level was for food preparation, laundry and storage. A few doors were locked, only accessed infrequently by workers who wore no uniforms and never spoke. 'Beringer', actually Legrand, always escorted these people to and from the rooms.

Josef drew a floor layout to match Marcel's description, continually asking for verification of accuracy.

Twice during Marcel's employment, a loud engine had started up behind one of those doors. 'Beringer' checked on it regularly until it stopped. The chef marked the location on the floor layout.

Throughout the interrogation, Viktor sensed determination and pride from Marcel. More importantly, Marcel told the truth about everything.

A nod from Josef, and Viktor augmented Marcel's emotions with confidence and bravery. He needed the man to trust him fully and to agree to help them tomorrow. If Marcel showed any fear or reluctance, Viktor would stifle those negative emotions and reinforce the positive ones.

He turned to face the young man. "Marcel."

The chef smiled when he looked at Viktor. "Yes?"

"Do you work tomorrow?"

"I do. Most weeks I have Sundays off, but Monsieur Beringer told me I had to work through the entire weekend."

Viktor nodded. "We need your help. We want to see and hear what's going on inside the house."

Marcel ran his fingers through his hair. "You want me to plant bugs? They'll catch me."

Nudging the man's emotions back into positive territory, Viktor explained, "These bugs are small. They don't transmit anything."

"I don't understand. In spy movies, when someone plants a bug, the other guy finds out — with some kind of detector."

Viktor nodded. "If these devices transmitted radio waves, you'd be right — they could detect them. But these bugs record silently."

Josef placed a small case on the table and opened it. Inside were horn-rimmed frames that matched Marcel's glasses. In addition, there were half a dozen gray lumps that looked like used chewing gum.

He removed the eyeglass frame and showed it to Marcel. "We will match your prescription so you can wear these tomorrow at work." He pointed to the front of the hinge on the right side. "There's a camera right here."

Marcel studied the hinge. "I can't see it."

Viktor took the frame from Josef. "That's the idea. It will record everything you look at tomorrow and no one will know. After work, we'll return your original glasses. No risk on your part."

Marcel nodded. "I can do that."

Josef removed one of the gray lumps and showed it to the chef. "These record sound. They stick easily to furniture and can be removed with little effort."

Viktor asked, "When you bring breakfast to Monsieur Roy, do you set it on a table?"

Marcel nodded. "I place his meal on a tray at his seat. I place drinks on the end table."

Bolstering the chef's positive emotions, Viktor added, "Could you stick one of these 'pieces of gum' under the edge of the end table?"

The young man's eyes looked up to the right then slowly to the left before focusing back on Viktor. "I'm sure I could."

Viktor handed him two of the 'chewing gum' devices. "We want you to stick both of these under the table at breakfast and retrieve one of them after his last meal of the day. Leave the other one there. You can give us the one you retrieved when you get your glasses back."

****

It was after midnight by the time Viktor returned to his hotel. All he wanted to do was go upstairs and collapse on the bed. He opened the door to his room, turned on the light, and fastened the security chain.

Someone's here. He could sense one person in his bathroom, but there could be more. Whoever it was, their anxiety and stress screamed in Viktor's head. But the tense emotions faded as calm and determination pushed them into the background. What kind of person can do that? *Professional. An assassin!*

He thought about running out of the room, but the security chain would slow him down. His mind raced. Did he ... or they ... have a gun pointed at the door right now? If he forced himself into the assassin's head and raised his fear or anxiety, would his trigger finger twitch? *Risky without seeing him.*

Keeping his eye on the bathroom door, Viktor walked backwards toward the phone by his bed, but didn't touch it. The assassin wouldn't know if he picked it up. With a loud voice, he said, "Front desk." Then he moved quickly away from the phone.

Suddenly, the bathroom door opened and a young man with closely cropped hair leaped out, gun aimed at the bed. He showed no sign of surprise as he smoothly shifted his aim toward Viktor.

Sensing the assassin's confusion, Viktor synchronized his mind with the man's emotions and projected fear into his assailant's head.

He saw the man flinch when the silenced gun fired and a lamp next to Viktor crashed to the floor.

Viktor jumped away from the lamp. He increased the intensity of the emotions.

Another bullet hit the wall near Viktor's foot before the gun dropped to the floor. The assassin's eyes rolled up, as if in a trance. He shook as his legs gave out beneath him and he dropped to the floor, vomiting.

It looked like the man was no longer a threat, but Viktor didn't take a chance. He carefully stepped around the assassin and the vomit, picked up the gun, and pointed it at the motionless body lying on the floor. He bent over and felt a pulse. *He's still alive.*

He backed away and sat on the bed, holding the gun in his hand. Any minute now, his headache would come. *My curse.* Maybe this time, Viktor would lose his sight completely. The thought terrified him.

The pain hit so hard he doubled over and almost dropped the gun. He searched through the blurred images to find the man lying on the floor.

Viktor didn't think calling the police would be a good idea. He called Josef.

****

Two hours later, Viktor sat on the bed. His headache had passed and his vision cleared. The assassin was gone and there were guards at the door.

Viktor looked at Josef, the only other person in the room, sitting in a chair near the TV. "What's the plan?"

"If the man who attacked you ever recovers from his stroke, we'll interrogate him. But our official report states a man died and the police are withholding his name until the family can be notified. Whoever ordered the hit will believe you're dead. If they observed your assailant being taken away, they'll believe you're the victim."

"I guess I'm sleeping in the command center tonight."

Josef nodded. "We set up a bed for you. The important thing is for you to stay out of sight."

"How do I get out of here without being seen?"

"Follow me," said Josef. "We'll take the service elevator. My car's nearby."

"I hope everything goes well with Marcel tomorrow. I can't stay in hiding very long."

Inner Sanctum
Chapter 46

Béziers, France

Sunday morning before dawn, Marcel drove by the front of the house where he worked, then turned left onto the private drive leading to the back door one level below the front. This was his normal routine. He didn't intend to change it.

The camera glasses fit better than the ones he wore every day. They hadn't slid down his nose even once since he put them on. As instructed, he walked a bit slower than normal and looked around like a cameraman filming a movie.

At the back door, Marcel faced the security panel and waited for a green light, followed by a click. No one noticed anything different with the glasses, just like Viktor had promised. He walked inside, slowly moving his head around to view the hallway and each door.

Wait 'til I tell my friends I talked to a real celebrity. Viktor promised to pay Marcel well if he did a good job. He even offered to recommend him for a chef's job at several exclusive restaurants. *Maybe I can buy a new car.*

When he arrived at the kitchen, Marcel took the tray of croissants from the refrigerator. They looked good. He had prepared them the previous night before his encounter with Viktor. Now it was time to pop them into the oven.

He brewed a carafe of coffee and pulled the pastries out of the oven a few minutes before seven. Then he waited for Monsieur Roy to press the buzzer letting Marcel know he wanted his breakfast. When it sounded, he placed the coffee and two croissants on a tray, threw a napkin across his forearm, headed upstairs in the elevator and stepped out into the main room.

Typing on his laptop computer, Monsieur Roy appeared oblivious to the presence of the chef.

Marcel moved his head to the right then to the left, recording everything with the secret camera in his glasses. He carried breakfast over to the man Viktor called a terrorist.

Monsieur Roy glanced up from his computer. "Just put the tray on the end table."

With a smile and a bow, Marcel did as he was told. He stuck two bugs under the edge of the table. Then he stepped back in front of his boss. "Is there anything else, sir?"

A dismissive wave of his hand was the only response.

I took a great picture of your face, asshole. They're going to nail you. He turned and walked toward the elevator.

****

Viktor sat in the command center watching drone videos of the puppet master's home while Josef typed away on a keyboard. "Too bad those bugs don't transmit. I'd love to know what's going on inside."

On the screen, they had watched while Marcel arrived at the back door three hours ago. Now, Legrand arrived and entered the building through the front door.

Josef shook his head. "Patience. We'll get audio of the entire day once Marcel leaves — video, too — but only where our young chef has been."

"I like Marcel. He's excited about helping us."

"We're going to need his help." Josef shook his head. "French police won't approve an assault without compelling evidence."

"I know you've been developing a plan. When the police finally say yes, how do we get in?"

Josef displayed the house layout on a large screen. "The difficult part is to eliminate power completely without giving advance warning." He pointed to the left side of the house. "One electric company brings power in here and the other company does it on the opposite side."

"You mentioned that before. But it's not a problem because we can get both companies to kill power at once — if the police authorize it."

Josef pointed to a spot on the floor layout near the back of the building. "You remember Marcel talking about the loud engine? He said it came from here."

Viktor nodded. "An emergency generator?"

"I'm certain. And I would be surprised if they didn't have a battery backup, too."

"You have a plan, right?"

Josef nodded and displayed a list on the screen:

Step 1: Power companies kill electricity. House goes on battery backup.
Step 2: Generator starts once batteries discharge. Heat signature visible.
Step 3: Kill generator without warning.

Viktor tugged on his eye patch. "I understand killing power and going to batteries, and it makes sense the generator will kick on and create heat. But what does step three mean?"

Josef turned away from the monitor and faced Viktor. "I considered several options, but most of them are risky. If we send in a repair technician for a fake service call, Legrand will escort him. If we send a team to the generator vent, the security system will warn Girard. We need something sudden that can be done from a distance."

"You can't take out a generator with a sniper bullet, no matter how powerful."

"You're right." Josef smiled. "But a Hellfire missile fired from a Predator drone can take it out."

Viktor gasped. "Hellfire? That'll destroy the place — including the precious computer data. You can't be serious."

Josef pulled up the cross-sectional diagram of a missile. "In the standard configuration, it would be very destructive. But we'll use a warhead with no explosives — only a tungsten-carbide penetrator. Since the missile travels faster than the speed of sound, it'll penetrate the building above the vents and smash into the generator. And, just to be sure, we'll fire a second one into the hole made by the first."

Viktor knew the Fist of Freedom had smart people and access to the best technology, but this plan was amazing. "You think the French police will approve?"

"We'll see." Josef smirked. "We have to kill internet access and jam their satellite link, too, but that's not a problem."

****

Later that evening, Viktor returned to the command center carrying the camera glasses and one of the audio bugs. He met Marcel earlier at Jean Jaurès Square and told him to stay home from work in the morning.

Four men in dark clothing, military types, huddled around Josef.

Viktor held the glasses over his head. "Marcel came through."

Josef looked up. "This is Mike and his team. They'll be assisting us."

The men nodded silently and Viktor returned the greeting.

Josef took the glasses and bug and uploaded them to the computer. He motioned for Viktor and the assault team to sit before two large computer monitors. One, a split screen, showed the floor layout of the house next to the sketch of the puppet master. The other displayed the video from Marcel's camera.

The audio played through speakers, synchronized with the video.

While they watched and listened, Josef and Mike each made comments to confirm accuracy or to identify differences in the floor layout on the lower level. Later, when the image moved out of the elevator, they got their first glimpse of the upper level. Much of it was a single large room. Five large, flat monitors hung from the ceiling, each screen totally black.

As they watched the video, the image approached a solitary man sitting in a chair typing on a laptop. The motion stopped in front of the chair and the puppet master's face filled the screen. He didn't say much, but his voice came through strong. He spoke French like a true Frenchman.

Viktor stared at him, then at the sketch. It was the same man. Somehow, he appeared more evil on the video. *You killed Father. Shot Mother.*

Dueling emotions coursed through his body. Hatred and anger would have to wait. It might harm the others in the room and he'd probably miss something important on the screen. Better to focus on the task at hand.

Later, the video image moved toward the elevator. Josef paused it when the doors opened. "We can study that later. I sent the puppet master's image to our analysts. Perhaps we'll get a match. Now we'll listen to the bug under the end table."

A graph of the audio signal replaced the video. It looked like tiny waves above and below a horizontal line.

Josef typed a few commands on his keyboard. "I'll fast forward until something significant appears." The wavy lines wiggled faster, then suddenly much larger waves filled the screen. He backed up and pressed play. "This matches the time Legrand walked into the house."

Viktor and the others listened while the puppet master spoke to another man, who would have to be Legrand. "Did you take him out?"

Legrand spoke more softly than his boss. "I'm certain Prazsky's dead. I don't yet have confirmation, but officials report an important man died in his hotel room. We also saw a body removed."

Viktor's heart pounded. "Sonofabitch! It's him. No doubt anymore." *This cold-hearted bastard sent the assassin. Killed Father. Shot Mother. All those people killed in Turkey, Prague. The fire in Dresden.* Viktor wanted to scream but he needed to listen.

The audio continued with the puppet master. "Didn't your assassin verify the kill?"

"I haven't heard from him yet. He may be busy avoiding capture."

Arrogance and disgust intruded into the puppet master's voice. "Find him. Eliminate him."

"Yes, Your Grace."

A chill went through Viktor's body. *Your Grace? Like royalty?*

Strong emotions disappeared from the master's voice and he changed subjects. "Did the warhead begin its journey before the alert was raised?"

Warhead? What's this? Chemical? Nuke?

Viktor sensed strong emotions of alarm from Josef, who frantically typed a few commands into the computer.

Josef pointed to the message on the screen. "This alert came out today ... this morning."

Empty Quiver: Khushab, Pakistan

Legrand's recorded voice responded to his boss. "The alert was too late to stop it. The warhead's on its way. Unless they encounter a problem, we'll hear nothing until it detonates."

Josef paused the sound and barked orders to Mike and his team. "Keep reviewing the audio. Use your headsets."

The horror of it all hit Viktor. "Empty Quiver? ... A nuclear bomb?"

Josef nodded. He hit speed dial and yelled into the phone. "We have your goddamn evidence. They've got a nuke and they're gonna use it."

Assault
Chapter 47

Béziers, France

Two hours later, Viktor glanced out the mobile command center window at the moonlit parking lot one kilometer south of the puppet master's house.

He turned to Josef. "Where's the damn French RAID team?"

"Patience, Viktor. They landed at the airport twenty minutes ago. They should be here soon."

Viktor thought about his father's killer sitting comfortably in the house up the road. *The puppet master.* His name was Charles Girard — identified from the video image of his face — a wealthy French investor with an expensive villa in Nice, three hundred kilometers to the east. The most recent picture available was ten years old. "Did Mike's team get inside Girard's holiday home?"

Josef shook his head. "Security is tight. Any attempt to enter the house in Nice might alert him. We can't risk tipping Girard off. Béziers is our priority."

Viktor wanted to rush the house immediately. Girard and Legrand were here. *They killed Father.* They've killed hundreds of innocent people, now they had a nuclear weapon. They could kill thousands, perhaps more. But the assault relied upon the element of surprise. "What are they doing to find the warhead?"

"NATO went on critical alert early this morning after Empty Quiver was declared." Josef projected a map of southern Asia on a screen, a red star highlighting a location in northeastern

Pakistan. "Since the nuclear material was stolen from Khushab, the physical search is primarily focused on Pakistan and its neighbors, India and Afghanistan. No telling where it is now. They've had five days to hide it."

"Can't they track nuclear materials via satellite?"

Josef nodded. "Every available European and American satellite in the region is searching and others are being repositioned to assist. So far, they've found nothing. Pakistan has engaged all available resources to find it — army, coast guard, maritime — even regional frontier and scout groups. NATO volunteered to help, in fact they demanded access for their experts to assist, but Pakistan refused the offer."

Refused? Are they crazy? "Terrorists have a nuclear bomb and Pakistan refuses assistance? Will NATO go in without their permission?"

"I'm sure they're considering the options. NATO teams are searching throughout India and Afghanistan."

Viktor looked at the screens monitoring the house. "They must know the entire world is searching for their warhead. Are you sure Girard's unaware of our assault plans?"

"He's been a master of hiding his involvement in the other attacks. He must feel confident in his anonymity."

Headlights flashed across Viktor's face. "It's them. It must be. Two armored personnel carriers."

Josef stood and opened the door.

A tall man wearing black head-to-toe assault gear, shield raised on his helmet, walked up to meet him, gloved hand extended. "Commander Foss here."

"Director Filipek," said Josef, as he stepped aside allowing Foss to enter. He motioned toward a seat and added, "This is Viktor Prazsky."

Viktor shook the commander's hand. *Intense focus. A real professional.*

Foss looked around the command center and nodded in approval. "My team's ready for the assault. Two additional teams are on their way from Paris and Bordeaux for backup. Is Legrand still inside?"

Viktor had hoped to grab Legrand when he left for the day, but it didn't work out. "He's still there."

"Too bad," said Foss. "We can't wait. Cut their power and suit up. We've got everything you need." Turning to Viktor he added, "You'll go on my vehicle with Red Team for the frontal attack. Director Filipek will go with Blue Team to the back door."

****

Inside the house, Legrand stood before Girard, who had adopted the name Ajax when he became grand master. Legrand explained the situation. "They've been searching for our warhead all day. I didn't expect them to discover it missing so quickly, but we're prepared. We have it under constant surveillance by satellite and drone. Should it be discovered, our associate will detonate it remotely."

Three short, high-pitched beeps interrupted them and the room lighting briefly blinked red. Ajax slammed his glass on the end table, cognac splashing on the floor. "How the hell did we lose two power feeds at once? You said this couldn't happen."

Legrand raised his hand. "The batteries will last thirty minutes. I'll go check on the generator to make sure it's ready if we need it." He turned to leave, then stopped at the elevator. "I'm going to arm the doors."

On his way to the generator, Legrand called the hot line of the diesel fuel supplier to make sure they were prepared to deliver fuel as long as required. One light on the generator panel indicated loss of primary power and a second light indicated the batteries were on-line. A gauge showed about twenty minutes of battery power remained. Before being completely discharged, the generator would start up automatically.

Legrand looked at the video monitor on the wall. He saw no obstructions outside the house to block the exhaust vent.

Next, he called the hot lines of both power companies servicing the house. Neither one had an estimate of service restoral. On his way to the elevator, he stopped to arm the back door.

On the main floor, Legrand armed the front door before approaching Ajax. "Everything's ready."

Five high-pitched beeps, accompanied by flashing red lights, signaled the end of battery power. The muffled sound of a powerful engine confirmed the engagement of the generator.

Ajax glared at Legrand. "I don't like—"

Suddenly, the lights went out. A loud bang and a powerful tremor hit the house. Dim red lights shone at the door along the rear wall.

****

Viktor waited for the command team to alert them when a heat signature appeared. That meant the generator kicked in and the assault would begin.

The radio crackled before announcing, "Heat signature. Go! Go!'

Viktor's assault vehicle raced toward the house with Josef's vehicle following in hot pursuit. Viktor stood on the rear running board, secured by a safety strap while hanging onto a grab rail. Commander Foss and four others hung onto the sides.

Viktor heard the missile slam into the back of the house. He watched smoke and dirt rise over the roof in the moonlight. But it wasn't an explosion — just a loud thud. He hung on while the Red Team vehicle crashed through the front gate and came to a stop. Viktor released the quick disconnect on his strap and jumped off. He slapped down his face shield, turned on his helmet light, and joined the rest of the team at the front door. Then he felt the vibration from the second missile striking the back of the house.

Three men lined up behind a blast shield on the left side of the door and three to the right. Viktor was the last man on the right. He was told to wait for an 'all clear' signal, but he didn't plan to wait. He needed to get inside. He needed to see the people responsible for terrorizing his country and his family.

One man quickly placed charges on six points around the door before retreating behind the blast shield. He shouted a warning. "Going hot!"

The door exploded into the house where a dim red light illuminated the entrance. The same man threw a flash-bang grenade through the smoke-filled doorway.

The point man disappeared into the smoke hugging the left side. Another man crouched low entering to the right.

A loud bang and a flash came from somewhere inside on the left.

Viktor sensed pain and fear from someone inside the door.

Before he could process what happened, someone yelled, "Stop! Man down! ... Repeat. Man down!"

Commander Foss yelled into his communicator. "Blue Team! Blue Team! This is Red Leader. Stand down! ... Repeat. Stand down! Doors armed! Booby trapped!"

One man backed out of the doorway pulling his partner by the shoulders. Viktor sensed no emotions at all from the limp body of the man whose heels dragged over the stone floor. Two team members rushed forward and moved the injured man away from the door, then removed his helmet.

Foss wasted no time. "Command, this is Red Leader. Send medical immediately. Man down. Critical. ... Has Paris arrived?"

A voice on his communicator responded. "Red Leader, this is Command. Medical on its way. Paris is here."

"Need sappers now. Two teams. Will Paris respond?"

"Affirmative."

Sappers. Viktor remembered the term from his Army days. *Minesweepers.*

Foss continued to bark orders. "Red Leader here. Suspects may have escaped. Request full alert including Europol and Interpol."

Escaped. That's why Josef was concerned about the tunnels. Girard delayed pursuit long enough to escape.

The medical team arrived and rushed over to the fallen man. One of the emergency responders checked for a pulse and shook his head. The Red Team loaded the body onto a stretcher and into a vehicle for transport. As he left, Viktor sensed sadness and anger from the men, but they showed no outward sign of mourning.

Two more assault vehicles arrived. *Probably Paris.* One of them pulled up to the front door and the other disappeared behind the house.

Five men jumped off the running boards. One of them rushed up to Commander Foss, who showed him the entrance. Three men unloaded blast shields plus several bulky suits that looked like something an astronaut would wear. The last man used a joystick control unit, operating a track-mounted robot, backing it out of the vehicle.

Once on the ground, the robot extended a long arm holding a one-meter bar at a right angle on the end, forming a "T". The robot operator unloaded several boxes of half-meter chains and fist-sized balls. One at a time, he attached ten chains to the bar, each with a ball on the end. They looked like something you'd see on a medieval mace. When he was done, he raised the arm and the bar high in the air. He rotated the bar on the end, flailing the attached balls at a frightening speed.

Foss gave a thumbs up and the chains stopped spinning.

The five-man sapper team from Paris donned bulky suits, carried their blast shields, and followed the robot toward the door. The robot arm angled the bar to fit inside the door then angled it back to allow straight-on entry. When the operator pressed a switch, the rapid, pounding sound, like a jackhammer, was a clear sign the chains were swinging and the balls were smashing on the floor.

The robot crept forward until an explosion blew smoke and debris out the doorway. The robot jumped. The jackhammer sound stopped briefly before starting up once again. The robot proceeded without incident into the house. The sappers came next followed slowly by the Red Team and Viktor.

****

After triggering two explosives near the entrance to the back door, Josef and the Blue Team followed the second sapper team and their robot inside. Their night vision goggles cut through the darkness. Several doors lined the hallway exactly as they appeared in Marcel's video. Using a simple battering ram, they broke through each one before the robot probed for explosives.

One-by-one, they cleared seven rooms without incident — storerooms, supply rooms, the kitchen, and the generator room. The non-explosive missiles had destroyed the equipment. No people were found.

One door remained at the end of the hallway to the right. When they broke through, the robot entered, setting off an explosion.

The Blue Team leader turned to Josef. "I think they went this way."

After the sappers cleared the entrance, Josef followed the Blue Team inside, where they found a roughly carved limestone tunnel, barely taller than the average man and not much wider than a man's shoulders.

They needed to probe the tunnel with the robot so their progress slowed. Twenty meters further, three tunnels split off in different directions.

Blue Leader removed his night vision goggles and signaled the others to do the same. Then he turned on a light and assessed the situation.

Josef shook his head. "This could take hours. We need to bring the other robot down here. They got away."

Agrippina
Chapter 48

Béziers, France

It was approaching noon when Viktor entered the Fist of Freedom command center. He had spent most of the night rummaging through Legrand's home.

The RAID team was still working their way through the maze of tunnels and the rest of Girard's house.

Josef, the only person inside the command center, looked up from the computer console, a tired smile on his face. "You look like shit, Viktor. Did you get any sleep?"

"Have you looked in a mirror lately? I had as much sleep as you did." Viktor glanced at the steaming cup on the table. "I hope you didn't drink it all."

"We've got plenty." Josef pointed at the counter.

Viktor poured himself a cup — black. The rich aroma of fresh coffee penetrated the fog in his brain. One sip made him smile. "Thanks." *Another sip to clear my head.*

Josef got right down to business. "Marcel retrieved the second audio bug. Legrand mentioned a collaborator monitoring the nuke by satellite or drone. It's possible he can trigger it remotely. I notified Commander Foss."

"Damn!" Viktor set his cup down and took a seat. "It might be on a ship. We found some information on Legrand's computer."

Josef sat upright in his chair. "What did you find?"

"Mike's team did a thorough job on Legrand's home. The laptop didn't have strong encryption. They had no difficulty breaking in. We discovered Legrand repeatedly searched for information on a transport ship, the *Agrippina*, which travels to ports near Pakistan. I passed the information on to Foss. Maybe that's where they'll find the nuke."

"That's the best lead we have. If it's on the *Agrippina*, NATO and our other allies will use all their resources to stop it."

Viktor nodded. *Terrorists with a nuke. No country wants that.* "I have news on another front. Legrand communicated regularly with Salafi Brotherhood — with Murat Bayik. And we have the Sarajevo address where Bayik's holed up. Mike's team plans to take him down."

Josef raised an eyebrow. "I don't suppose Legrand kept financial data on his computer."

"He didn't make it easy, but we have a lead. Mike broke into his wall safe. In addition to a few thousand euros and some stock certificates, we found correspondence with his lawyers. Nothing specific or incriminating. French police brought his lawyers in for questioning early this morning. They'll freeze any accounts they can identify."

"I hope the team we sent to Legrand's home in Saint-Tropez comes up with something useful."

"Not to mention Girard's home in Nice." Viktor sipped his coffee. "Speaking of Girard, do we know where he is?"

A frown formed on Josef's face. "We have nothing to go on. French police continue to work their way through the maze of tunnels. It looks like they escaped through a crypt in the old cemetery one kilometer north of the house. Once outside the crypt, they managed to avoid cameras and left no trail. So far, we found three other exits, but none of them showed any sign of recent activity."

"No trail? The nuke's still on the loose, and so are the men who control it. We may have slowed these guys down, but we haven't stopped them."

"We'll get them. We've seized a treasure trove of information. More importantly, we'll stop the bomb."

Viktor wasn't optimistic. "Tell me about their main computer. What treasure trove have you found?"

"The good news is our assault took them by surprise. It appears they didn't have a chance to destroy anything. Of course, the permanent data was encrypted with a strong algorithm. It'll take some time to crack it."

"So, we get nothing from the computer for a week, a month, maybe never?"

"No, it's not like that. We have the best cryptanalysts on it. Meanwhile, an unencrypted cache still holds recently accessed data which revealed valuable information. They paid at least fifty thousand euros to Gupta Steel. I'm not sure of the significance, but I hope it has something to do with the nuke. I gave the invoice to Commander Foss, I'm sure he can make sense of it."

Viktor glanced at his watch. "Speaking of Foss, we have a videoconference coming up."

Josef logged them into the meeting with NATO Command Center Operations in Uedem, Germany, thirty kilometers east of the Dutch border. This was the team responsible to locate and recover the nuclear weapon. Foss flew there overnight.

The words STAND BY appeared on the large computer screen. Small images of Josef and Viktor appeared on the left side, along with similar images of other attendees on both sides.

When Commander Foss joined the call, his face filled the center of the screen. Over his shoulder was the NATO logo. He began the briefing in English, the common language understood by all attendees. "Our analysts tell us the warhead is aboard the cargo transport ship *Agrippina*, which left Mundra, India, yesterday. It's scheduled to arrive at its next port, Salalah, Oman, in three days. The ship carries more than five hundred containers, stacked like boxes along the upper deck. We believe one of them, from Gupta Steel, contains the bomb. It's located ten rows aft of the bow — two layers below the top."

Josef clicked on the screen. His face replaced the commander's. "When do we go in?"

The image of Foss returned to the center of the screen. "Tonight. But before we go over the assault, I need to explain a few things. Although I'm convinced the missing plutonium is now integrated into a nuclear warhead on the *Agrippina*, we cannot assume this to be true. For that reason, NATO and our other allies have deployed teams to search for the missing Pakistani nuclear material. In addition, America and France continue to search the globe with their satellites."

Foss took a drink of water before continuing. "My team is responsible to locate and neutralize the suspected nuclear warhead on the *Agrippina*. Due to the urgency and the location of the ship, we have put together a team of NATO plus Indian and Sri Lankan personnel and resources. The *Agrippina* is a commercial ship. We reached the captain on a secure channel and notified him of the operation we've planned. He's agreed to cooperate, and he's informed his crew to stay below decks. Director Filipek has some precautionary information about the warhead."

Josef's face moved to the center of the screen. "We have reason to believe the terrorists have a collaborator who is monitoring their warhead using commercial earth observation satellites. I doubt any nation state would let them use their military satellites, unless they felt they could survive nuclear retaliation. This collaborator could have the ability to detonate the weapon remotely if he sees anyone threatening it. To keep them from using drones to monitor it, Commander Foss has directed the *Agrippina* to adjust her course to a more southerly route. That should put it about seven kilometers from the nearest ship, a course that would also minimize casualties in the event of a nuclear blast."

Commander Foss took over. "The operation will be launched from the Indian aircraft carrier, *INS Veera*. Captain Singh, where are you now?"

The face of a different man appeared in the center of the screen. He wore an Indian naval officer's uniform. The windows behind him looked out to the open sea. "My ship is in the Arabian Sea, seven kilometers south of the target. We're supporting three teams for this operation — our own air support, the Sri Lankan Air Mobile Brigade, and the newly formed French nuclear bomb disposal team. Commander Patel, please brief them on air operations."

Another Indian officer appeared on the screen, wearing a camouflage jump suit. "Before the assault, we will launch an early warning aircraft. It will maintain a position one kilometer from the target, acting as the command center for our drone operation. We'll carry two specially configured drones that will take turns flying over the *Agrippina,* projecting a cone of electromagnetic radiation that will jam all radio communication to or from the ship. The terrorists can't trigger the bomb as long as the drone is in the air. In addition, our helicopter crew will deliver the assault team and the bomb disposal team to the *Agrippina*."

A man in a khaki shirt with a maroon beret appeared on screen. "My name is Colonel Perera. I am the leader of the Sri Lankan Air Mobile Brigade. We're on the *Veera*. Commander Patel's helicopter crew will insert my team on the *Agrippina* once the jammer is activated. We'll cover the container with RF shielding fabric as an extra precaution against the terrorists triggering the bomb. Once the shield is in place, the drone will not be required."

Commander Foss's image appeared on the screen. "We won't hear from the French team. They're still en route to the *Veera*. We face another challenge with this operation. Once the helicopter approaches the *Agrippina*, it will enter the electromagnetic cone below the drone where electronic communication is not possible. No radio, no phone, no GPS. The helicopter crew and the assault team will have to use visual cues to navigate and communicate."

Josef clicked on the screen again. "How will we observe the operation?"

Foss responded. "The Americans are repositioning a satellite to give us a view of the ship, the containers, and the assault team. In addition, the drone and the command aircraft will deliver video from their vantage points. Nevertheless, we will have no audio. To minimize the terrorist's view of the operation, we'll wait until dark. The assault begins at 1900 Zulu — midnight local time. Wind and sea conditions should be favorable. Fortunately, the American satellite delivers excellent hi-resolution infrared images."

Arabian Sea, 500 kilometers west of Mundra, India

On the flight deck of the *INS Veera,* Colonel Perera's eight-man assault team double-checked their equipment, ensuring it was securely stowed inside the Sea King transport helicopter. Five rolls of RF insulating fabric were wrapped up like carpet and attached firmly to the bulkhead. The four-man Indian flight crew went through their checklists in preparation for liftoff.

At 1900 Zulu, Perera received a message from the Indian command aircraft. They just launched the jamming drone. *If they're watching in the dark, they know we're onto them. But they can't detonate it.*

The Sri Lankan team strapped in. The copter lifted off and headed toward the *Agrippina.*

Perera spotted the jamming drone a hundred meters above the ship, making a slow circle in the sky. He stepped to the open door while the copter descended. He counted the rows of containers from the bow and located his target. Then he stood at the side of the opening.

Twenty meters above the *Agrippina*, the copter slowed its descent and maintained altitude. The wind and sea were mild. The pilot held his position expertly.

Two men stepped to the opening, checked their hookup, and tugged on the rope to ensure a good connection.

Perera yelled, "Drop."

One man tossed his deployment bag out the door, which pulled the rope and unwound it on its fast trip to the ship below.

A quick glance verified the rope was all the way down, free of tangles. Perera gave a thumbs up.

Without hesitation, the man stepped on the skid. He faced the colonel and grasped the rope.

Perera yelled, "Go!"

The man jumped and dropped a third of the way to the ship before braking, then released before braking again. Two more times and he landed on the deck. He moved away from the drop spot — a textbook rappel. The second man followed the first.

Two men brought the fabric rolls to the door and attached one of them to a rope. One at a time they dropped each roll down to the ship, braking the fall before it hit the deck. The men on the ship below untied them and secured them to the side.

After they lowered all the rolls, the remaining men rappelled to the ship. Once Perera touched down and released his rope, he pointed his flashlight at the copter and waved it back and forth, sending the Sea King away It would return soon with the French bomb disposal team.

Three container rows forward, one of the team members signaled with his flashlight. He had been assigned to locate the

Gupta Steel container. The rest of the men grabbed their gear and the fabric rolls before joining him.

The men untied and spread the fabric across the tops of several rows, then they clipped the ends together to form a gigantic tablecloth. All eight men demonstrated their expertise and cooperation in positioning it over one container, draping the sides down three layers below. A Faraday cage now shielded all electronic communication under this cloth. The jamming drone would no longer be needed.

The team moved to the starboard side and lifted the fabric exposing the entry doors of the boxes below. One man attached a rope to the top container and rappelled down to the door marked *Gupta Steel.* Using a specially designed hollow bar, he released each latch, opened the door on the right and jumped into the container. The rest followed.

Once inside, they found hundreds of pieces of machinery and equipment secured to the floors and sides. The search for the warhead could be daunting, but they knew it must be connected to an antenna in order to receive the signal for remote detonation.

Perera gave the order. "Everyone spread out. Search along the edge of the ceiling. Anything unusual, call out."

Eight flashlight beams searched the upper reaches of the container. A few minutes later, a man yelled out, "Got it." The sound came from the opposite end of the cavernous box.

The colonel made his way to the end of the container. He looked up to the point where the man shined his flashlight. A white cube filled the upper corner. The terrorists must have cut the metal from that part of the container and replaced it with fiberglass to allow access for the antenna.

Perera pointed to a cable attached to the cube in the corner. It was routed along the wall, disappearing out of sight. "Trace the cable. The bomb should be on the other end."

Two men worked together until they found the cable entering a cabinet. One man studied the seams along the box and inserted a crowbar into a small opening.

"Stop!" Perera shouted, "It could be booby trapped. Don't do anything to the box or the cable. We'll wait for the bomb disposal team."

A metallic sound came from the far side of the container, followed by a distant voice. "Colonel Perera?"

"In the back," shouted the colonel.

A French major was followed by seven enlisted men. "If that's the bomb, we'll disarm it."

Fugitives
Chapter 49

Prague, Czech Republic

Charles Girard, grand master of Arcadian Hand, spent the past week on the run with Henre Legrand. The man who ruined everything for them, Viktor Prazsky, was in Prague.

Revenge brought Girard to the city where he checked into a hotel suite. He washed and dried his face, then looked in the mirror. *That's the face everyone's searching for.* He hated wearing the moustache and the curly wig, but he had no choice.

When Girard stepped out of the bathroom, Legrand spoke. "They go out to dinner most evenings. Usually around seven."

Girard walked over to the chair near the television. "Damn Prazskys. Our faces are all over the news. We can't walk down the street or go to a restaurant without wearing these annoying disguises." He opened a bottle of cognac and poured himself a glass. "He stole my money, too."

"They froze your accounts," said Legrand.

Girard slammed his fist on the chair. "Frozen …. stolen. They have it and I don't." He lifted the glass to his lips and swallowed half the brown liquid. "Everyone abandoned me. No one will help."

"I'm here, Your Grace."

He looked Legrand in the eyes. "You're the only one I can count on." He downed the rest of the drink. "We'll get Prazsky tomorrow at dinner. You'll be the bait. I'll be the trap."

"You're confident this plan is going to work?"

"Yes. But if we can't get Prazsky, we'll grab his wife."

****

The next evening at the Ottokar Cafe, Viktor shared a table for four with Louise. It was only the two of them, but he liked to sit next to her. Today was their 'three-month wedding anniversary' — silly, but worth celebrating.

He gazed into her eyes. "I don't know how you do it."

His wife smiled. "Do what, Viktor?"

"Get more beautiful every day." He placed his hand on hers. "I thought women lost their beauty over time, but you keep getting better."

"It's the miracle of makeup, my dear."

Someone caught Viktor's attention at the front of the restaurant. A man with a familiar face staring into the window. *Legrand*! His heart pounded. *No sudden moves ... yet.* He looked at Louise and spoke calmly. "Don't react to what I say."

Louise nodded almost imperceptibly.

"Legrand is standing outside the window."

Keeping her head still, Louise's eyes searched for Legrand.

Viktor sensed her nervousness and fear. He gently squeezed her hand. "When I leave, stay here and call Josef. Tell him about Legrand."

Slowly pushing his chair back, Viktor looked around the room and prepared to stand.

Legrand turned and walked away.

Viktor sprung from his seat and ran outside. He turned right and chased a man who was running away, gradually closing the gap.

When the man turned right, Viktor followed him and turned the corner into an alley. The poor lighting hampered his vision until he got closer. It was Legrand.

Now Viktor was close enough to sense emotions. The man wasn't afraid, he was excited. Synchronizing their brainwaves, Viktor reinforced the excitement, then shifted it to fear, panic and sheer terror. Legrand's emotions followed when Viktor increased the intensity.

Legrand's legs stopped, but his upper body kept moving. He fell face down in the alley and banged his head on the stone pavement.

A dark Land Rover, half a block away, startled Viktor as it pulled away from its parking spot and drove off. Could be an accomplice, or simply someone who didn't want to be a witness.

As he walked up to Legrand's limp form, his headache struck. A sharp pain hit Viktor like a spike in the temple, dropping him to his knees. *Damn curse!* A loud ringing sound drowned out everything around him. He looked at Legrand. The man wasn't going to get up on his own.

Viktor pulled out his phone. His ears continued to ring. He texted Josef.

I have Legrand. Not moving. Come now. Near Ottokar Café. Can't talk.

Josef texted back.

On my way. Need directions.

Viktor texted Josef directions to the alley.

Then he texted Louise, but she didn't respond. He texted her again. The ringing in his ears was fading. He called her on the phone. After a few rings, it went to voice mail. He tried again with the same results. *Something's wrong.*

Legrand's not going anywhere. He ran back to the restaurant as fast as he could.

Inside, a young man was clearing the table where he left Louise. Viktor ran up to him. "Where did the lady go? The one who was sitting here?"

The young man looked up. "She was told her husband — that's you, isn't it?"

"Yes. What was she told?"

"That you were injured. She should come right away."

His mind raced. *Sonofabitch! Who? Not Legrand.* "Who told her? What did he look like?"

"Umm ... he was tall. Curly hair — brown. He had a mustache and wore glasses."

Who the hell could it be? It wasn't Girard ... he wouldn't show his face in public. Viktor made a call. As soon as Josef answered, Viktor yelled, "Louise is missing — taken. Find her cell phone."

****

Louise sat naked, a gag stuffed in her mouth, tied to a chair in the main bedroom of a hotel suite. She couldn't make a sound. With her legs and arms tightly bound, she couldn't move either. She dared not try to move the chair for fear Girard would hurt her.

Back at the restaurant, she hadn't recognized him. Some kind of disguise. Said Viktor was hurt. He led Louise outside and stuck a pistol in her ribs, then pushed her into a Land Rover. He jammed the gun in her ribs and told her to drive to the hotel.

Now Girard stood before Louise, holding her cell phone in his hand. "When I call your husband, you will tell him to do everything I say."

She shook her head back and forth in defiance.

He punched her in the face — hard. She wasn't sure if she had passed out, but she felt dizzy. Her nose hurt. *Maybe it's broken.* Something wet and warm ran over her lips. It ran down her chest, a thin red stream flowing between her naked breasts.

Girard smiled — a cruel smile. He waved a hunting knife in front of her face. "You will do exactly as I say, or I will skin you like a deer." He placed the blade under her left breast and lifted it. "Perhaps I'll start here."

He set the knife on the table and reached for her chin. "When I remove your gag, you will not yell. You will only talk when I say so." He forced her to look at him. "Do you understand?"

No choice. She slowly nodded.

Girard removed the gag. Then he inserted the SIM card in her phone, turned it on and placed a call.

Louise remembered Viktor telling her the phone can only be tracked when it's turned on. *This man knows it, too.* Things didn't look good for a rescue.

Girard screamed into the phone. "No — this is not Louise. I have your wife. You will listen and follow my directions. If not, she dies. It will be slow and painful."

Louise strained to hear Viktor's voice, but couldn't understand a thing.

"You can talk to her, but make it quick." Girard put it on speakerphone.

Viktor's voice came through loud and clear. "Louise. Are you all right? Did he hurt you?"

She couldn't let Girard hurt Viktor. She had to warn him, no matter the consequences. "Stay away. He'll kill you."

Girard grabbed the knife and stabbed the point into the center of her left hand, driving it straight through, into the arm of the chair.

Louise screamed. The pain was intense. She tried to get out of the chair, but she couldn't break free. The legs lifted briefly from the floor before crashing back again.

Viktor yelled, "Louise!"

Girard turned off the speaker and held the phone to his ear. "Follow my directions without fail." His voice was calm but demanding. "If I see anyone other than you, she dies ... Wait for my call." He turned off the phone and removed the SIM card.

Louise hoped the bleeding would stop when Girard wrapped a towel around her hand. *Must need me alive for a while*. It was clear he planned to kill Viktor and then her. *Gotta take a chance ... but can't be stupid.*

She studied everything in sight. Ideas ran through her head. If she tried anything and failed, he would hurt her — maybe kill her. No escape plan seemed viable.

****

Viktor sat in his car in the restaurant parking lot talking on the phone. "Did you get that, Josef?"

"We got a rough location before he turned off the phone. They're in Old Town, near the square. We have it narrowed down to a two-block area. The GPS in her cell didn't have time to be more accurate. I sent a map to your phone. We'll have a team there in five minutes."

Viktor looked at the map, drove out of the lot and headed toward Old Town. "Tell them to stay outside the area you marked. He threatened to kill her if he sees anyone but me. When I go in, tell them to wait ten minutes before approaching."

"I will. Be prepared. Most of the buildings are multi-story apartments and hotels. He may be in one of those units."

"Text me if you get a better fix on the location when he calls."

"We will, Viktor. And if you're close enough when he calls, you can follow his signal like a beacon."

"I'll have to move fast. He didn't leave the phone on very long after the last call."

"We've got your back, Viktor."

****

The air circulating through the room blew constantly across Louise's naked body. She shivered from the cold. Her entire face throbbed and her hand felt like the knife was still in it. Blood from her nose was drying on her chest. The towel on her hand got bloodier every minute.

Girard activated the phone again and called Viktor. "Your wife's a good-looking woman, but she doesn't look happy ... She's alive — for now." He turned it to speakerphone and held it in front of Louise. "Go ahead."

Viktor's voice warmed her heart, but he sounded out of breath. "Louise! Did he hurt you?"

"I'm okay. I'm hurt, but okay."

Before Girard could turn off the speakerphone, she added, "I love you."

Holding the phone to his ear, Girard spoke. "Go directly to Petrin Park. The funicular train. Wait there until I call ... I don't care where ... Listen, just go to the—"

A loud bang came from the entry door. Louise could see Viktor from her chair in the back room. He had a gun aimed in her direction.

Girard crouched behind Louise, grabbed her by the hair and held a knife to her throat. "Drop the gun or I slit her open."

Viktor held the gun steady. "It's over, Girard. Do you want to die?"

"Your lovely wife is the one who will die." He pulled her hair backward, exposing the full length of her throat. "Drop your gun now."

Viktor dropped his gun.

Girard stood. He dropped his knife and raised a pistol, aiming it at Viktor.

"No!" yelled Louise. She shoved her chair backwards into Girard.

The gun fired and Viktor jerked backward. Blood turned his shirt red. He dropped to the floor.

Girard grabbed her by the shoulder and pressed his gun into the side of Louise's head. "You bitch! You—"

Suddenly, his grip on her released. The gun dropped and Girard collapsed at her feet.

Viktor hadn't moved. He must have used his *gift*. Both her husband and her tormenter lay motionless on the floor. How long would Girard stay down?

Louise tried to stand, struggling with the chair. As she rose, the chair rose with her. She aimed the legs at the man who shot Viktor, forcefully dropping herself and the chair onto him. She couldn't tell how badly she hurt him. She raised the chair again and slammed it down. She did it again — and again.

Closure
Chapter 50

Carcassonne, France

Viktor sat in the Restaurant Percival in Carcassonne across from Louise. Her long, blonde hair spilled over her well-tanned shoulders. Her inviting breasts threatened to escape from the scoop neck of her blouse.

He reached out and took her right hand. "It looks like you're in a medieval painting." He nodded toward the large window behind her. "The sun's shining brightly on two towers and the wall of Count's Castle. You complete the painting perfectly."

Her smile brightened. "You know how to flatter a woman." She held up her bandaged left hand. "They could call the painting, *The Wounded Woman and the Castle.*"

"A few more surgeries and we'll both be good as new." Viktor picked up a glass of Perrier and clinked it with Louise's. "To the love of my life. I know it's not wine or beer, but it goes better with pain medicine."

"You smooth talker." She winked. "Are you trying to seduce me?"

"Guilty as charged."

A man in a traditional white chef's jacket and tall hat walked over to the table and bowed. "Monsieur Prazsky, Madame Prazsky. It is a pleasure to see you again."

Viktor turned to him and smiled. "Marcel. We're glad we had a chance to thank you for your help. I see they made you a chef."

"Senior Chef, thanks to you." He shifted his gaze to Louise. "I admire your husband. He saved the world, but he didn't forget a person as insignificant as me."

Louise patted Viktor's hand and looked at Marcel. "He's the best. And he never forgets a friend." She sat back in her chair. "I know the media gave Viktor most of the credit for taking down Girard and his terrorist network, but he told me he couldn't have done it without you."

Viktor wanted to mention Marcel's role in locating the nuclear warhead, but the public was not told of the incident. The media repeated rumors, but officials declined comment. "I hate that phrase, 'Saved the world.' Besides, the media ignored the contributions of people like you." He stood up and extended a hand. "If anyone 'saved the world', it would start with you."

Marcel smiled and shook Viktor's hand. "I saw the press release. It's hard to believe. My boss — former boss — the mastermind behind the killing. I thought Muslims did this out of hatred. But it was really Girard who did it — for the money."

Viktor sat down. "Did you read the Europol press release?"

With a shake of his head, Marcel responded, "No, not really. I saw what they said on TV. It's all over the papers and the Internet, too. Everyone's talking about it." He glanced at his watch. "It was good seeing you, but I must get back to work." With a bow, he left.

Louise sipped her water. "No one reads those boring press releases ... except you."

Viktor leaned forward. "There are things in the report I didn't know. Legrand must be spilling everything. I knew they arrested everyone in Salafi Brotherhood and Arcadian Spear, but I didn't know they got so many Al Qaida and Daesh cells — assassins, too."

"You know, honey. You might have truly 'saved the world.' Girard was a major cause of terrorism for years. And now he's gone. It's over."

"I wish it were true. And I know things will get better … for a while. But humans didn't become the top predators in the world because of their peaceful nature."

"You're so cynical."

"You ever hear of the scorpion and the frog?"

"Are you going to tell me a story?"

"Of course." Viktor scratched his scar and recited from memory:

> *A scorpion asked a frog to carry him over the river.*
>
> *The frog objected because he expected the scorpion to sting and kill him.*
>
> *The scorpion explained that killing the frog would doom them both.*
>
> *Halfway across the river, the scorpion stung the frog.*
>
> *The dying frog asked the drowning scorpion why he did it.*
>
> *The scorpion explained it was simply his nature.*

"And that's your lesson for the day?"

"That's it. Hate and greed are part of human nature. Even at the expense of our future survival."

Val d'Oise, France

The owner of an old two-story farmhouse, located fifty kilometers northwest of Paris, rented rooms and garage space to individuals and families who preferred the rural life to the bustle of the city. Jean Berger rented a small bedroom on the second floor, which he converted to an office. It was here that he hosted the weekly meetings of the Tribulation Warriors.

On a cool morning in November, Jean sat behind a simple desk, addressing five of his loyal members. "French voters are stupid. They are afraid to leave the European Union so we let Brussels rule our lives. We are overrun by filthy immigrants. Muslims and filthy people from Eastern Europe. It is time we did something about it."

One of the men spoke up. "They take our jobs and kill innocent people. Time they learned France is for Frenchmen."

Jean listened to them vent about sharia law, women hiding their faces behind veils and Muslim men attacking French women.

All he had to do was tell them where and how. "Our friends and benefactors are scared and hiding. Many of them have been arrested. We do not have enough money to buy explosives so we make them ourselves. We are on our own. But that has never stopped us before and it will not stop us now."

He let them cheer and brag, reinforcing each other's anger and determination.

"We will destroy the largest mosque in Paris. When my cousin, Philippe, finishes making the explosives, we will steal a truck and—"

A large explosion rocked the room. Jean ran to the window. Flames and smoke engulfed one of the garages.

"*Philippe!*"

Frankfurt, Germany

The sun reflected off the west face of Darmstadt Bank's glass and steel headquarters building, standing proudly fifty stories above Frankfurt. On the thirty-seventh floor, Ethan Vance, a British venture capitalist, sat on one side of a long table in a conference room. Around the table sat twelve other British financiers.

Lord Moore, the man at the head of the table, had been CEO of Nelson Price Bank, until the European financial center moved from London to Frankfurt, following the British exit from the EU.

Ethan's investments were primarily in technology and security. Nearly half of them were British, and those investments suffered a drop in sales to Europe. He needed a strategy to move toward a truly European portfolio.

Moore interrupted his thoughts. "Ethan. I asked you if anyone questioned you about money laundering or terrorist financing."

Ethan reached for his phone and located the information. "British investigators grilled me three weeks ago, and Europe sent someone earlier this week." He looked at the faces around the table. "They have nothing. I told them nothing. And that's what each of us need to do." *What a bunch of scared rabbits.*

Across the table, a man wiped the sweat from his forehead. "They arrested a man who used to give me excellent investment advice. Right after Girard died."

Another man described two arrests in the French Council of Ministers.

Ethan silently listened to the complaints and fears of everyone. Girard's partners had guaranteed riskless investments to all of them, but those days were gone. And these idiots had no idea what to do.

After the meeting, Ethan found a quiet corner to talk to his aide. "Go forward with the action in Paris. You suggested a reliable group."

"Tribulation Warriors."

"Do it."

"As you wish, Your Grace."

About the Author

After living most of my life in Pennsylvania working in technology, my wife and I moved to sunny Florida. I've always been interested in science, world issues and beer. In 1971, Uncle Sam sent me to Tonkin Gulf on the USS Midway. I programmed my first computer in 1966, then worked in the computer industry for my entire civilian career.

Nowadays, my wife and I love to travel. I've been to 44 of the 50 states, and 35 countries on five continents, visiting breweries and brewpubs along the way.

If you enjoyed this novel, I would appreciate your review on Amazon or wherever you buy your books. I'd also love to hear from you via email (mark.pryor@pryorpatch.com), and I invite you to visit my website to keep up with my writing (www.pryorpatch.com).